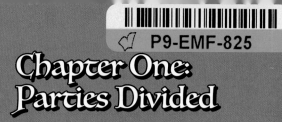

Chapter One:
Parties Divided

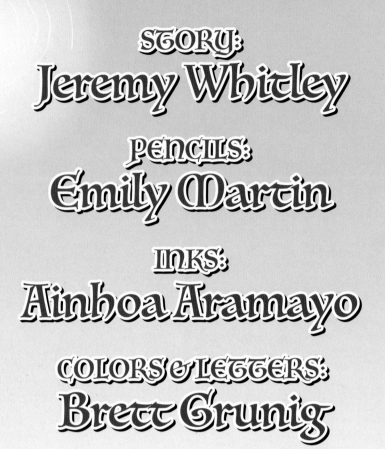

STORY:
Jeremy Whitley

PENCILS:
Emily Martin

INKS:
Ainhoa Aramayo

COLORS & LETTERS:
Brett Grunig

COVER A: Onyinye Anakor   COVER B: Emily Martin

EDITORS:
Alicia Whitley (script)
Nicole D'Andria (comic)

Bryan Seaton: Publisher/ CEO • Shawn Gabborin: Editor In Chief
Jason Martin: Publisher-Danger Zone • Nicole D'Andria: Marketing Director/Editor
Jim Dietz: Social Media Manager • Danielle Davison: Executive Administrator
Chad Cicconi: Still Waiting For His Princess • Shawn Pryor: President of Creator Relations

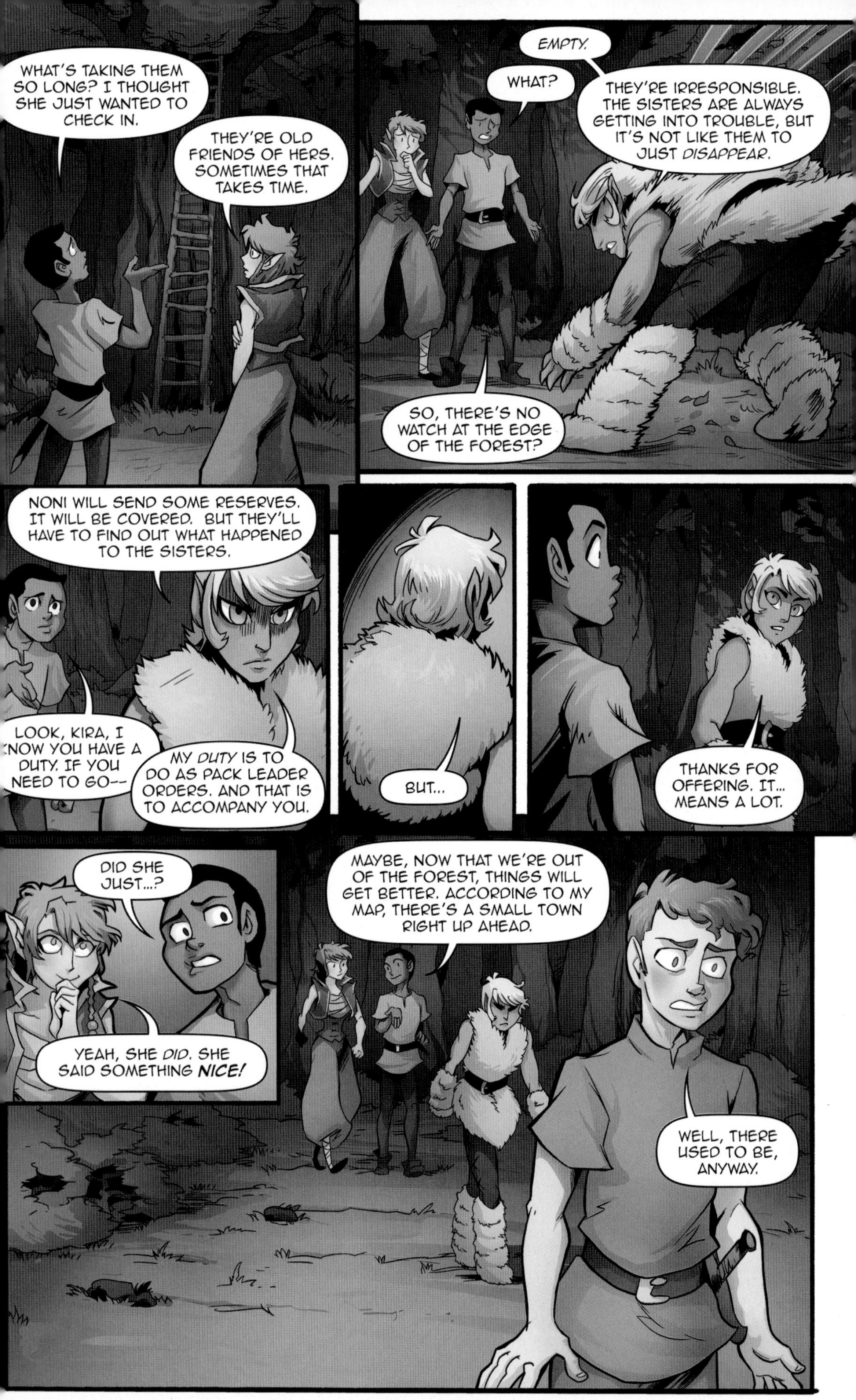
WHAT'S TAKING THEM SO LONG? I THOUGHT SHE JUST WANTED TO CHECK IN.
THEY'RE OLD FRIENDS OF HERS. SOMETIMES THAT TAKES TIME.
EMPTY.
WHAT?
THEY'RE IRRESPONSIBLE. THE SISTERS ARE ALWAYS GETTING INTO TROUBLE, BUT IT'S NOT LIKE THEM TO JUST DISAPPEAR.
SO, THERE'S NO WATCH AT THE EDGE OF THE FOREST?
NONI WILL SEND SOME RESERVES. IT WILL BE COVERED. BUT THEY'LL HAVE TO FIND OUT WHAT HAPPENED TO THE SISTERS.
LOOK, KIRA, I KNOW YOU HAVE A DUTY. IF YOU NEED TO GO--
MY DUTY IS TO DO AS PACK LEADER ORDERS. AND THAT IS TO ACCOMPANY YOU.
BUT...
THANKS FOR OFFERING. IT... MEANS A LOT.
DID SHE JUST...?
YEAH, SHE DID. SHE SAID SOMETHING NICE!
MAYBE, NOW THAT WE'RE OUT OF THE FOREST, THINGS WILL GET BETTER. ACCORDING TO MY MAP, THERE'S A SMALL TOWN RIGHT UP AHEAD.
WELL, THERE USED TO BE, ANYWAY.

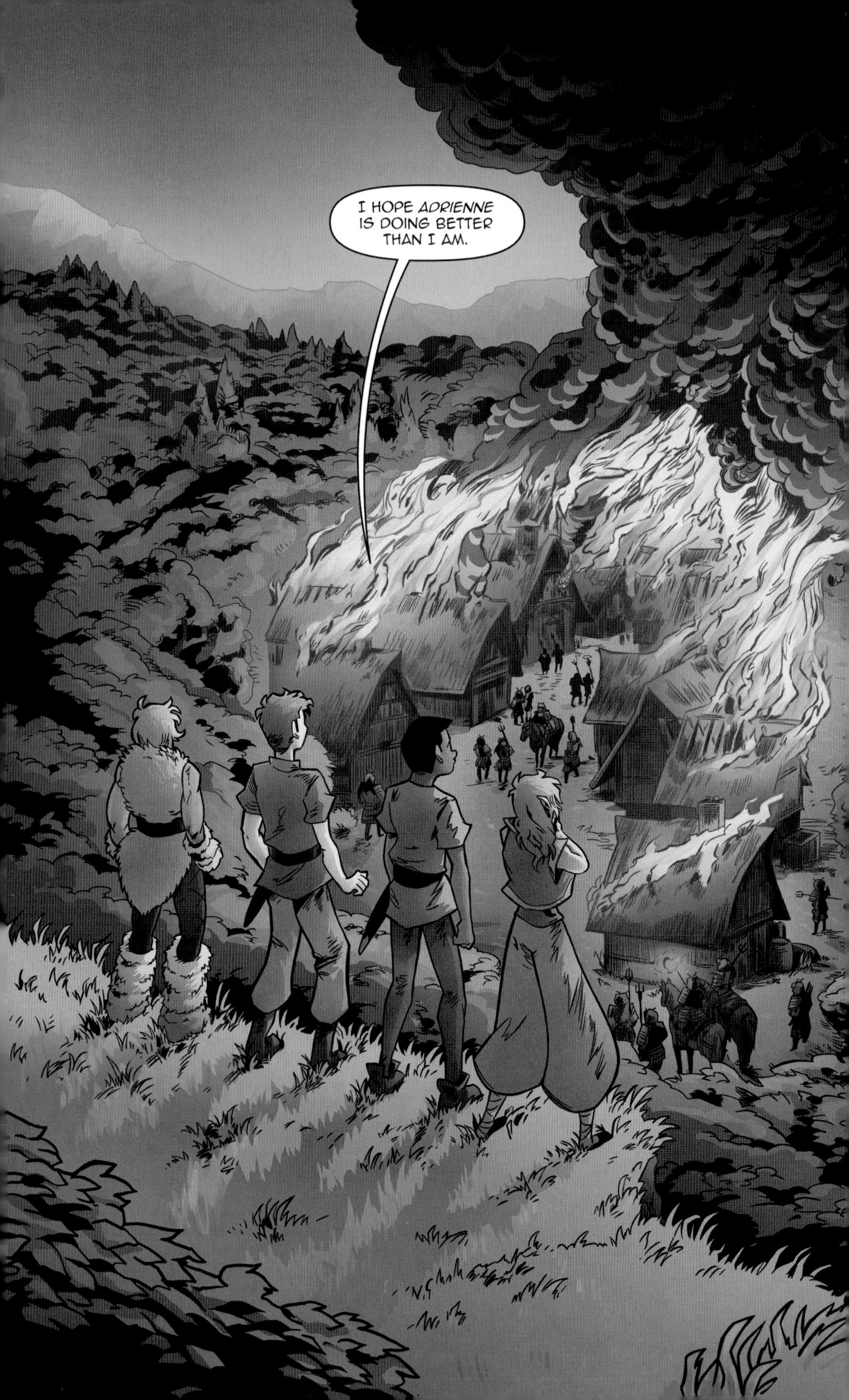
I HOPE ADRIENNE IS DOING BETTER THAN I AM.

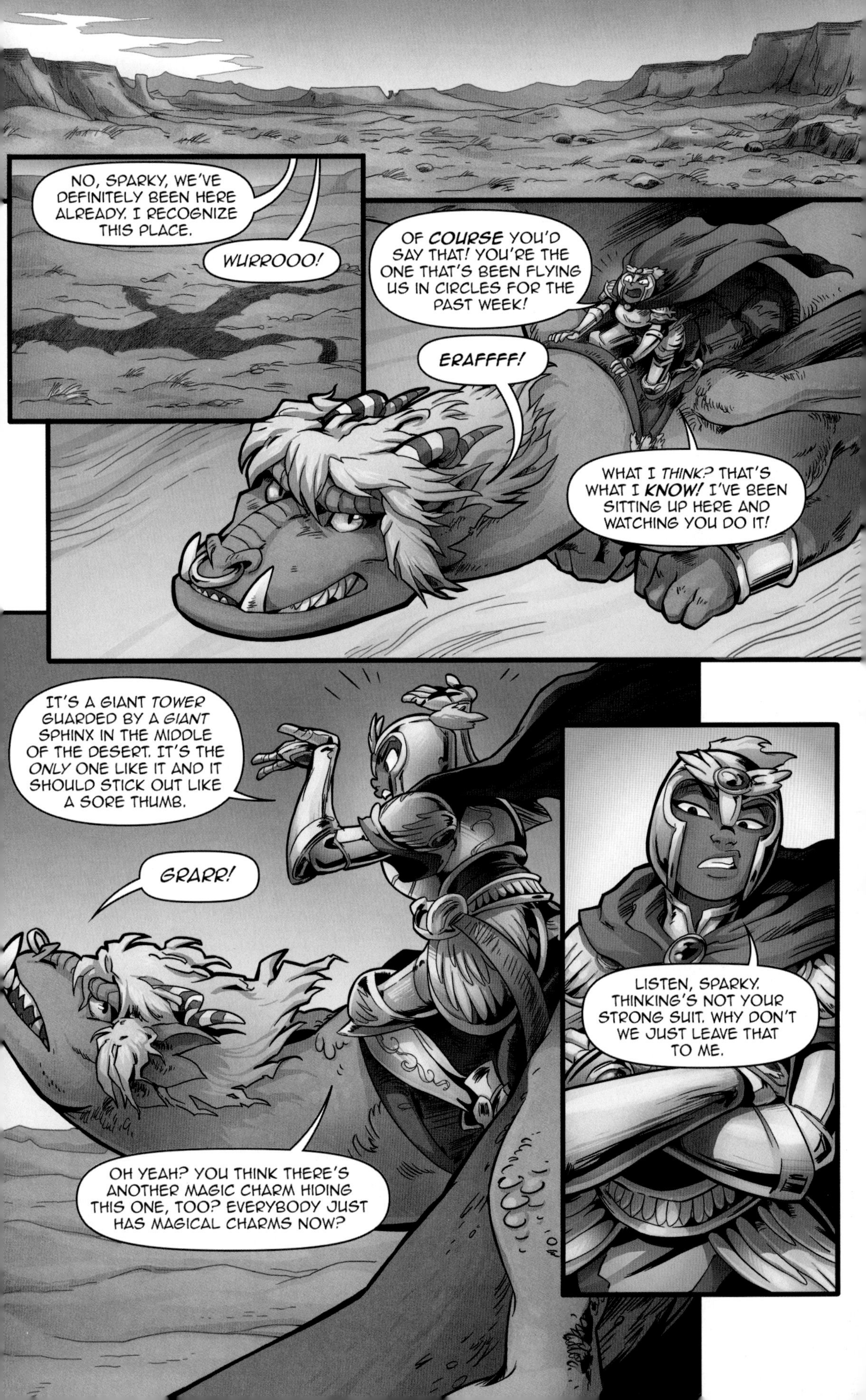

NO, SPARKY, WE'VE DEFINITELY BEEN HERE ALREADY. I RECOGNIZE THIS PLACE.
WURROOO!
OF COURSE YOU'D SAY THAT! YOU'RE THE ONE THAT'S BEEN FLYING US IN CIRCLES FOR THE PAST WEEK!
ERAFFFF!
WHAT I THINK? THAT'S WHAT I KNOW! I'VE BEEN SITTING UP HERE AND WATCHING YOU DO IT!
IT'S A GIANT TOWER GUARDED BY A GIANT SPHINX IN THE MIDDLE OF THE DESERT. IT'S THE ONLY ONE LIKE IT AND IT SHOULD STICK OUT LIKE A SORE THUMB.
GRARR!
OH YEAH? YOU THINK THERE'S ANOTHER MAGIC CHARM HIDING THIS ONE, TOO? EVERYBODY JUST HAS MAGICAL CHARMS NOW?
LISTEN, SPARKY. THINKING'S NOT YOUR STRONG SUIT. WHY DON'T WE JUST LEAVE THAT TO ME.

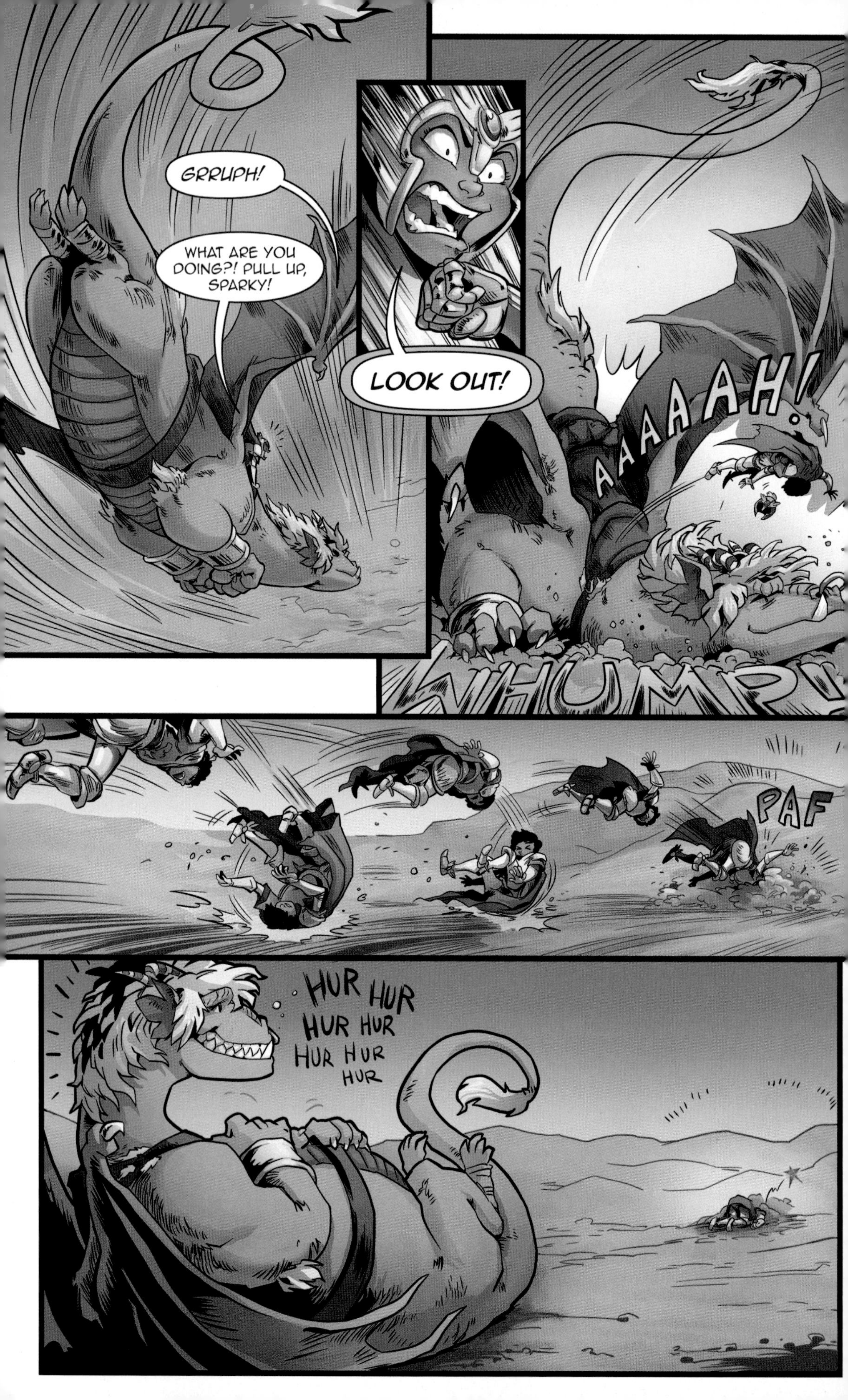
GRRUPH!
WHAT ARE YOU DOING?! PULL UP, SPARKY!
LOOK OUT!
AAAAAAH!
WHUMP!
PAF
HUR HUR
HUR HUR
HUR HUR
HUR

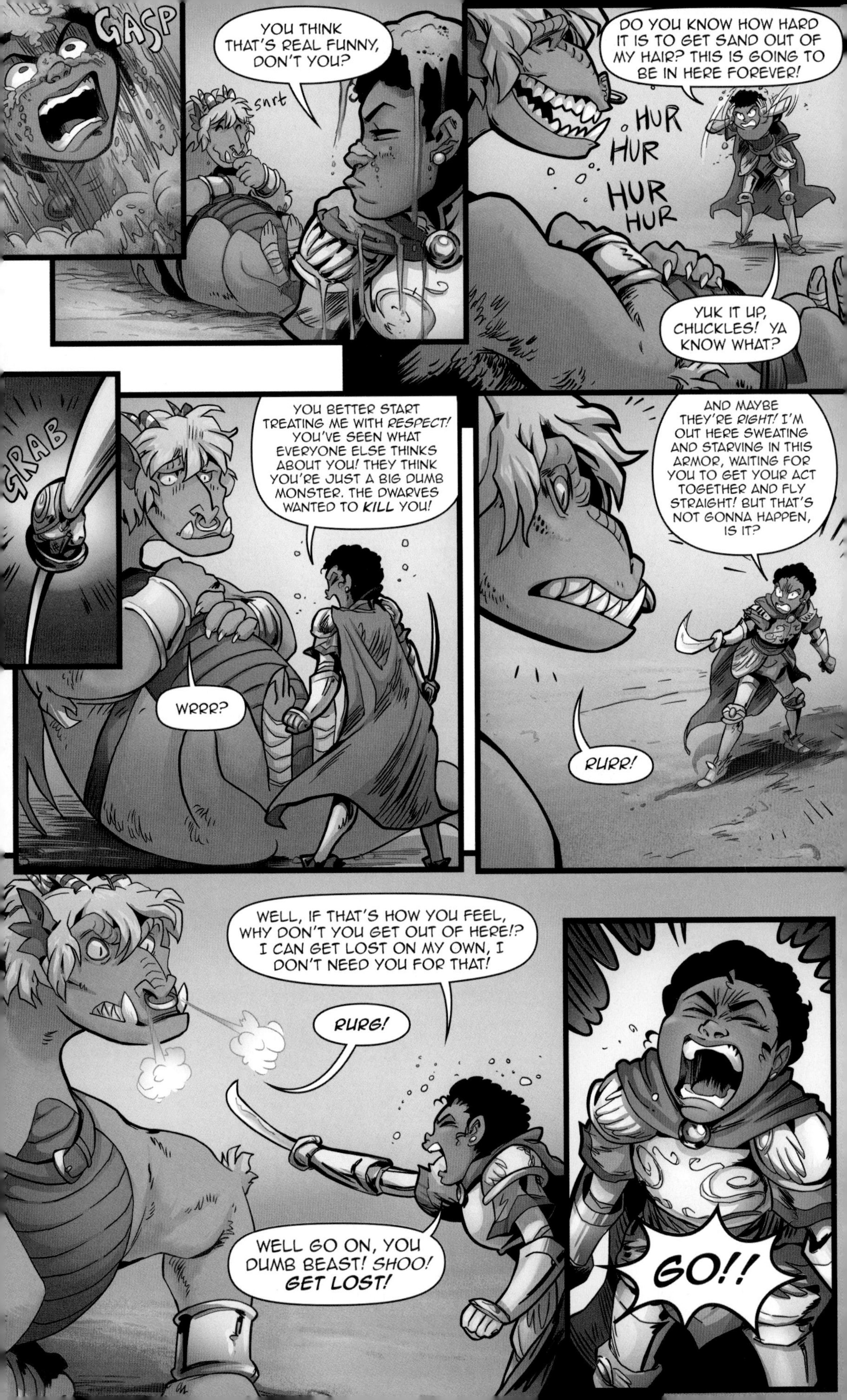

GASP
YOU THINK THAT'S REAL FUNNY, DON'T YOU?
snrt
DO YOU KNOW HOW HARD IT IS TO GET SAND OUT OF MY HAIR? THIS IS GOING TO BE IN HERE FOREVER!
HUR HUR HUR HUR
YUK IT UP, CHUCKLES! YA KNOW WHAT?
GRAB
YOU BETTER START TREATING ME WITH *RESPECT*! YOU'VE SEEN WHAT EVERYONE ELSE THINKS ABOUT YOU! THEY THINK YOU'RE JUST A BIG DUMB MONSTER. THE DWARVES WANTED TO ***KILL*** YOU!
WRRR?
AND MAYBE THEY'RE *RIGHT*! I'M OUT HERE SWEATING AND STARVING IN THIS ARMOR, WAITING FOR YOU TO GET YOUR ACT TOGETHER AND FLY STRAIGHT! BUT THAT'S NOT GONNA HAPPEN, IS IT?
RURR!
WELL, IF THAT'S HOW YOU FEEL, WHY DON'T YOU GET OUT OF HERE!? I CAN GET LOST ON MY OWN, I DON'T NEED YOU FOR THAT!
RURG!
WELL GO ON, YOU DUMB BEAST! *SHOO!* ***GET LOST!***
GO!!

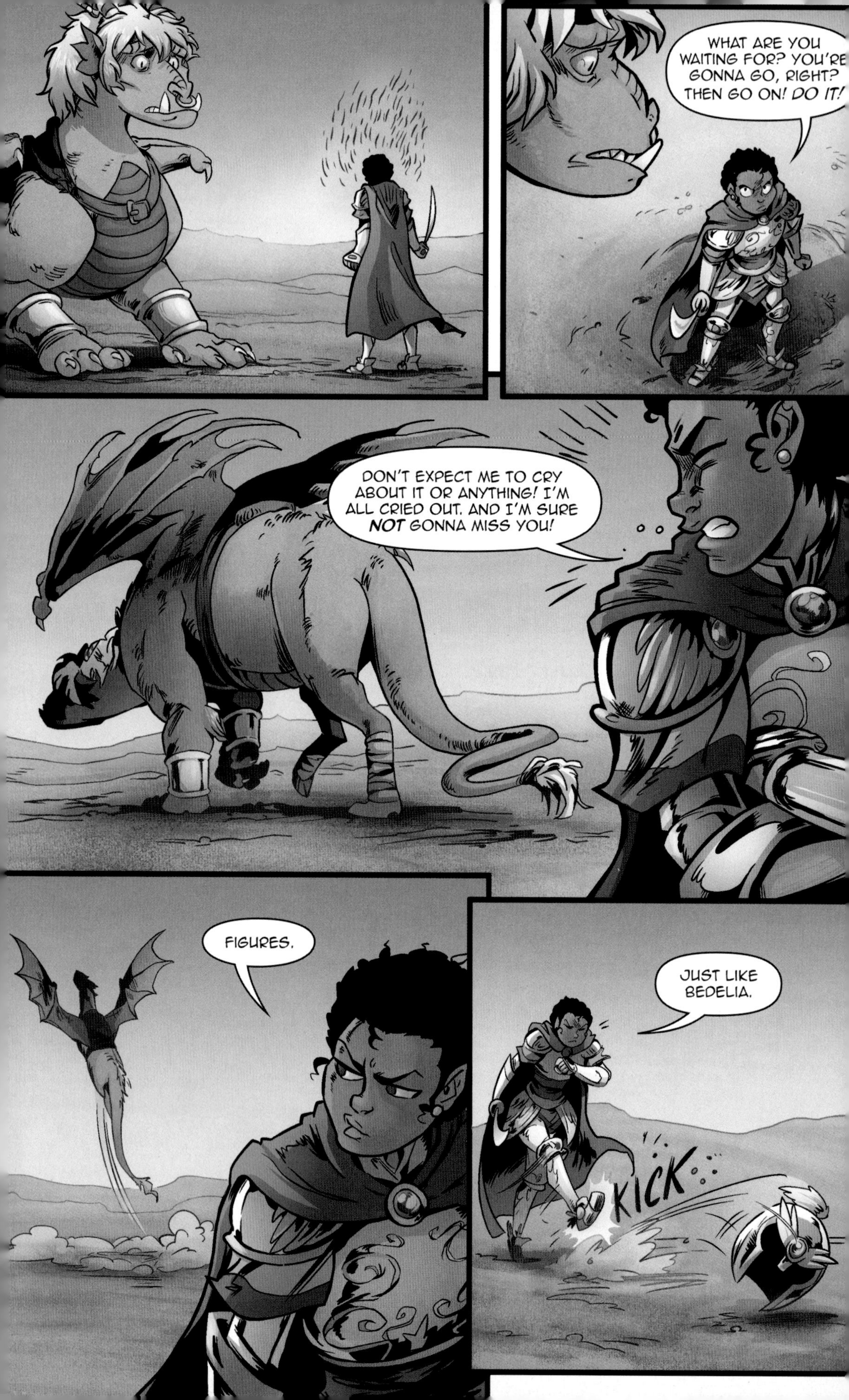
WHAT ARE YOU WAITING FOR? YOU'RE GONNA GO, RIGHT? THEN GO ON! *DO IT!*
DON'T EXPECT ME TO CRY ABOUT IT OR ANYTHING! I'M ALL CRIED OUT. AND I'M SURE ***NOT*** GONNA MISS YOU!
FIGURES.
JUST LIKE BEDELIA.
KICK

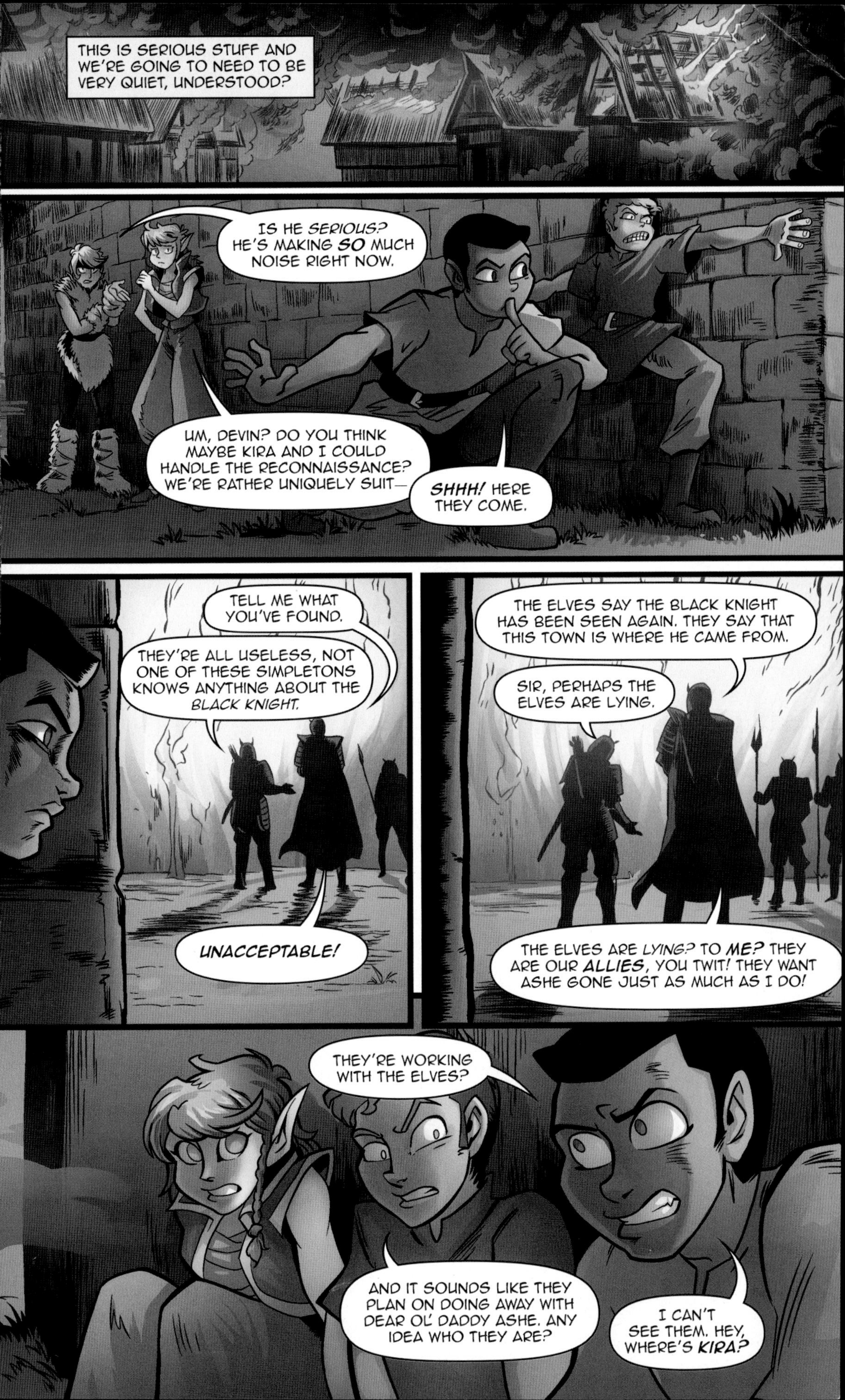
THIS IS SERIOUS STUFF AND WE'RE GOING TO NEED TO BE VERY QUIET, UNDERSTOOD?
IS HE *SERIOUS?* HE'S MAKING **SO** MUCH NOISE RIGHT NOW.
UM, DEVIN? DO YOU THINK MAYBE KIRA AND I COULD HANDLE THE RECONNAISSANCE? WE'RE RATHER UNIQUELY SUIT—
SHHH! HERE THEY COME.
TELL ME WHAT YOU'VE FOUND.
THEY'RE ALL USELESS, NOT ONE OF THESE SIMPLETONS KNOWS ANYTHING ABOUT THE *BLACK KNIGHT.*
UNACCEPTABLE!
THE ELVES SAY THE BLACK KNIGHT HAS BEEN SEEN AGAIN. THEY SAY THAT THIS TOWN IS WHERE HE CAME FROM.
SIR, PERHAPS THE ELVES ARE LYING.
THE ELVES ARE *LYING?* TO ***ME?*** THEY ARE OUR **ALLIES**, YOU TWIT! THEY WANT ASHE GONE JUST AS MUCH AS I DO!
THEY'RE WORKING WITH THE ELVES?
AND IT SOUNDS LIKE THEY PLAN ON DOING AWAY WITH DEAR OL' DADDY ASHE. ANY IDEA WHO THEY ARE?
I CAN'T SEE THEM. HEY, WHERE'S ***KIRA?***

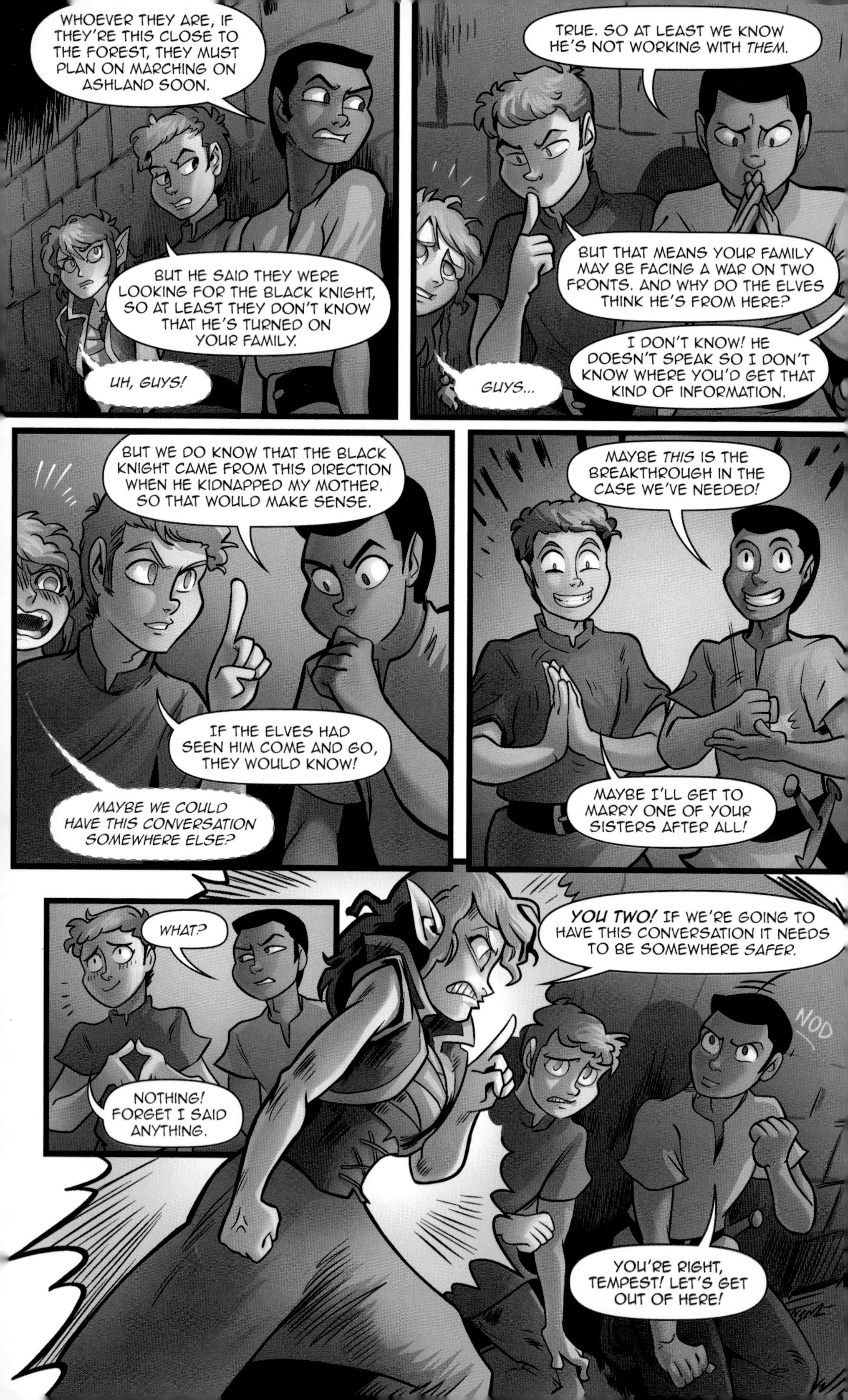
WHOEVER THEY ARE, IF THEY'RE THIS CLOSE TO THE FOREST, THEY MUST PLAN ON MARCHING ON ASHLAND SOON.
BUT HE SAID THEY WERE LOOKING FOR THE BLACK KNIGHT, SO AT LEAST THEY DON'T KNOW THAT HE'S TURNED ON YOUR FAMILY.
UH, GUYS!
TRUE. SO AT LEAST WE KNOW HE'S NOT WORKING WITH *THEM*.
BUT THAT MEANS YOUR FAMILY MAY BE FACING A WAR ON TWO FRONTS. AND WHY DO THE ELVES THINK HE'S FROM HERE?
GUYS...
I DON'T KNOW! HE DOESN'T SPEAK SO I DON'T KNOW WHERE YOU'D GET THAT KIND OF INFORMATION.
BUT WE DO KNOW THAT THE BLACK KNIGHT CAME FROM THIS DIRECTION WHEN HE KIDNAPPED MY MOTHER. SO THAT WOULD MAKE SENSE.
IF THE ELVES HAD SEEN HIM COME AND GO, THEY WOULD KNOW!
MAYBE WE COULD HAVE THIS CONVERSATION SOMEWHERE ELSE?
MAYBE *THIS* IS THE BREAKTHROUGH IN THE CASE WE'VE NEEDED!
MAYBE I'LL GET TO MARRY ONE OF YOUR SISTERS AFTER ALL!
WHAT?
NOTHING! FORGET I SAID ANYTHING.
YOU TWO! IF WE'RE GOING TO HAVE THIS CONVERSATION IT NEEDS TO BE SOMEWHERE *SAFER*.
NOD
YOU'RE RIGHT, TEMPEST! LET'S GET OUT OF HERE!

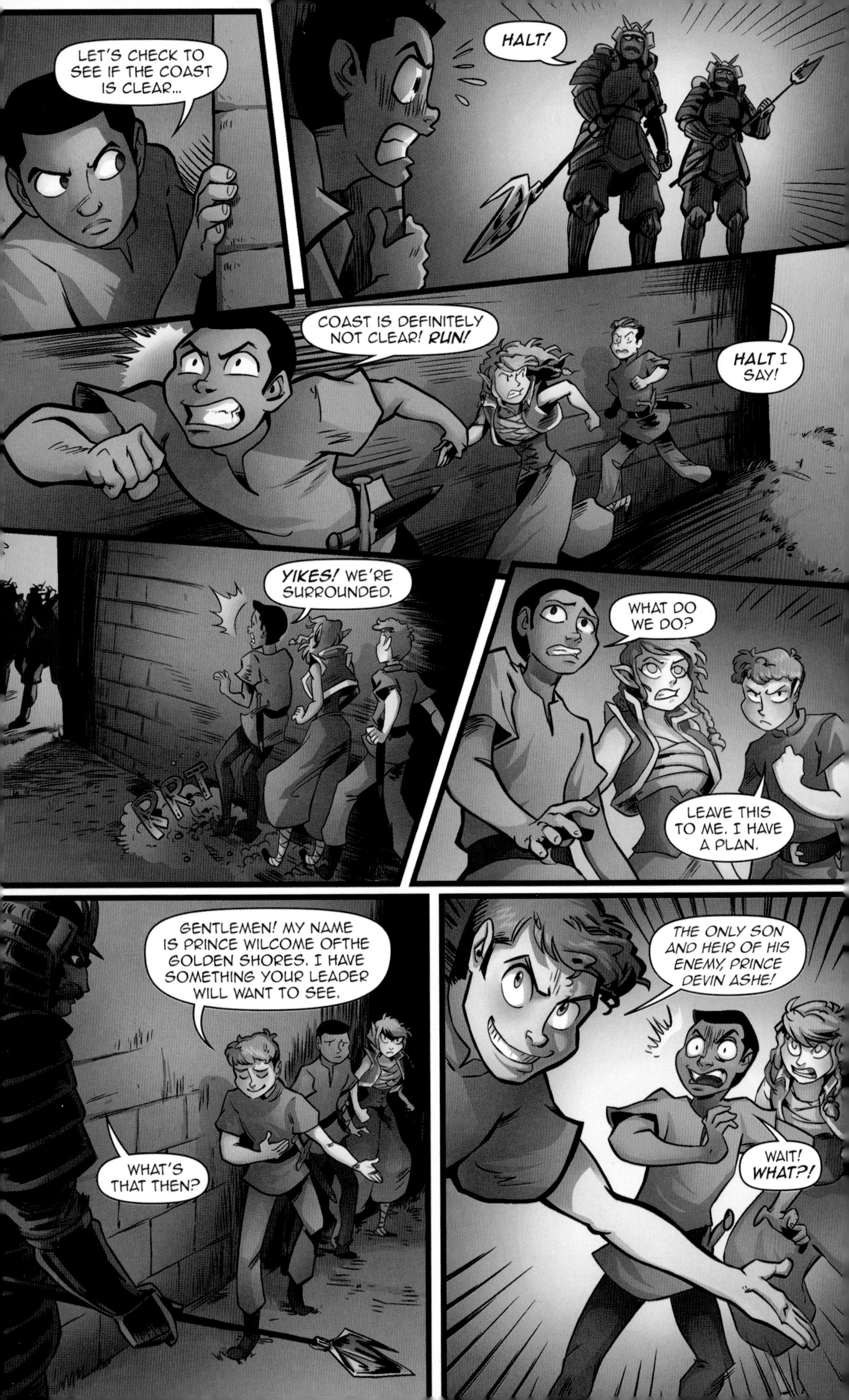
LET'S CHECK TO SEE IF THE COAST IS CLEAR...
HALT!
COAST IS DEFINITELY NOT CLEAR! RUN!
HALT I SAY!
YIKES! WE'RE SURROUNDED.
RRRT
WHAT DO WE DO?
LEAVE THIS TO ME. I HAVE A PLAN.
GENTLEMEN! MY NAME IS PRINCE WILCOME OFTHE GOLDEN SHORES. I HAVE SOMETHING YOUR LEADER WILL WANT TO SEE.
WHAT'S THAT THEN?
THE ONLY SON AND HEIR OF HIS ENEMY, PRINCE DEVIN ASHE!
WAIT! WHAT?!

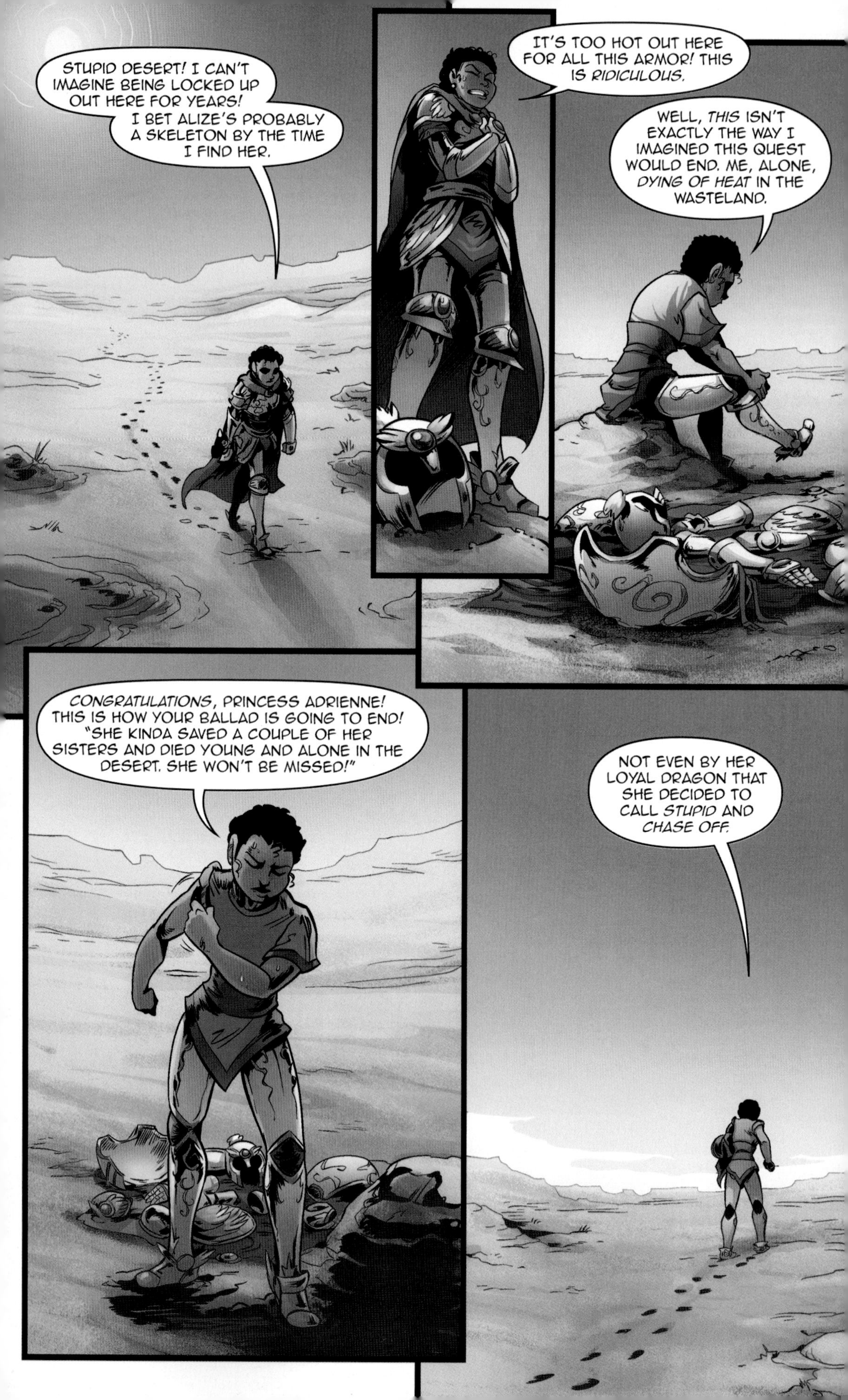
STUPID DESERT! I CAN'T IMAGINE BEING LOCKED UP OUT HERE FOR YEARS!
I BET ALIZE'S PROBABLY A SKELETON BY THE TIME I FIND HER.
IT'S TOO HOT OUT HERE FOR ALL THIS ARMOR! THIS IS RIDICULOUS.
WELL, THIS ISN'T EXACTLY THE WAY I IMAGINED THIS QUEST WOULD END. ME, ALONE, DYING OF HEAT IN THE WASTELAND.
CONGRATULATIONS, PRINCESS ADRIENNE! THIS IS HOW YOUR BALLAD IS GOING TO END! "SHE KINDA SAVED A COUPLE OF HER SISTERS AND DIED YOUNG AND ALONE IN THE DESERT. SHE WON'T BE MISSED!"
NOT EVEN BY HER LOYAL DRAGON THAT SHE DECIDED TO CALL STUPID AND CHASE OFF.

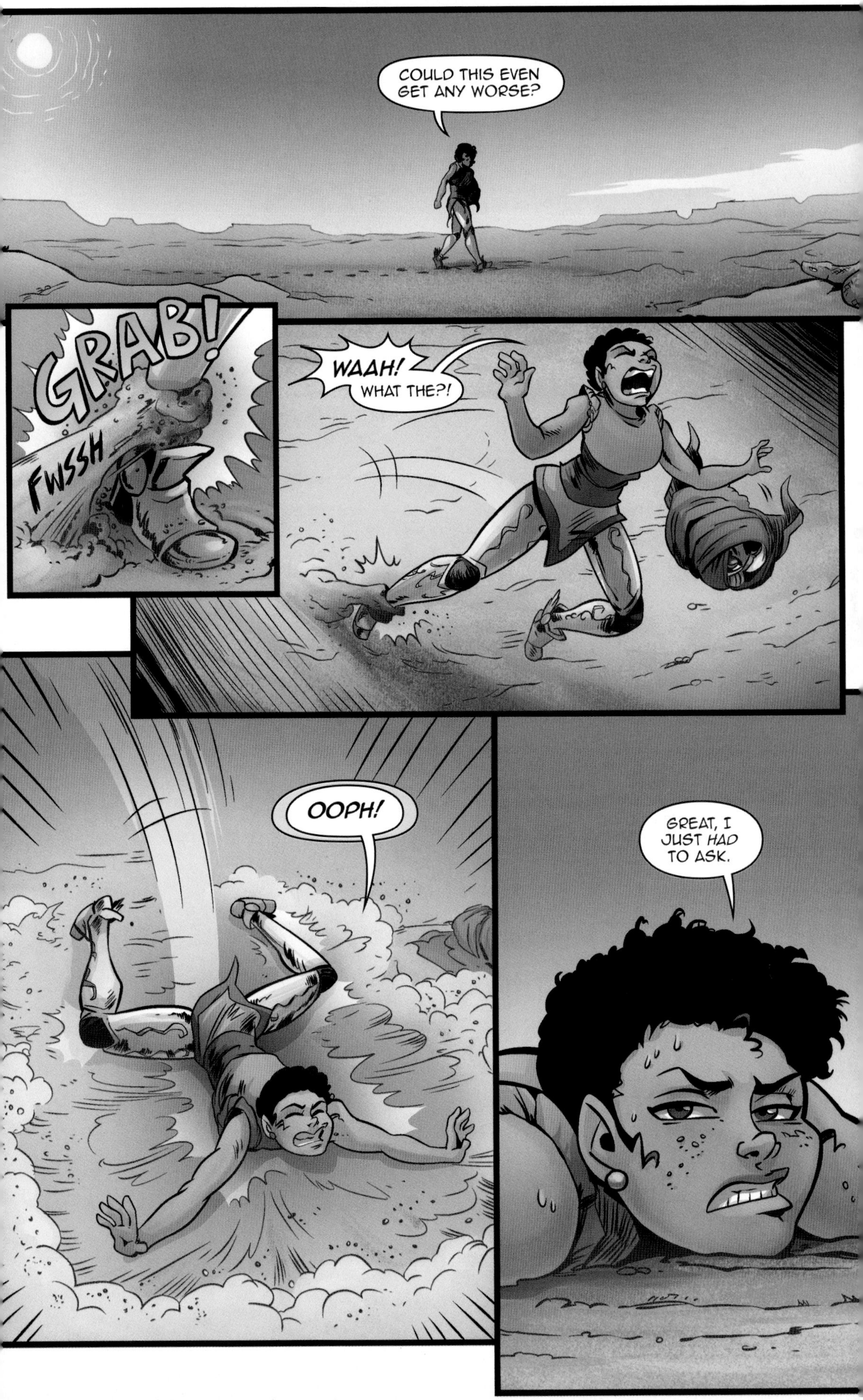
COULD THIS EVEN GET ANY WORSE?
GRAB!
FWSSH
WAAH!
WHAT THE?!
OOPH!
GREAT, I JUST *HAD* TO ASK.

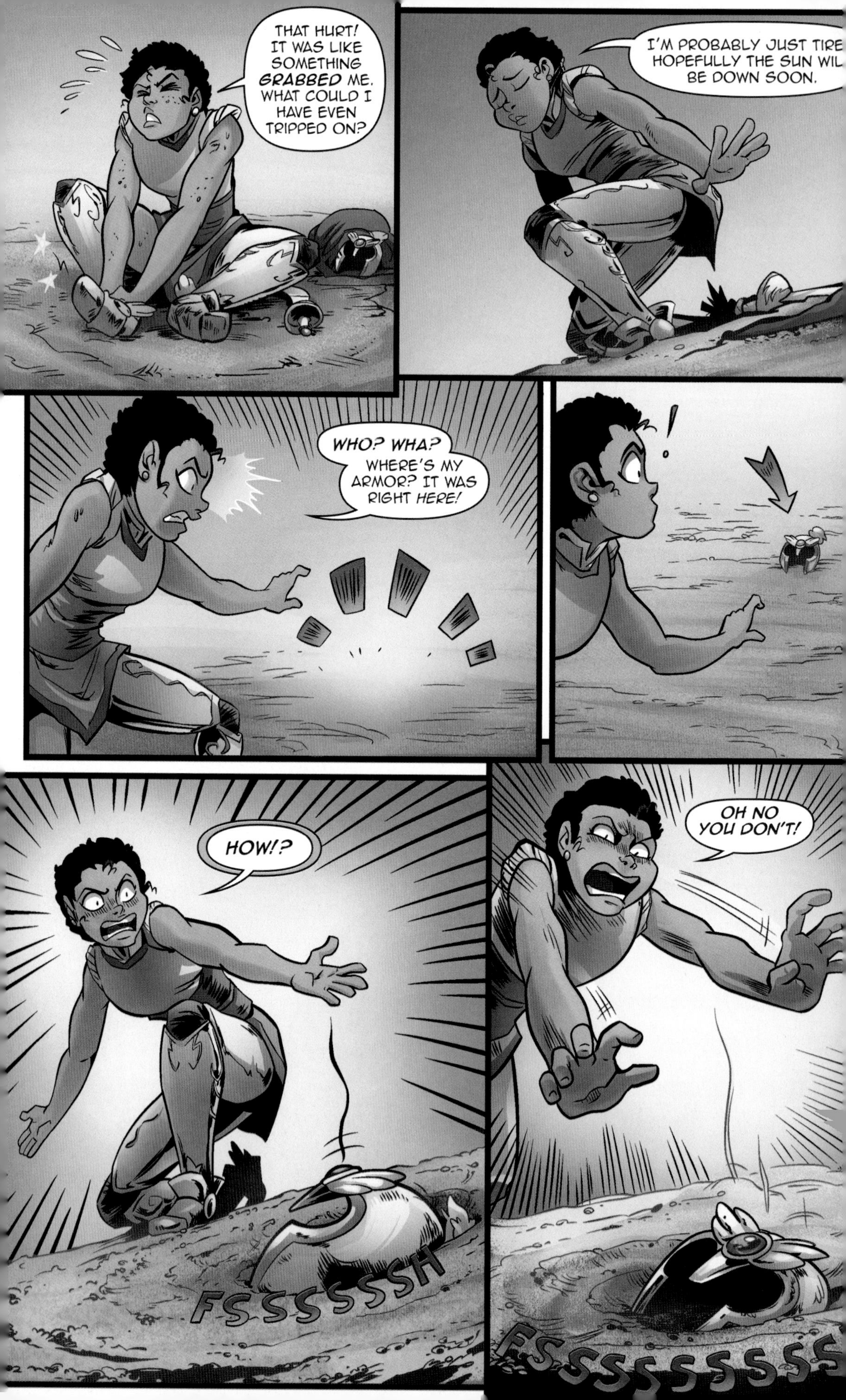
THAT HURT! IT WAS LIKE SOMETHING GRABBED ME. WHAT COULD I HAVE EVEN TRIPPED ON?
I'M PROBABLY JUST TIRE HOPEFULLY THE SUN WIL BE DOWN SOON.
WHO? WHA? WHERE'S MY ARMOR? IT WAS RIGHT HERE!
!
HOW!?
FSSSSSSSH
OH NO YOU DON'T!
FSSSSSSSSSS

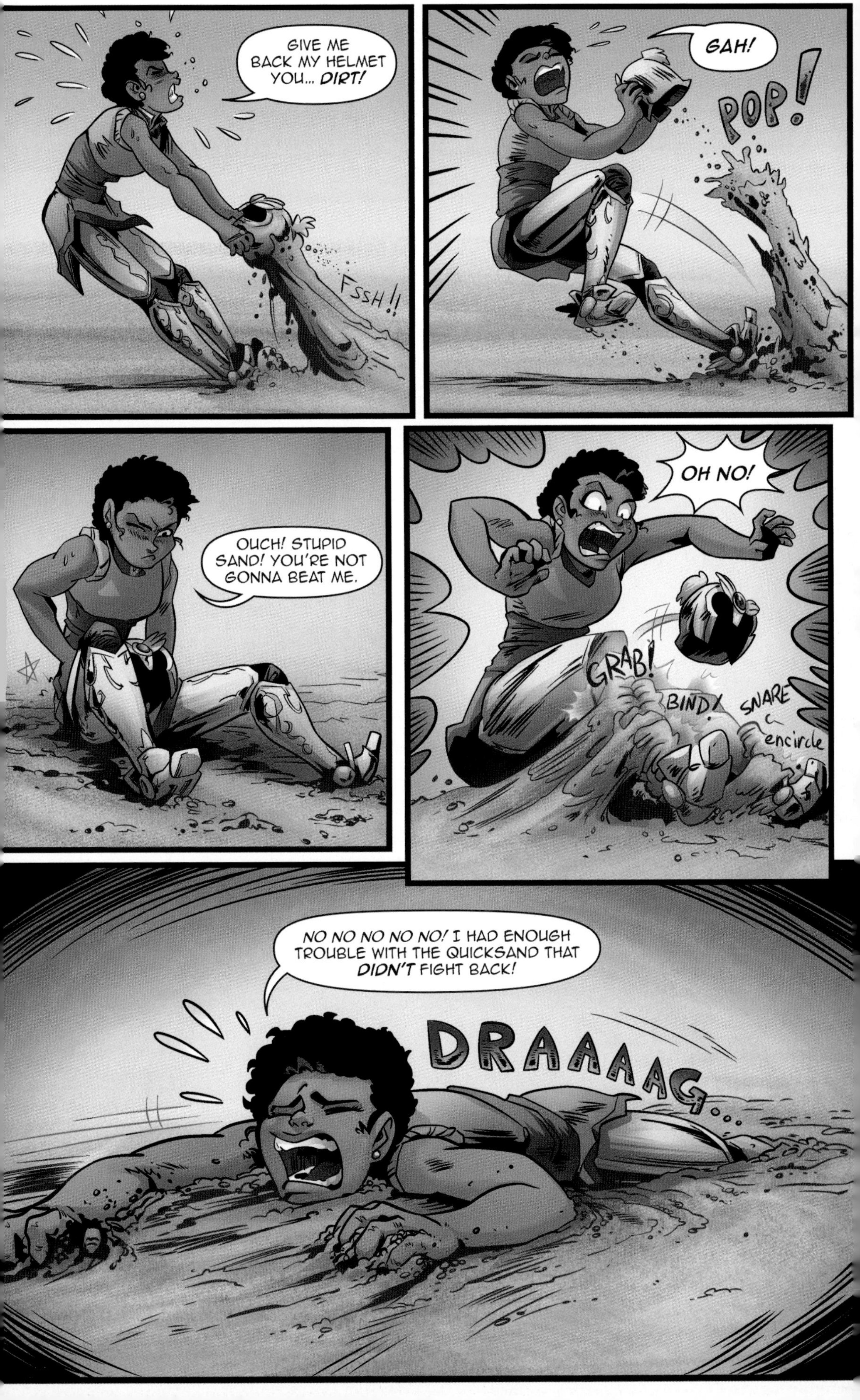
GIVE ME BACK MY HELMET YOU... DIRT!
FSSH!!
GAH!
POP!
OUCH! STUPID SAND! YOU'RE NOT GONNA BEAT ME.
OH NO!
GRAB!
BIND!
SNARE
encircle
NO NO NO NO NO! I HAD ENOUGH TROUBLE WITH THE QUICKSAND THAT DIDN'T FIGHT BACK!
DRAAAAG...

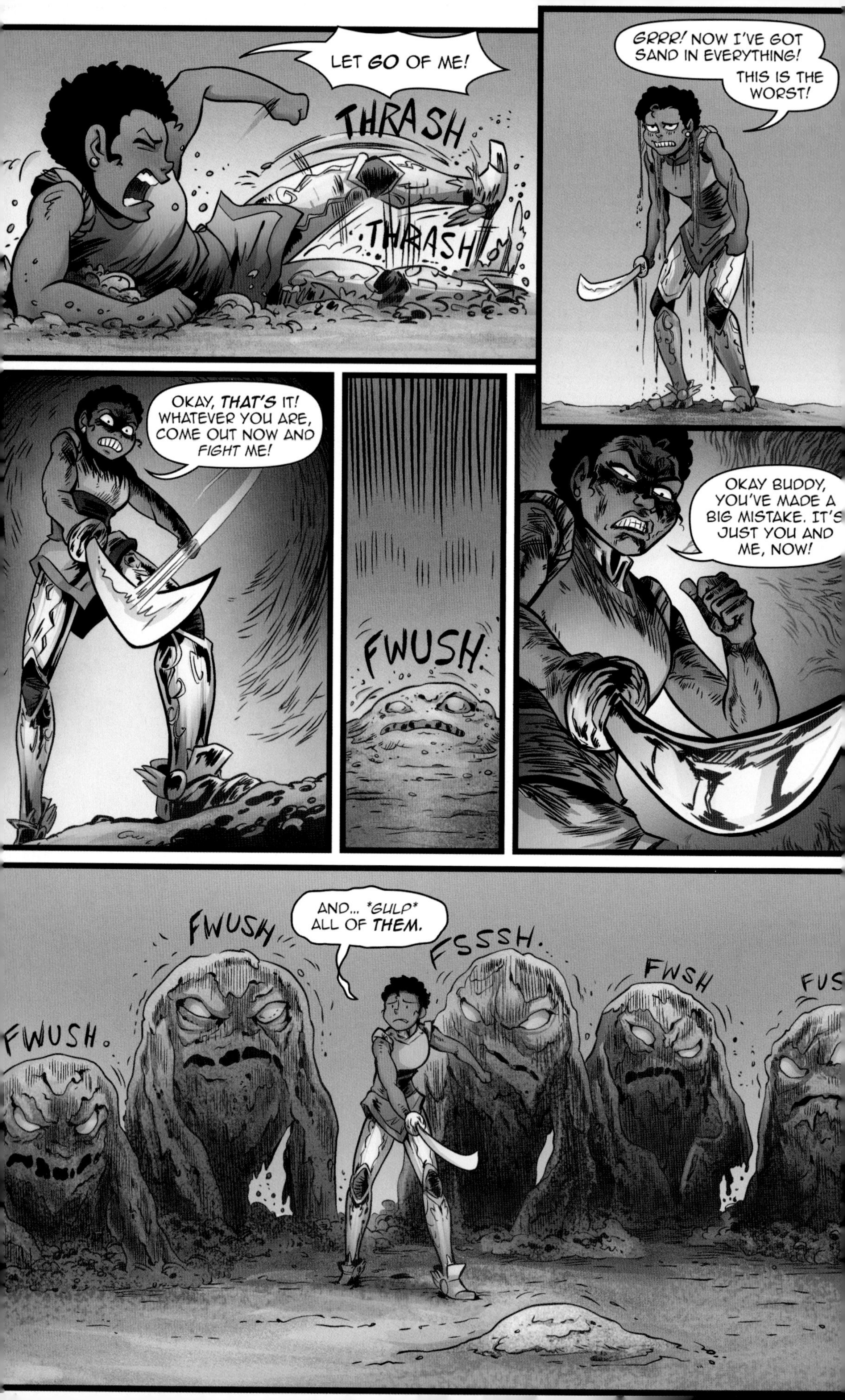

LET GO OF ME!
THRASH
THRASH
GRRR! NOW I'VE GOT SAND IN EVERYTHING!
THIS IS THE WORST!
OKAY, THAT'S IT! WHATEVER YOU ARE, COME OUT NOW AND FIGHT ME!
FWUSH.
OKAY BUDDY, YOU'VE MADE A BIG MISTAKE. IT'S JUST YOU AND ME, NOW!
FWUSH
AND... *GULP* ALL OF THEM.
FSSSH.
FWSH
FWUSH.

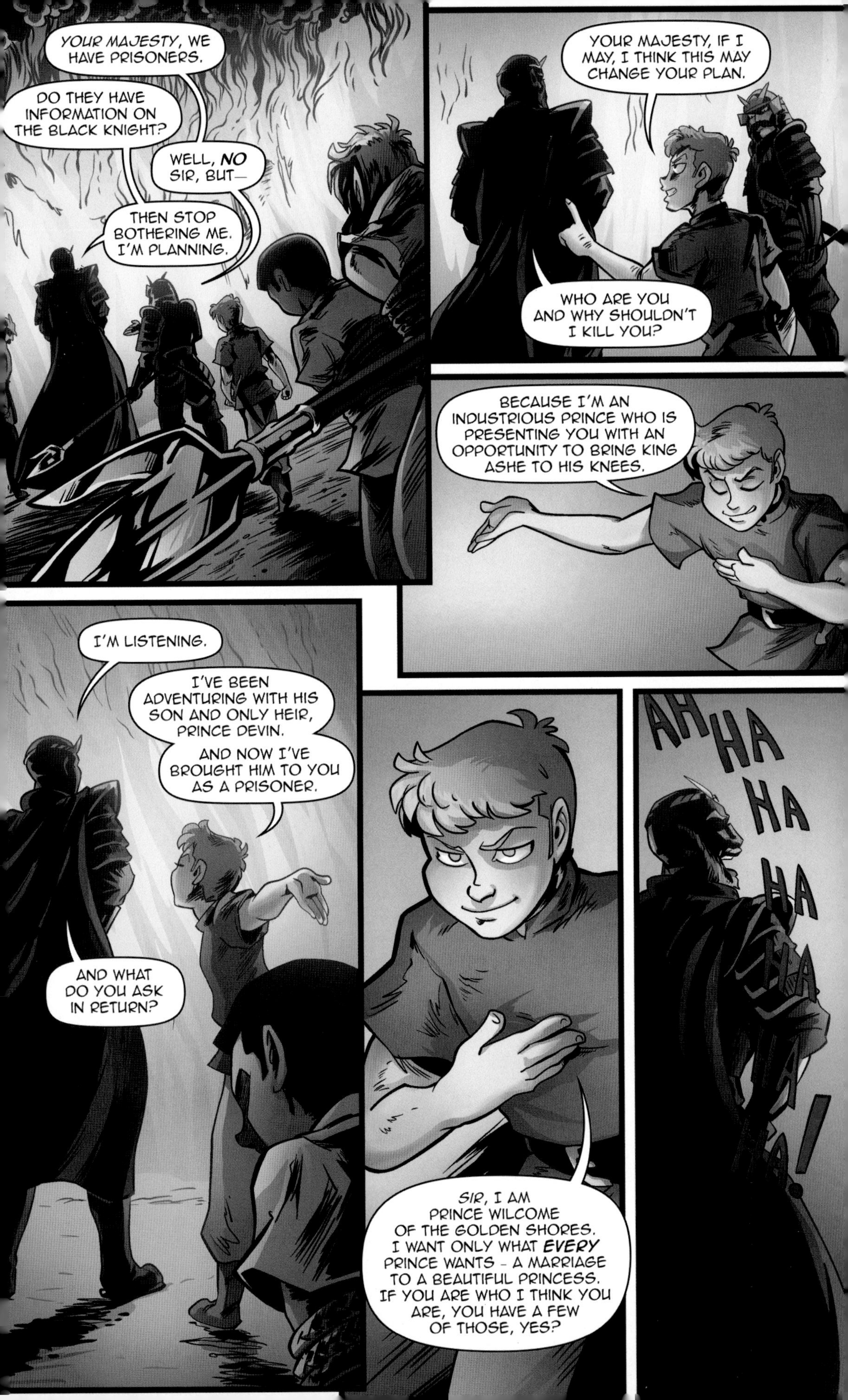
YOUR MAJESTY, WE HAVE PRISONERS.
DO THEY HAVE INFORMATION ON THE BLACK KNIGHT?
WELL, **NO** SIR, BUT—
THEN STOP BOTHERING ME. I'M PLANNING.
YOUR MAJESTY, IF I MAY, I THINK THIS MAY CHANGE YOUR PLAN.
WHO ARE YOU AND WHY SHOULDN'T I KILL YOU?
BECAUSE I'M AN INDUSTRIOUS PRINCE WHO IS PRESENTING YOU WITH AN OPPORTUNITY TO BRING KING ASHE TO HIS KNEES.
I'M LISTENING.
I'VE BEEN ADVENTURING WITH HIS SON AND ONLY HEIR, PRINCE DEVIN.
AND NOW I'VE BROUGHT HIM TO YOU AS A PRISONER.
AND WHAT DO YOU ASK IN RETURN?
SIR, I AM PRINCE WILCOME OF THE GOLDEN SHORES. I WANT ONLY WHAT ***EVERY*** PRINCE WANTS - A MARRIAGE TO A BEAUTIFUL PRINCESS. IF YOU ARE WHO I THINK YOU ARE, YOU HAVE A FEW OF THOSE, YES?
AHHAHAHAHAHAHA!

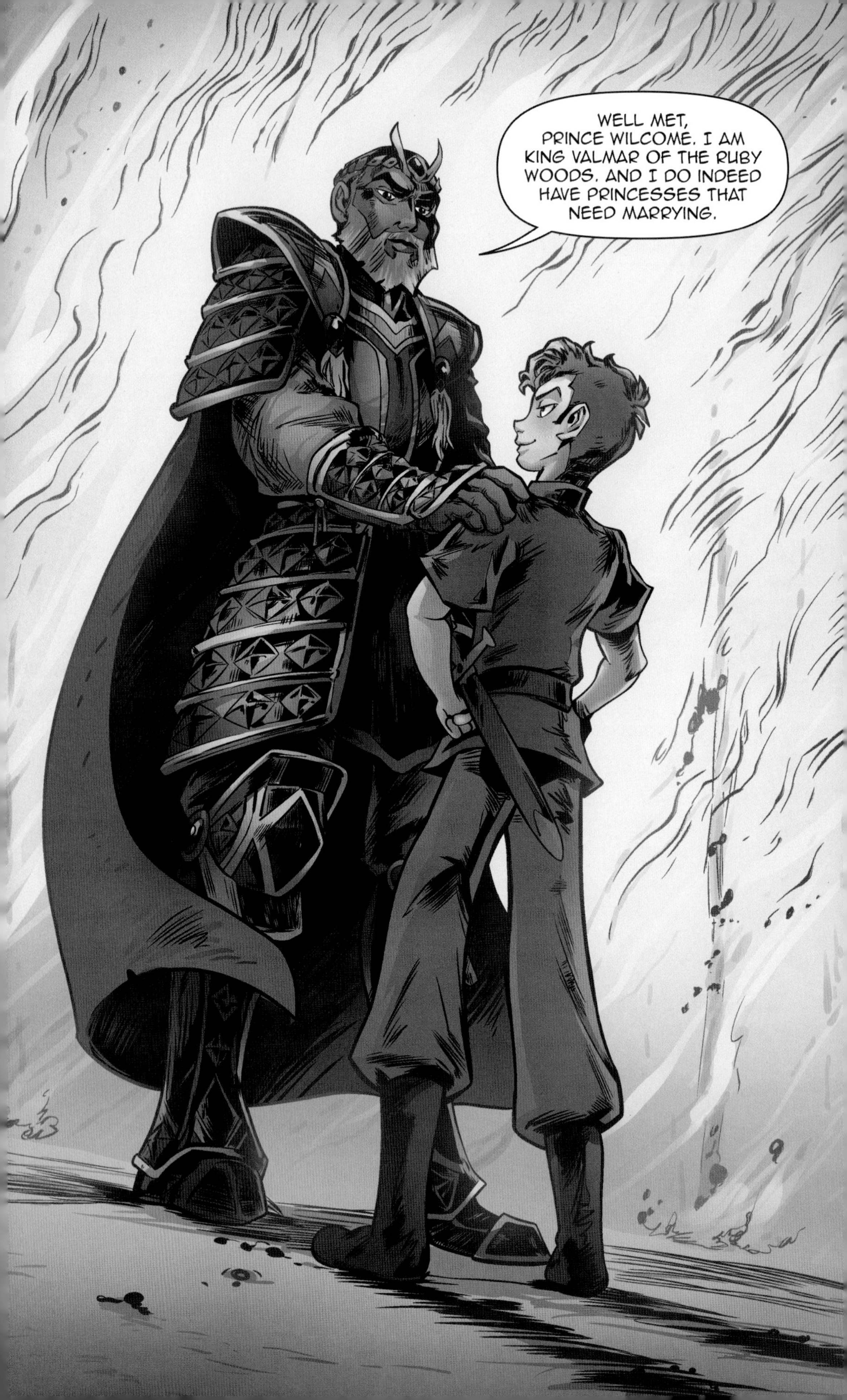
WELL MET, PRINCE WILCOME. I AM KING VALMAR OF THE RUBY WOODS. AND I DO INDEED HAVE PRINCESSES THAT NEED MARRYING.

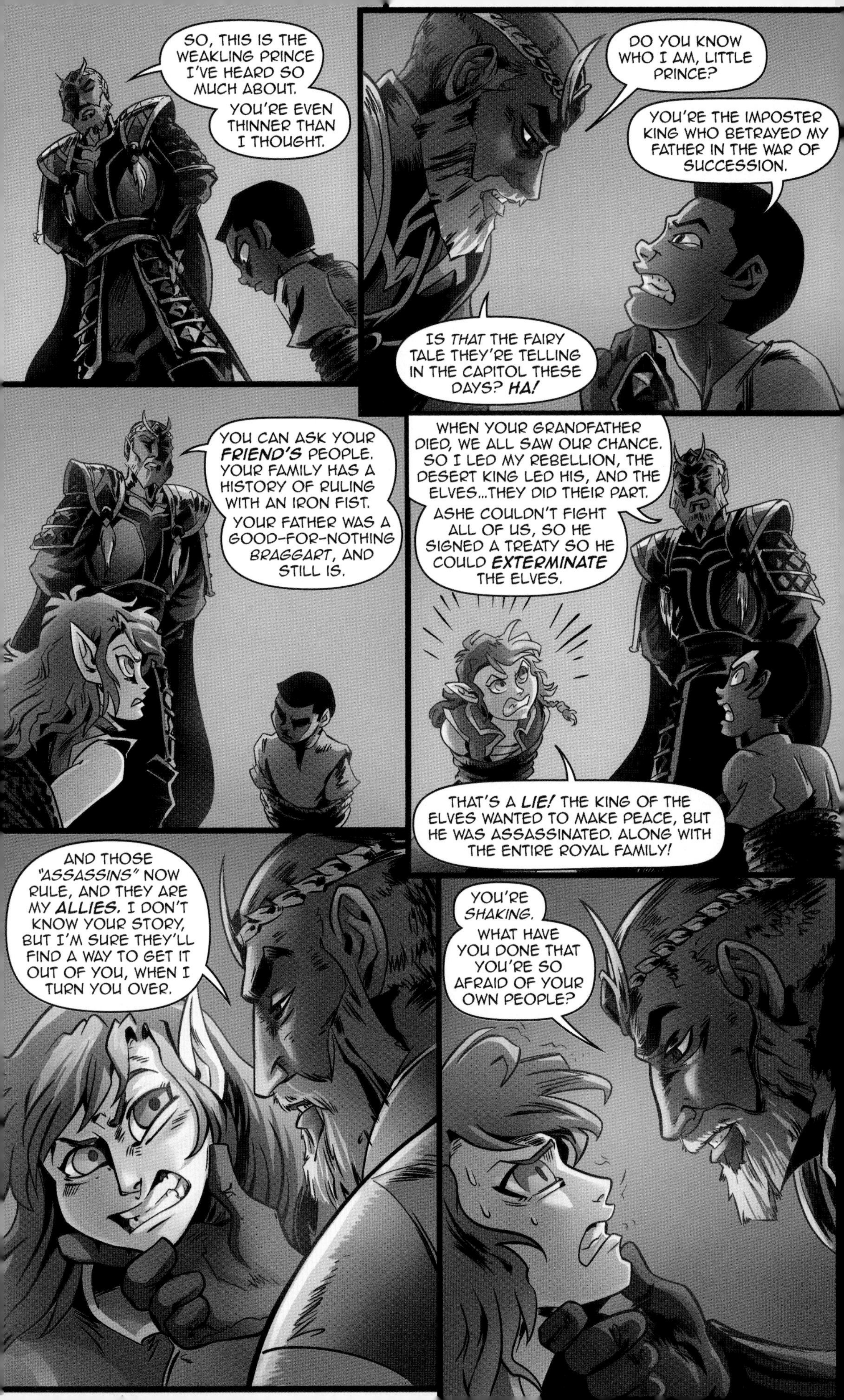
SO, THIS IS THE WEAKLING PRINCE I'VE HEARD SO MUCH ABOUT.
YOU'RE EVEN THINNER THAN I THOUGHT.
DO YOU KNOW WHO I AM, LITTLE PRINCE?
YOU'RE THE IMPOSTER KING WHO BETRAYED MY FATHER IN THE WAR OF SUCCESSION.
IS *THAT* THE FAIRY TALE THEY'RE TELLING IN THE CAPITOL THESE DAYS? ***HA!***
YOU CAN ASK YOUR ***FRIEND'S*** PEOPLE. YOUR FAMILY HAS A HISTORY OF RULING WITH AN IRON FIST.
YOUR FATHER WAS A GOOD-FOR-NOTHING *BRAGGART*, AND STILL IS.
WHEN YOUR GRANDFATHER DIED, WE ALL SAW OUR CHANCE. SO I LED MY REBELLION, THE DESERT KING LED HIS, AND THE ELVES...THEY DID THEIR PART.
ASHE COULDN'T FIGHT ALL OF US, SO HE SIGNED A TREATY SO HE COULD ***EXTERMINATE*** THE ELVES.
THAT'S A ***LIE!*** THE KING OF THE ELVES WANTED TO MAKE PEACE, BUT HE WAS ASSASSINATED. ALONG WITH THE ENTIRE ROYAL FAMILY!
AND THOSE *"ASSASSINS"* NOW RULE, AND THEY ARE MY ***ALLIES.*** I DON'T KNOW YOUR STORY, BUT I'M SURE THEY'LL FIND A WAY TO GET IT OUT OF YOU, WHEN I TURN YOU OVER.
YOU'RE *SHAKING.*
WHAT HAVE YOU DONE THAT YOU'RE SO AFRAID OF YOUR OWN PEOPLE?

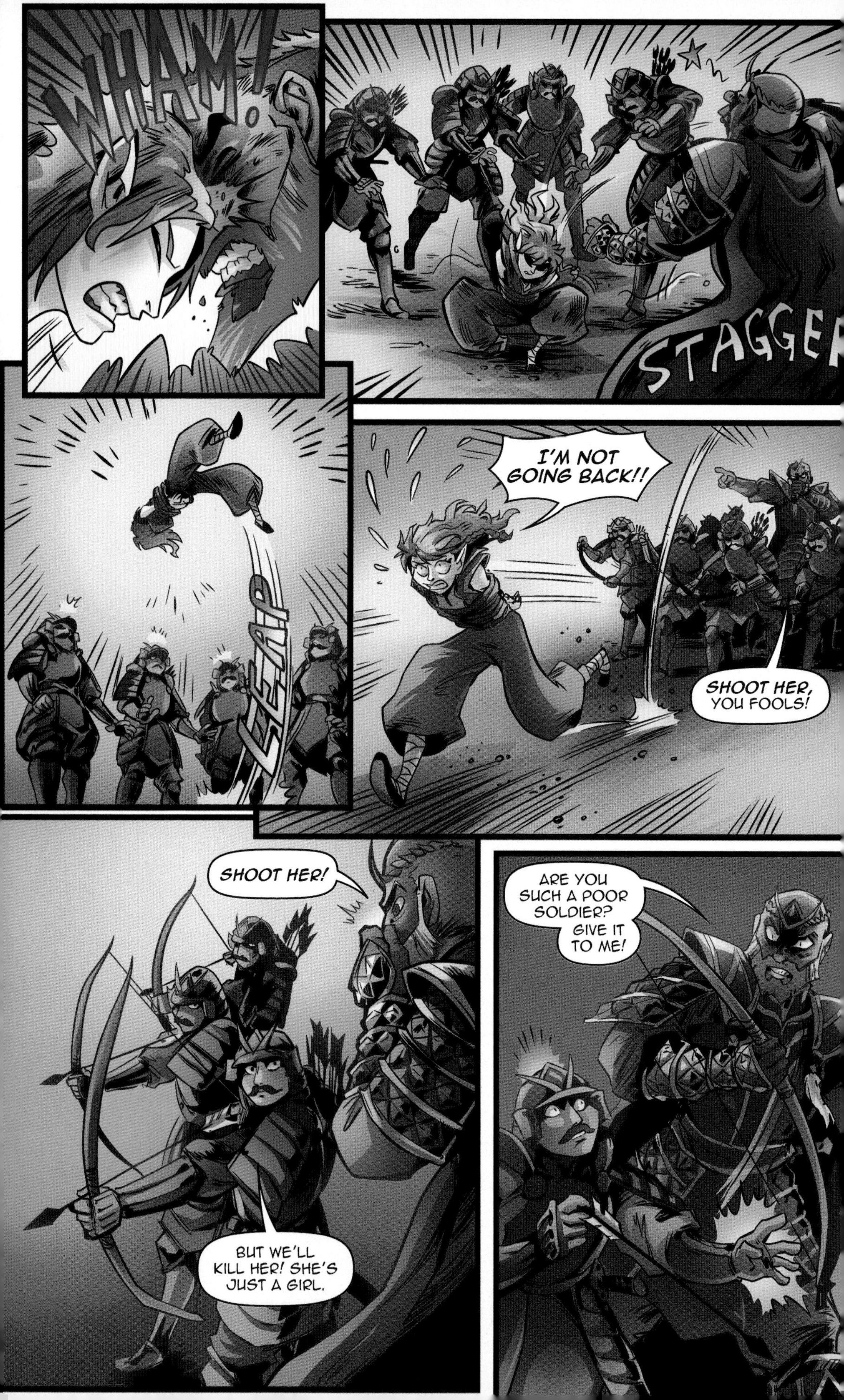
WHAM!
STAGGER
LEAP
I'M NOT GOING BACK!!
SHOOT HER, YOU FOOLS!
SHOOT HER!
BUT WE'LL KILL HER! SHE'S JUST A GIRL.
ARE YOU SUCH A POOR SOLDIER? GIVE IT TO ME!

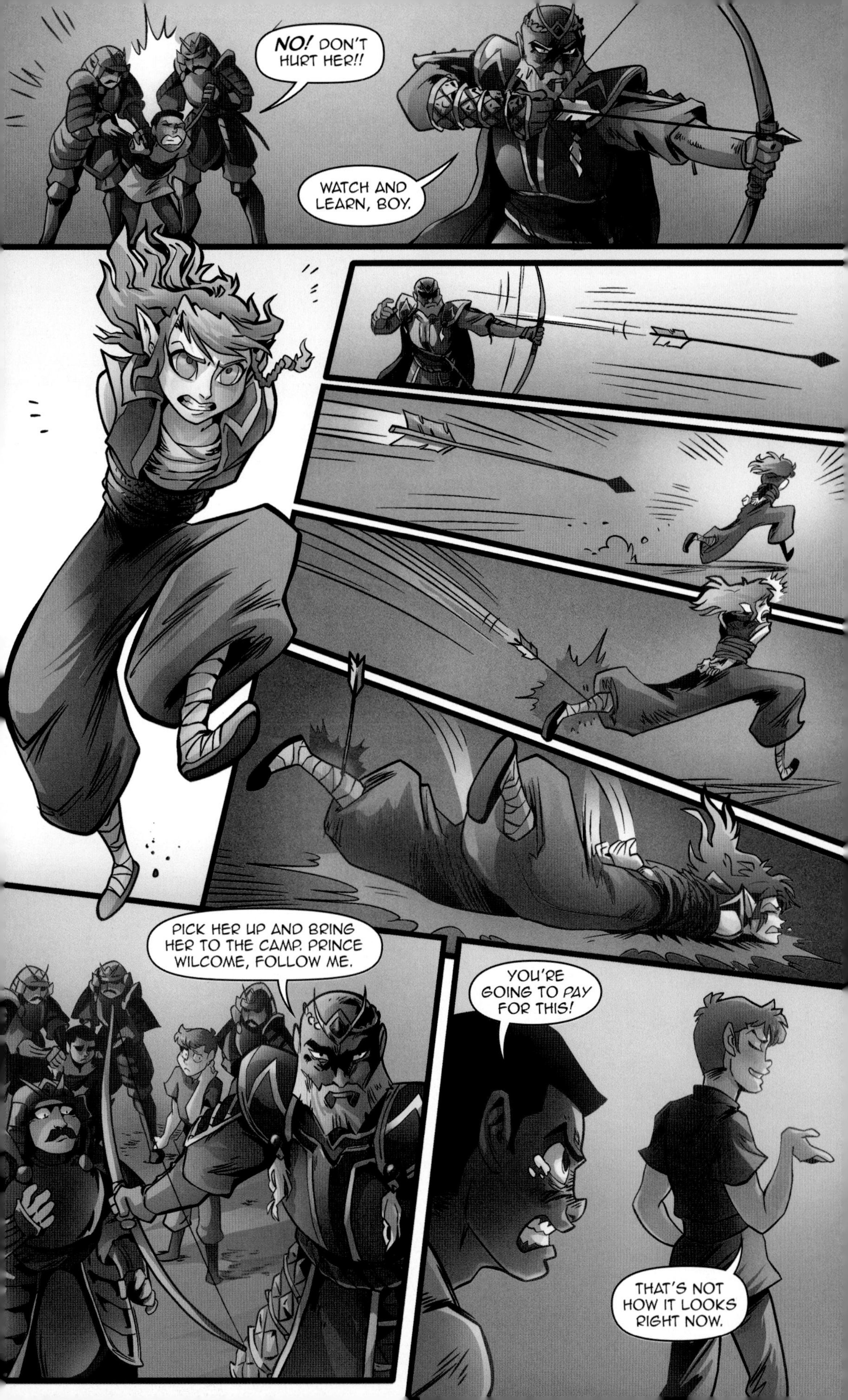
NO! DON'T HURT HER!!
WATCH AND LEARN, BOY.
PICK HER UP AND BRING HER TO THE CAMP. PRINCE WILCOME, FOLLOW ME.
YOU'RE GOING TO PAY FOR THIS!
THAT'S NOT HOW IT LOOKS RIGHT NOW.

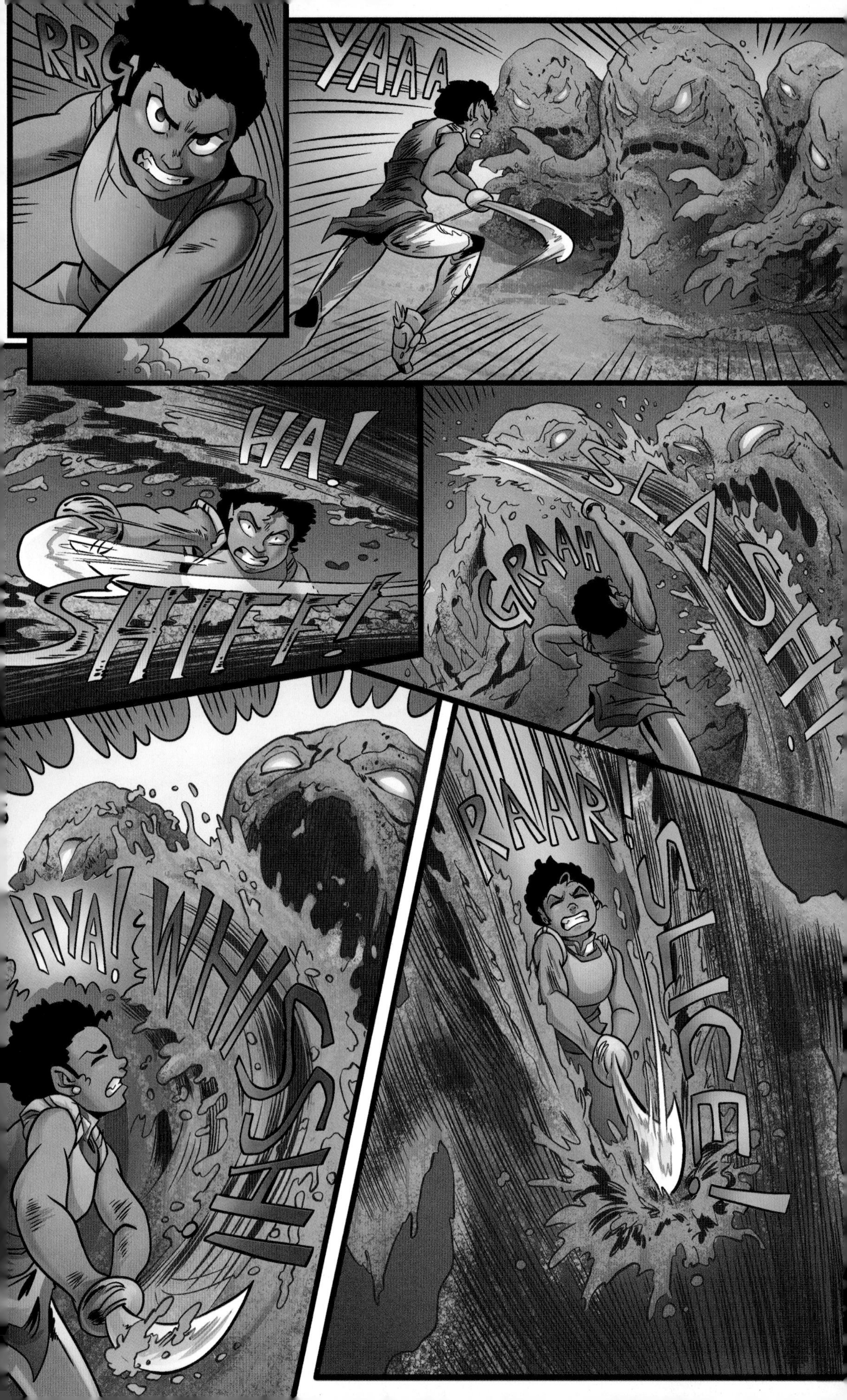
RRG
YAAA
HA!
SHIFF!
SLASH!
GRAAH
HYA!
WHISSH!
RAAR!
SLICE!

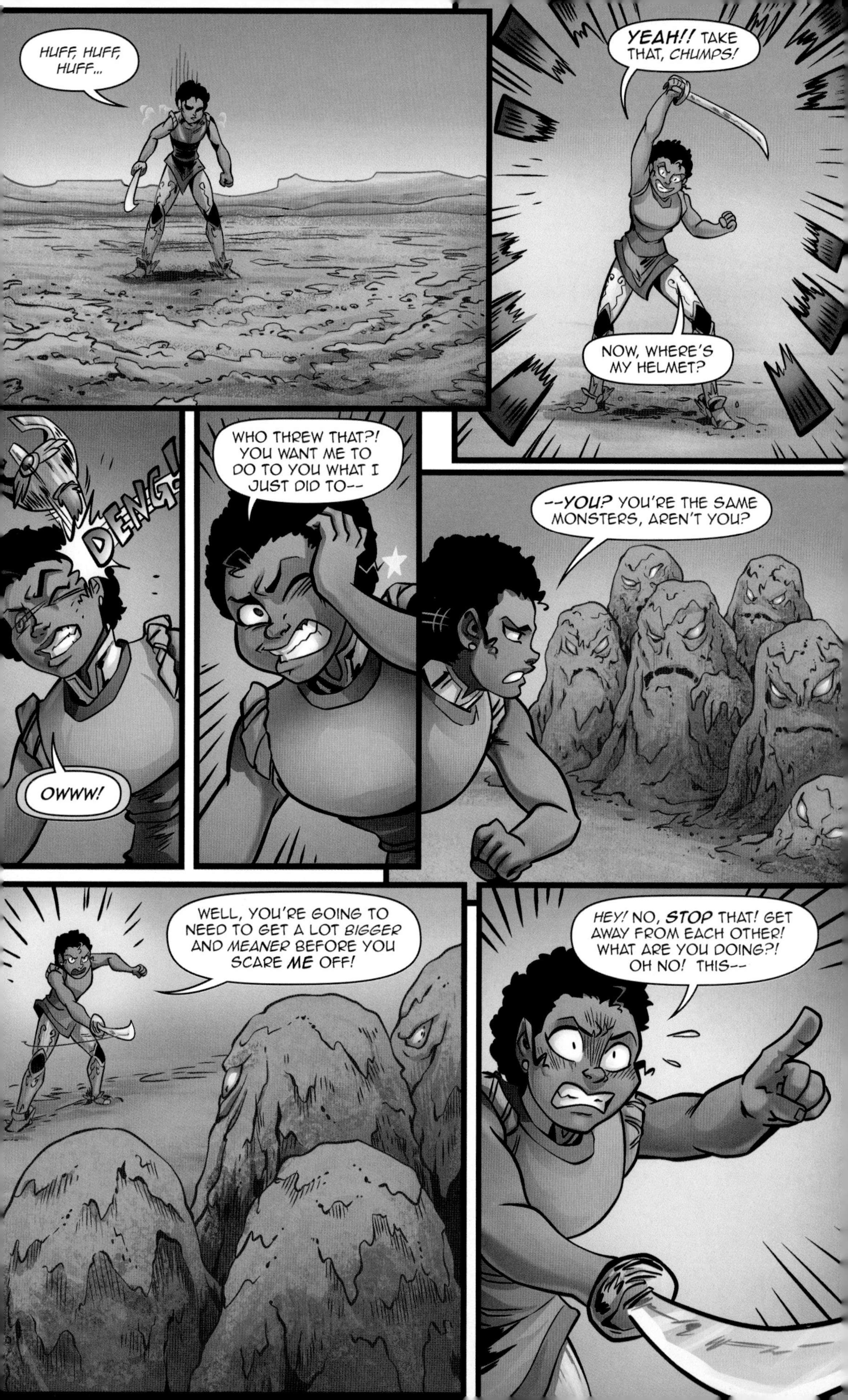
HUFF, HUFF, HUFF...
YEAH!! TAKE THAT, CHUMPS!
NOW, WHERE'S MY HELMET?
DENG!
OWWW!
WHO THREW THAT?! YOU WANT ME TO DO TO YOU WHAT I JUST DID TO--
--YOU? YOU'RE THE SAME MONSTERS, AREN'T YOU?
WELL, YOU'RE GOING TO NEED TO GET A LOT BIGGER AND MEANER BEFORE YOU SCARE ME OFF!
HEY! NO, STOP THAT! GET AWAY FROM EACH OTHER! WHAT ARE YOU DOING?! OH NO! THIS--

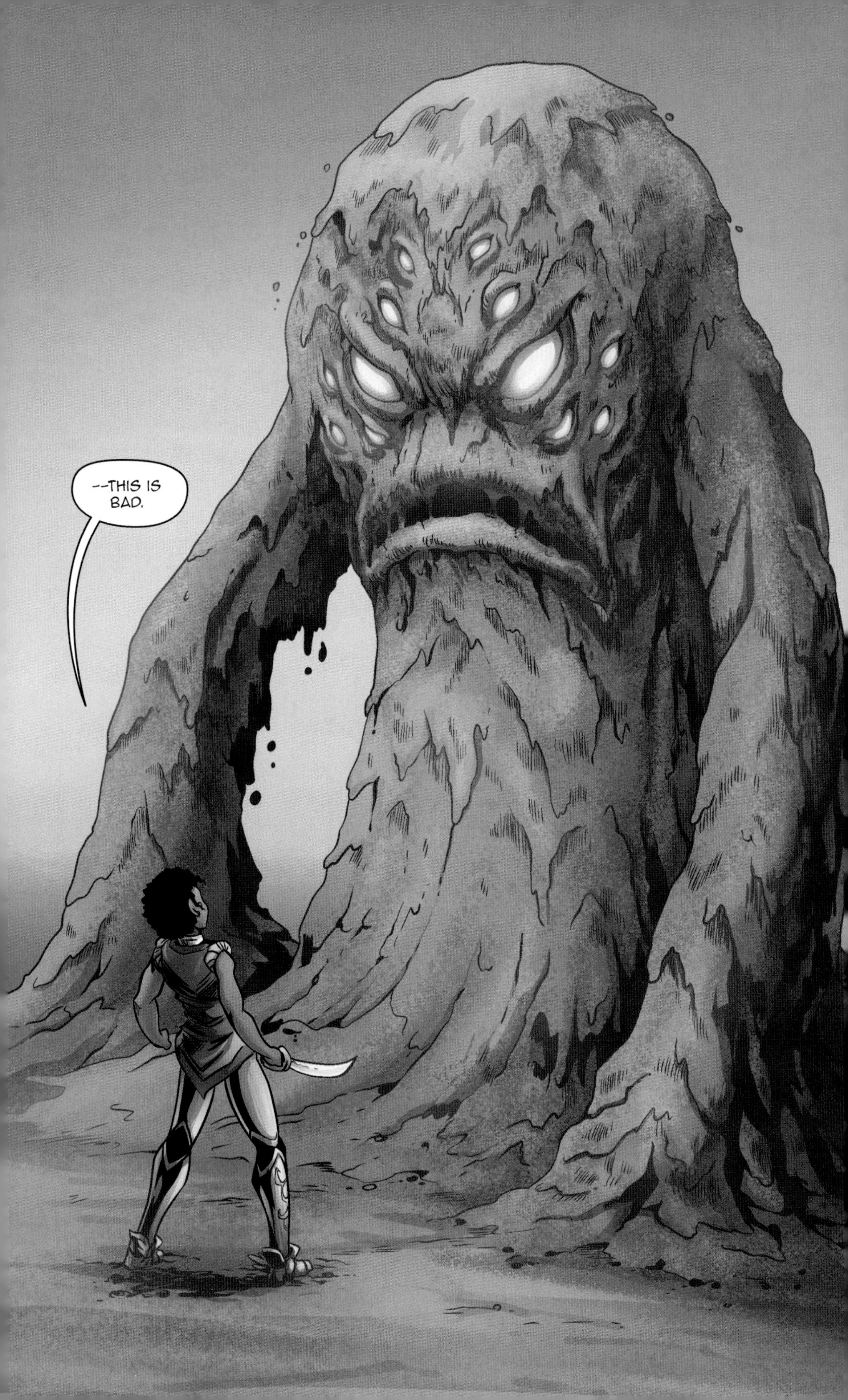
--THIS IS
BAD.

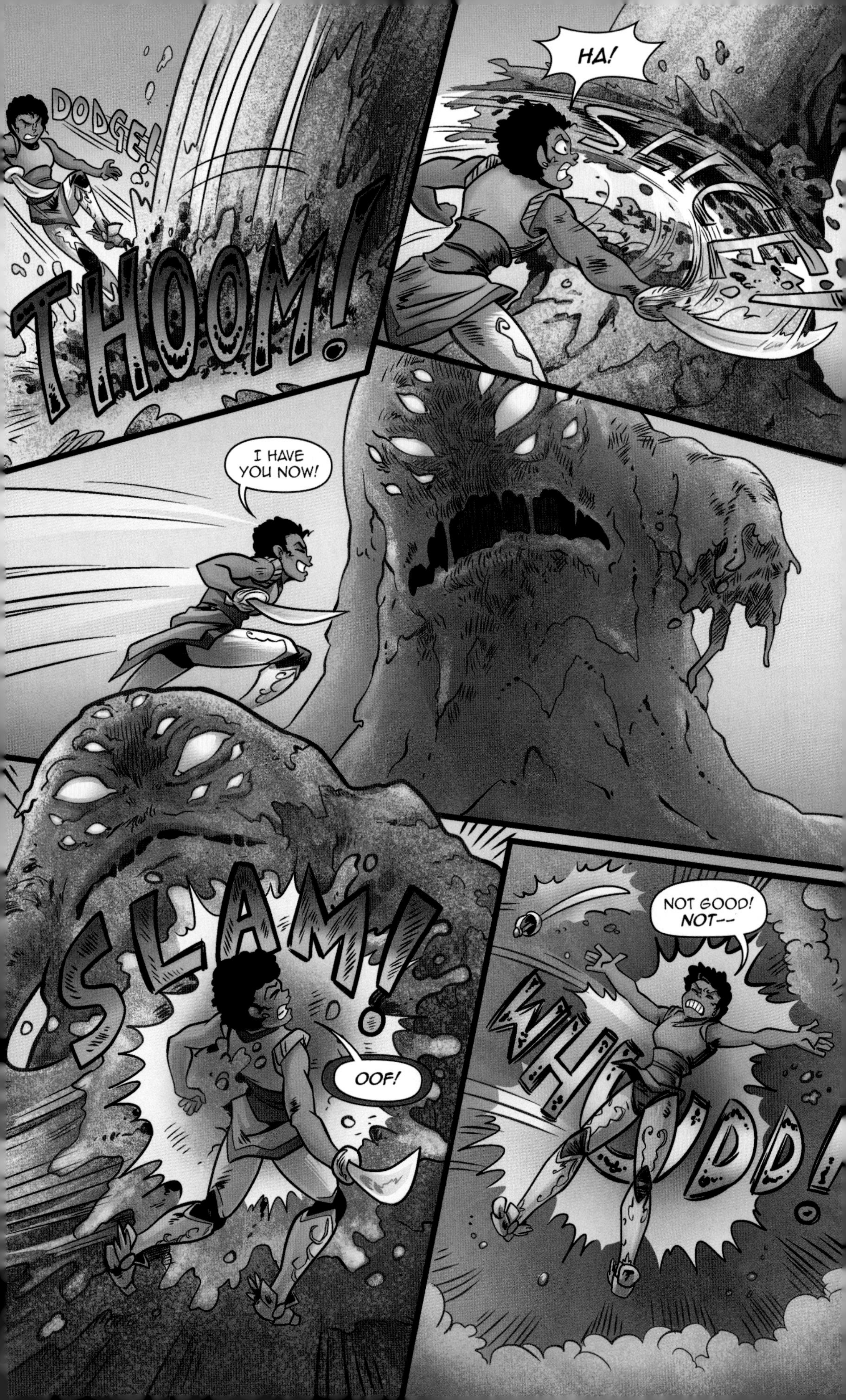
DODGE!
THOOM!
HA!
I HAVE YOU NOW!
SLAM!
OOF!
NOT GOOD! NOT--

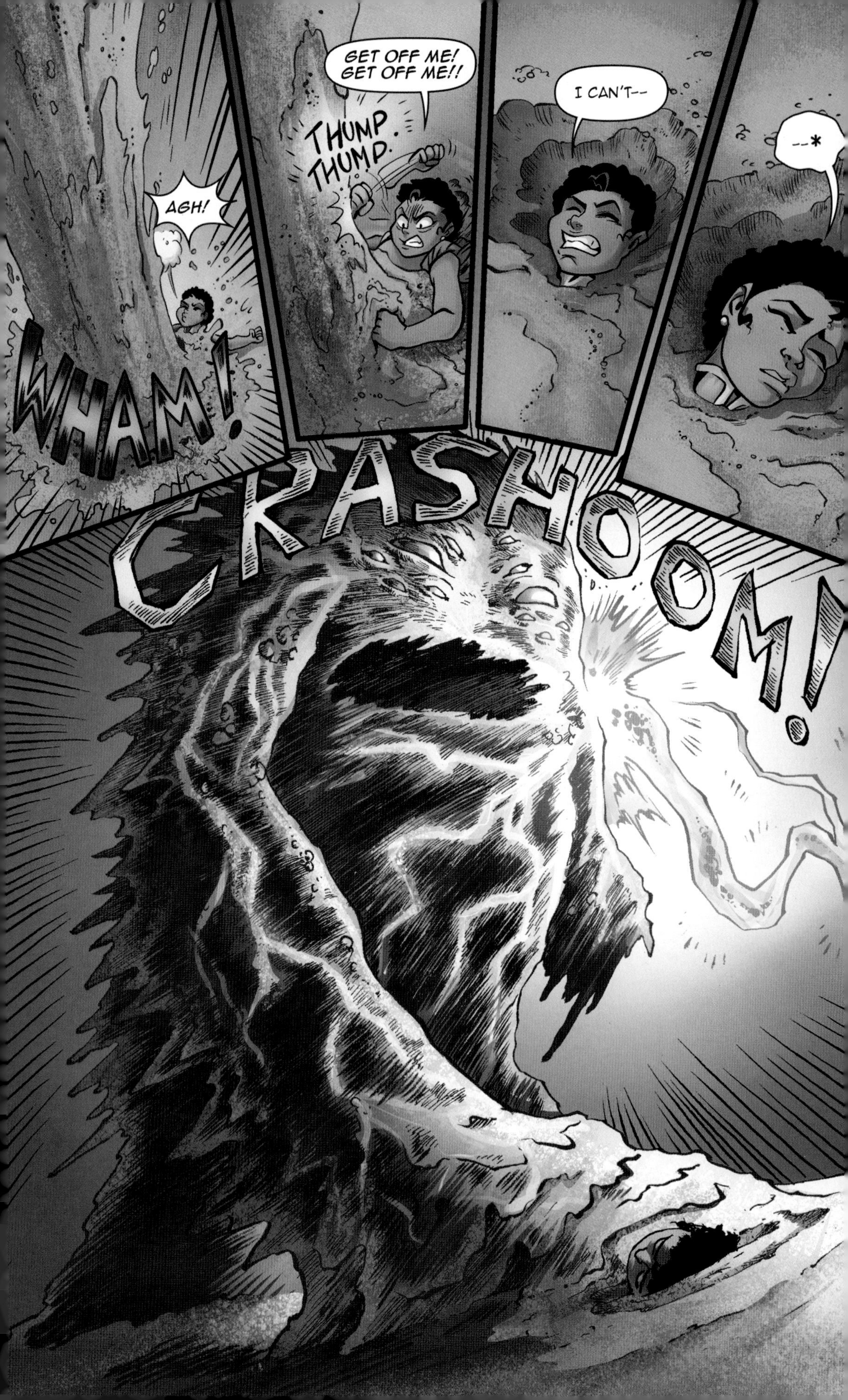
AGH!
WHAM!
GET OFF ME! GET OFF ME!!
THUMP THUMP
I CAN'T--
--*
CRASHOOOM!

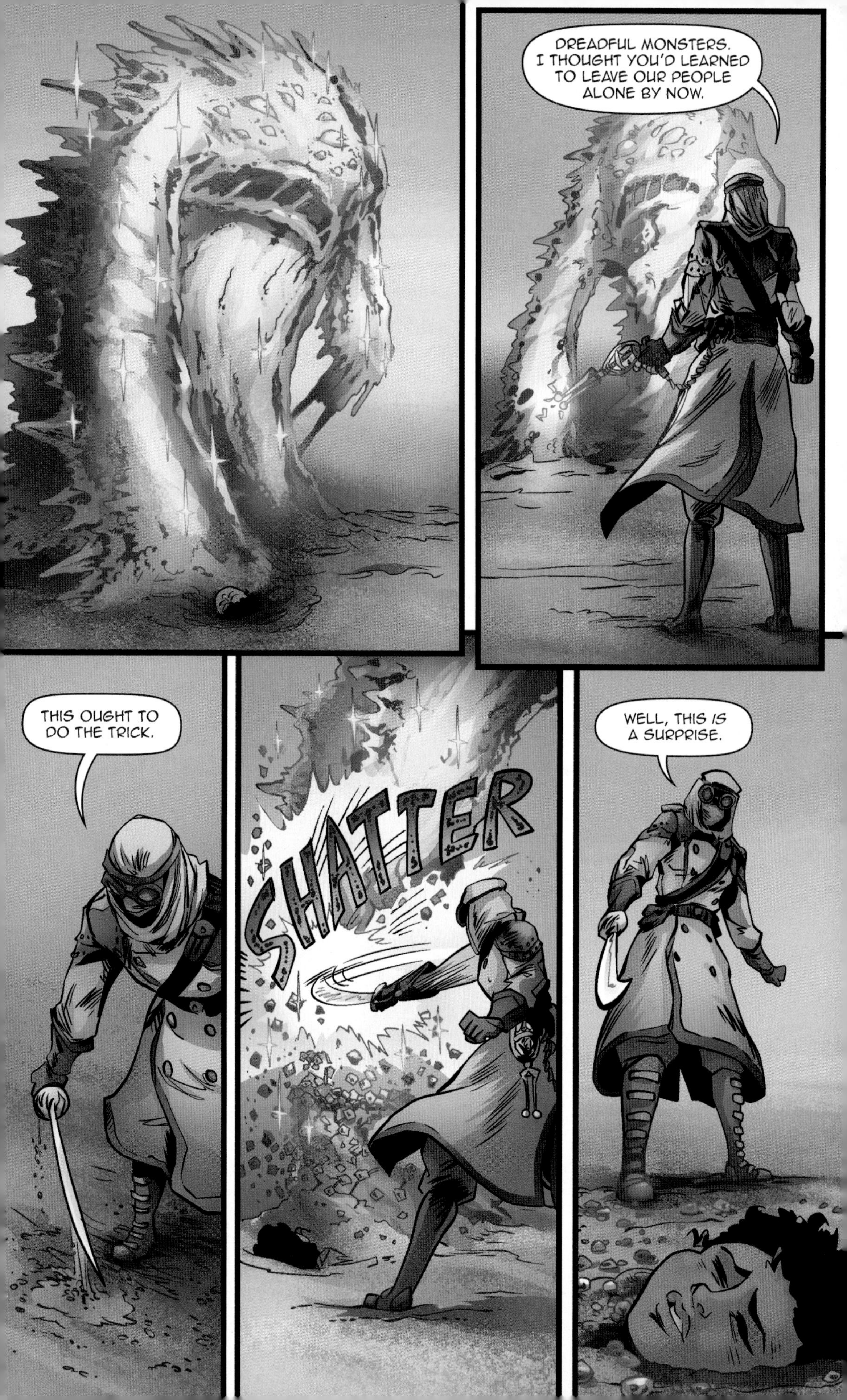
DREADFUL MONSTERS. I THOUGHT YOU'D LEARNED TO LEAVE OUR PEOPLE ALONE BY NOW.
THIS OUGHT TO DO THE TRICK.
SHATTER
WELL, THIS *IS* A SURPRISE.

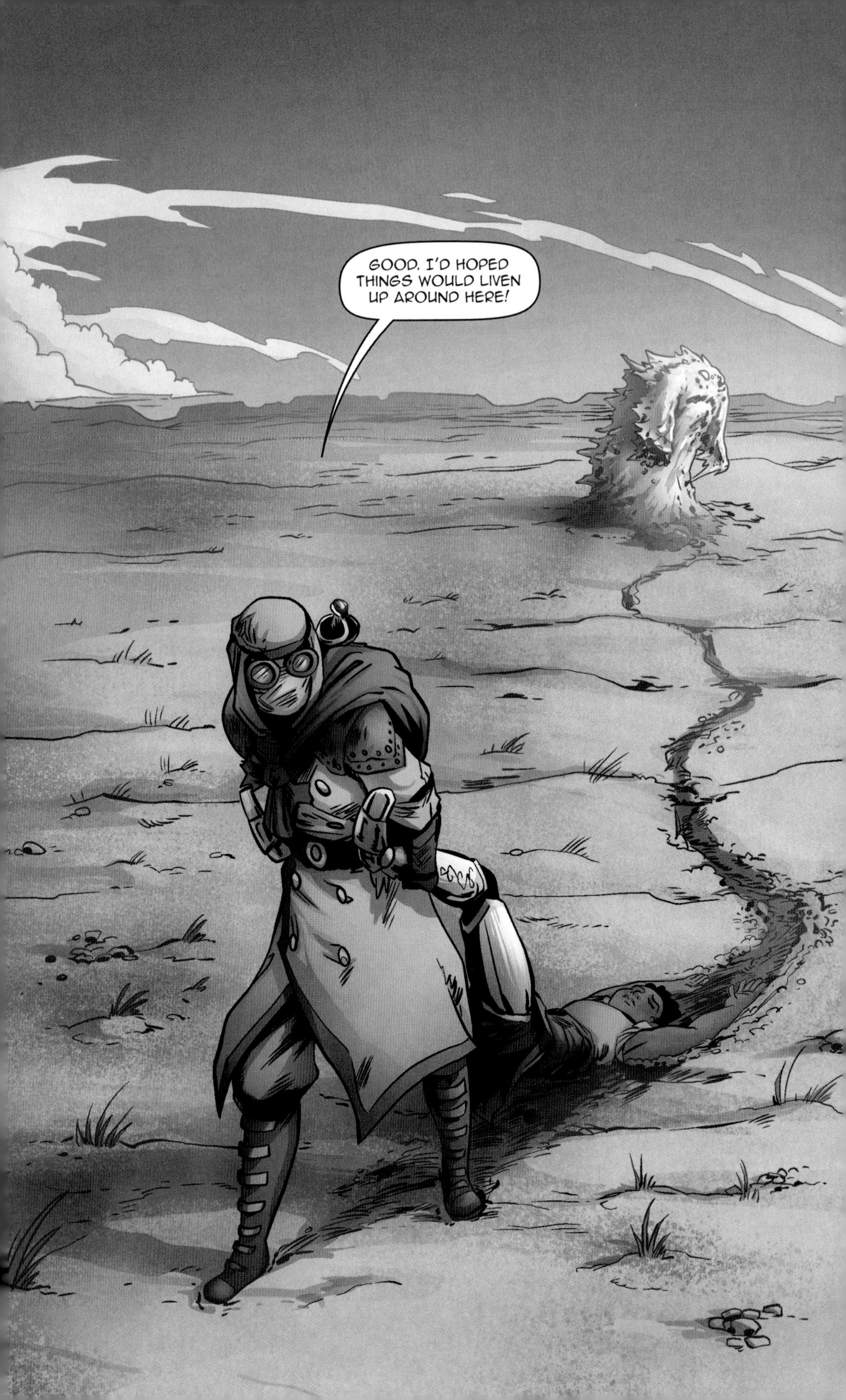
GOOD. I'D HOPED THINGS WOULD LIVEN UP AROUND HERE!

Page 20:

Panel 1: Adrienne rears back to slash with her sword. The sand creatures are reaching out for her.

ADRIENNE
Yaa!

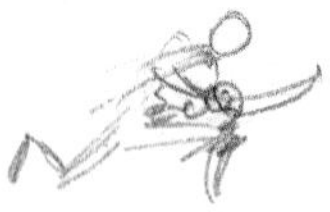

Panel 2: Adrienne slashes through one of the sand creatures.

ADRIENNE
Ha!

SFX
Slice.

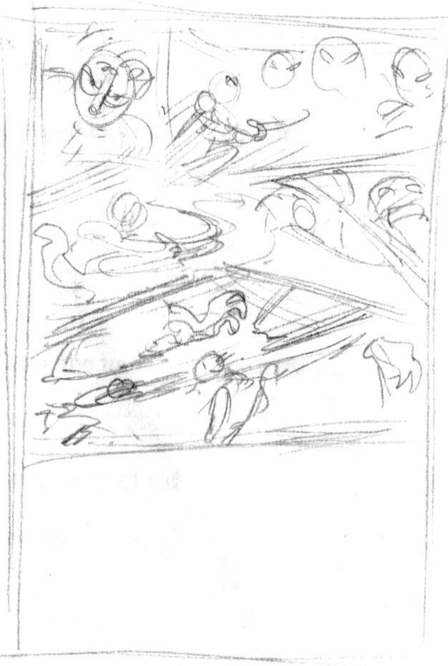

Panel 3: Adrienne cuts two sand creatures diagonally.

ADRIENNE
Raar!

SFX
Shing!

Panel 4: Adrienne slices through two more.

ADRIENNE
Graaa!

SFX
Swish!

Panel 5: Adrienne swings down through the last sand creature, cutting them in half.

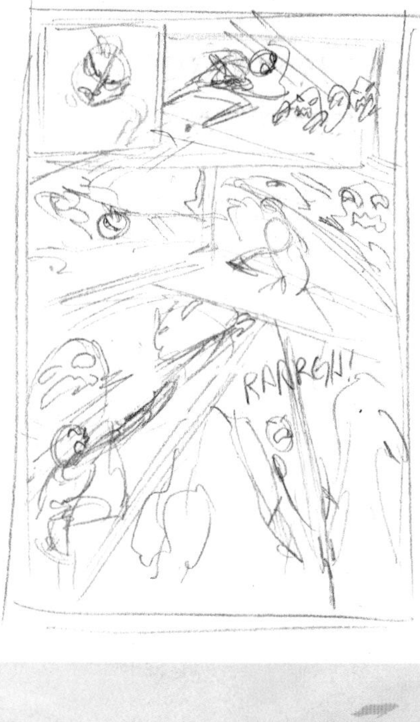

ARTIST EMILY MARTIN'S NOTES
ON ORIGINAL SCRIPT PAGES
TEXT BY JEREMY WHITLEY

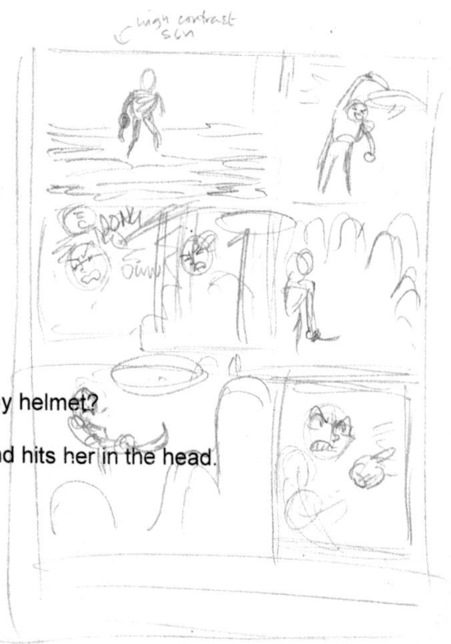
high contrast scn

Page 21:
Panel 1: Adrienne stands alone in the sand. She is panting.

ADRIENNE
Huff huff huff...

Panel 2: Adrienne holds her sword up over her head.

ADRIENNE
Yeah! Take that chumps! Now where's my helmet?

Panel 3: Adrienne's helmet comes flying in from off panel and hits her in the head.

SFX
Dong!

ADRIENNE
Owww!

Panel 4: Adrienne rubs the sore spot where she was hit as she turns to look where the helmet came from.

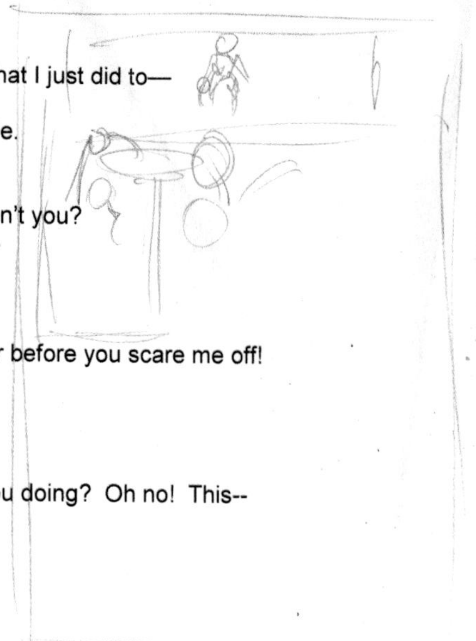

ADRIENNE
Who threw that?! You want me to do to you what I just did to—

Panel 5: Six identical sand monsters approach from the side.

ADRIENNE
--You? You're the same monsters aren't you?

Panel 6: Adrienne lifts her sword again.

ADRIENNE
Well you're going to need to get a lot bigger and meaner before you scare me off!

Panel 7: Adrienne's face. She suddenly looks panicked.

ADRIENNE
No, stop that! Get away from each other! What are you doing? Oh no! This--

ARTIST EMILY MARTIN'S NOTES ON ORIGINAL SCRIPT PAGES
TEXT BY JEREMY WHITLEY

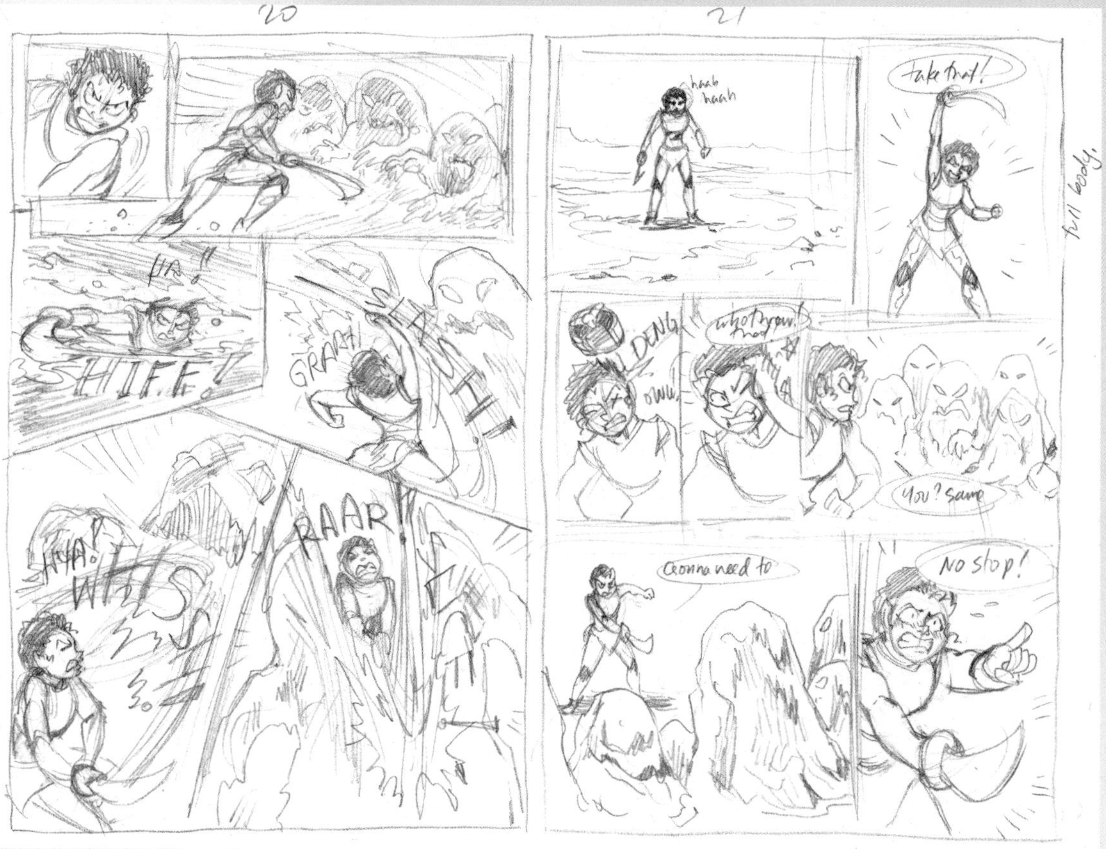

20
21
HA!
SHIFF!
GRAAH
HYA!
RAAR!
haah haah
take that!
full body.
DENG
oww
You? same
Gonna need to
No stop!

THUMBNAILS FOR PAGES 20 & 21

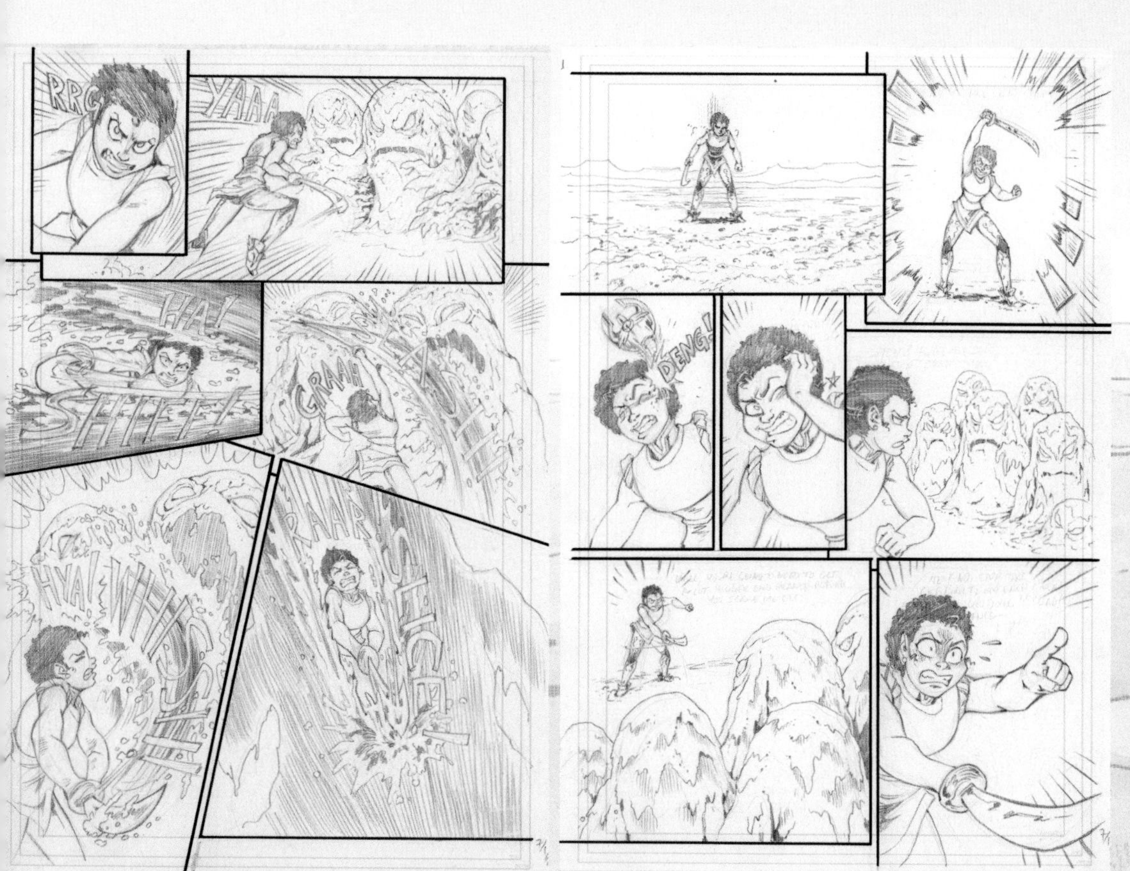

RRG
YAAA
HA!
SHIFF!
GRAAH
HYA!
RAAR
DENG!

PENCILS FOR PAGES 20 & 21

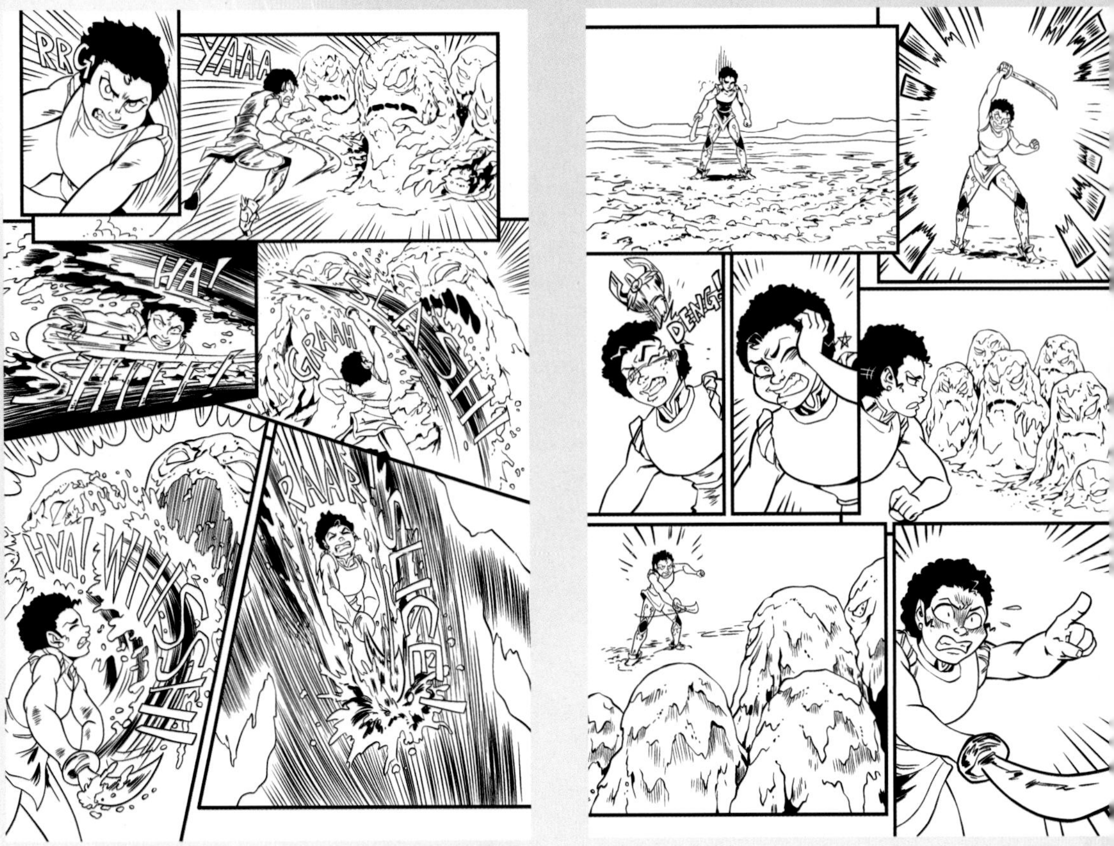
RRG
YAAA
HA!
SHIFF!
GRAAH
SLASH!
HYA!
RAAR!
SLICE!
DENG!

INKS FOR PAGES 20 & 21

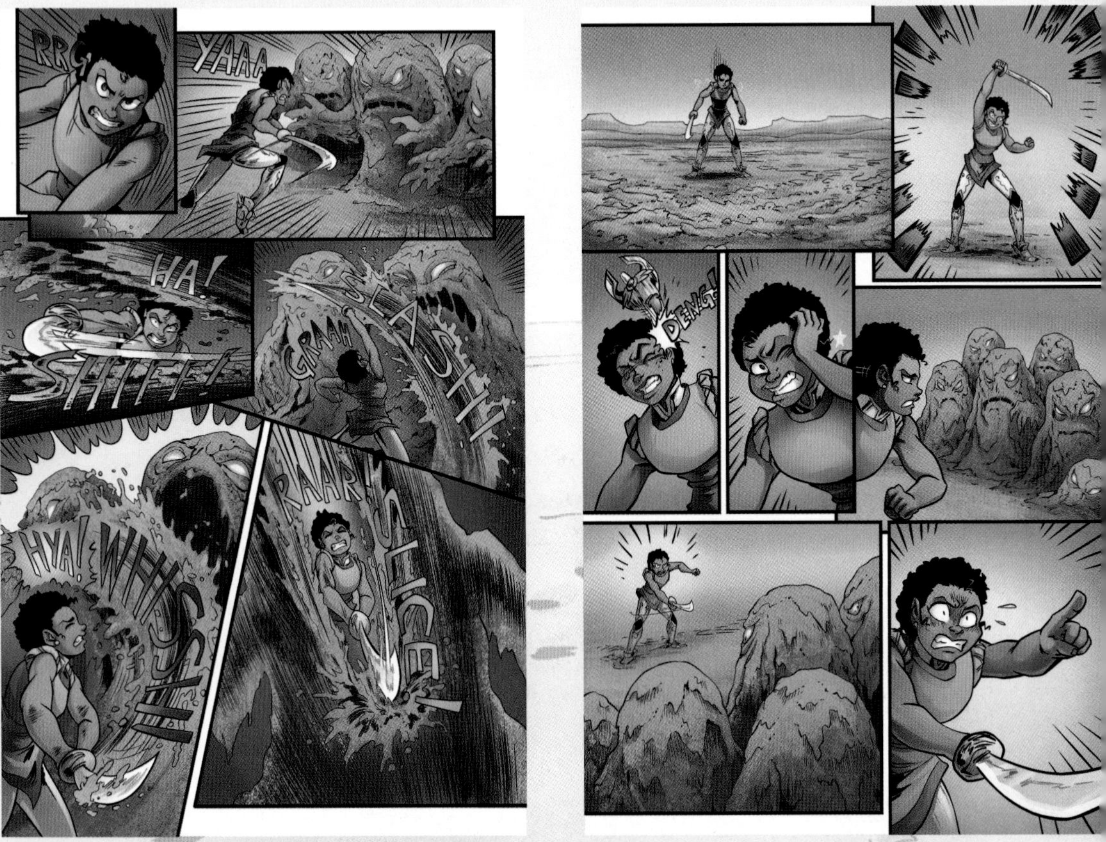
RRG
YAAA
HA!
SHIFF!
GRAAH
SLASH!
HYA!
RAAR!
SLICE!
DENG!

COLORS FOR PAGES 20 & 21

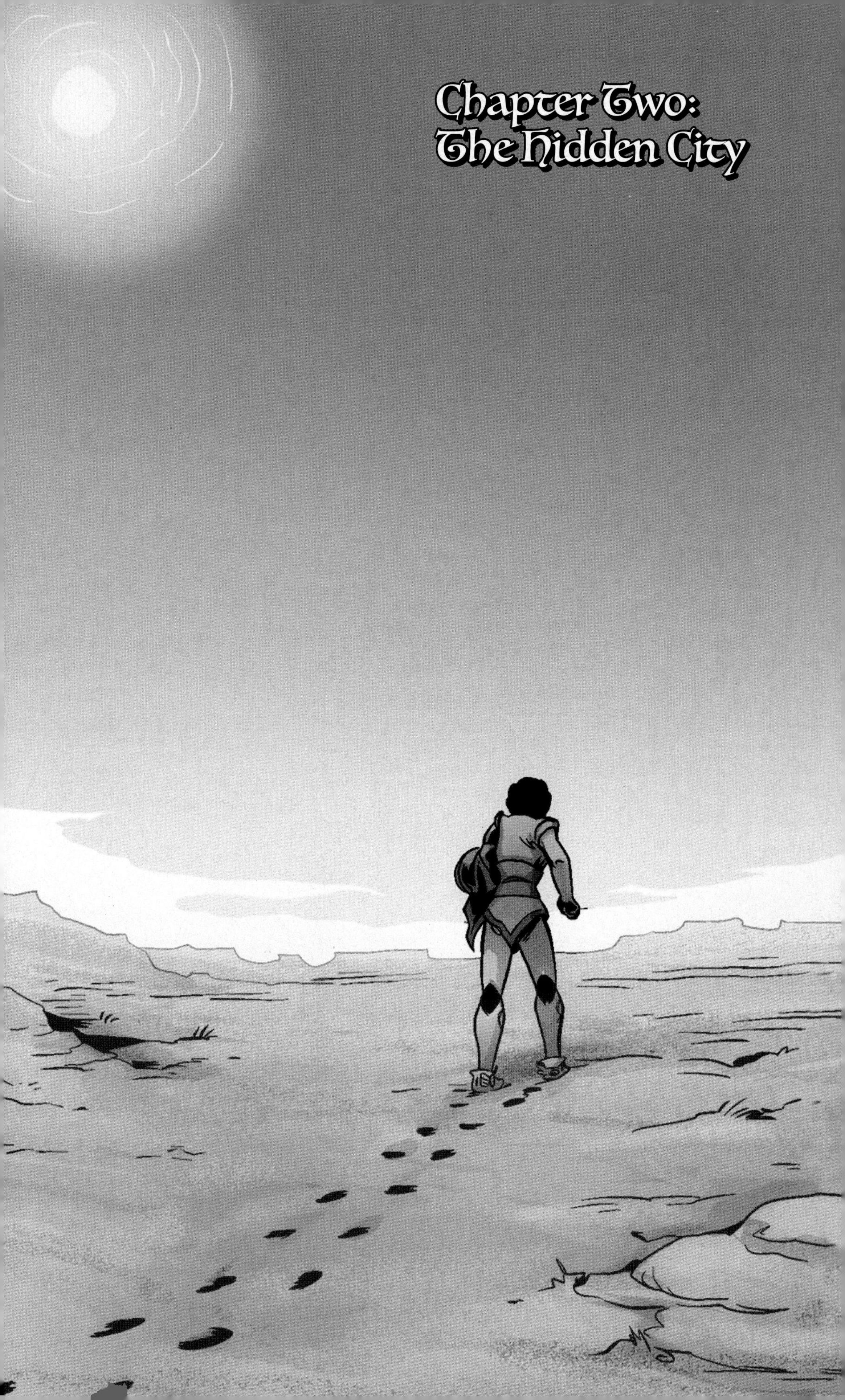
Chapter Two:
The Hidden City

STORY:
Jeremy Whitley

PENCILS:
Emily Martin

INKS:
Ainhoa Aramayo (Pages 1-15)
& Christine Hipp (Pages 16-24)

COLORS & LETTERS:
Brett Grunig

COVER A: Emily Martin   **COVER B:** Onyinye Anakor

EDITORS:
Alicia Whitley (script)
Nicole D'Andria (comic)

Bryan Seaton: Publisher/ CEO • **Shawn Gabborin:** Editor In Chief
Jason Martin: Publisher-Danger Zone • **Nicole D'Andria:** Marketing Director/Editor
Jim Dietz: Social Media Manager • **Danielle Davison:** Executive Administrator
Chad Cicconi: Still Waiting For His Princess • **Shawn Pryor:** President of Creator Relations

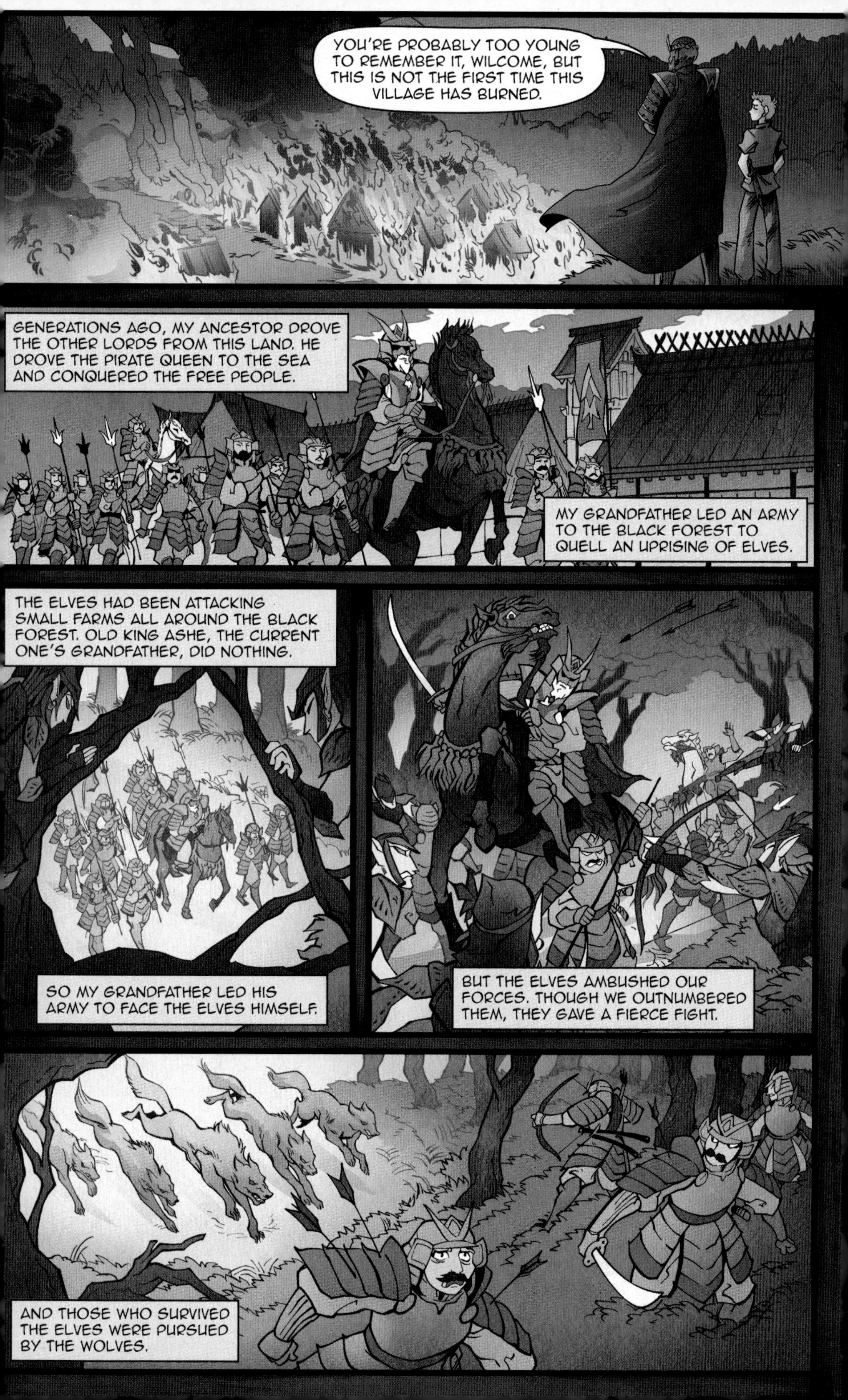
YOU'RE PROBABLY TOO YOUNG TO REMEMBER IT, WILCOME, BUT THIS IS NOT THE FIRST TIME THIS VILLAGE HAS BURNED.
GENERATIONS AGO, MY ANCESTOR DROVE THE OTHER LORDS FROM THIS LAND. HE DROVE THE PIRATE QUEEN TO THE SEA AND CONQUERED THE FREE PEOPLE.
MY GRANDFATHER LED AN ARMY TO THE BLACK FOREST TO QUELL AN UPRISING OF ELVES.
THE ELVES HAD BEEN ATTACKING SMALL FARMS ALL AROUND THE BLACK FOREST. OLD KING ASHE, THE CURRENT ONE'S GRANDFATHER, DID NOTHING.
SO MY GRANDFATHER LED HIS ARMY TO FACE THE ELVES HIMSELF.
BUT THE ELVES AMBUSHED OUR FORCES. THOUGH WE OUTNUMBERED THEM, THEY GAVE A FIERCE FIGHT.
AND THOSE WHO SURVIVED THE ELVES WERE PURSUED BY THE WOLVES.

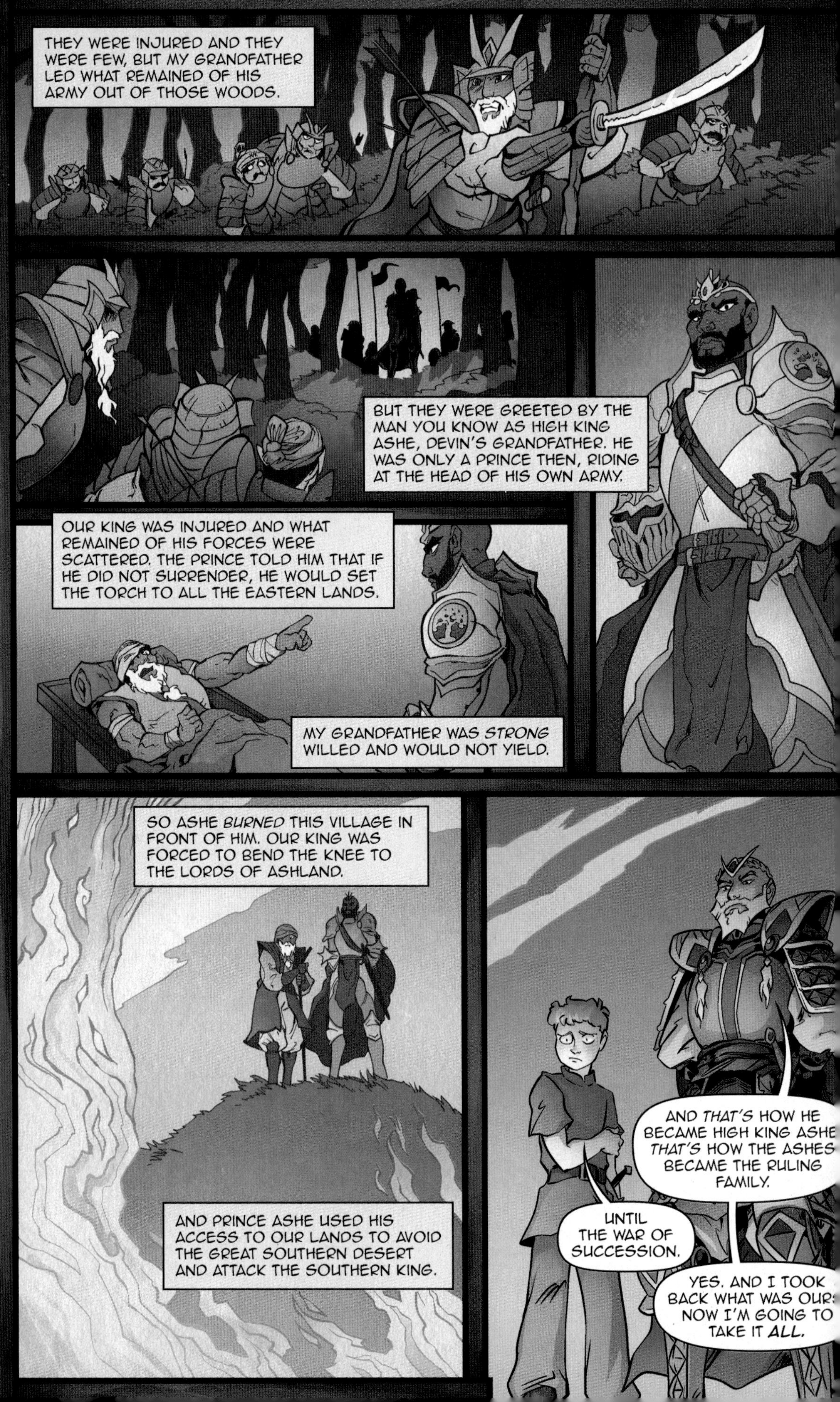
THEY WERE INJURED AND THEY WERE FEW, BUT MY GRANDFATHER LED WHAT REMAINED OF HIS ARMY OUT OF THOSE WOODS.
BUT THEY WERE GREETED BY THE MAN YOU KNOW AS HIGH KING ASHE, DEVIN'S GRANDFATHER. HE WAS ONLY A PRINCE THEN, RIDING AT THE HEAD OF HIS OWN ARMY.
OUR KING WAS INJURED AND WHAT REMAINED OF HIS FORCES WERE SCATTERED. THE PRINCE TOLD HIM THAT IF HE DID NOT SURRENDER, HE WOULD SET THE TORCH TO ALL THE EASTERN LANDS.
MY GRANDFATHER WAS *STRONG* WILLED AND WOULD NOT YIELD.
SO ASHE *BURNED* THIS VILLAGE IN FRONT OF HIM. OUR KING WAS FORCED TO BEND THE KNEE TO THE LORDS OF ASHLAND.
AND PRINCE ASHE USED HIS ACCESS TO OUR LANDS TO AVOID THE GREAT SOUTHERN DESERT AND ATTACK THE SOUTHERN KING.
AND *THAT'S* HOW HE BECAME HIGH KING ASHE *THAT'S* HOW THE ASHES BECAME THE RULING FAMILY.
UNTIL THE WAR OF SUCCESSION.
YES. AND I TOOK BACK WHAT WAS OUR NOW I'M GOING TO TAKE IT *ALL*.

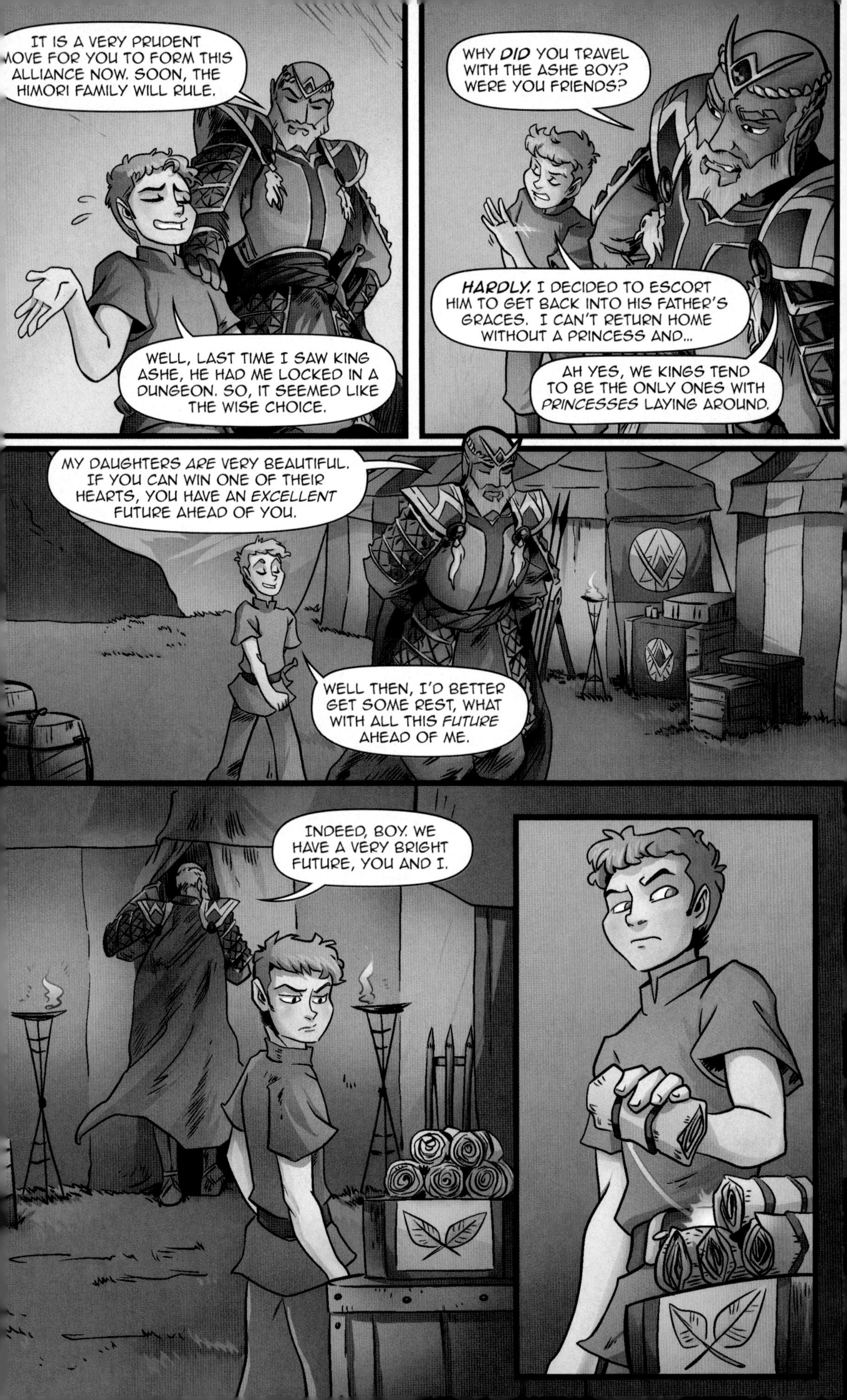
IT IS A VERY PRUDENT MOVE FOR YOU TO FORM THIS ALLIANCE NOW. SOON, THE HIMORI FAMILY WILL RULE.
WELL, LAST TIME I SAW KING ASHE, HE HAD ME LOCKED IN A DUNGEON. SO, IT SEEMED LIKE THE WISE CHOICE.
WHY *DID* YOU TRAVEL WITH THE ASHE BOY? WERE YOU FRIENDS?
HARDLY. I DECIDED TO ESCORT HIM TO GET BACK INTO HIS FATHER'S GRACES. I CAN'T RETURN HOME WITHOUT A PRINCESS AND...
AH YES, WE KINGS TEND TO BE THE ONLY ONES WITH *PRINCESSES* LAYING AROUND.
MY DAUGHTERS *ARE* VERY BEAUTIFUL. IF YOU CAN WIN ONE OF THEIR HEARTS, YOU HAVE AN *EXCELLENT* FUTURE AHEAD OF YOU.
WELL THEN, I'D BETTER GET SOME REST, WHAT WITH ALL THIS *FUTURE* AHEAD OF ME.
INDEED, BOY. WE HAVE A VERY BRIGHT FUTURE, YOU AND I.

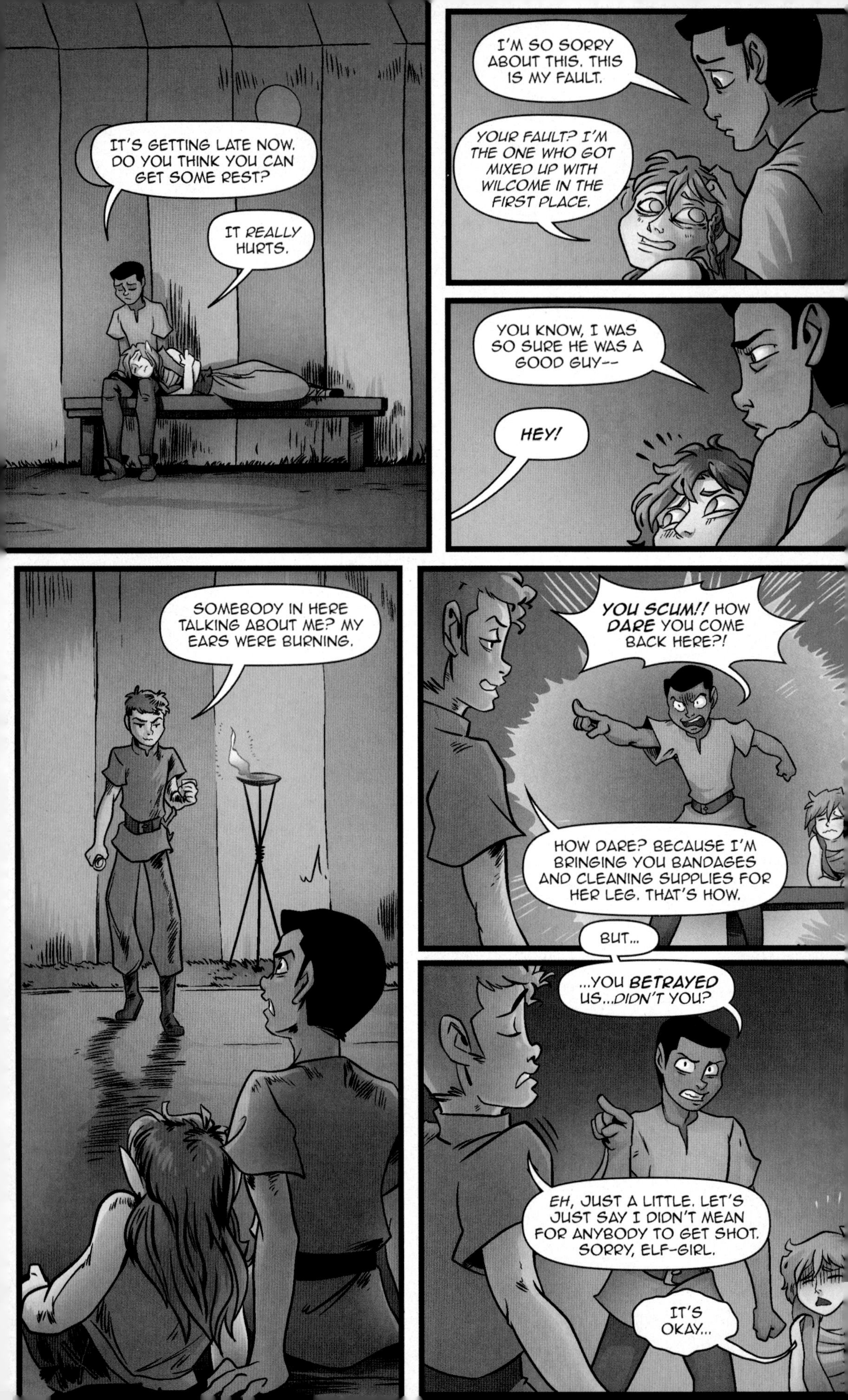
IT'S GETTING LATE NOW. DO YOU THINK YOU CAN GET SOME REST?
IT *REALLY* HURTS.
I'M SO SORRY ABOUT THIS. THIS IS MY FAULT.
YOUR FAULT? I'M THE ONE WHO GOT MIXED UP WITH WILCOME IN THE FIRST PLACE.
YOU KNOW, I WAS SO SURE HE WAS A GOOD GUY--
HEY!
SOMEBODY IN HERE TALKING ABOUT ME? MY EARS WERE BURNING.
YOU SCUM!! HOW ***DARE*** YOU COME BACK HERE?!
HOW DARE? BECAUSE I'M BRINGING YOU BANDAGES AND CLEANING SUPPLIES FOR HER LEG. THAT'S HOW.
BUT...
...YOU ***BETRAYED*** US...*DIDN'T* YOU?
EH, JUST A LITTLE. LET'S JUST SAY I DIDN'T MEAN FOR ANYBODY TO GET SHOT. SORRY, ELF-GIRL.
IT'S OKAY...

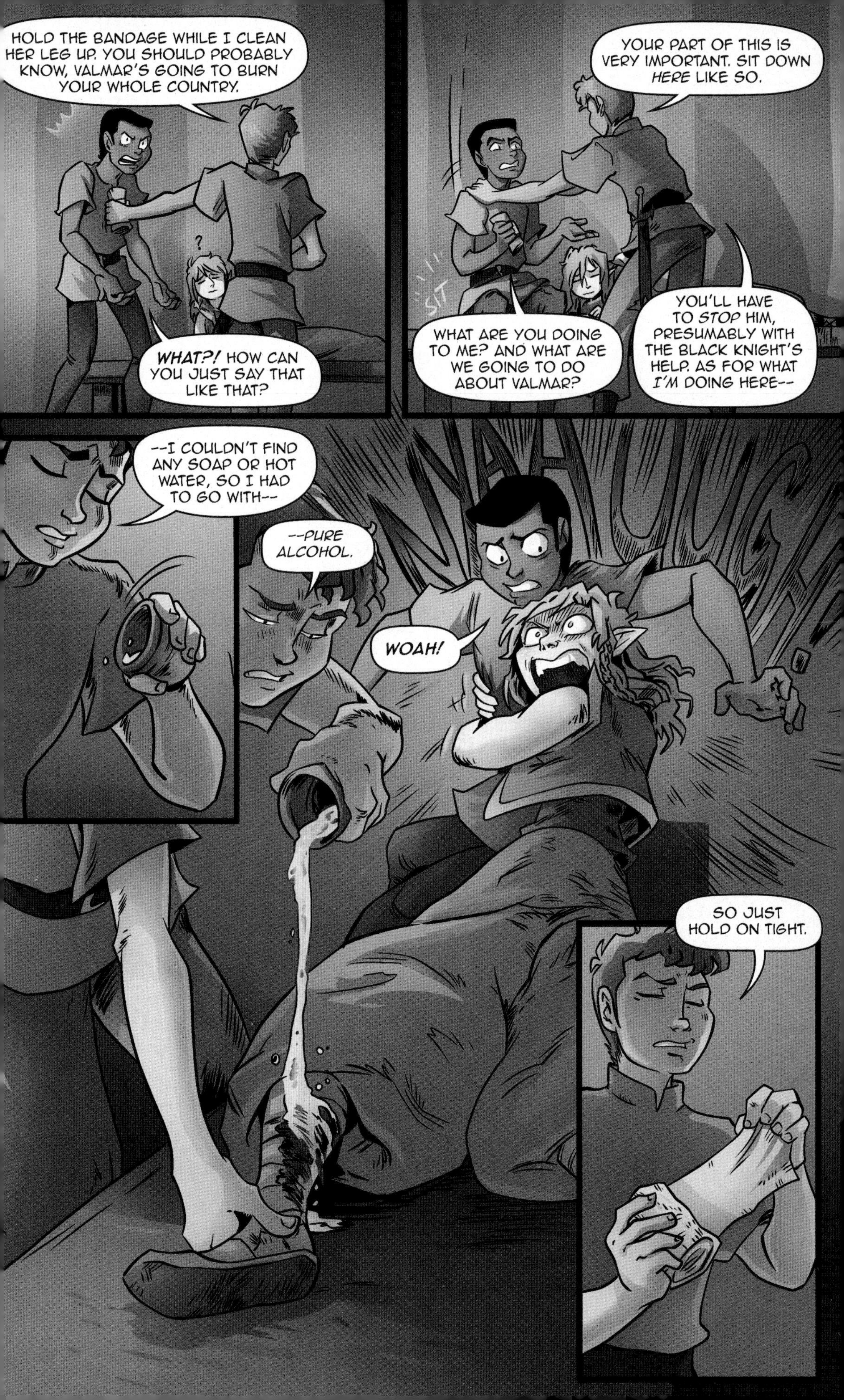

HOLD THE BANDAGE WHILE I CLEAN HER LEG UP. YOU SHOULD PROBABLY KNOW, VALMAR'S GOING TO BURN YOUR WHOLE COUNTRY.
?
WHAT?! HOW CAN YOU JUST SAY THAT LIKE THAT?
YOUR PART OF THIS IS VERY IMPORTANT. SIT DOWN HERE LIKE SO.
SIT
WHAT ARE YOU DOING TO ME? AND WHAT ARE WE GOING TO DO ABOUT VALMAR?
YOU'LL HAVE TO STOP HIM, PRESUMABLY WITH THE BLACK KNIGHT'S HELP. AS FOR WHAT I'M DOING HERE--
--I COULDN'T FIND ANY SOAP OR HOT WATER, SO I HAD TO GO WITH--
--PURE ALCOHOL.
NYAHUUGH!
WOAH!
SO JUST HOLD ON TIGHT.

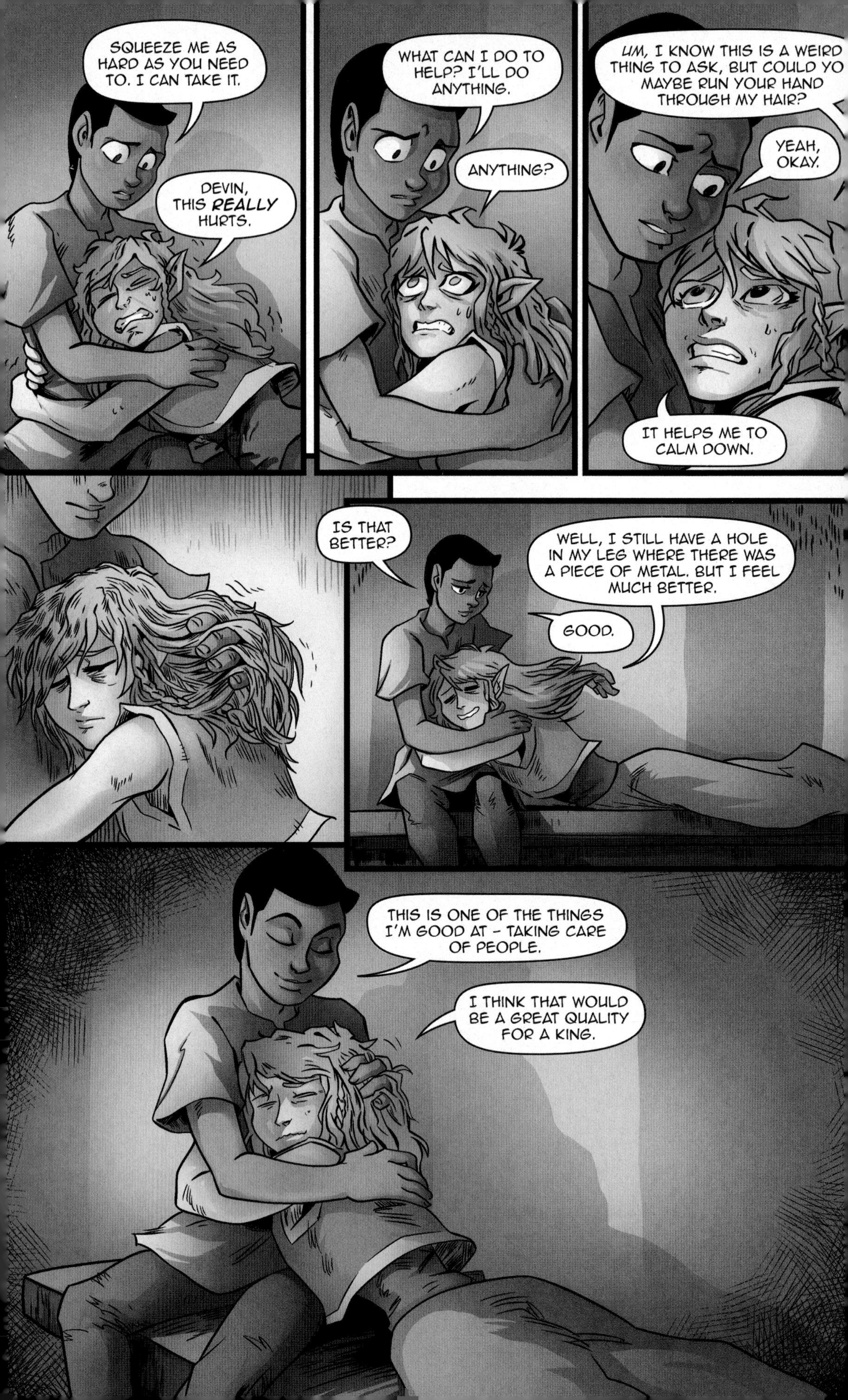
SQUEEZE ME AS HARD AS YOU NEED TO. I CAN TAKE IT.
DEVIN, THIS **REALLY** HURTS.
WHAT CAN I DO TO HELP? I'LL DO ANYTHING.
ANYTHING?
UM, I KNOW THIS IS A WEIRD THING TO ASK, BUT COULD YO MAYBE RUN YOUR HAND THROUGH MY HAIR?
YEAH, OKAY.
IT HELPS ME TO CALM DOWN.
IS THAT BETTER?
WELL, I STILL HAVE A HOLE IN MY LEG WHERE THERE WAS A PIECE OF METAL. BUT I FEEL MUCH BETTER.
GOOD.
THIS IS ONE OF THE THINGS I'M GOOD AT - TAKING CARE OF PEOPLE.
I THINK THAT WOULD BE A GREAT QUALITY FOR A KING.

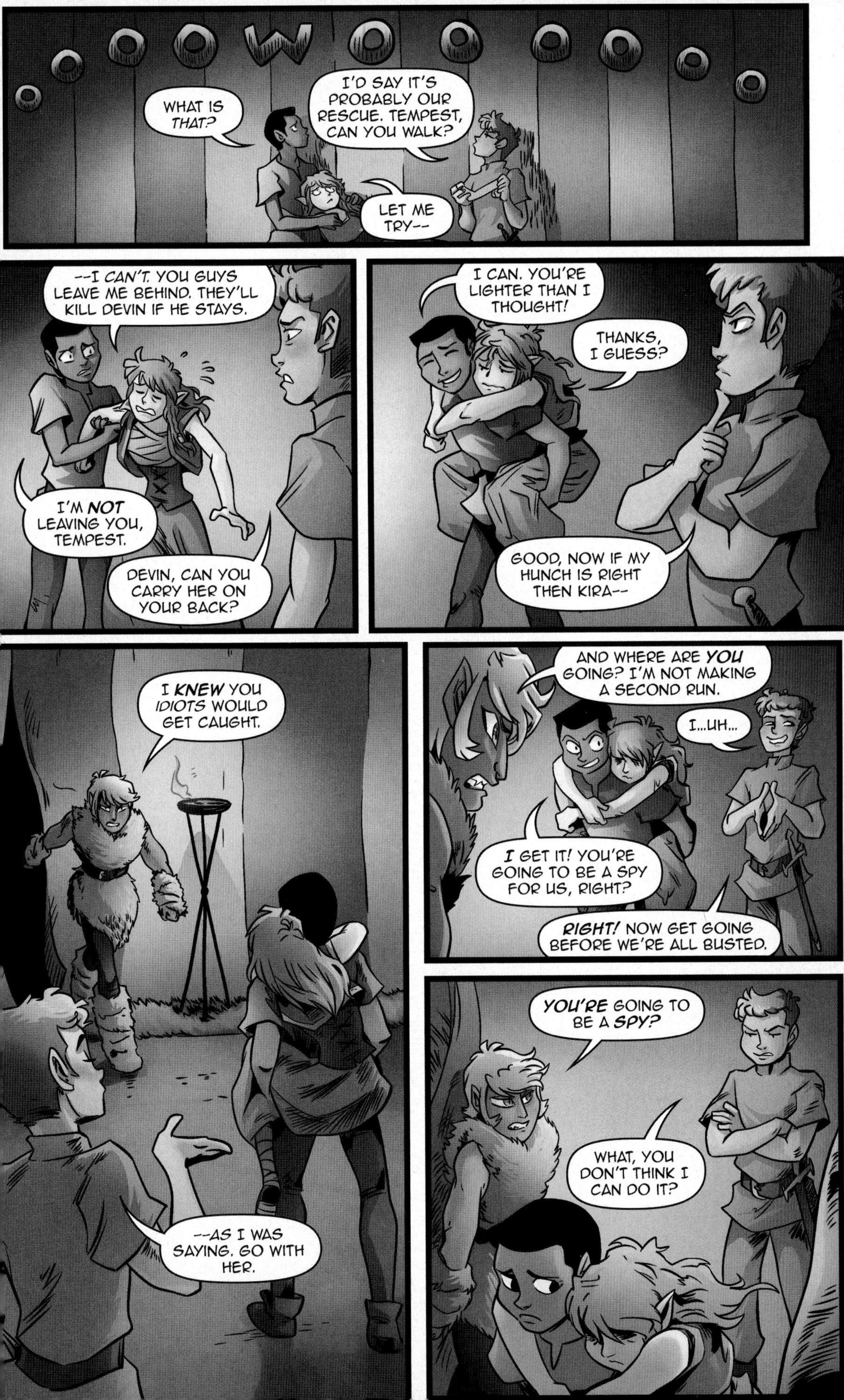
OOOOWOOOOOO
WHAT IS THAT?
I'D SAY IT'S PROBABLY OUR RESCUE. TEMPEST, CAN YOU WALK?
LET ME TRY--
--I CAN'T. YOU GUYS LEAVE ME BEHIND. THEY'LL KILL DEVIN IF HE STAYS.
I'M NOT LEAVING YOU, TEMPEST.
DEVIN, CAN YOU CARRY HER ON YOUR BACK?
I CAN. YOU'RE LIGHTER THAN I THOUGHT!
THANKS, I GUESS?
GOOD, NOW IF MY HUNCH IS RIGHT THEN KIRA--
I KNEW YOU IDIOTS WOULD GET CAUGHT.
--AS I WAS SAYING. GO WITH HER.
AND WHERE ARE YOU GOING? I'M NOT MAKING A SECOND RUN.
I...UH...
I GET IT! YOU'RE GOING TO BE A SPY FOR US, RIGHT?
RIGHT! NOW GET GOING BEFORE WE'RE ALL BUSTED.
YOU'RE GOING TO BE A SPY?
WHAT, YOU DON'T THINK I CAN DO IT?

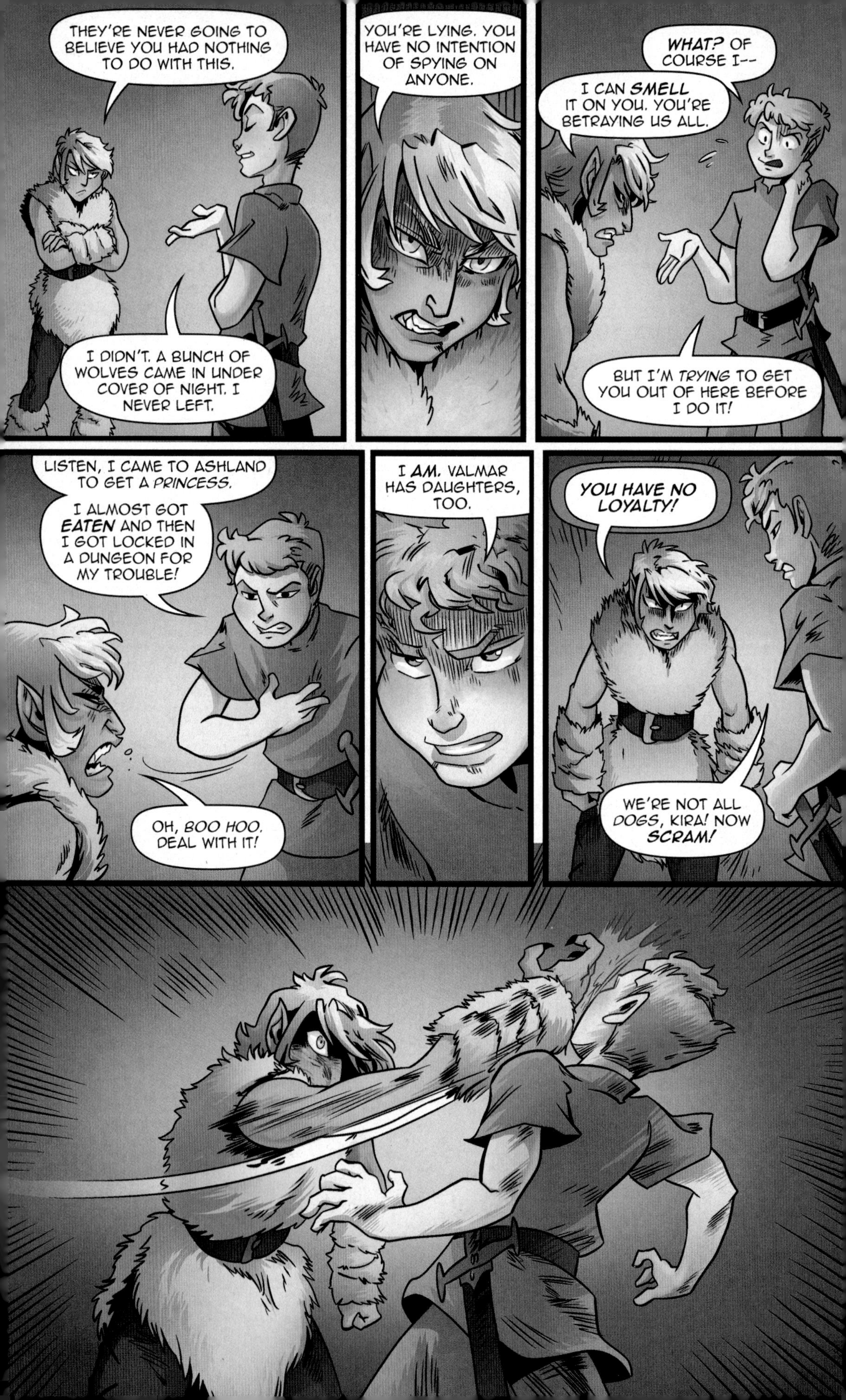
THEY'RE NEVER GOING TO BELIEVE YOU HAD NOTHING TO DO WITH THIS.
I DIDN'T. A BUNCH OF WOLVES CAME IN UNDER COVER OF NIGHT. I NEVER LEFT.
YOU'RE LYING. YOU HAVE NO INTENTION OF SPYING ON ANYONE.
WHAT? OF COURSE I--
I CAN SMELL IT ON YOU. YOU'RE BETRAYING US ALL.
BUT I'M TRYING TO GET YOU OUT OF HERE BEFORE I DO IT!
LISTEN, I CAME TO ASHLAND TO GET A PRINCESS.
I ALMOST GOT EATEN AND THEN I GOT LOCKED IN A DUNGEON FOR MY TROUBLE!
OH, BOO HOO. DEAL WITH IT!
I AM. VALMAR HAS DAUGHTERS, TOO.
YOU HAVE NO LOYALTY!
WE'RE NOT ALL DOGS, KIRA! NOW SCRAM!

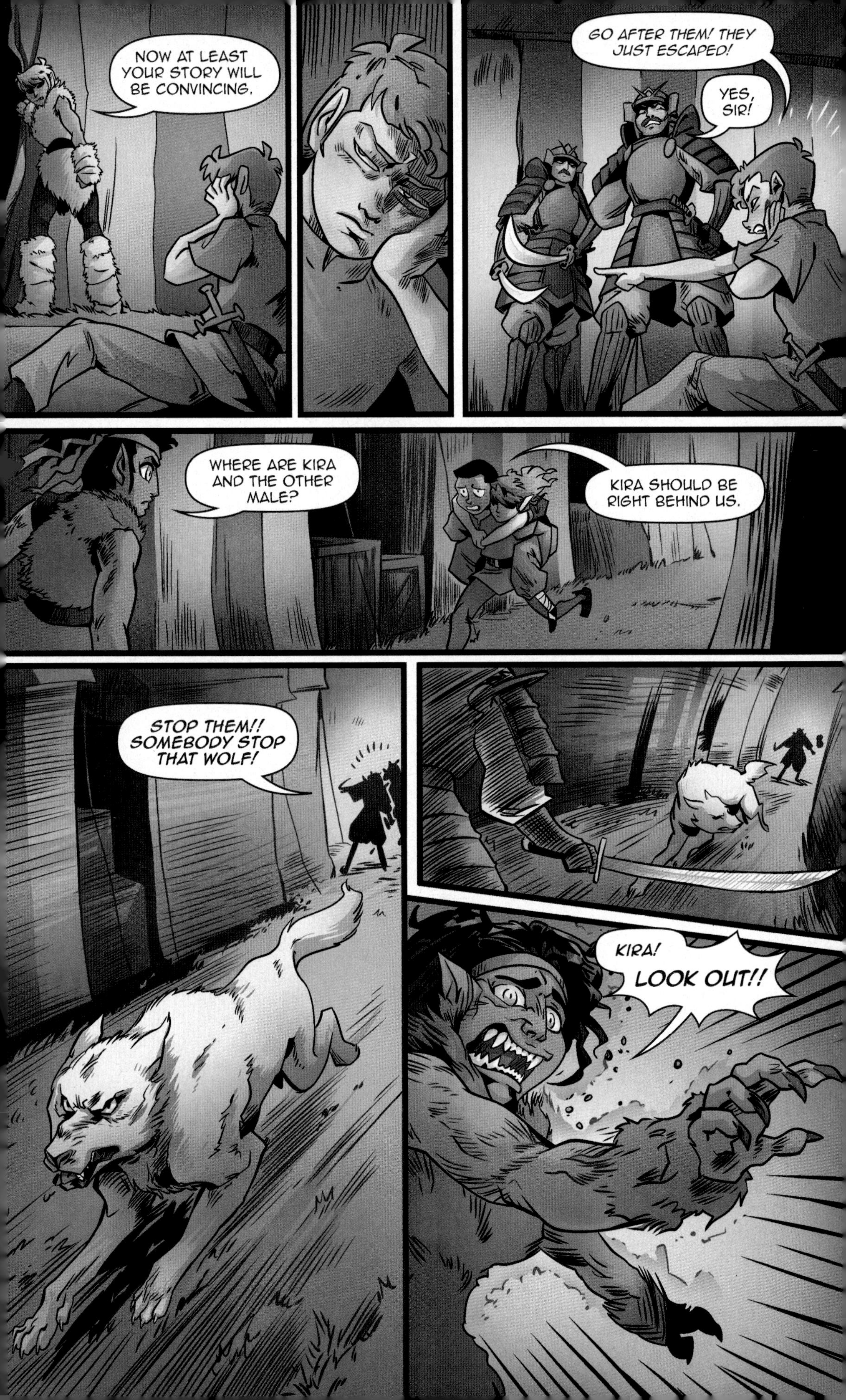
NOW AT LEAST YOUR STORY WILL BE CONVINCING.
GO AFTER THEM! THEY JUST ESCAPED!
YES, SIR!
WHERE ARE KIRA AND THE OTHER MALE?
KIRA SHOULD BE RIGHT BEHIND US.
STOP THEM!! SOMEBODY STOP THAT WOLF!
KIRA!
LOOK OUT!!

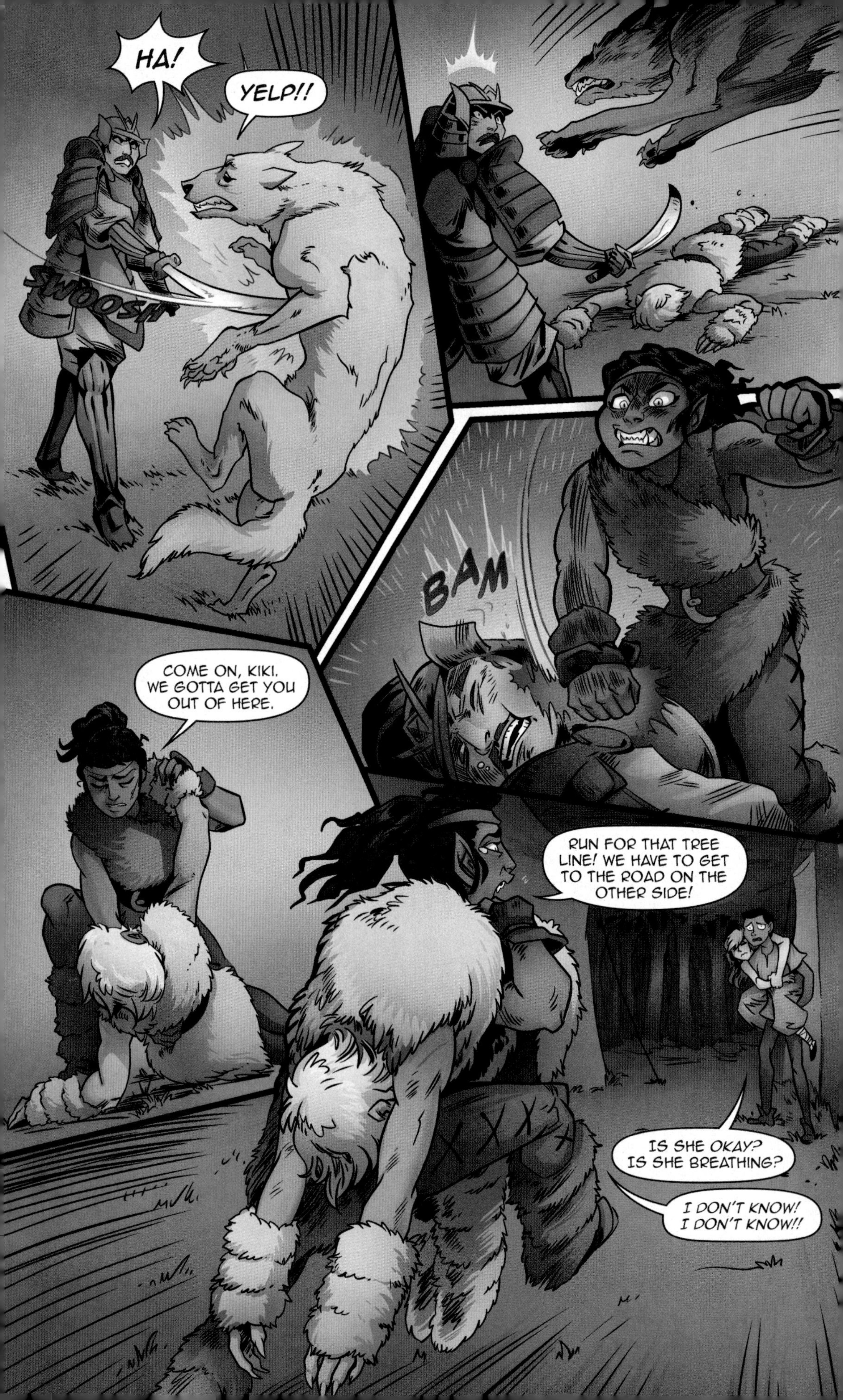
HA!
YELP!!
SWOOSH
BAM
COME ON, KIKI. WE GOTTA GET YOU OUT OF HERE.
RUN FOR THAT TREE LINE! WE HAVE TO GET TO THE ROAD ON THE OTHER SIDE!
IS SHE OKAY? IS SHE BREATHING?
I DON'T KNOW! I DON'T KNOW!!

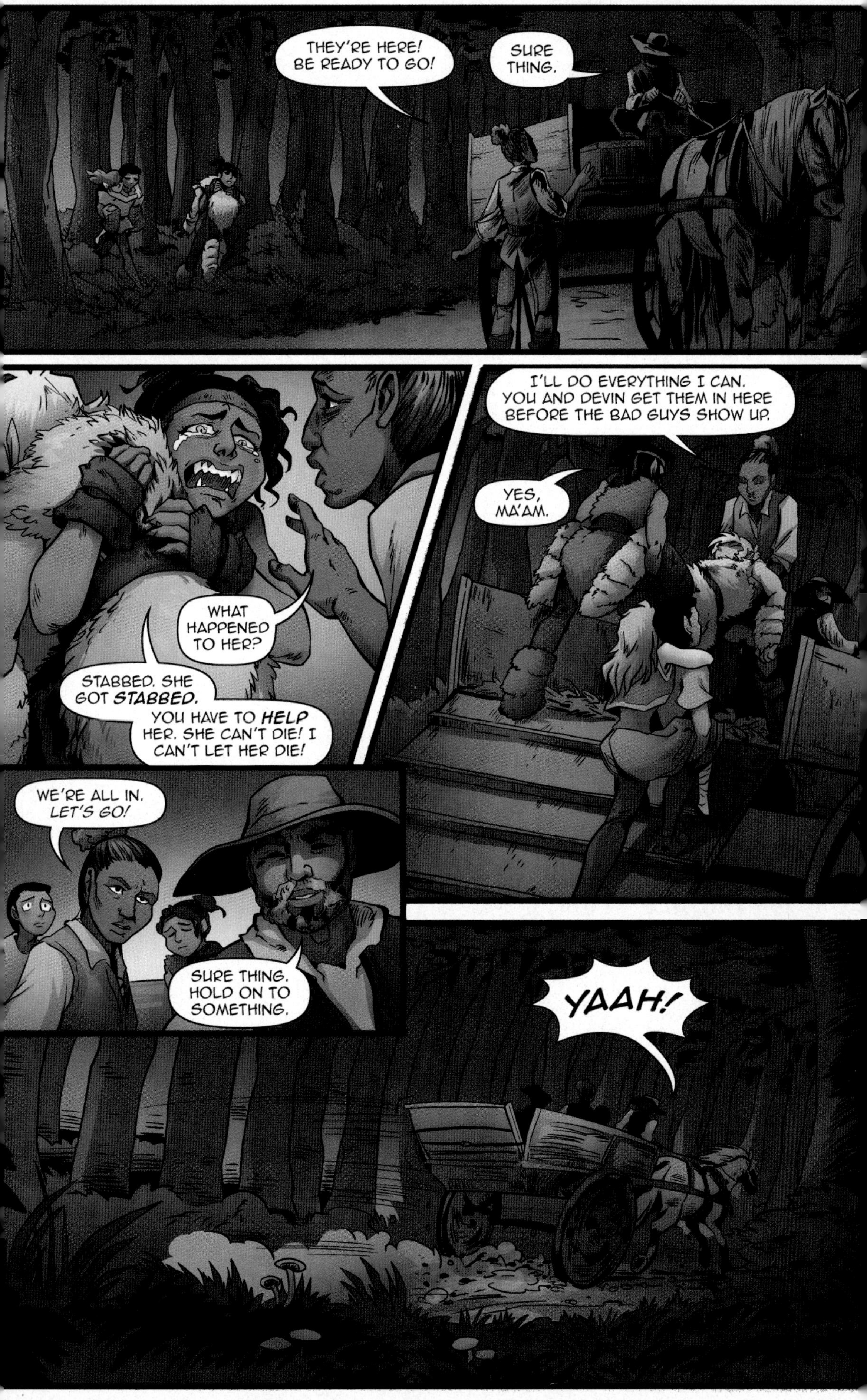
THEY'RE HERE! BE READY TO GO!
SURE THING.
WHAT HAPPENED TO HER?
STABBED. SHE GOT STABBED.
YOU HAVE TO HELP HER. SHE CAN'T DIE! I CAN'T LET HER DIE!
I'LL DO EVERYTHING I CAN. YOU AND DEVIN GET THEM IN HERE BEFORE THE BAD GUYS SHOW UP.
YES, MA'AM.
WE'RE ALL IN. LET'S GO!
SURE THING. HOLD ON TO SOMETHING.
YAAH!

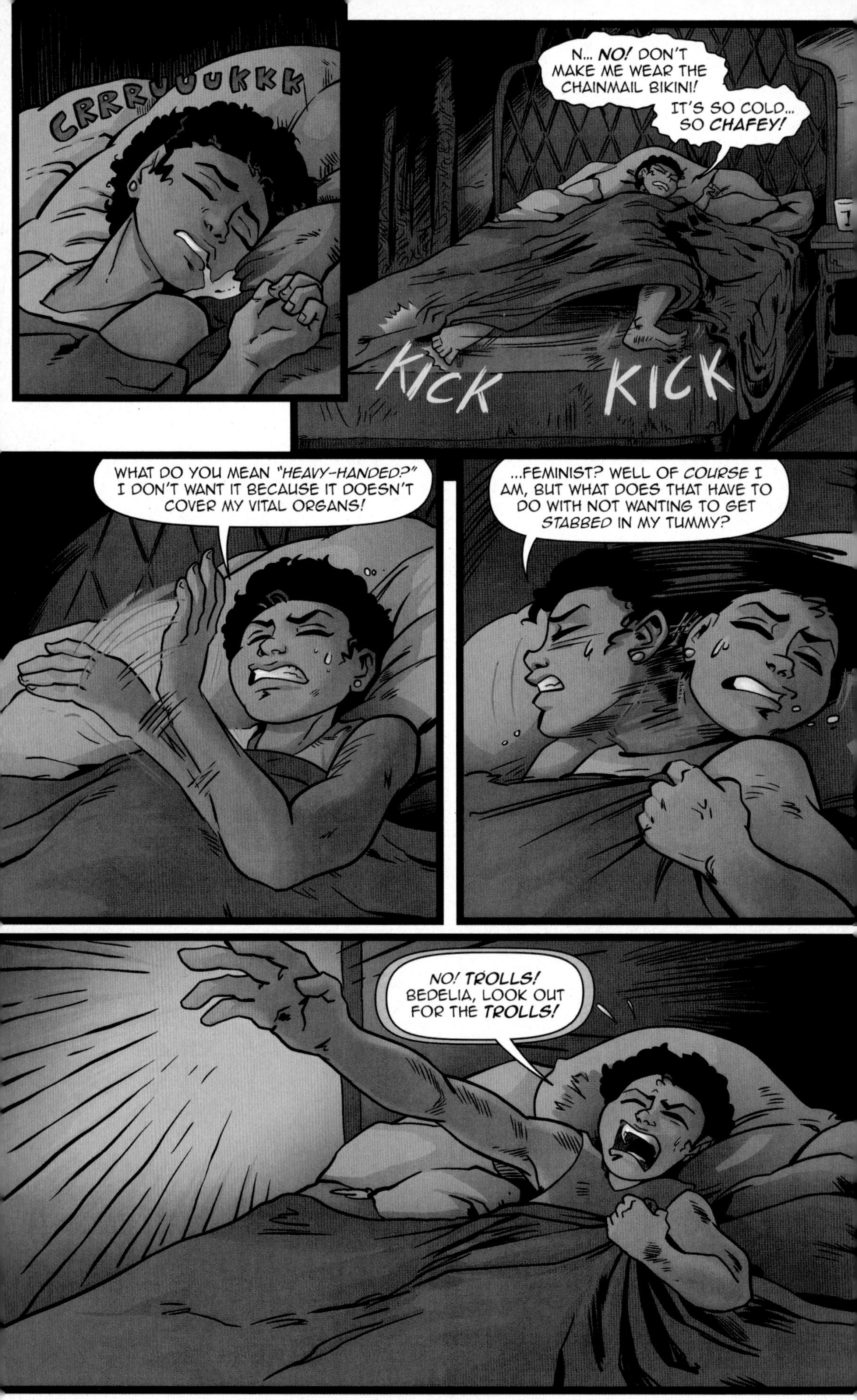
CRRRUUUUKKK
N... NO! DON'T MAKE ME WEAR THE CHAINMAIL BIKINI!
IT'S SO COLD... SO CHAFEY!
KICK
KICK
WHAT DO YOU MEAN "HEAVY-HANDED?" I DON'T WANT IT BECAUSE IT DOESN'T COVER MY VITAL ORGANS!
...FEMINIST? WELL OF COURSE I AM, BUT WHAT DOES THAT HAVE TO DO WITH NOT WANTING TO GET STABBED IN MY TUMMY?
NO! TROLLS! BEDELIA, LOOK OUT FOR THE TROLLS!

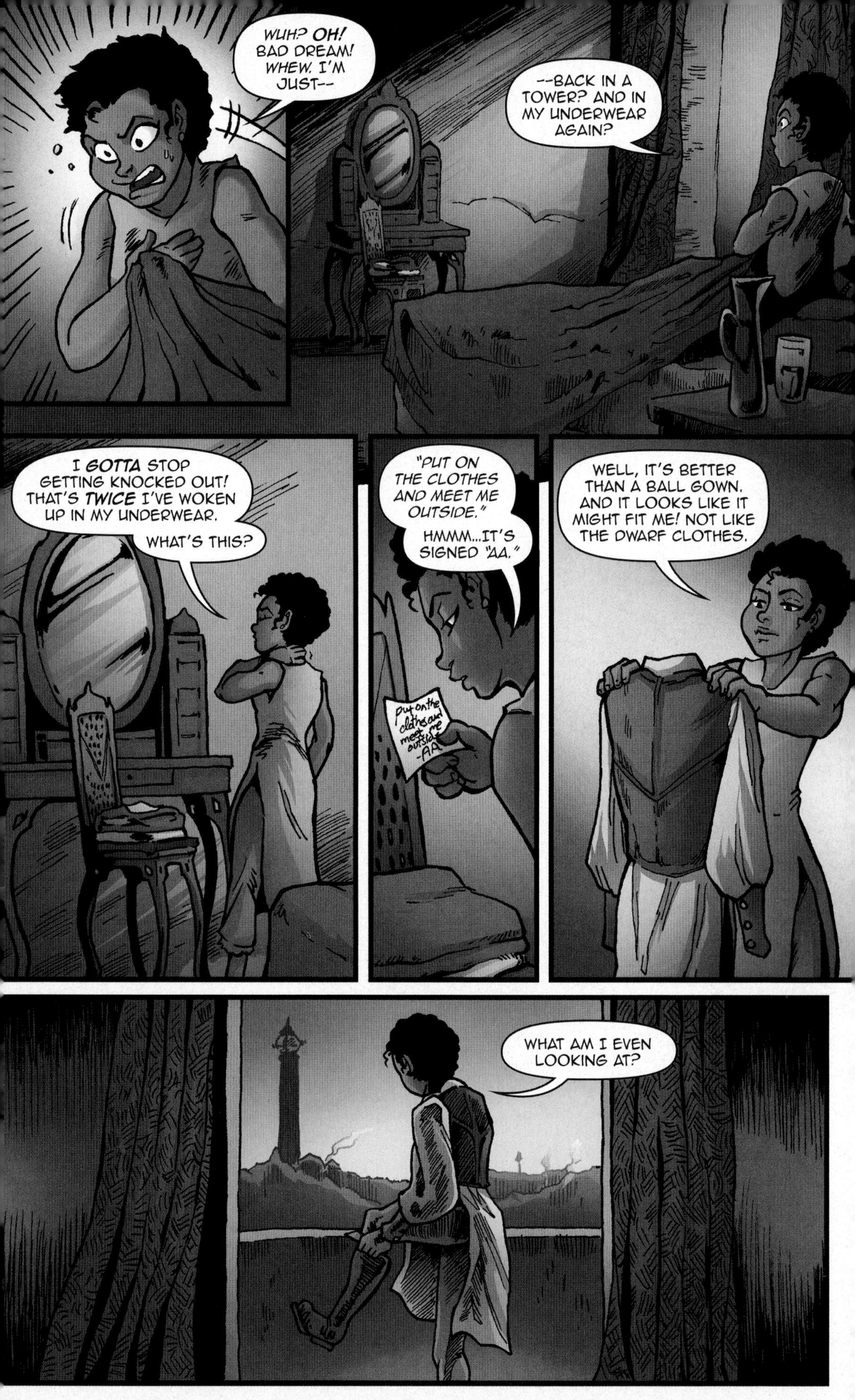
WUH? OH! BAD DREAM! WHEW. I'M JUST--
--BACK IN A TOWER? AND IN MY UNDERWEAR AGAIN?
I GOTTA STOP GETTING KNOCKED OUT! THAT'S TWICE I'VE WOKEN UP IN MY UNDERWEAR.
WHAT'S THIS?
"PUT ON THE CLOTHES AND MEET ME OUTSIDE."
HMMM...IT'S SIGNED "AA."
Put on the clothes and meet me outside -AA
WELL, IT'S BETTER THAN A BALL GOWN. AND IT LOOKS LIKE IT MIGHT FIT ME! NOT LIKE THE DWARF CLOTHES.
WHAT AM I EVEN LOOKING AT?

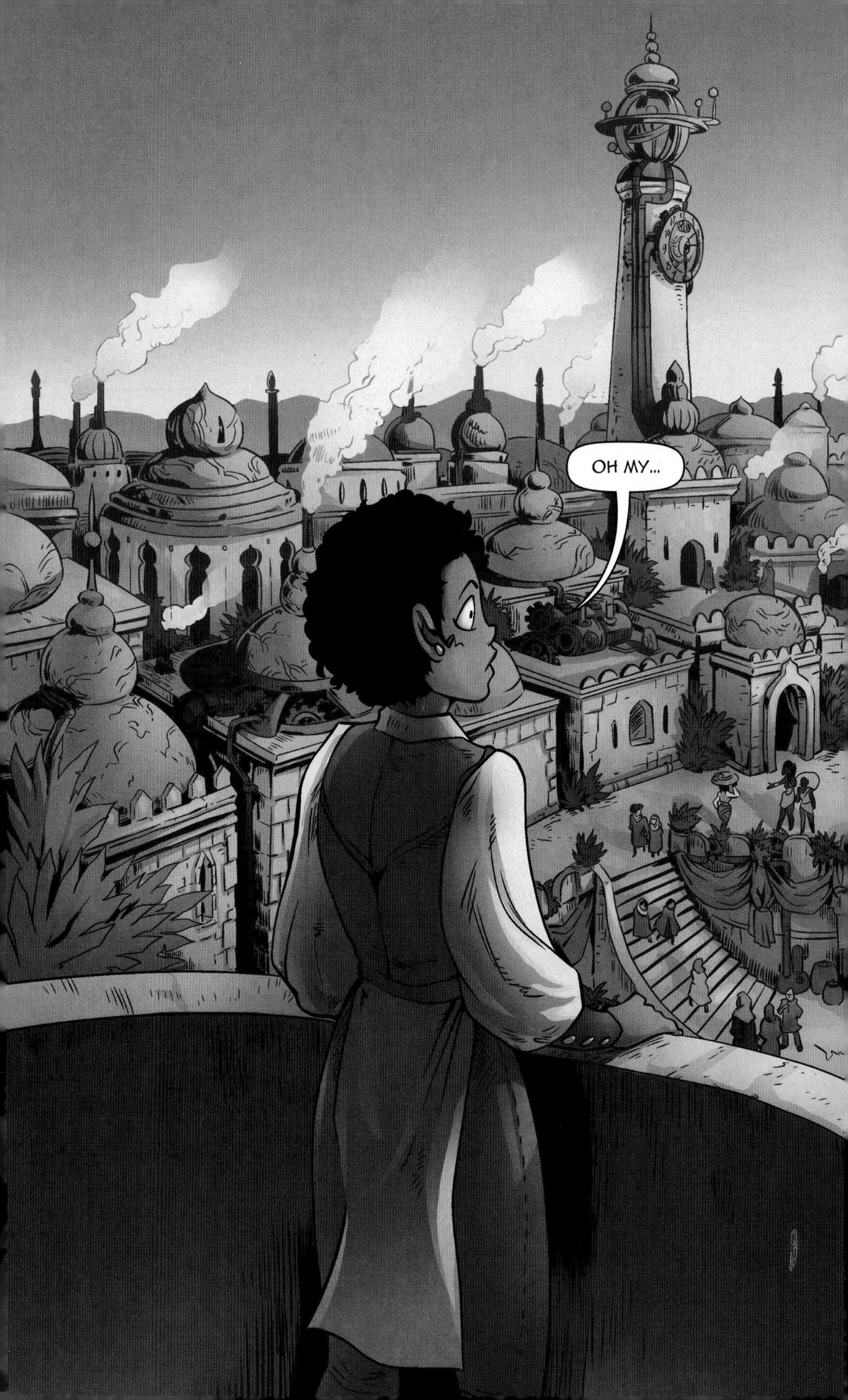
OH MY...

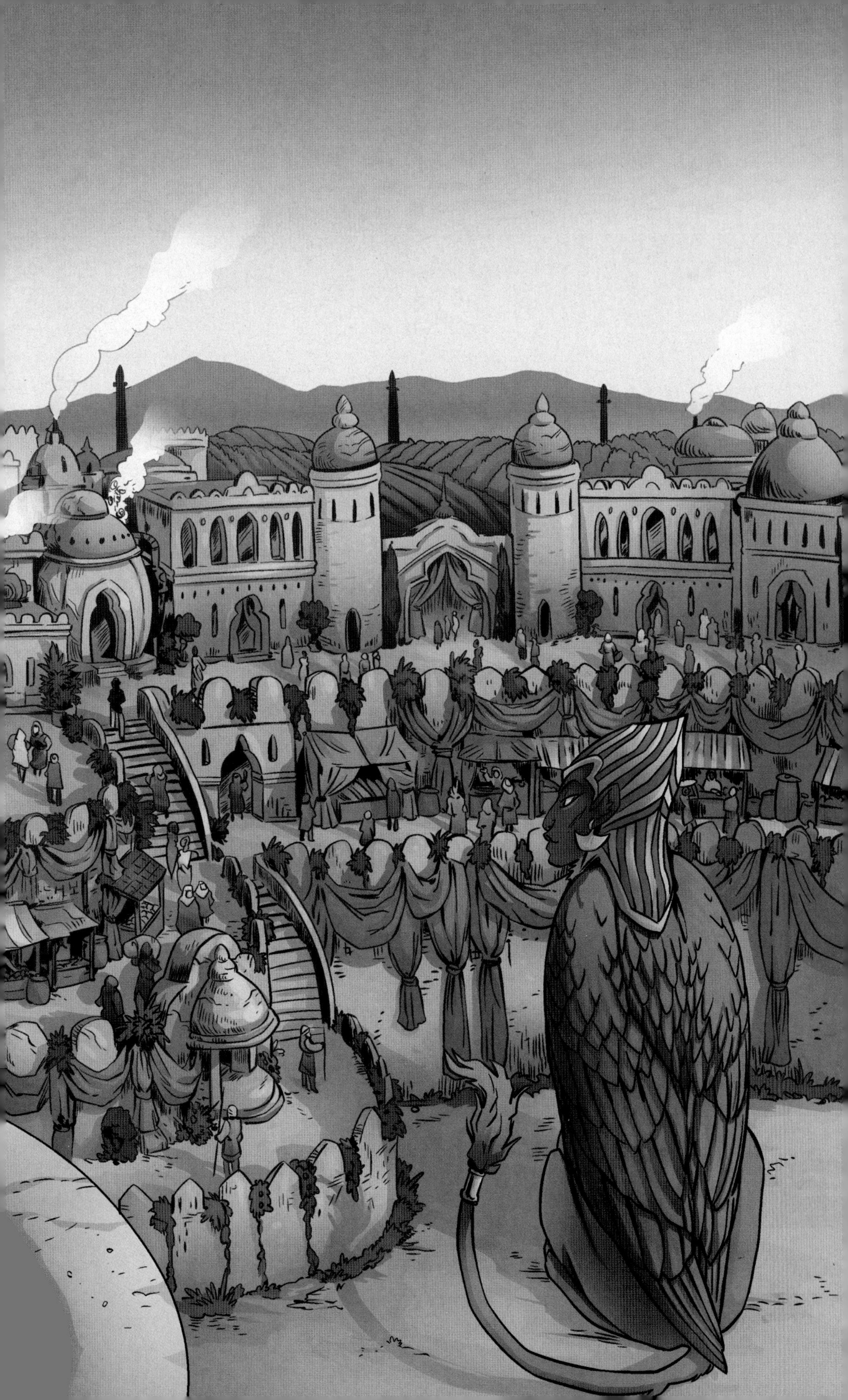

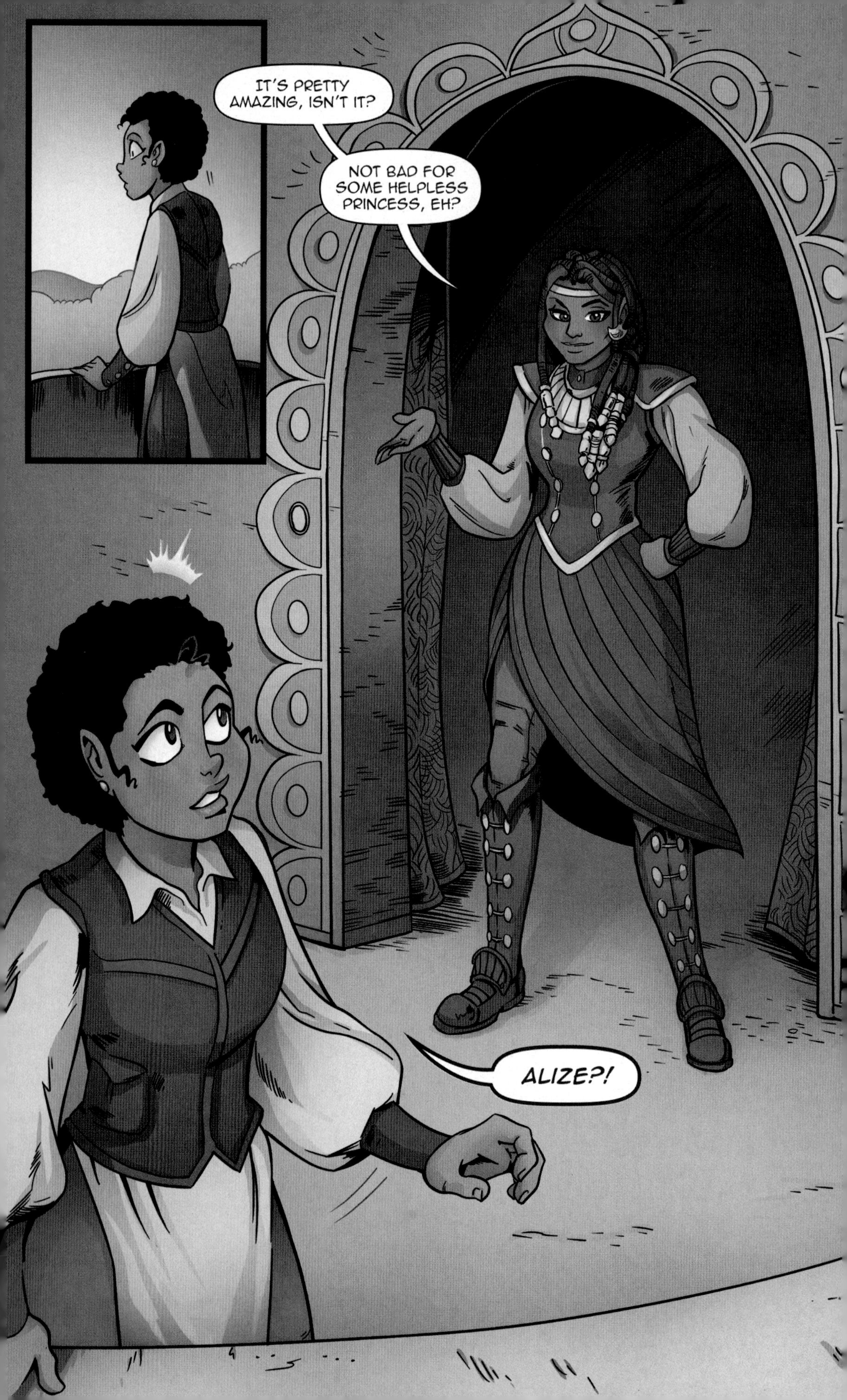
IT'S PRETTY AMAZING, ISN'T IT?
NOT BAD FOR SOME HELPLESS PRINCESS, EH?
ALIZE?!

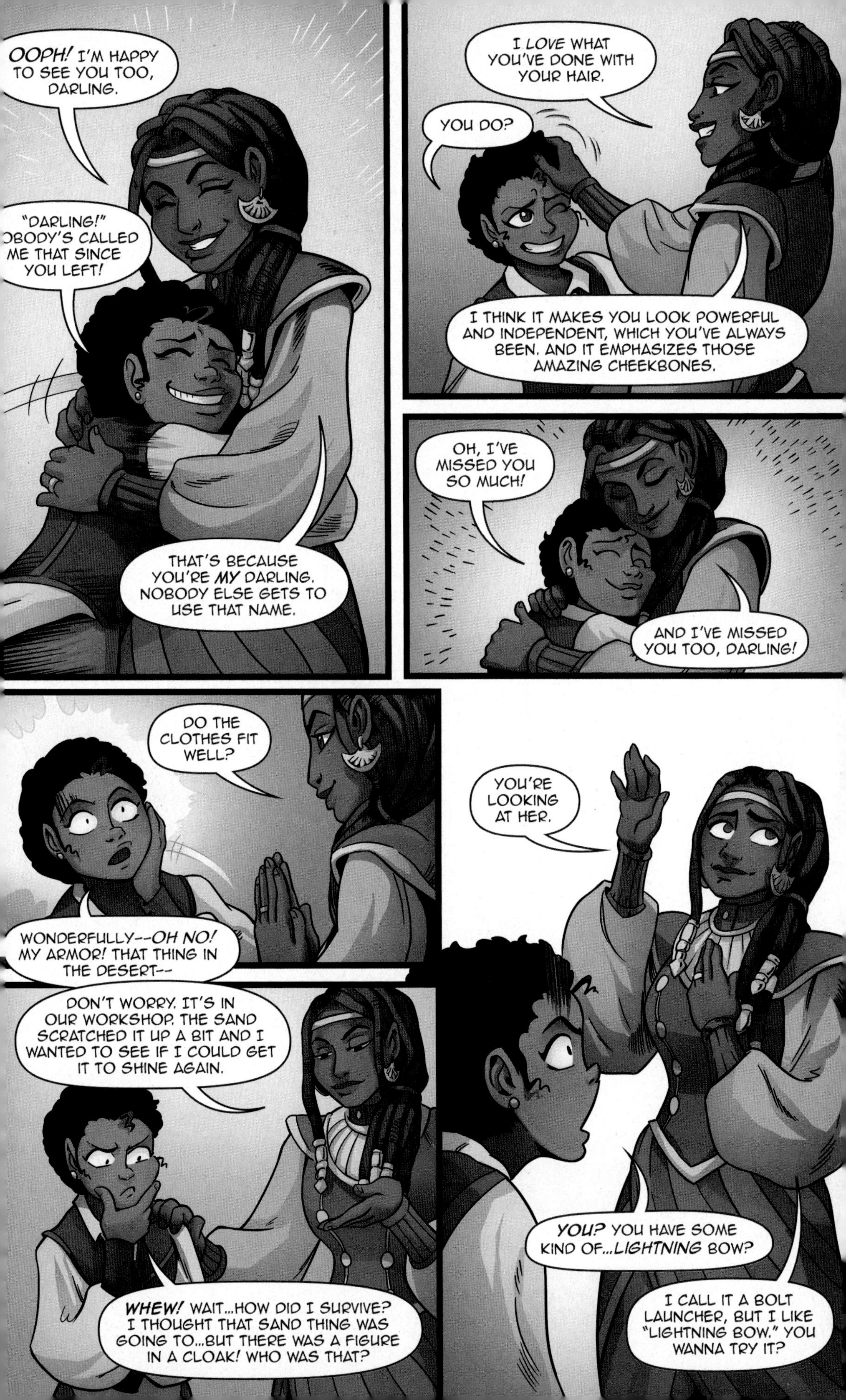
OOPH! I'M HAPPY TO SEE YOU TOO, DARLING.
"DARLING!" NOBODY'S CALLED ME THAT SINCE YOU LEFT!
THAT'S BECAUSE YOU'RE MY DARLING. NOBODY ELSE GETS TO USE THAT NAME.
I LOVE WHAT YOU'VE DONE WITH YOUR HAIR.
YOU DO?
I THINK IT MAKES YOU LOOK POWERFUL AND INDEPENDENT, WHICH YOU'VE ALWAYS BEEN. AND IT EMPHASIZES THOSE AMAZING CHEEKBONES.
OH, I'VE MISSED YOU SO MUCH!
AND I'VE MISSED YOU TOO, DARLING!
DO THE CLOTHES FIT WELL?
WONDERFULLY--OH NO! MY ARMOR! THAT THING IN THE DESERT--
DON'T WORRY. IT'S IN OUR WORKSHOP. THE SAND SCRATCHED IT UP A BIT AND I WANTED TO SEE IF I COULD GET IT TO SHINE AGAIN.
WHEW! WAIT...HOW DID I SURVIVE? I THOUGHT THAT SAND THING WAS GOING TO...BUT THERE WAS A FIGURE IN A CLOAK! WHO WAS THAT?
YOU'RE LOOKING AT HER.
YOU? YOU HAVE SOME KIND OF...LIGHTNING BOW?
I CALL IT A BOLT LAUNCHER, BUT I LIKE "LIGHTNING BOW." YOU WANNA TRY IT?

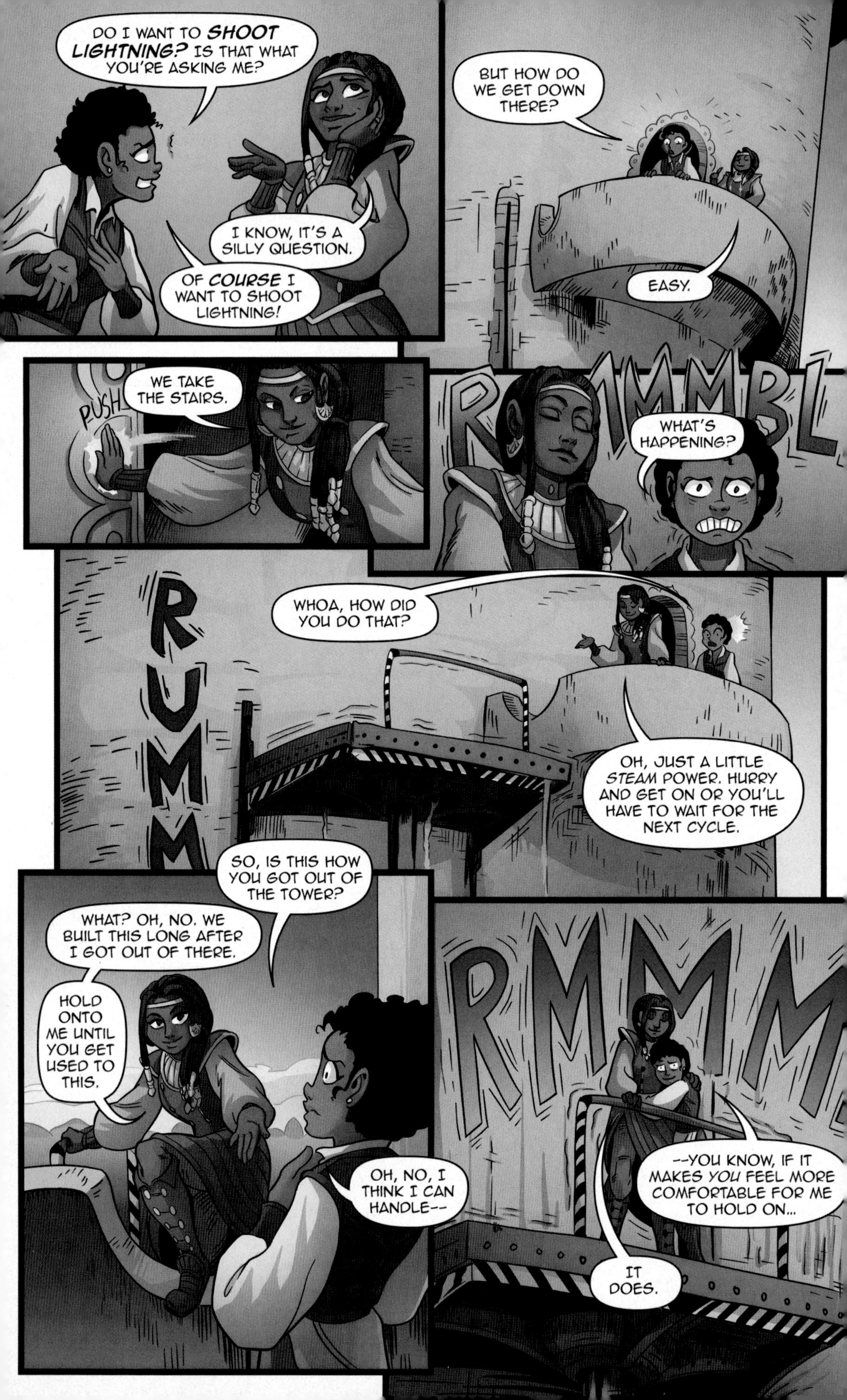
DO I WANT TO *SHOOT LIGHTNING?* IS THAT WHAT YOU'RE ASKING ME?
I KNOW, IT'S A SILLY QUESTION.
OF *COURSE* I WANT TO SHOOT LIGHTNING!
BUT HOW DO WE GET DOWN THERE?
EASY.
PUSH
WE TAKE THE STAIRS.
RMMMBL
WHAT'S HAPPENING?
RUMM
WHOA, HOW DID YOU DO THAT?
OH, JUST A LITTLE *STEAM* POWER. HURRY AND GET ON OR YOU'LL HAVE TO WAIT FOR THE NEXT CYCLE.
SO, IS THIS HOW YOU GOT OUT OF THE TOWER?
WHAT? OH, NO. WE BUILT THIS LONG AFTER I GOT OUT OF THERE.
HOLD ONTO ME UNTIL YOU GET USED TO THIS.
OH, NO, I THINK I CAN HANDLE--
RMMM
--YOU KNOW, IF IT MAKES *YOU* FEEL MORE COMFORTABLE FOR ME TO HOLD ON...
IT DOES.

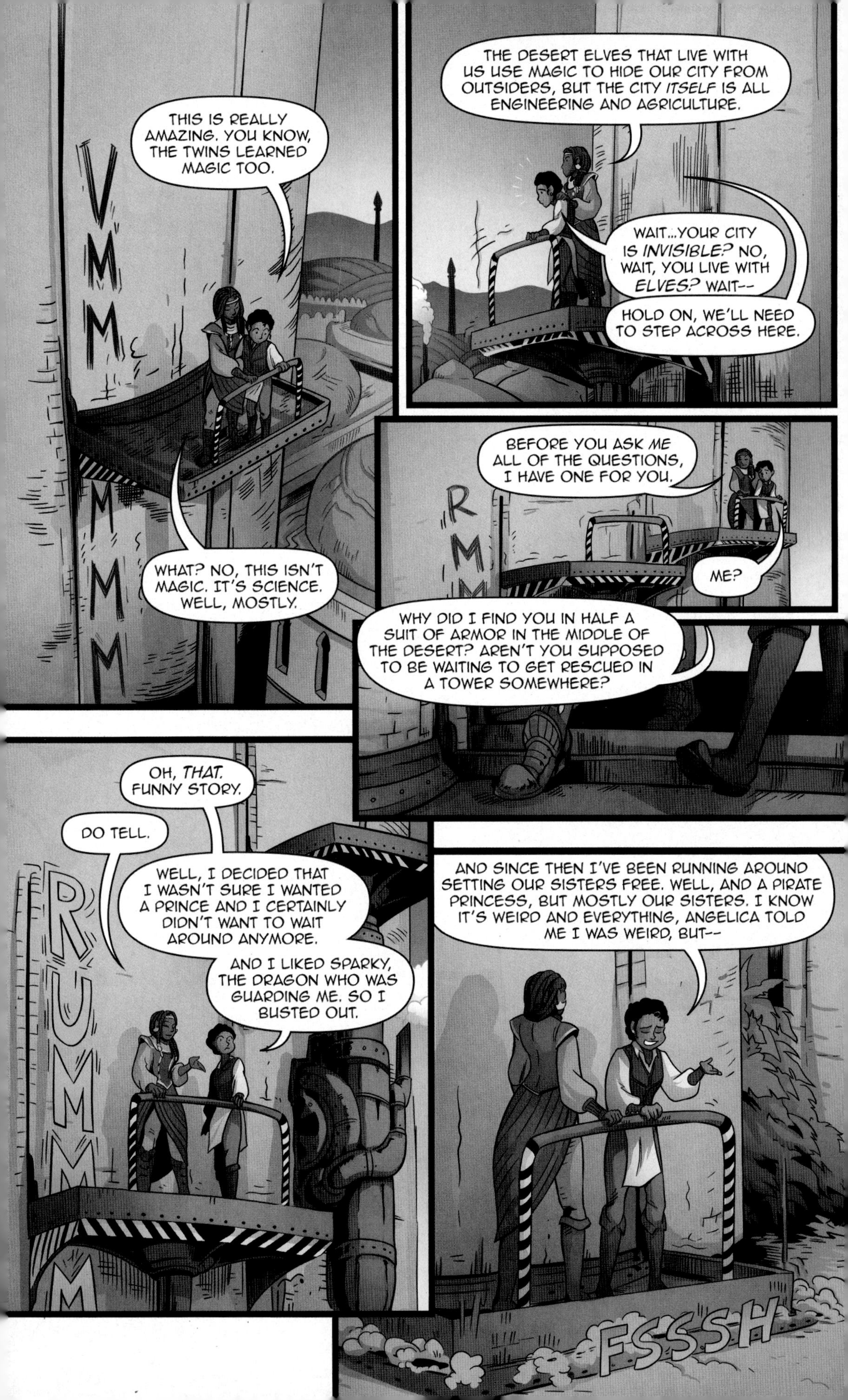
THIS IS REALLY AMAZING. YOU KNOW, THE TWINS LEARNED MAGIC TOO.
VMMMM
WHAT? NO, THIS ISN'T MAGIC. IT'S SCIENCE. WELL, MOSTLY.
THE DESERT ELVES THAT LIVE WITH US USE MAGIC TO HIDE OUR CITY FROM OUTSIDERS, BUT THE CITY ITSELF IS ALL ENGINEERING AND AGRICULTURE.
WAIT...YOUR CITY IS INVISIBLE? NO, WAIT, YOU LIVE WITH ELVES? WAIT--
HOLD ON, WE'LL NEED TO STEP ACROSS HERE.
BEFORE YOU ASK ME ALL OF THE QUESTIONS, I HAVE ONE FOR YOU.
RMM
ME?
WHY DID I FIND YOU IN HALF A SUIT OF ARMOR IN THE MIDDLE OF THE DESERT? AREN'T YOU SUPPOSED TO BE WAITING TO GET RESCUED IN A TOWER SOMEWHERE?
OH, THAT. FUNNY STORY.
DO TELL.
WELL, I DECIDED THAT I WASN'T SURE I WANTED A PRINCE AND I CERTAINLY DIDN'T WANT TO WAIT AROUND ANYMORE.
AND I LIKED SPARKY, THE DRAGON WHO WAS GUARDING ME. SO I BUSTED OUT.
RUMMM
AND SINCE THEN I'VE BEEN RUNNING AROUND SETTING OUR SISTERS FREE. WELL, AND A PIRATE PRINCESS, BUT MOSTLY OUR SISTERS. I KNOW IT'S WEIRD AND EVERYTHING, ANGELICA TOLD ME I WAS WEIRD, BUT--
FSSSH

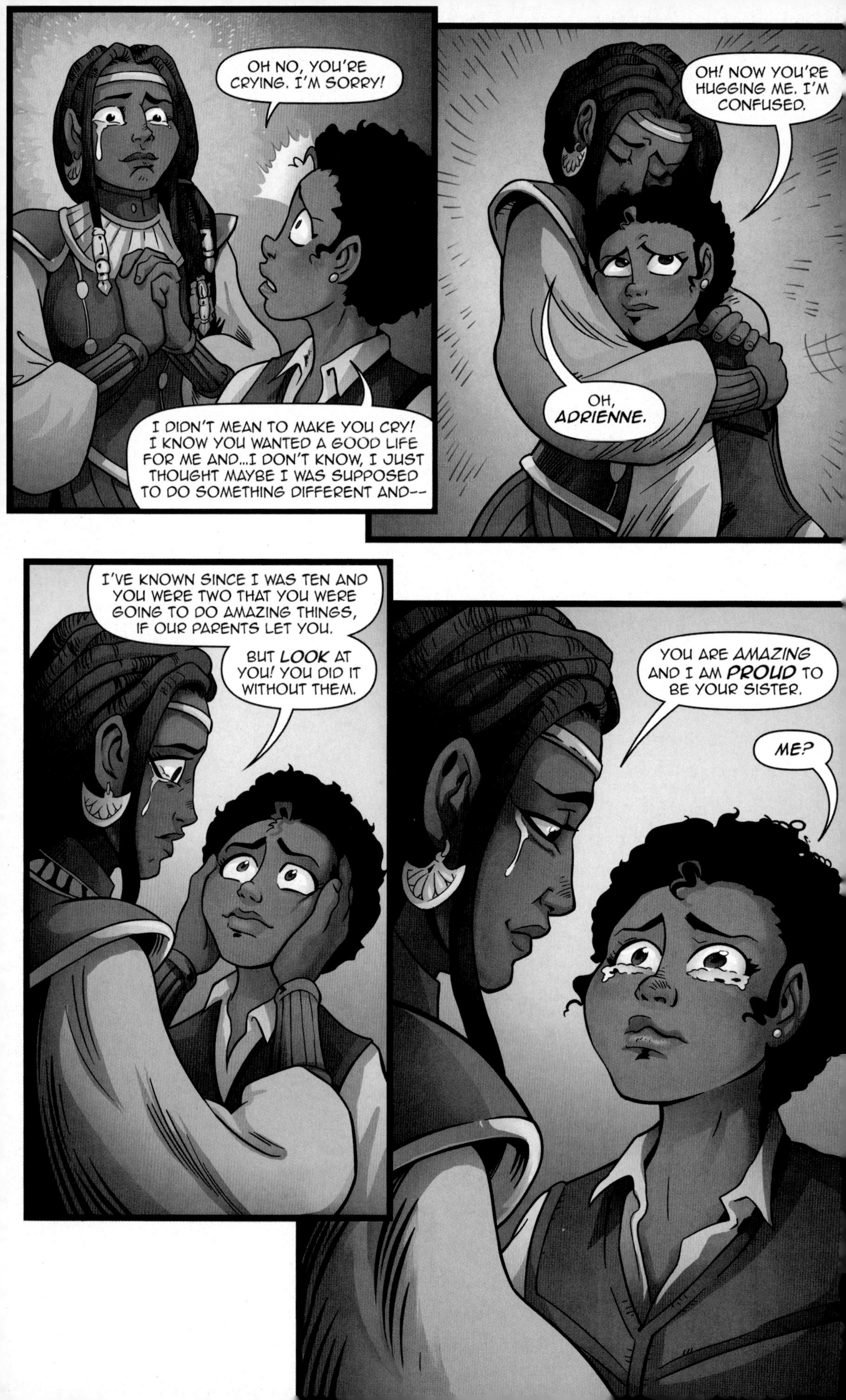
OH NO, YOU'RE CRYING. I'M SORRY!
I DIDN'T MEAN TO MAKE YOU CRY! I KNOW YOU WANTED A GOOD LIFE FOR ME AND...I DON'T KNOW, I JUST THOUGHT MAYBE I WAS SUPPOSED TO DO SOMETHING DIFFERENT AND--
OH! NOW YOU'RE HUGGING ME. I'M CONFUSED.
OH, ADRIENNE.
I'VE KNOWN SINCE I WAS TEN AND YOU WERE TWO THAT YOU WERE GOING TO DO AMAZING THINGS, IF OUR PARENTS LET YOU.
BUT LOOK AT YOU! YOU DID IT WITHOUT THEM.
YOU ARE AMAZING AND I AM PROUD TO BE YOUR SISTER.
ME?

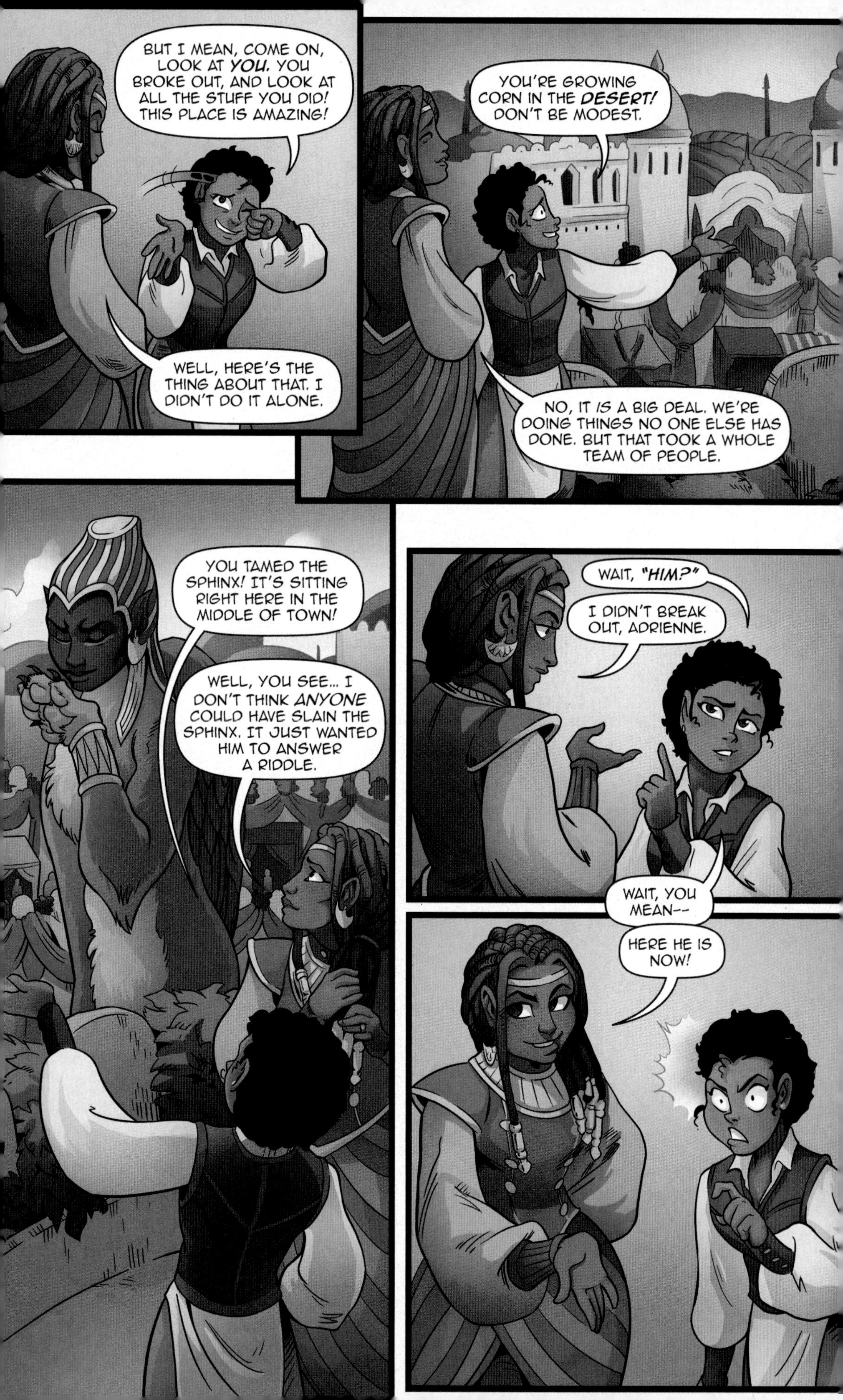
BUT I MEAN, COME ON, LOOK AT *YOU.* YOU BROKE OUT, AND LOOK AT ALL THE STUFF YOU DID! THIS PLACE IS AMAZING!
WELL, HERE'S THE THING ABOUT THAT. I DIDN'T DO IT ALONE.
YOU'RE GROWING CORN IN THE *DESERT!* DON'T BE MODEST.
NO, IT *IS* A BIG DEAL. WE'RE DOING THINGS NO ONE ELSE HAS DONE. BUT THAT TOOK A WHOLE TEAM OF PEOPLE.
YOU TAMED THE SPHINX! IT'S SITTING RIGHT HERE IN THE MIDDLE OF TOWN!
WELL, YOU SEE... I DON'T THINK *ANYONE* COULD HAVE SLAIN THE SPHINX. IT JUST WANTED HIM TO ANSWER A RIDDLE.
WAIT, *"HIM?"*
I DIDN'T BREAK OUT, ADRIENNE.
WAIT, YOU MEAN--
HERE HE IS NOW!

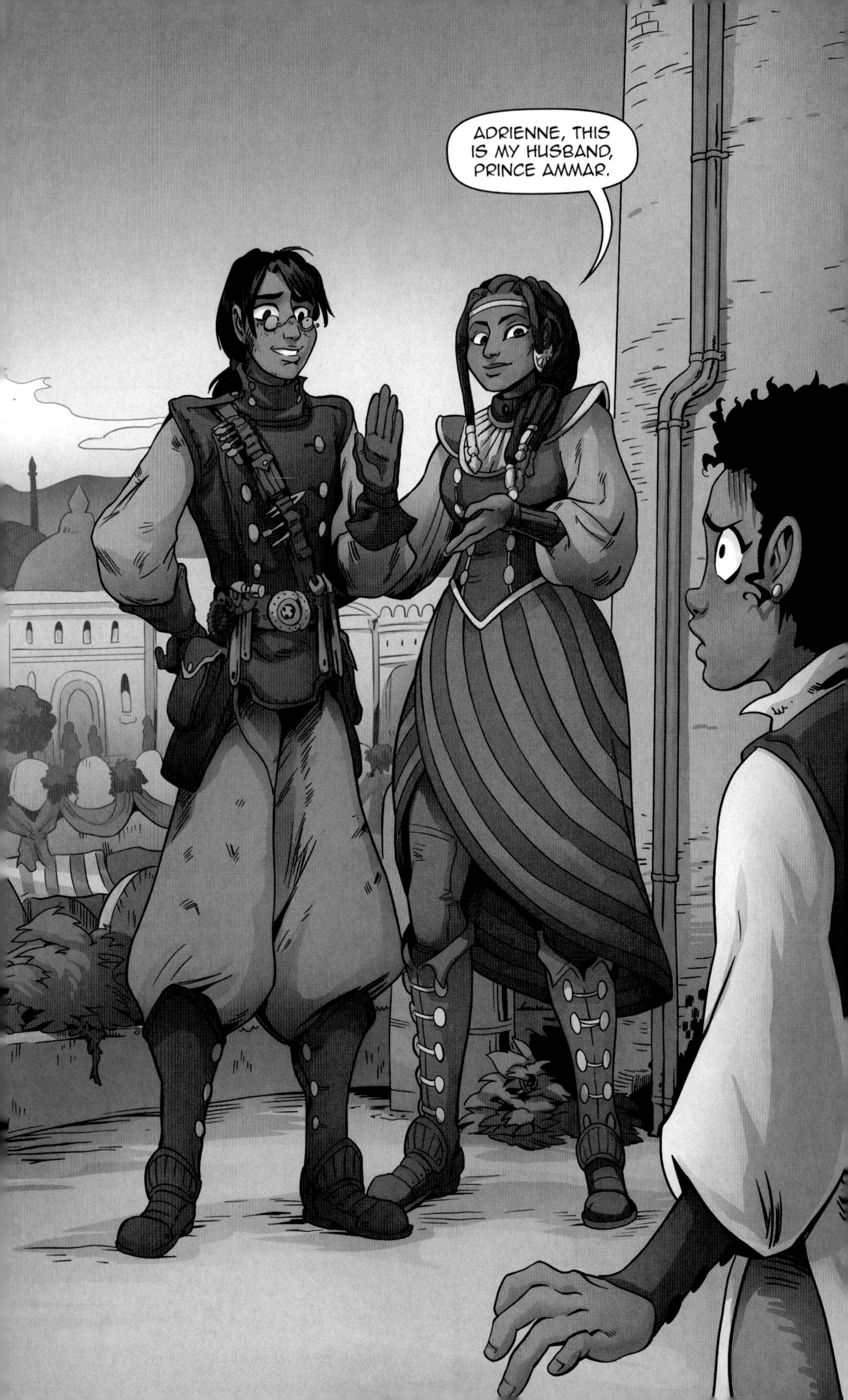
ADRIENNE, THIS IS MY HUSBAND, PRINCE AMMAR.

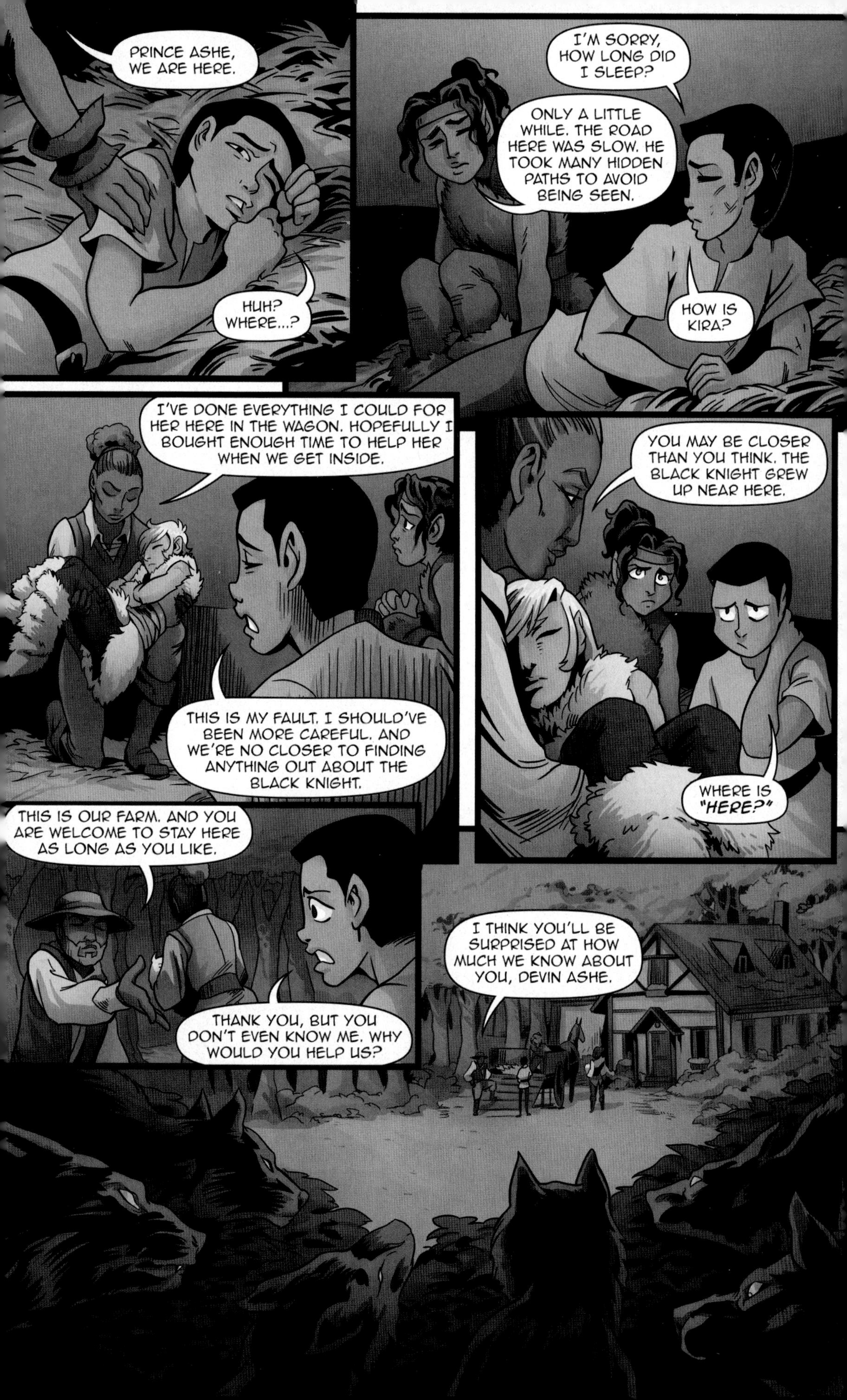
PRINCE ASHE, WE ARE HERE.
HUH? WHERE...?
I'M SORRY, HOW LONG DID I SLEEP?
ONLY A LITTLE WHILE. THE ROAD HERE WAS SLOW. HE TOOK MANY HIDDEN PATHS TO AVOID BEING SEEN.
HOW IS KIRA?
I'VE DONE EVERYTHING I COULD FOR HER HERE IN THE WAGON. HOPEFULLY I BOUGHT ENOUGH TIME TO HELP HER WHEN WE GET INSIDE.
THIS IS MY FAULT. I SHOULD'VE BEEN MORE CAREFUL. AND WE'RE NO CLOSER TO FINDING ANYTHING OUT ABOUT THE BLACK KNIGHT.
YOU MAY BE CLOSER THAN YOU THINK. THE BLACK KNIGHT GREW UP NEAR HERE.
WHERE IS *"HERE?"*
THIS IS OUR FARM. AND YOU ARE WELCOME TO STAY HERE AS LONG AS YOU LIKE.
THANK YOU, BUT YOU DON'T EVEN KNOW ME. WHY WOULD YOU HELP US?
I THINK YOU'LL BE SURPRISED AT HOW MUCH WE KNOW ABOUT YOU, DEVIN ASHE.

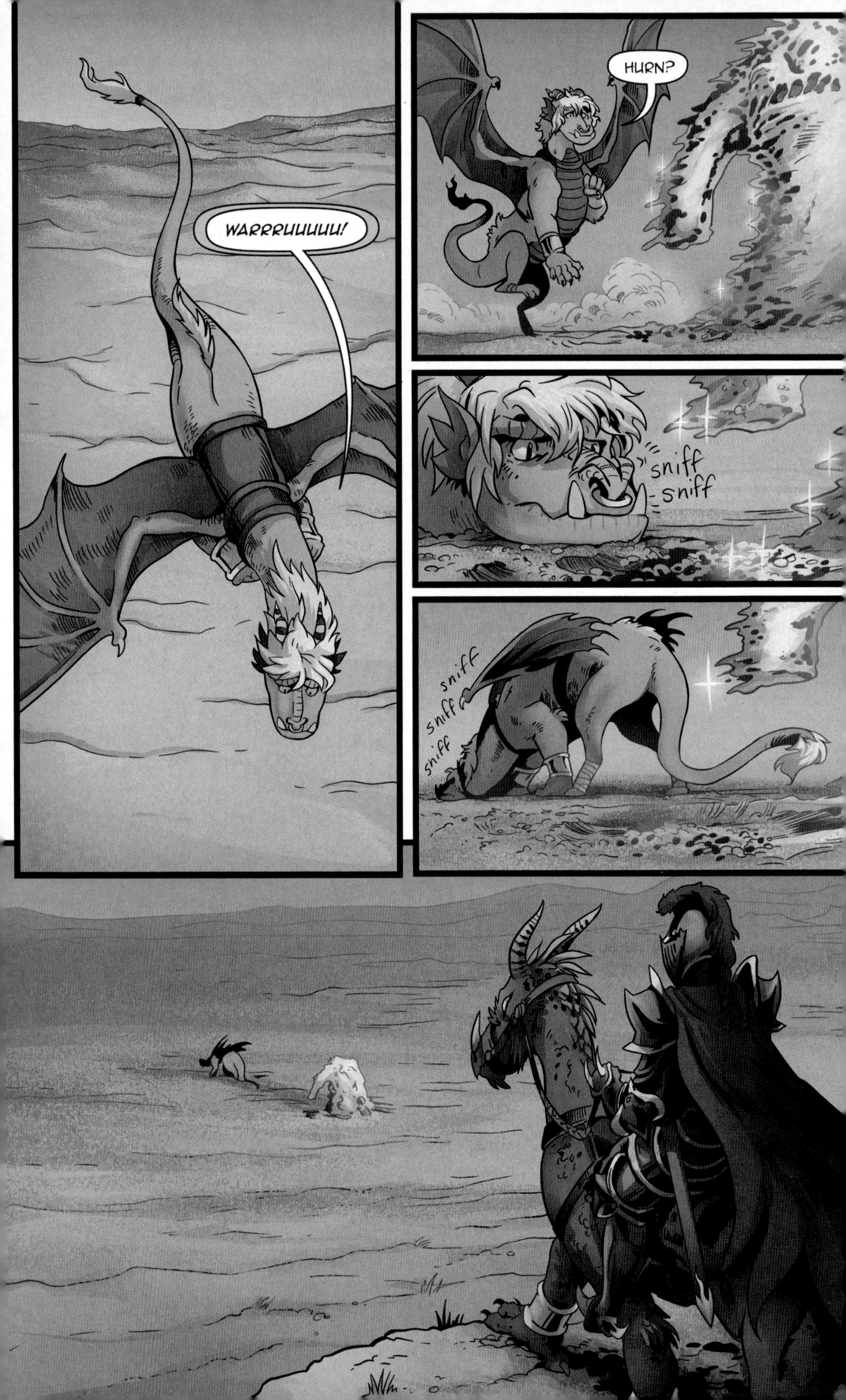
WARRRUUUUU!
HURN?
sniff
sniff
sniff
sniff
sniff

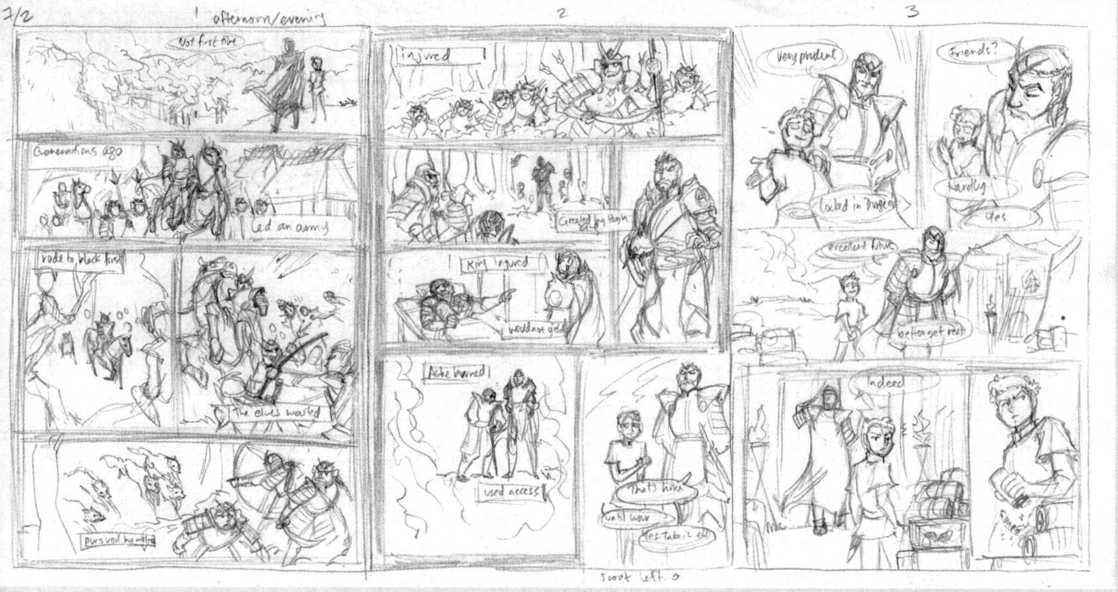

afternoon/evening
Not first time
Generations ago
Led an army
The elves waited
Injured
King injured
used access
That's him
Very prudent
Friends?
Hardly
Yes
better get rest
Indeed

THUMBNAILS FOR PAGES 1 – 3

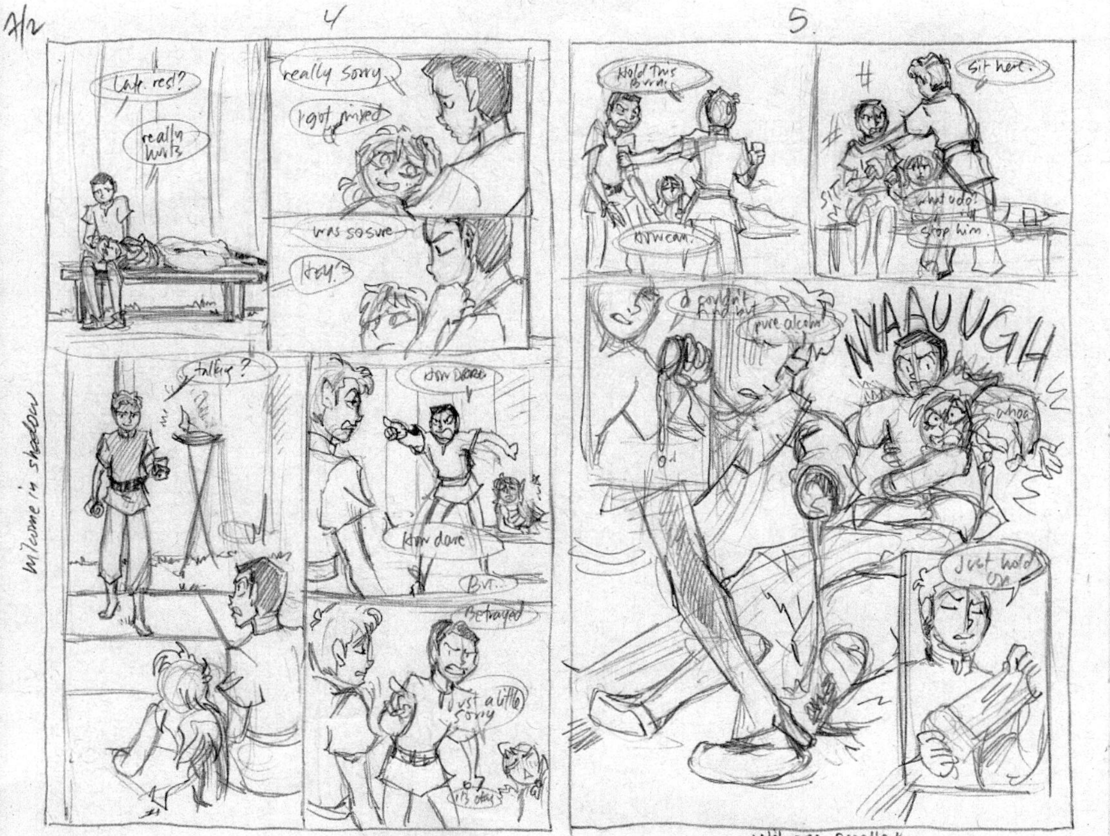

Late rest?
really hurts
really sorry
I got mixed
was so sure
talking?
How dare
How dare
But...
Betrayed
Just a little sorry
Sit here.
what u do?
Stop him.
pure alcohol
NAAUUGH
whoa
Just hold on
Welcome smaller

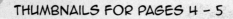

THUMBNAILS FOR PAGES 4 – 5

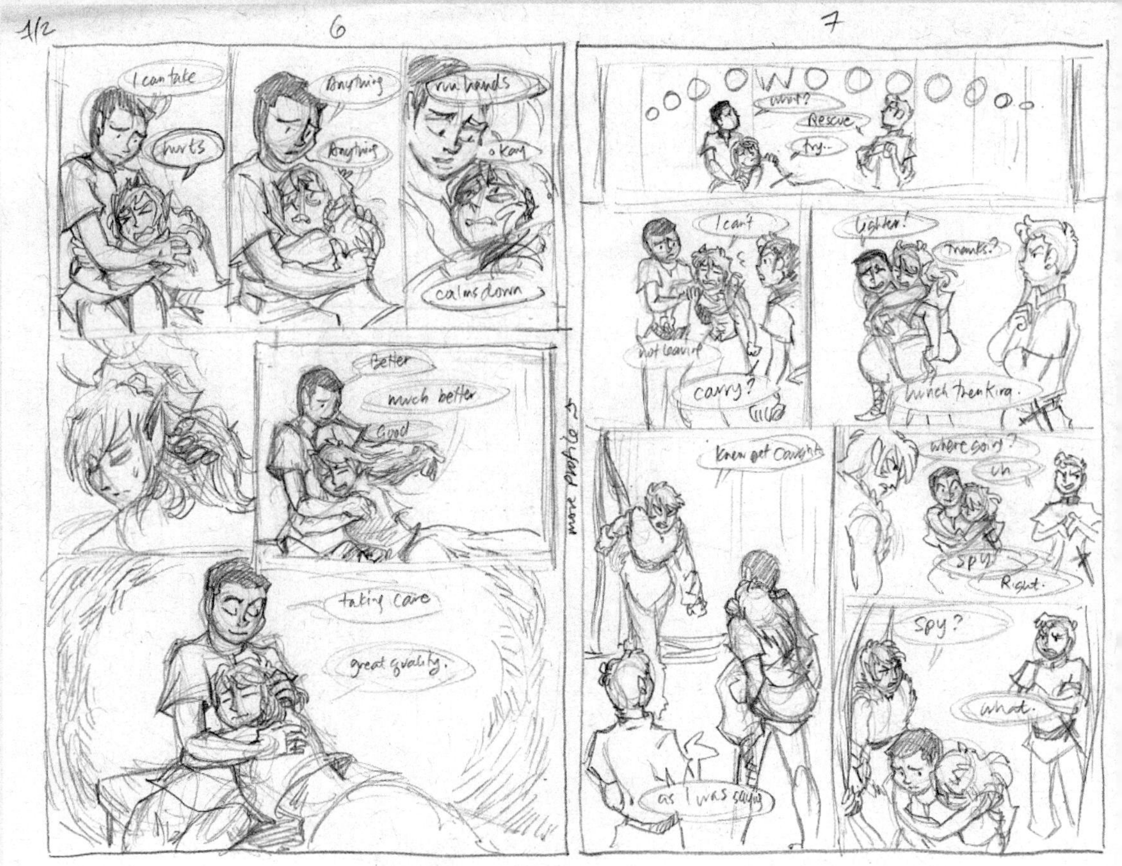
1/2
6
I can take
hurts
Anything
Anything
run hands
okay
calms down
Better
much better
Good
taking care
great quality.
7
what?
Rescue
try..
I can't
not leaving
carry?
lighter!
Thanks?
where going?
uh
Spy
Right.
Spy?
what.
as I was saying

THUMBNAILS FOR PAGES 6 - 7

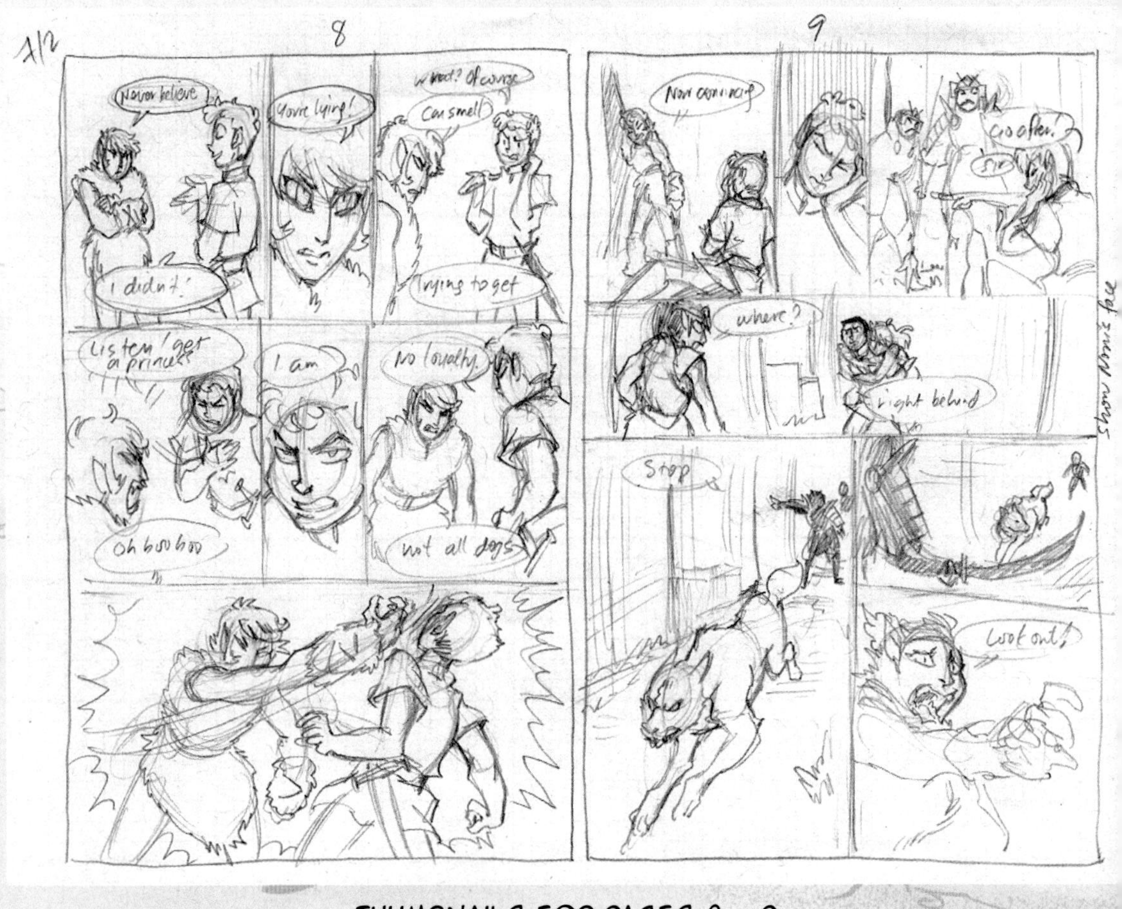
1/2
8
Never believe
You're lying!
what? Of course
Can smell
I didn't!
trying to get
Listen! get a princess
I am
No loyalty
oh boo hoo
not all dogs
9
where?
right behind
Stop
Look out!

THUMBNAILS FOR PAGES 8 - 9

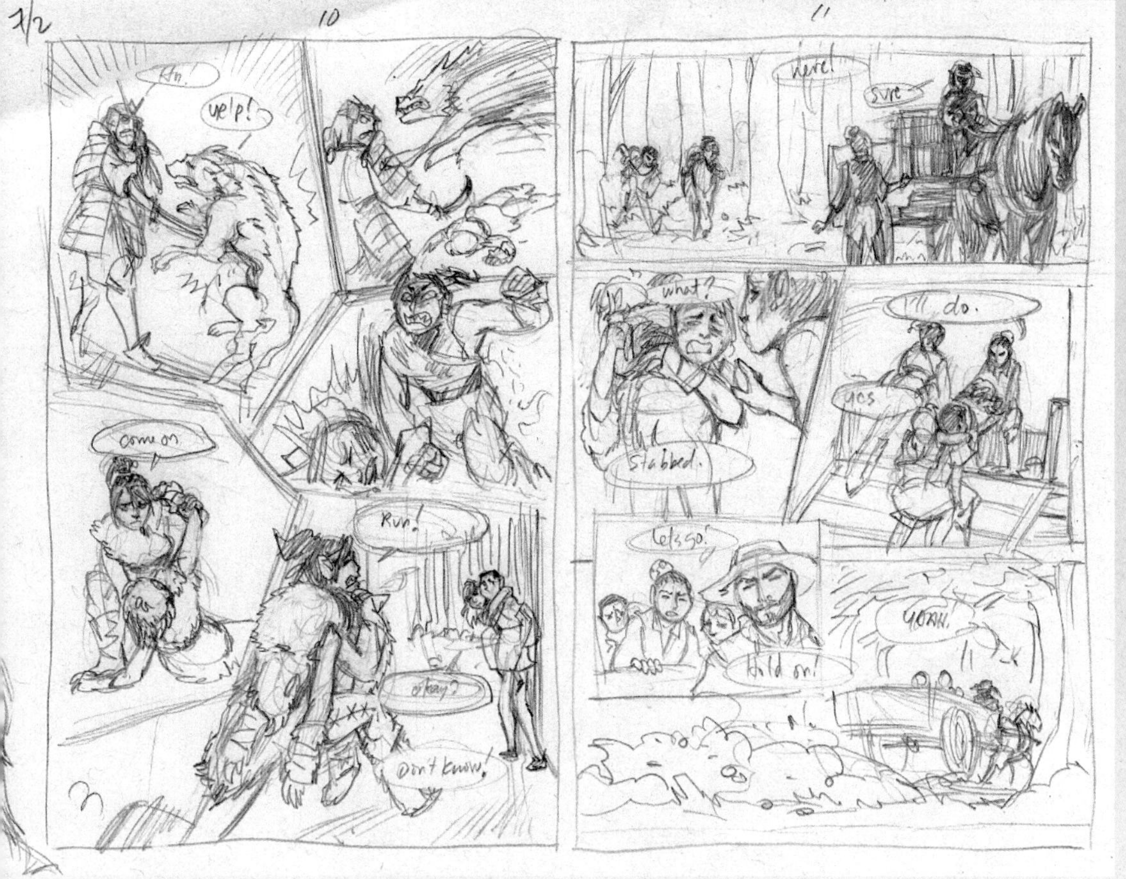
7/2
10
11
Run!
yelp!
come on
Run!
okay?
Don't know!
here!
Sure
what?
I'll do.
yes
stabbed.
Let's go!
Hold on!

THUMBNAILS FOR PAGES 10 - 11

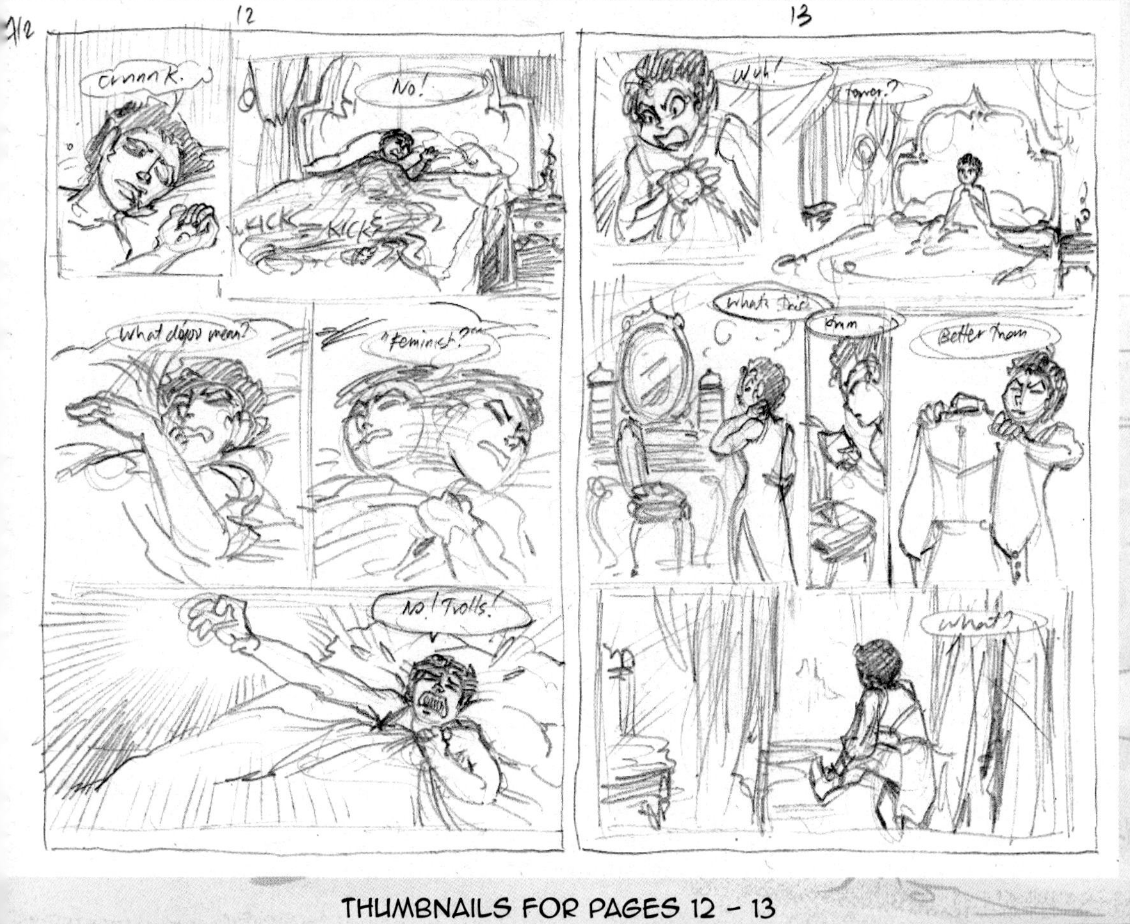
7/2
12
13
No!
KICK
KICK
What do you mean?
"Feminist?"
No! Trolls!
Wuh!
Tower?
Hmm
Better than
What?

THUMBNAILS FOR PAGES 12 - 13

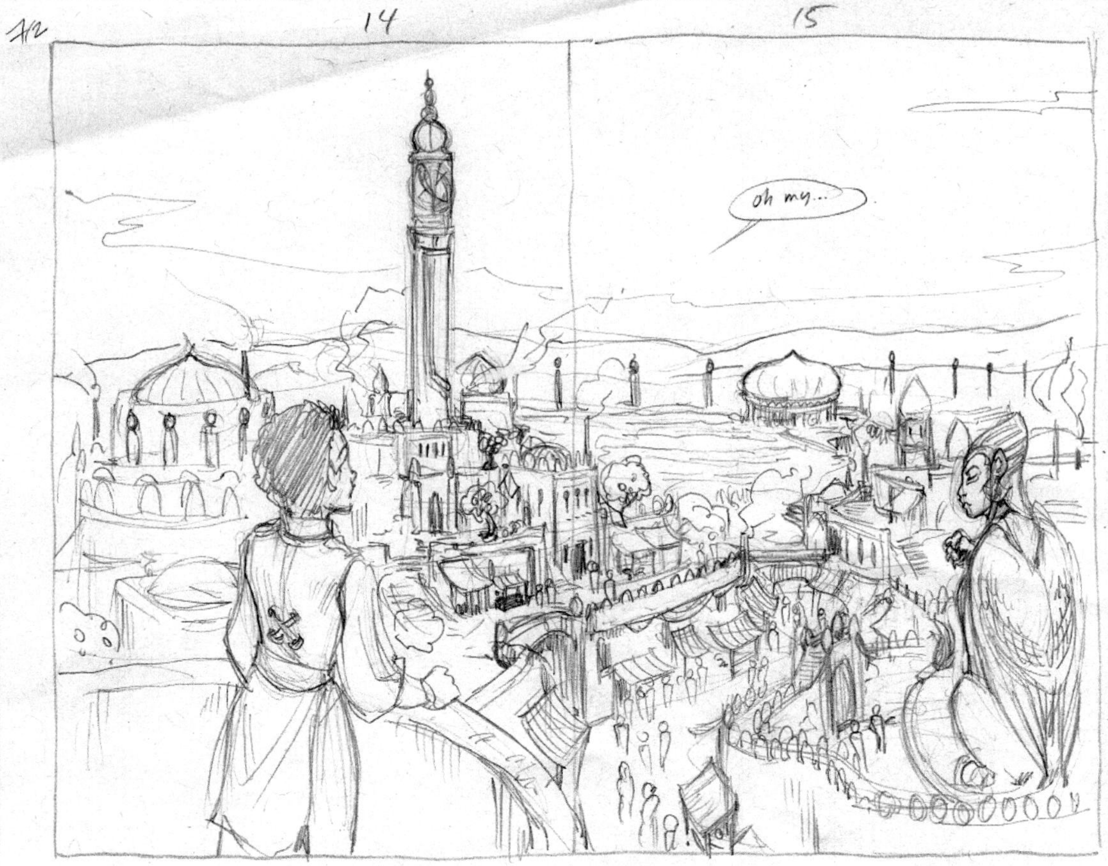
72
14
15
oh my...

THUMBNAILS FOR PAGES 14 – 15

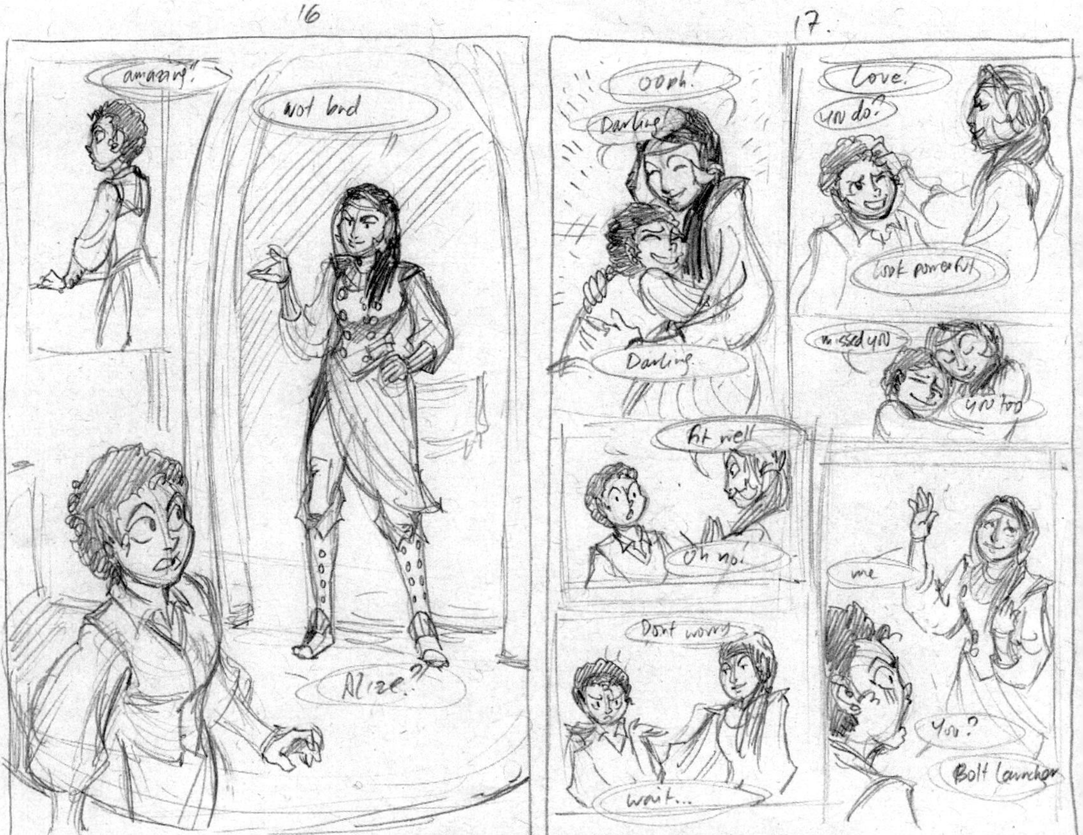
16
17.
amazing!
not bad
Alize?
Ooph!
Darling
Darling
Love!
you do?
look powerful
missed you
you too
fit well
Oh no!
Don't worry
wait...
me
You?
Bolt Launcher
Change Alize → taller

THUMBNAILS FOR PAGES 16 – 17

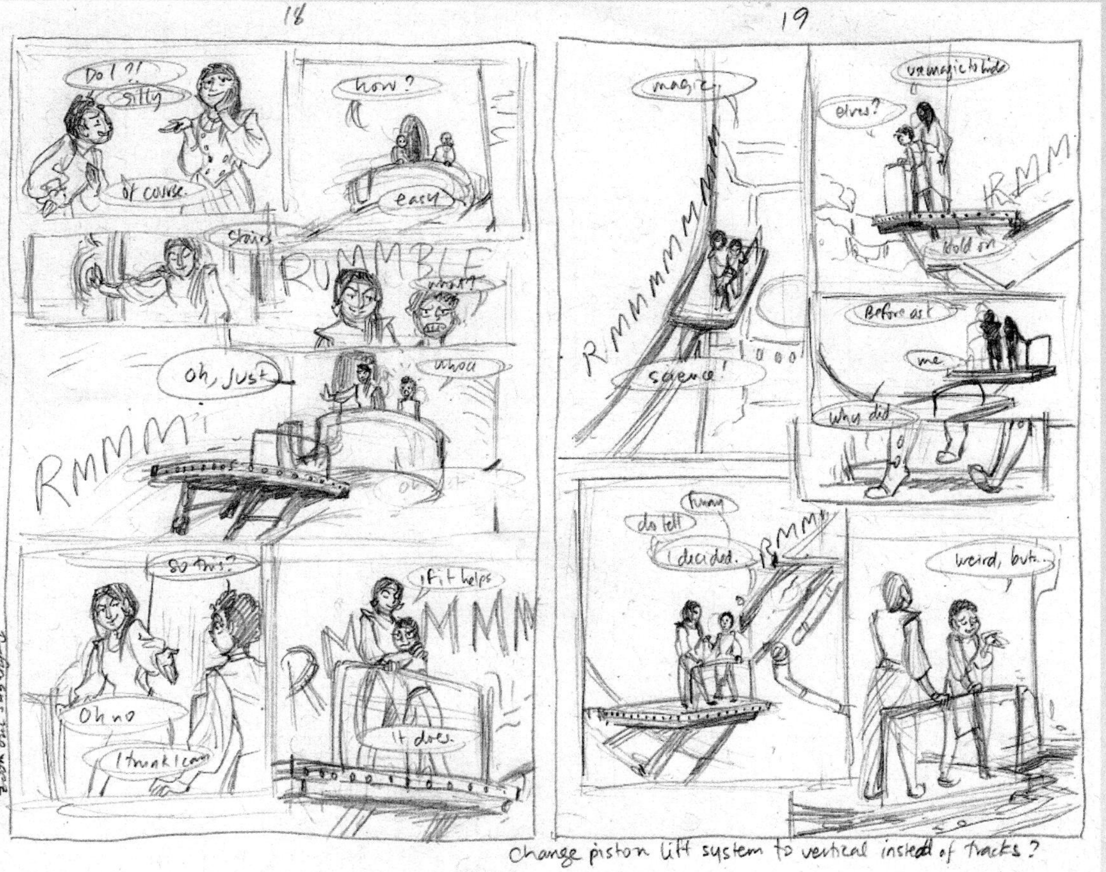
18
19
silly
Of course.
how?
easy
RUMMBLE
Oh, Just
RMMM
If it helps
RMMMM
It does.
Oh no
magic
science!
Elves?
RMMM
Hold on
Before ask
me
Why did
do tell
funny
I decided.
weird, but...
Change piston lift system to vertical instead of tracks?

THUMBNAILS FOR PAGES 18 – 19

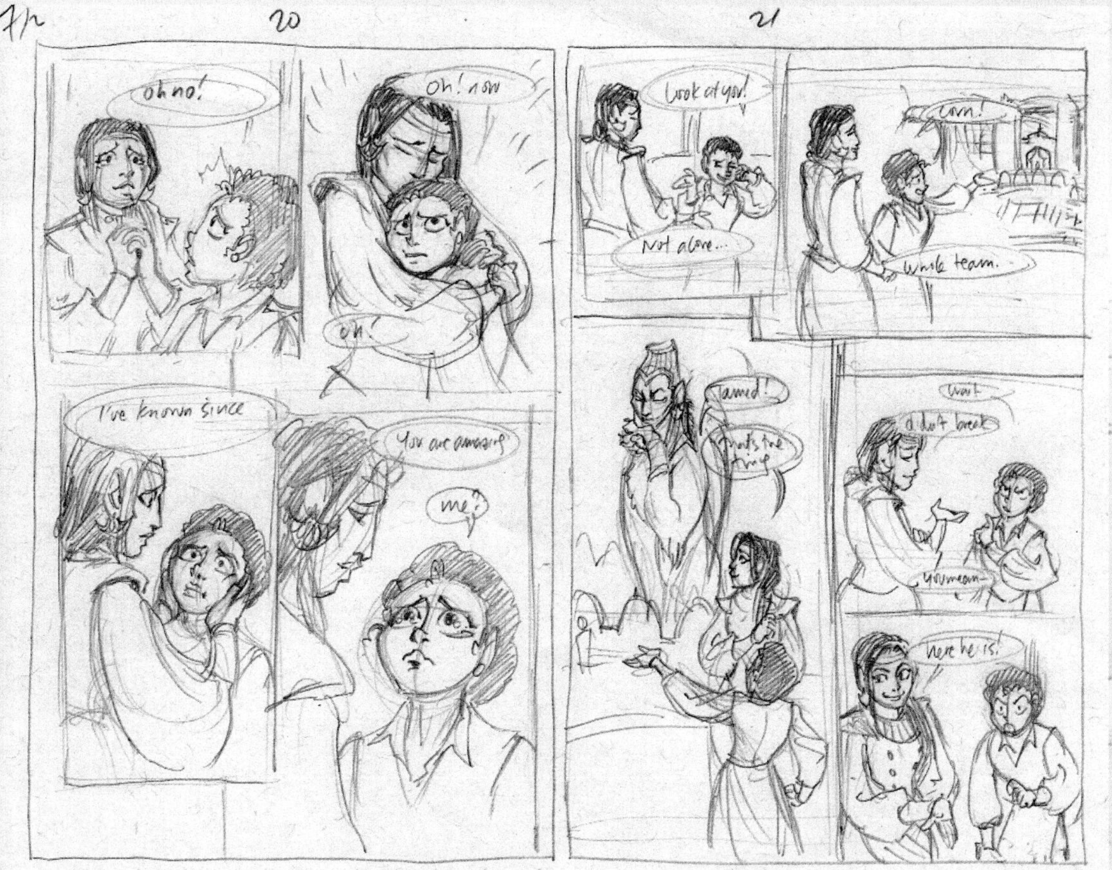
20
21
oh no!
Oh! now
oh!
I've known since
You are amazing
me?
Look at you!
Not alone...
Whole team.
Tamed!
Wait
Here he is!

THUMBNAILS FOR PAGES 20 – 21

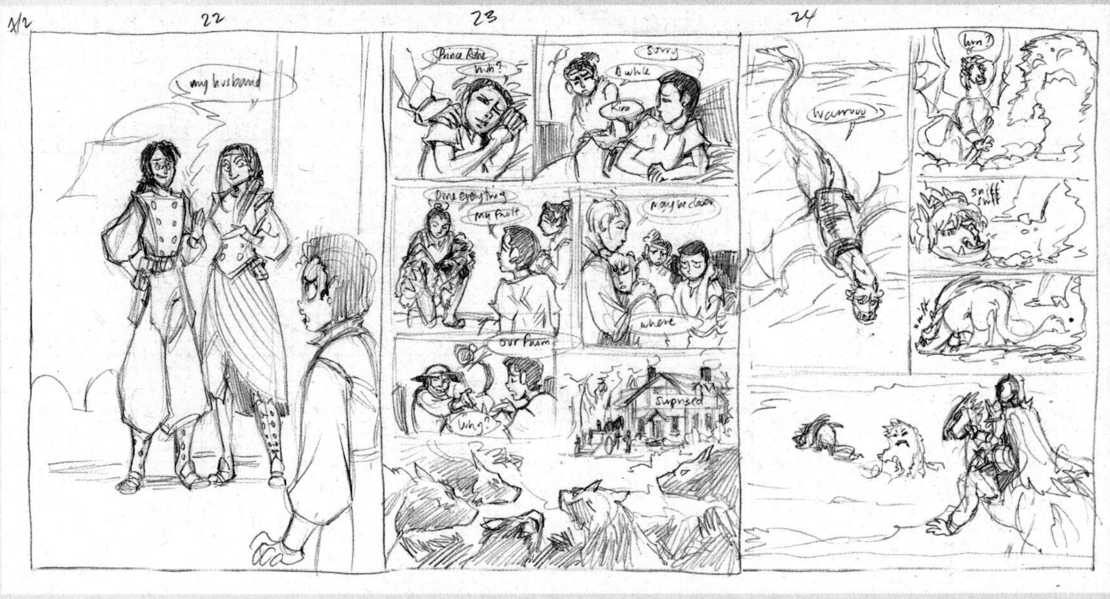
22
my husband
23
huh?
Sorry
Kira
Done everything
my fault
maybe closer
where
our farm
why?
surprised
24
sniff
sniff

THUMBNAILS FOR PAGES 22 - 24

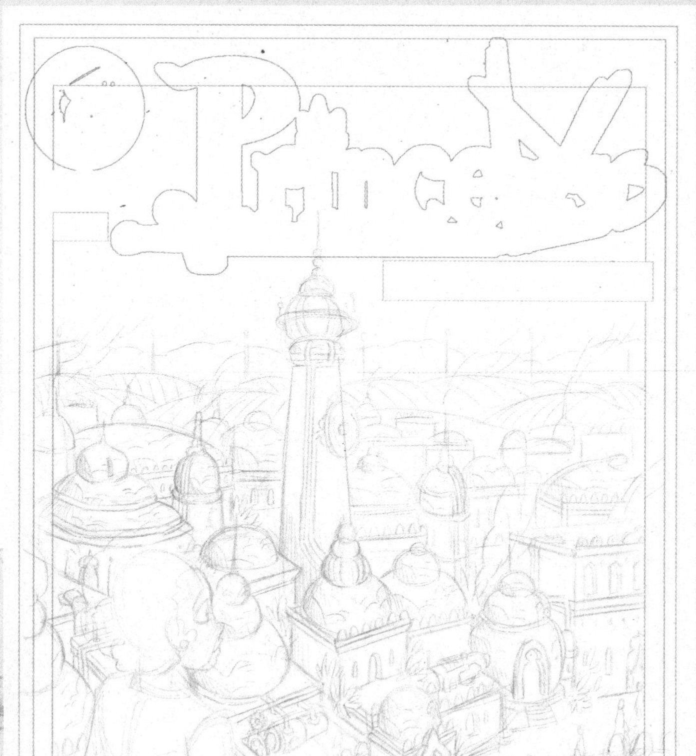

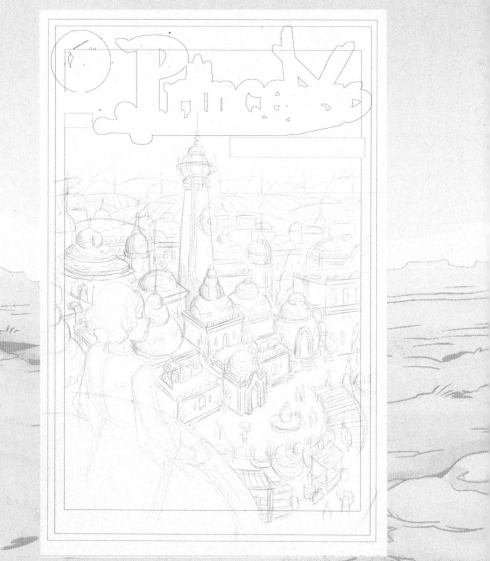

COVER BLUE LINES

Chapter Three: My Sister's House

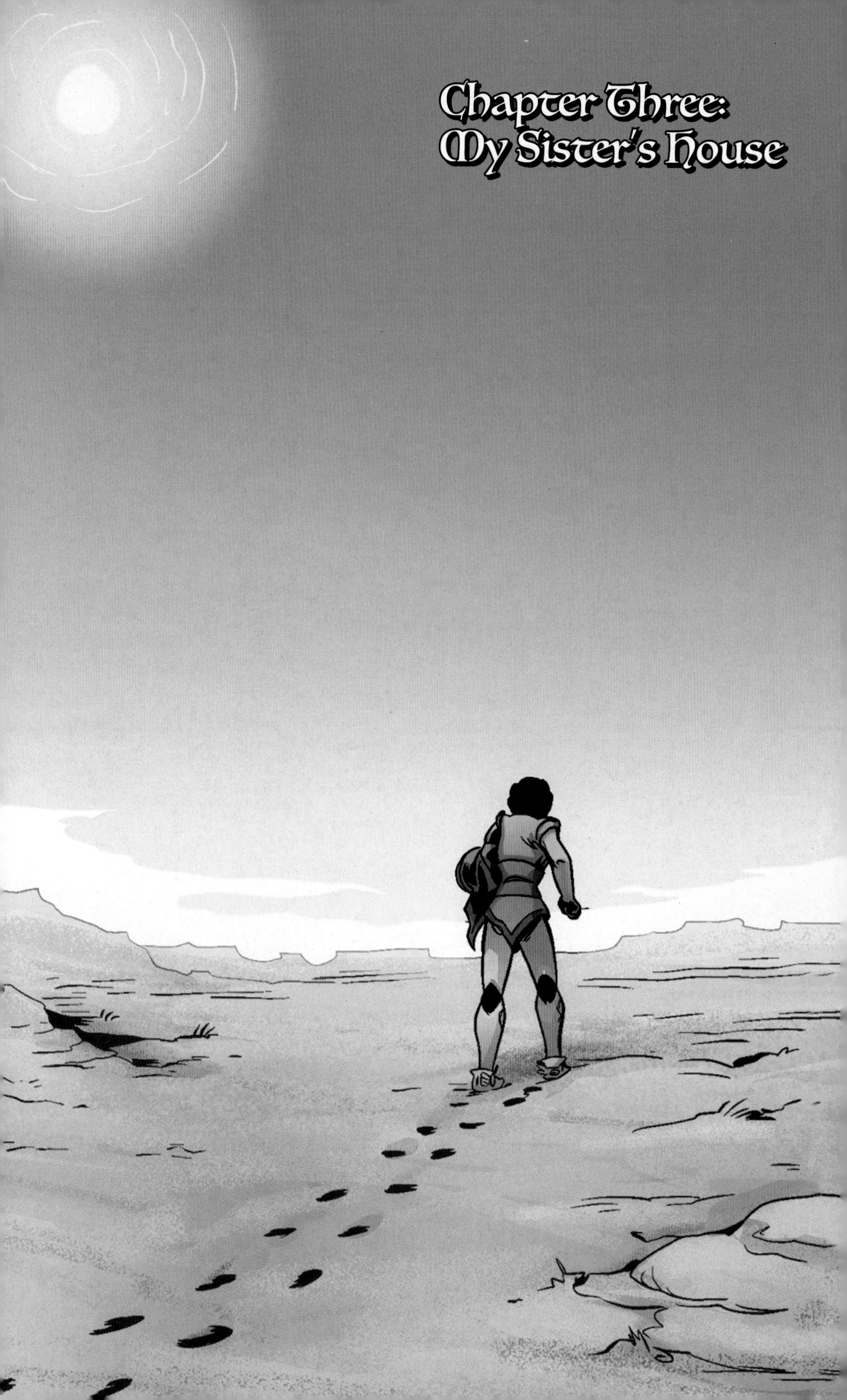

STORY:
Jeremy Whitley

PENCILS:
Emily Martin

INKS:
Christine Hipp

COLORS & LETTERS:
Brett Grunig

COVER A: Emily Martin   COVER B: Yesenia Moises

EDITORS:
Alicia Whitley (script)
Nicole D'Andria (comic)

Bryan Seaton: Publisher/ CEO • **Shawn Gabborin:** Editor In Chief
Jason Martin: Publisher-Danger Zone • **Nicole D'Andria:** Marketing Director/Editor
Jim Dietz: Social Media Manager • **Danielle Davison:** Executive Administrator
Chad Cicconi: Still Waiting For His Princess • **Shawn Pryor:** President of Creator Relations

PRINCELESS Vol. 7: FIND YOURSELF #3, August 2018. Copyright Jeremy Whitley, 2015. Published by Action Lab Comics. All rights reserved. All characters are fictional. Any likeness to anyone living or dead is purely coincidental. No part of this publication may be reproduced or transmitted without permission, except for small excerpts for review purposes. Second Printing. Printed in Canada.

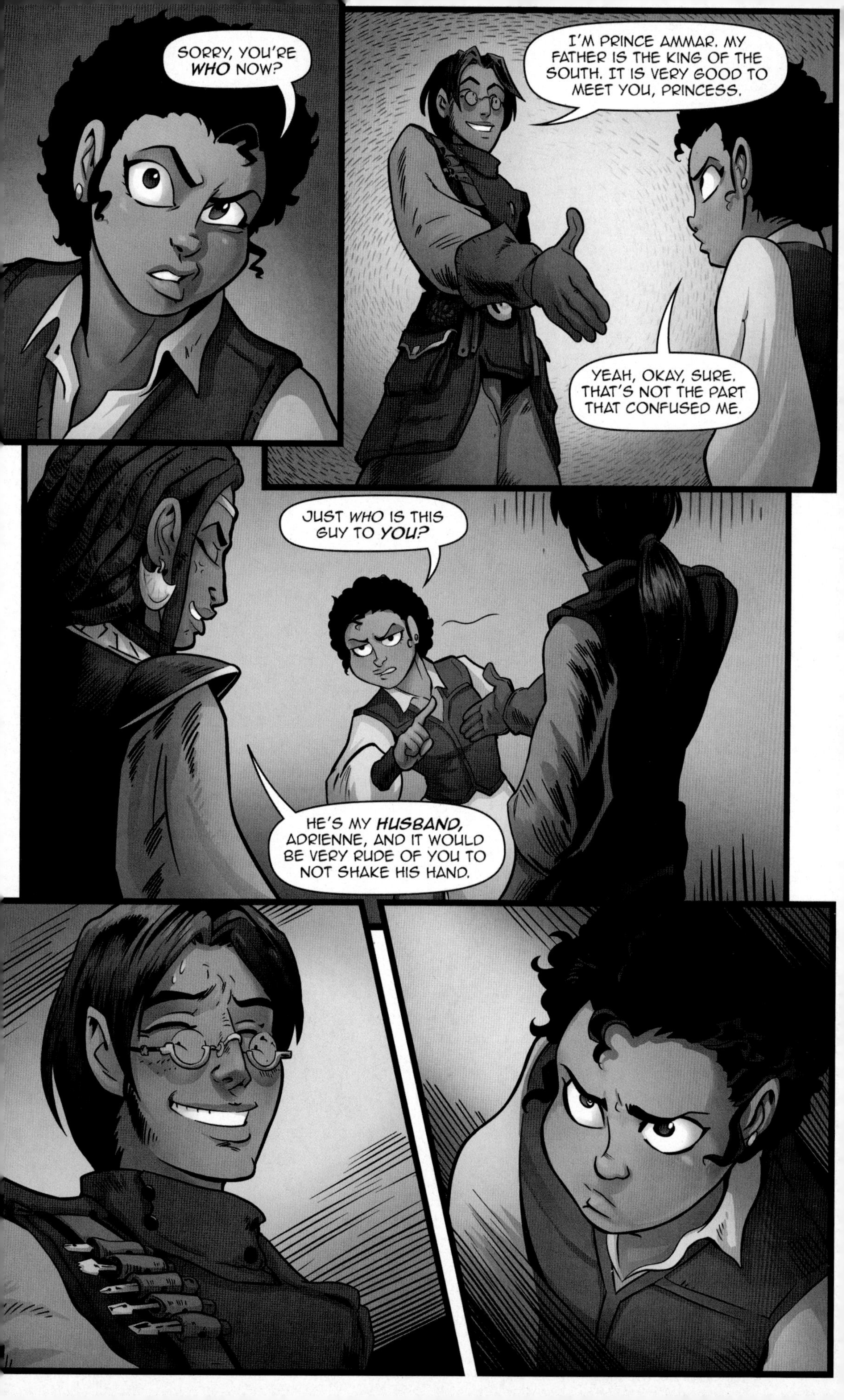
SORRY, YOU'RE *WHO* NOW?
I'M PRINCE AMMAR. MY FATHER IS THE KING OF THE SOUTH. IT IS VERY GOOD TO MEET YOU, PRINCESS.
YEAH, OKAY, SURE. THAT'S NOT THE PART THAT CONFUSED ME.
JUST *WHO* IS THIS GUY TO *YOU?*
HE'S MY **HUSBAND,** ADRIENNE, AND IT WOULD BE VERY RUDE OF YOU TO NOT SHAKE HIS HAND.

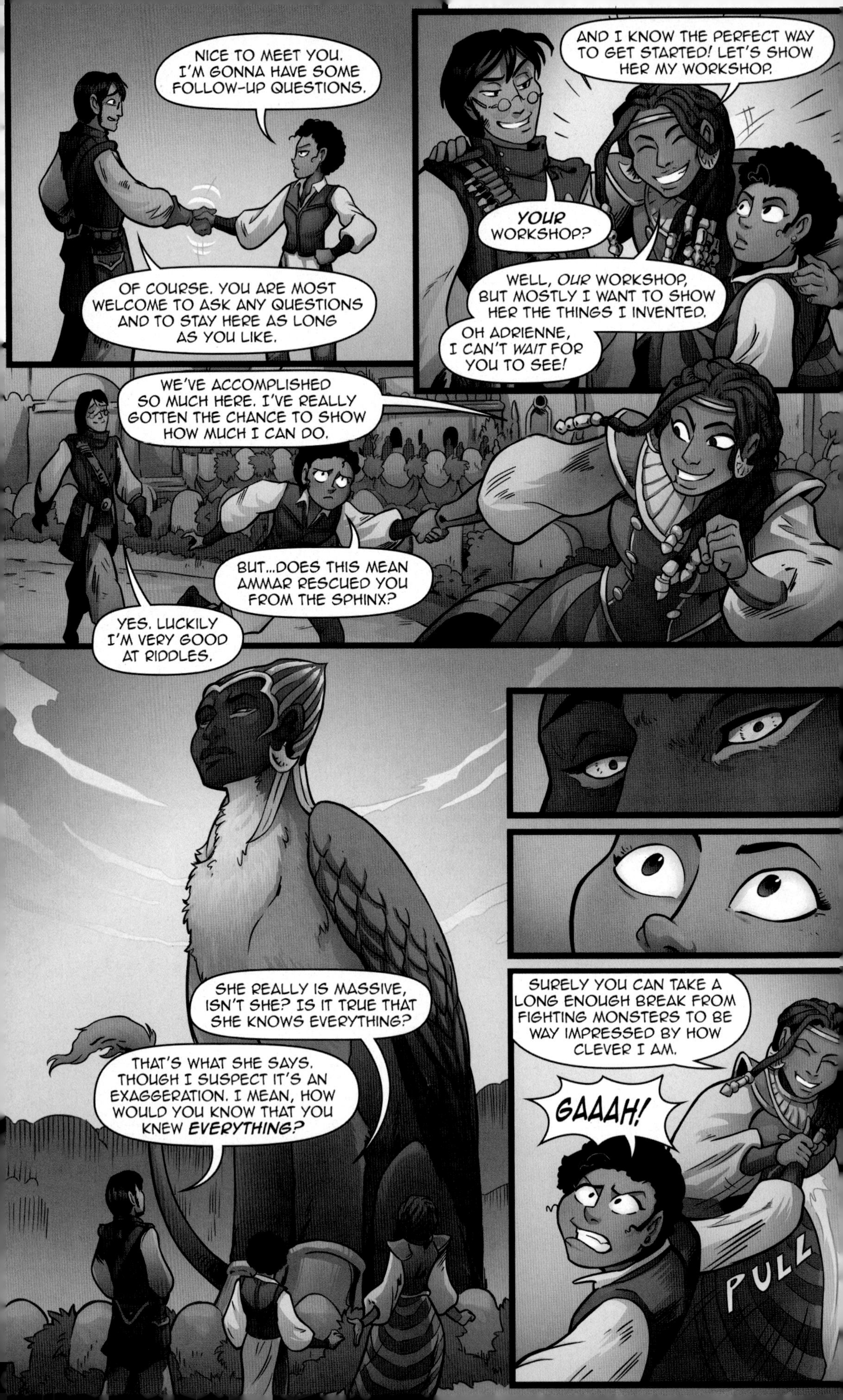
NICE TO MEET YOU. I'M GONNA HAVE SOME FOLLOW-UP QUESTIONS.
OF COURSE. YOU ARE MOST WELCOME TO ASK ANY QUESTIONS AND TO STAY HERE AS LONG AS YOU LIKE.
AND I KNOW THE PERFECT WAY TO GET STARTED! LET'S SHOW HER MY WORKSHOP.
YOUR WORKSHOP?
WELL, *OUR* WORKSHOP, BUT MOSTLY I WANT TO SHOW HER THE THINGS I INVENTED.
OH ADRIENNE, I CAN'T *WAIT* FOR YOU TO SEE!
WE'VE ACCOMPLISHED SO MUCH HERE. I'VE REALLY GOTTEN THE CHANCE TO SHOW HOW MUCH I CAN DO.
BUT...DOES THIS MEAN AMMAR RESCUED YOU FROM THE SPHINX?
YES. LUCKILY I'M VERY GOOD AT RIDDLES.
SHE REALLY IS MASSIVE, ISN'T SHE? IS IT TRUE THAT SHE KNOWS EVERYTHING?
THAT'S WHAT SHE SAYS. THOUGH I SUSPECT IT'S AN EXAGGERATION. I MEAN, HOW WOULD YOU KNOW THAT YOU KNEW *EVERYTHING?*
SURELY YOU CAN TAKE A LONG ENOUGH BREAK FROM FIGHTING MONSTERS TO BE WAY IMPRESSED BY HOW CLEVER I AM.
GAAAH!
PULL

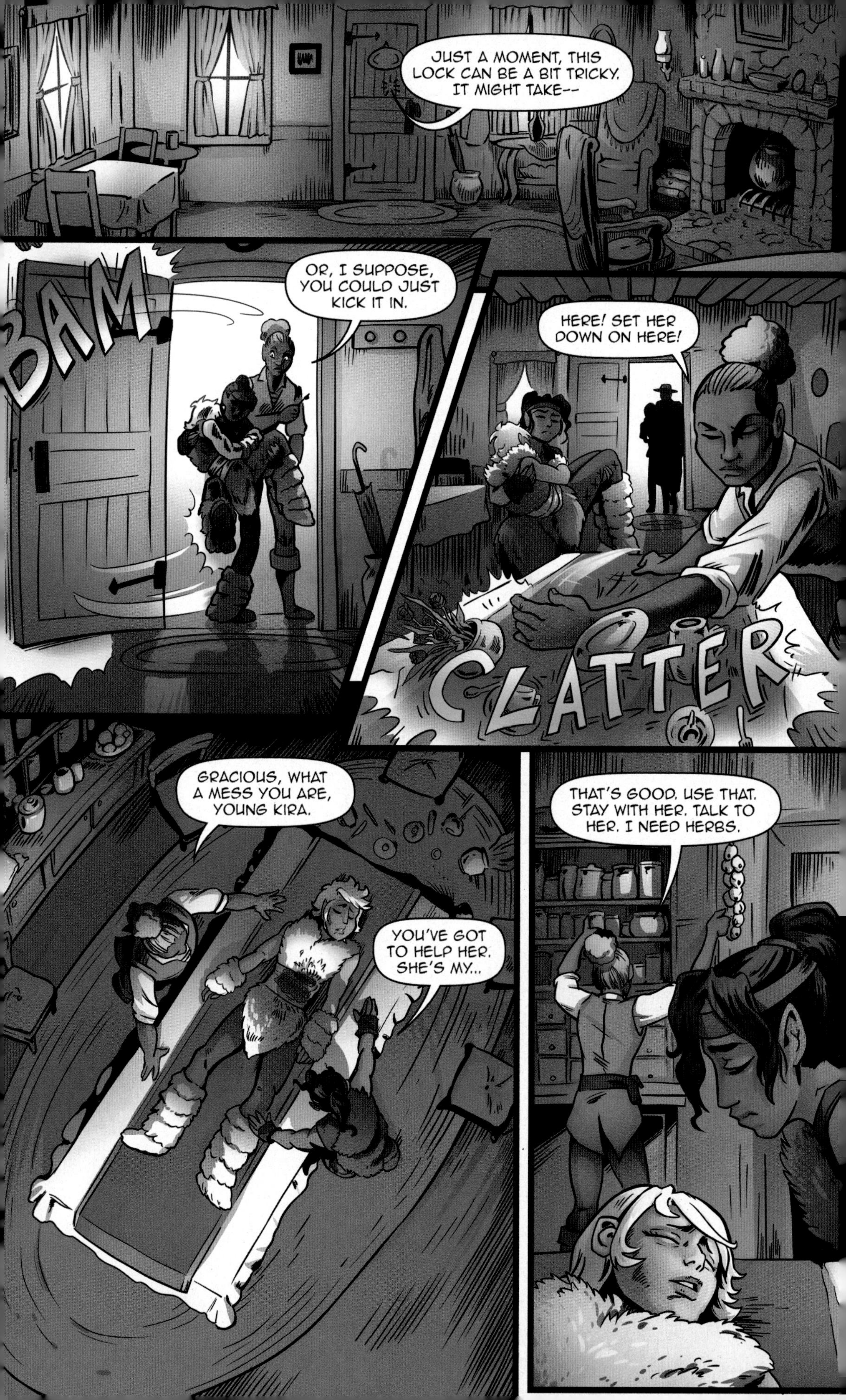
JUST A MOMENT, THIS LOCK CAN BE A BIT TRICKY. IT MIGHT TAKE--
BAM
OR, I SUPPOSE, YOU COULD JUST KICK IT IN.
HERE! SET HER DOWN ON HERE!
CLATTER
GRACIOUS, WHAT A MESS YOU ARE, YOUNG KIRA.
YOU'VE GOT TO HELP HER. SHE'S MY...
THAT'S GOOD. USE THAT. STAY WITH HER. TALK TO HER. I NEED HERBS.

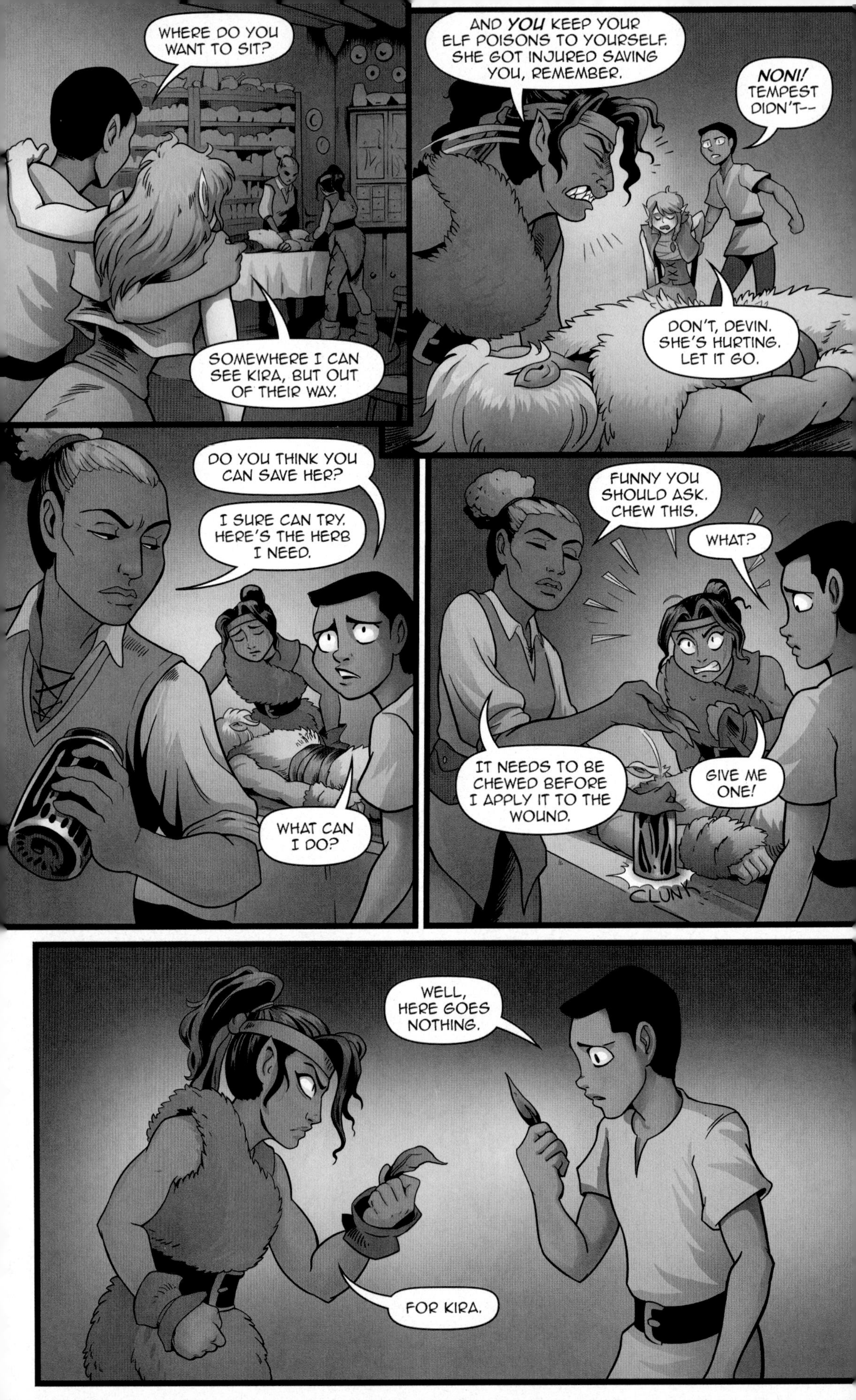
WHERE DO YOU WANT TO SIT?
SOMEWHERE I CAN SEE KIRA, BUT OUT OF THEIR WAY.
AND YOU KEEP YOUR ELF POISONS TO YOURSELF. SHE GOT INJURED SAVING YOU, REMEMBER.
NONI! TEMPEST DIDN'T--
DON'T, DEVIN. SHE'S HURTING. LET IT GO.
DO YOU THINK YOU CAN SAVE HER?
I SURE CAN TRY. HERE'S THE HERB I NEED.
WHAT CAN I DO?
FUNNY YOU SHOULD ASK. CHEW THIS.
WHAT?
IT NEEDS TO BE CHEWED BEFORE I APPLY IT TO THE WOUND.
GIVE ME ONE!
CLUNK
WELL, HERE GOES NOTHING.
FOR KIRA.

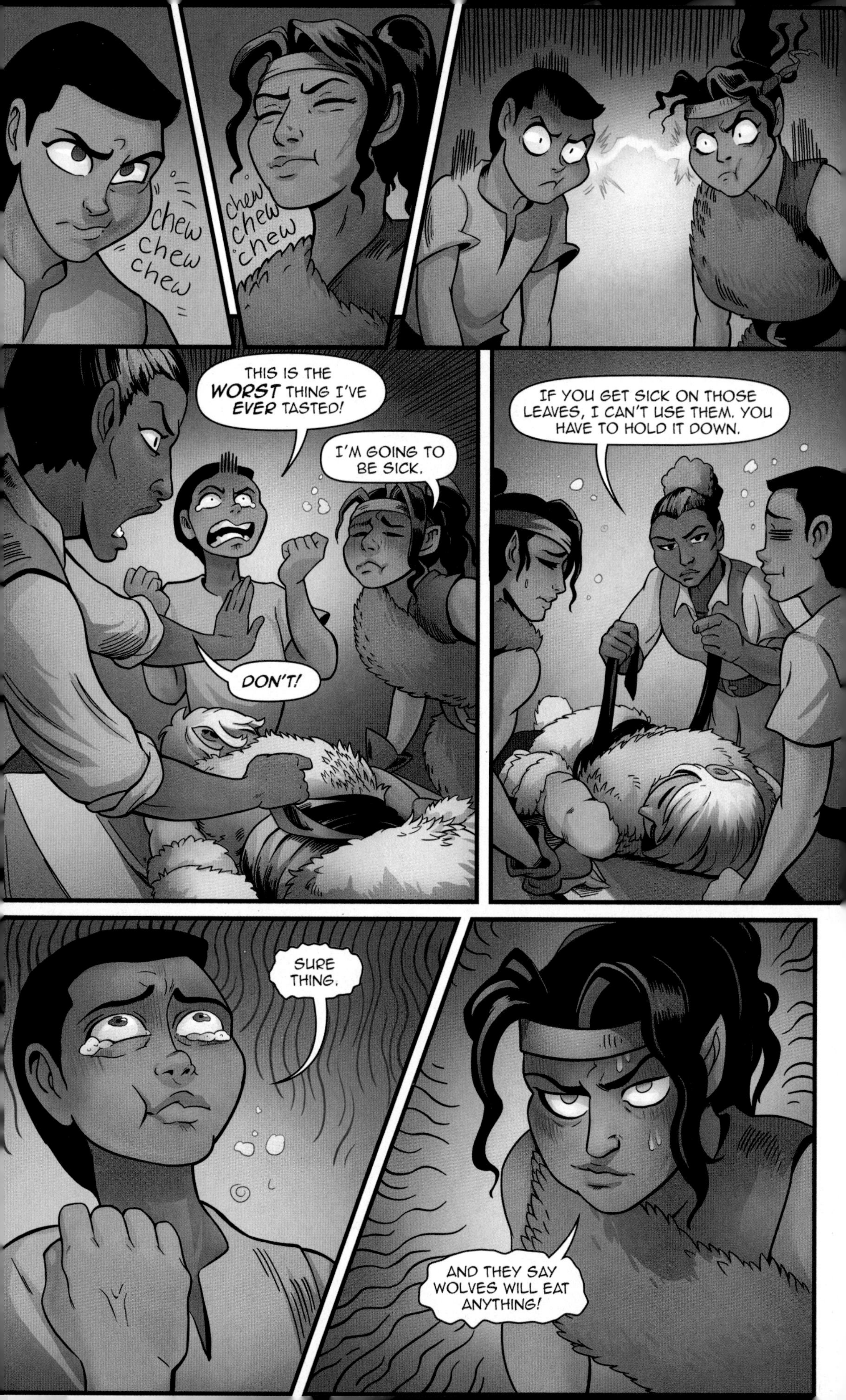
chew chew chew
chew chew chew
THIS IS THE WORST THING I'VE EVER TASTED!
I'M GOING TO BE SICK.
DON'T!
IF YOU GET SICK ON THOSE LEAVES, I CAN'T USE THEM. YOU HAVE TO HOLD IT DOWN.
SURE THING.
AND THEY SAY WOLVES WILL EAT ANYTHING!

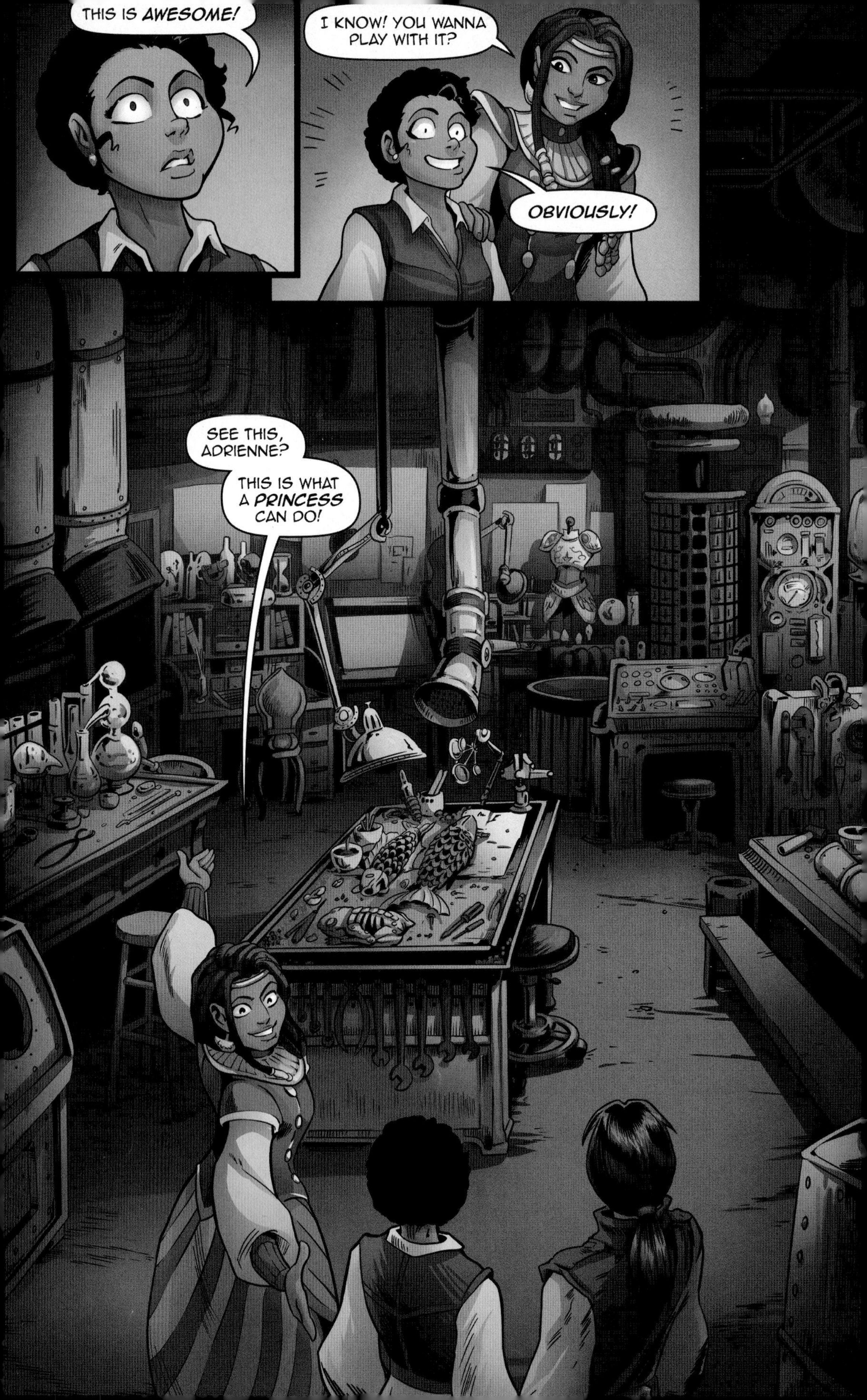
THIS IS AWESOME!
I KNOW! YOU WANNA PLAY WITH IT?
OBVIOUSLY!
SEE THIS, ADRIENNE?
THIS IS WHAT A PRINCESS CAN DO!

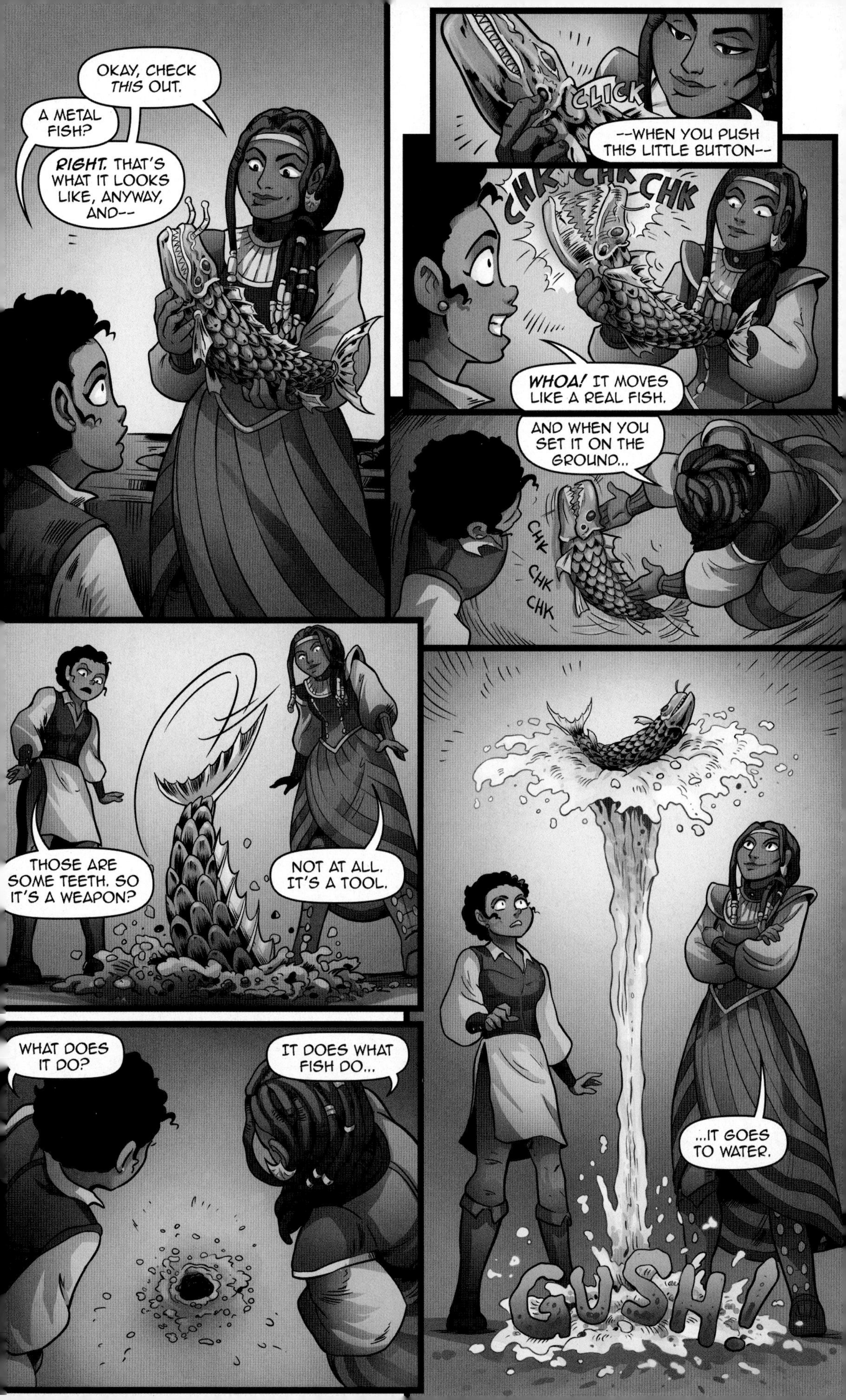
OKAY, CHECK *THIS* OUT.
A METAL FISH?
RIGHT. THAT'S WHAT IT LOOKS LIKE, ANYWAY, AND--
CLICK
--WHEN YOU PUSH THIS LITTLE BUTTON--
CHK CHK CHK
WHOA! IT MOVES LIKE A REAL FISH.
AND WHEN YOU SET IT ON THE GROUND...
CHK
CHK
CHK
THOSE ARE SOME TEETH. SO IT'S A WEAPON?
NOT AT ALL. IT'S A TOOL.
WHAT DOES IT DO?
IT DOES WHAT FISH DO...
...IT GOES TO WATER.
GUSH!

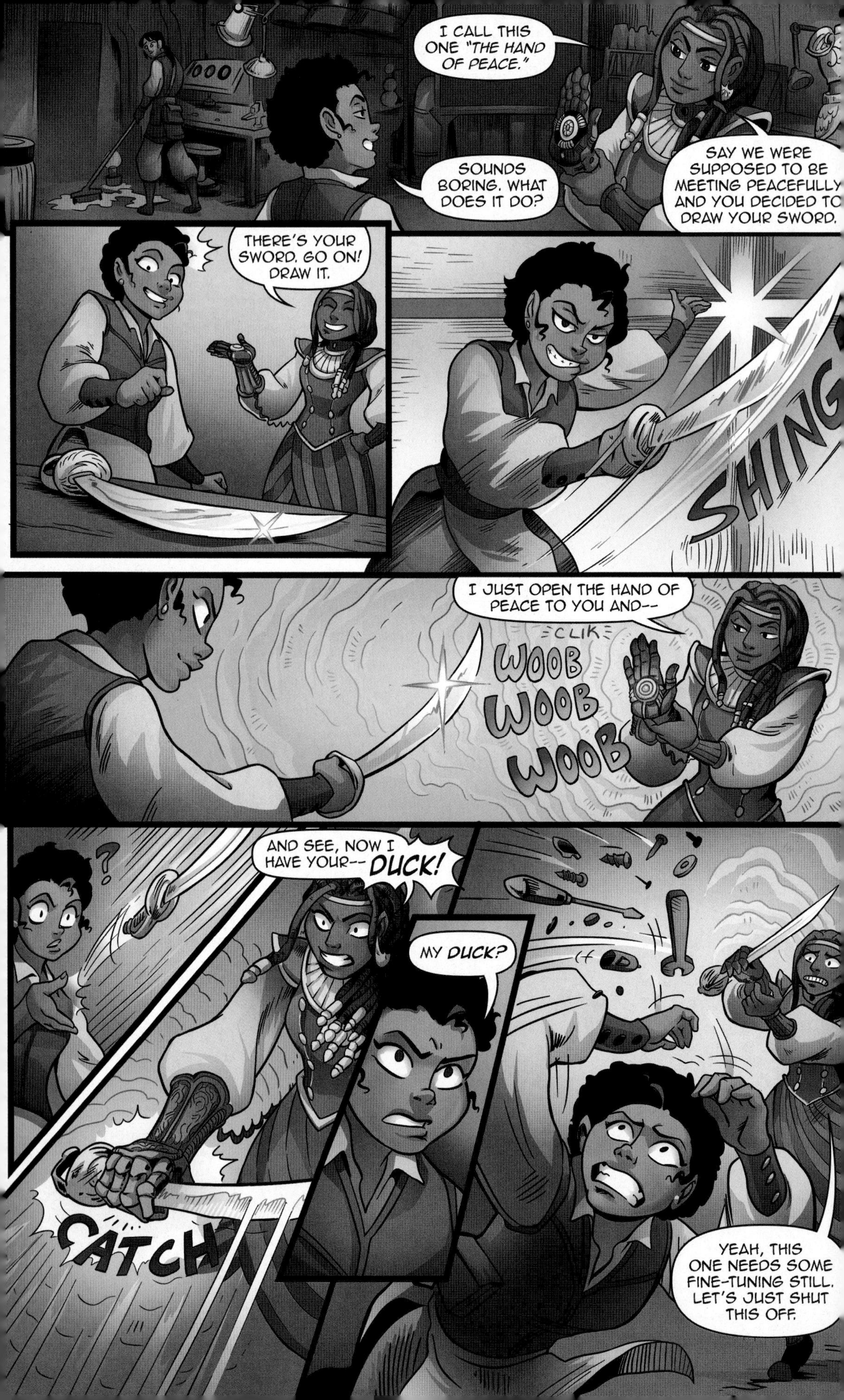
I CALL THIS ONE "THE HAND OF PEACE."
SOUNDS BORING. WHAT DOES IT DO?
SAY WE WERE SUPPOSED TO BE MEETING PEACEFULLY AND YOU DECIDED TO DRAW YOUR SWORD.
THERE'S YOUR SWORD. GO ON! DRAW IT.
SHING
I JUST OPEN THE HAND OF PEACE TO YOU AND--
CLIK
WOOB WOOB WOOB
?
AND SEE, NOW I HAVE YOUR-- DUCK!
MY DUCK?
CATCH
YEAH, THIS ONE NEEDS SOME FINE-TUNING STILL. LET'S JUST SHUT THIS OFF.

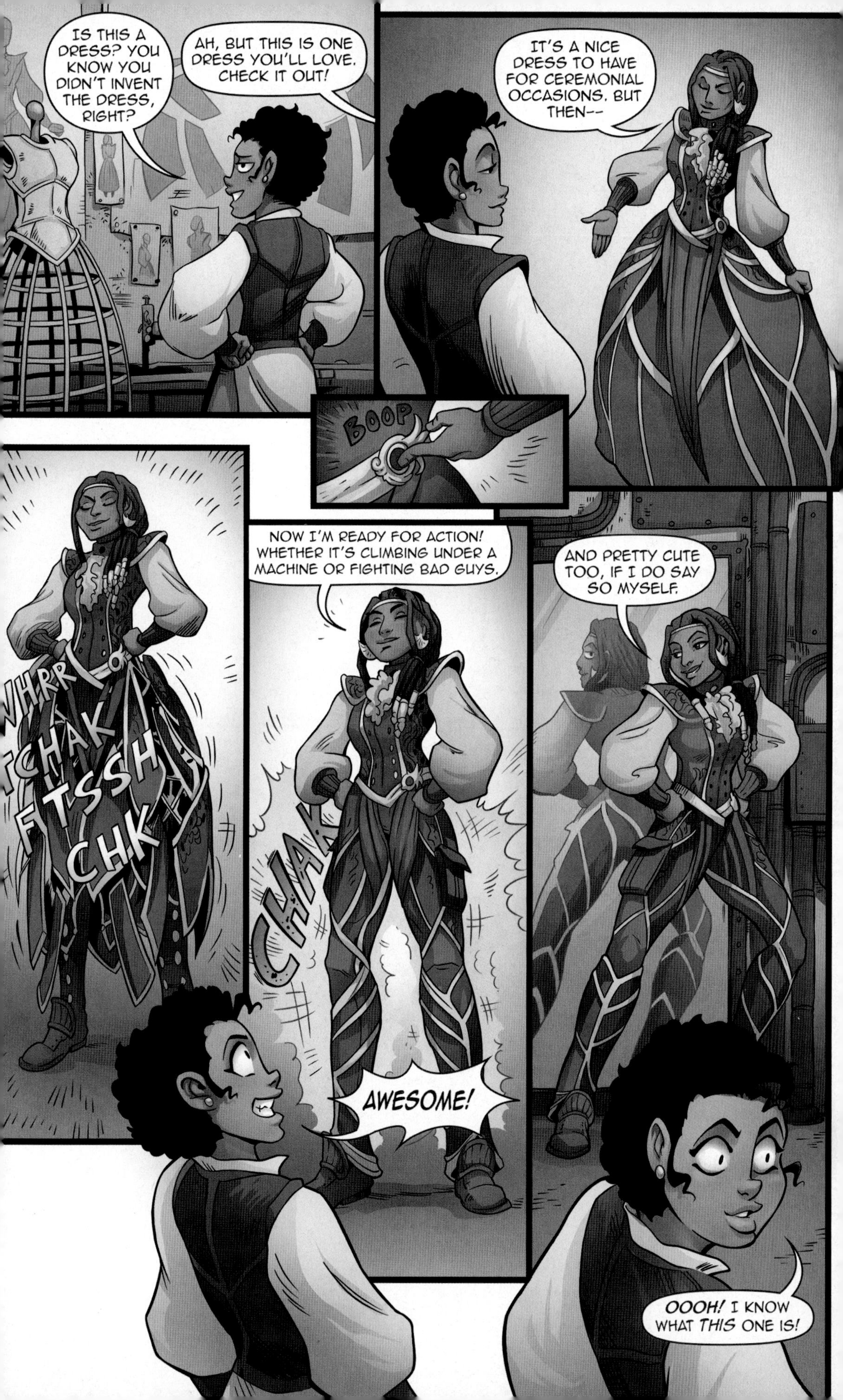
IS THIS A DRESS? YOU KNOW YOU DIDN'T INVENT THE DRESS, RIGHT?
AH, BUT THIS IS ONE DRESS YOU'LL LOVE. CHECK IT OUT!
IT'S A NICE DRESS TO HAVE FOR CEREMONIAL OCCASIONS. BUT THEN--
BOOP
WHRR
CHAK
FTSSH
CHK
NOW I'M READY FOR ACTION! WHETHER IT'S CLIMBING UNDER A MACHINE OR FIGHTING BAD GUYS.
CHAK
AWESOME!
AND PRETTY CUTE TOO, IF I DO SAY SO MYSELF.
OOOH! I KNOW WHAT *THIS* ONE IS!

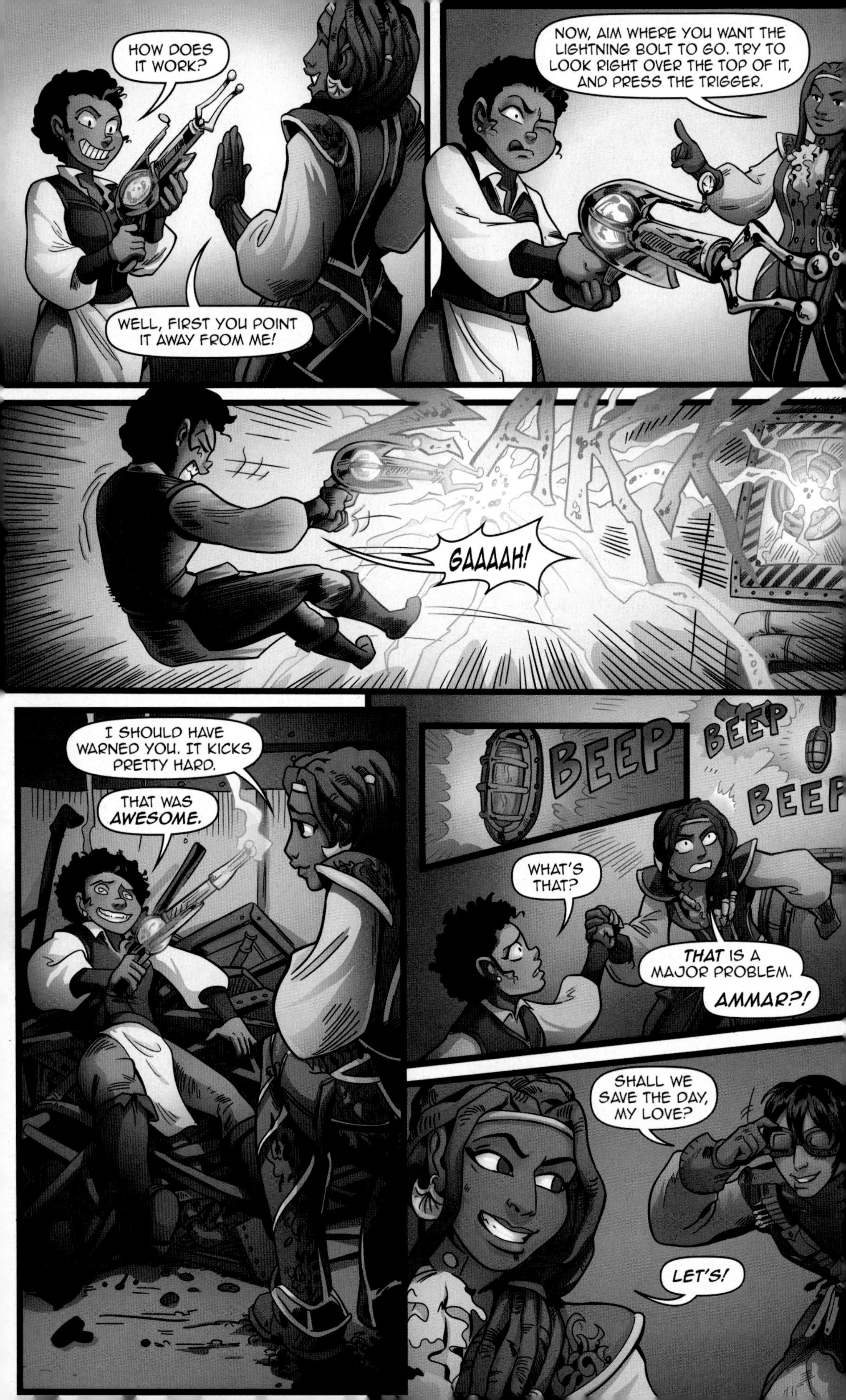
HOW DOES IT WORK?
WELL, FIRST YOU POINT IT AWAY FROM ME!
NOW, AIM WHERE YOU WANT THE LIGHTNING BOLT TO GO. TRY TO LOOK RIGHT OVER THE TOP OF IT, AND PRESS THE TRIGGER.
GAAAAH!
I SHOULD HAVE WARNED YOU. IT KICKS PRETTY HARD.
THAT WAS AWESOME.
BEEP
BEEP
BEEP
WHAT'S THAT?
THAT IS A MAJOR PROBLEM.
AMMAR?!
SHALL WE SAVE THE DAY, MY LOVE?
LET'S!

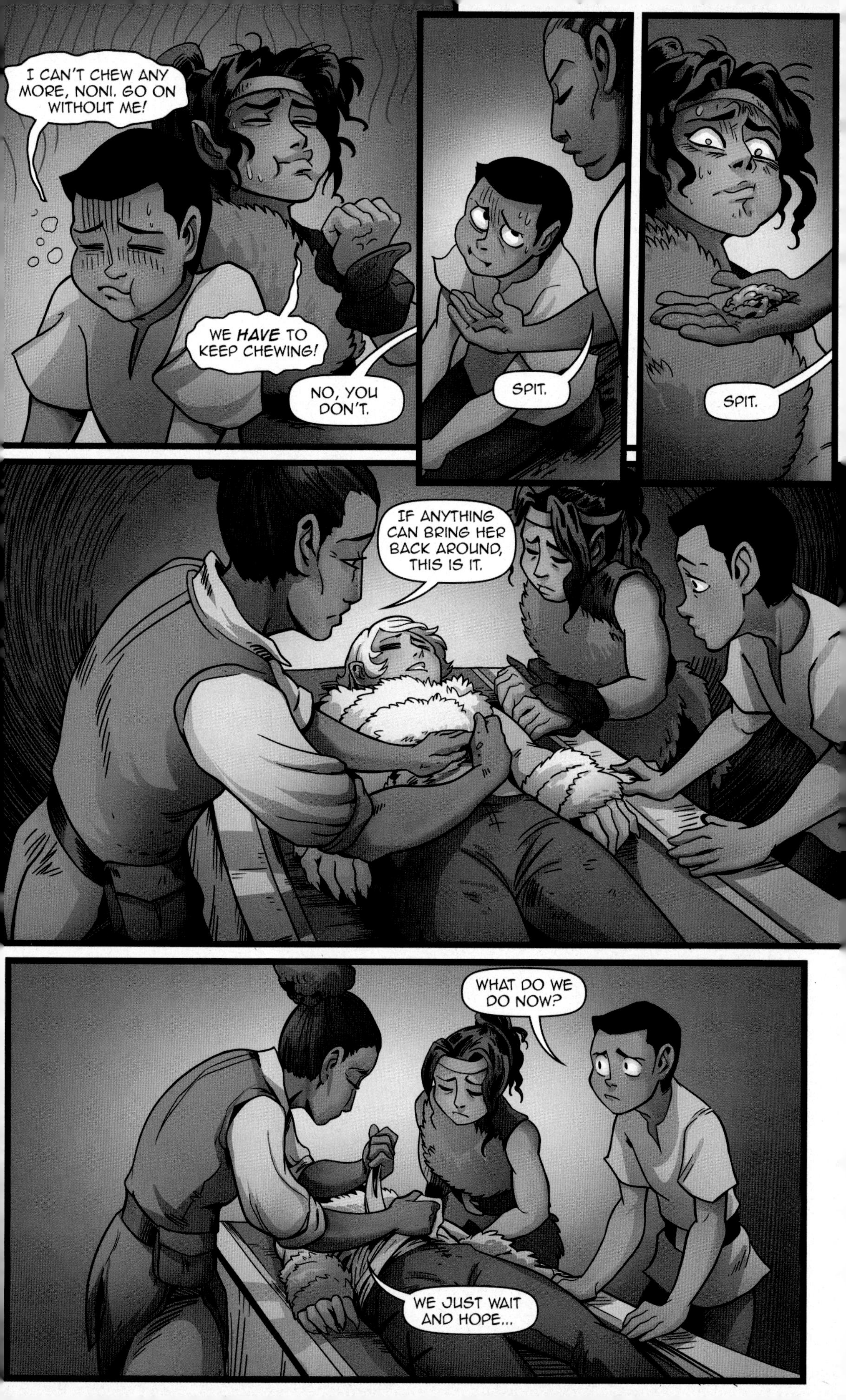
I CAN'T CHEW ANY MORE, NONI. GO ON WITHOUT ME!
WE *HAVE* TO KEEP CHEWING!
NO, YOU DON'T.
SPIT.
SPIT.
IF ANYTHING CAN BRING HER BACK AROUND, THIS IS IT.
WHAT DO WE DO NOW?
WE JUST WAIT AND HOPE...

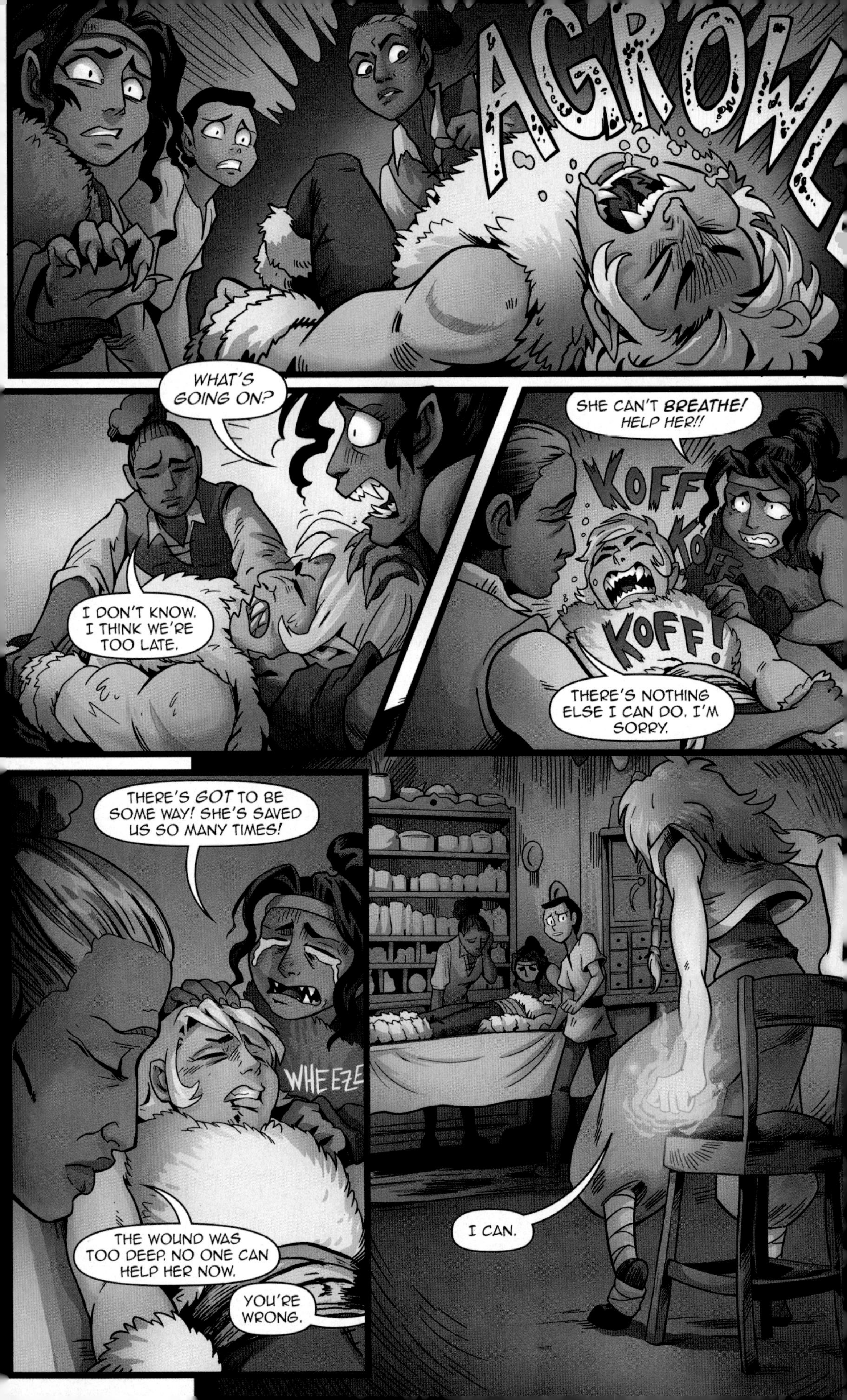
AGROWL
WHAT'S GOING ON?
I DON'T KNOW. I THINK WE'RE TOO LATE.
SHE CAN'T BREATHE! HELP HER!!
KOFF
KOFF
KOFF!
THERE'S NOTHING ELSE I CAN DO. I'M SORRY.
THERE'S GOT TO BE SOME WAY! SHE'S SAVED US SO MANY TIMES!
WHEEZE
THE WOUND WAS TOO DEEP. NO ONE CAN HELP HER NOW.
YOU'RE WRONG.
I CAN.

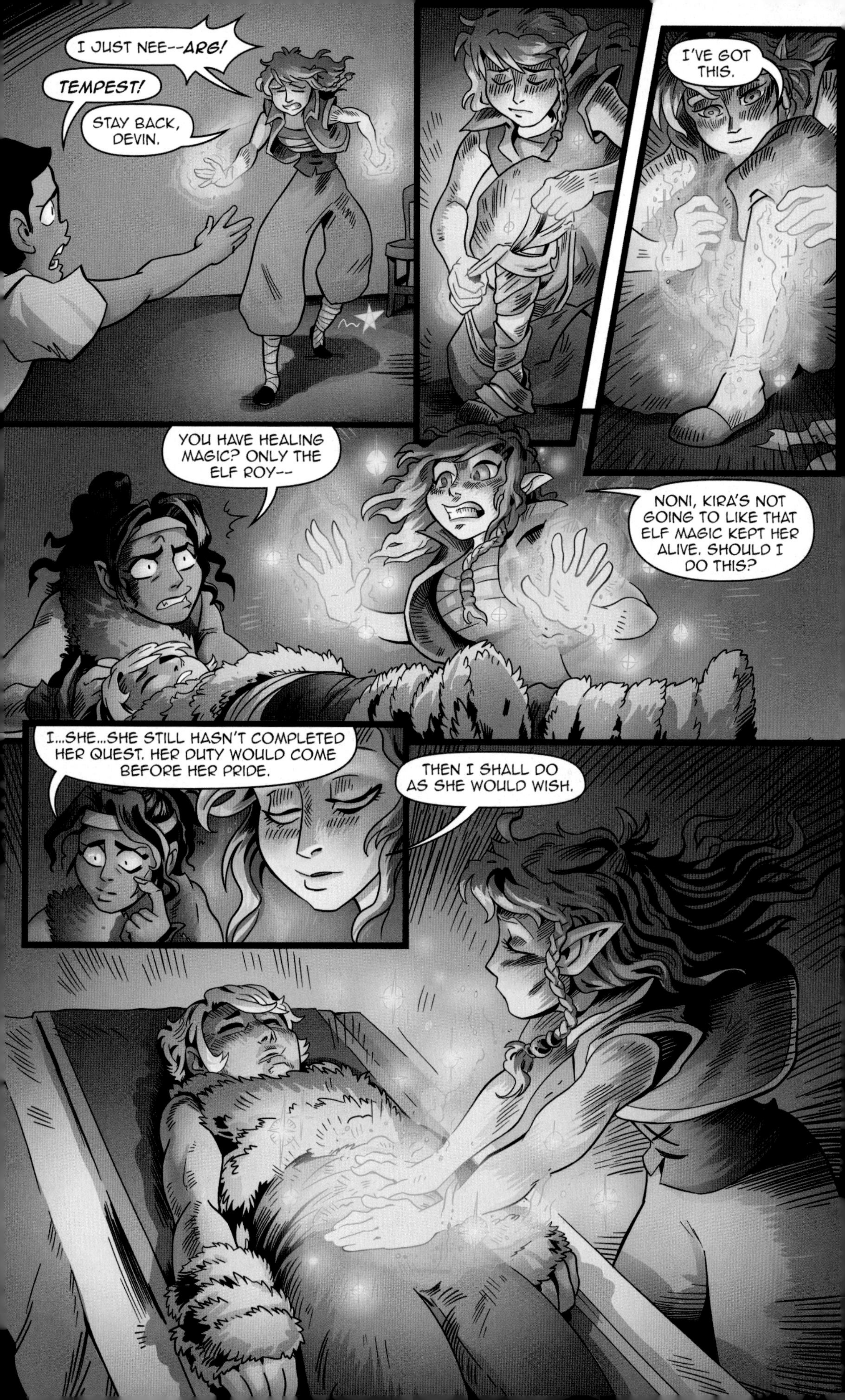
I JUST NEE--ARG!
TEMPEST!
STAY BACK, DEVIN.
I'VE GOT THIS.
YOU HAVE HEALING MAGIC? ONLY THE ELF ROY--
NONI, KIRA'S NOT GOING TO LIKE THAT ELF MAGIC KEPT HER ALIVE. SHOULD I DO THIS?
I...SHE...SHE STILL HASN'T COMPLETED HER QUEST. HER DUTY WOULD COME BEFORE HER PRIDE.
THEN I SHALL DO AS SHE WOULD WISH.

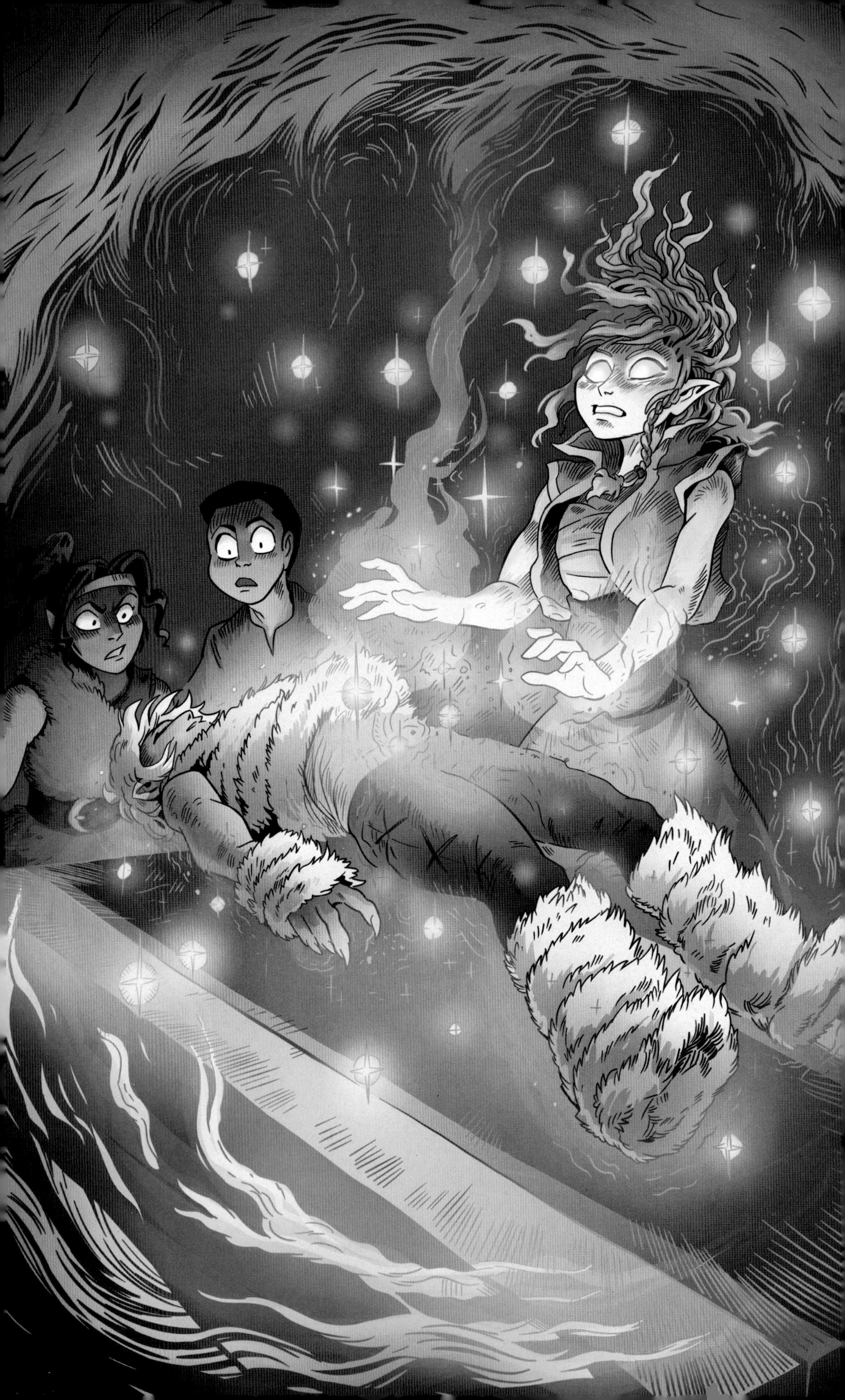

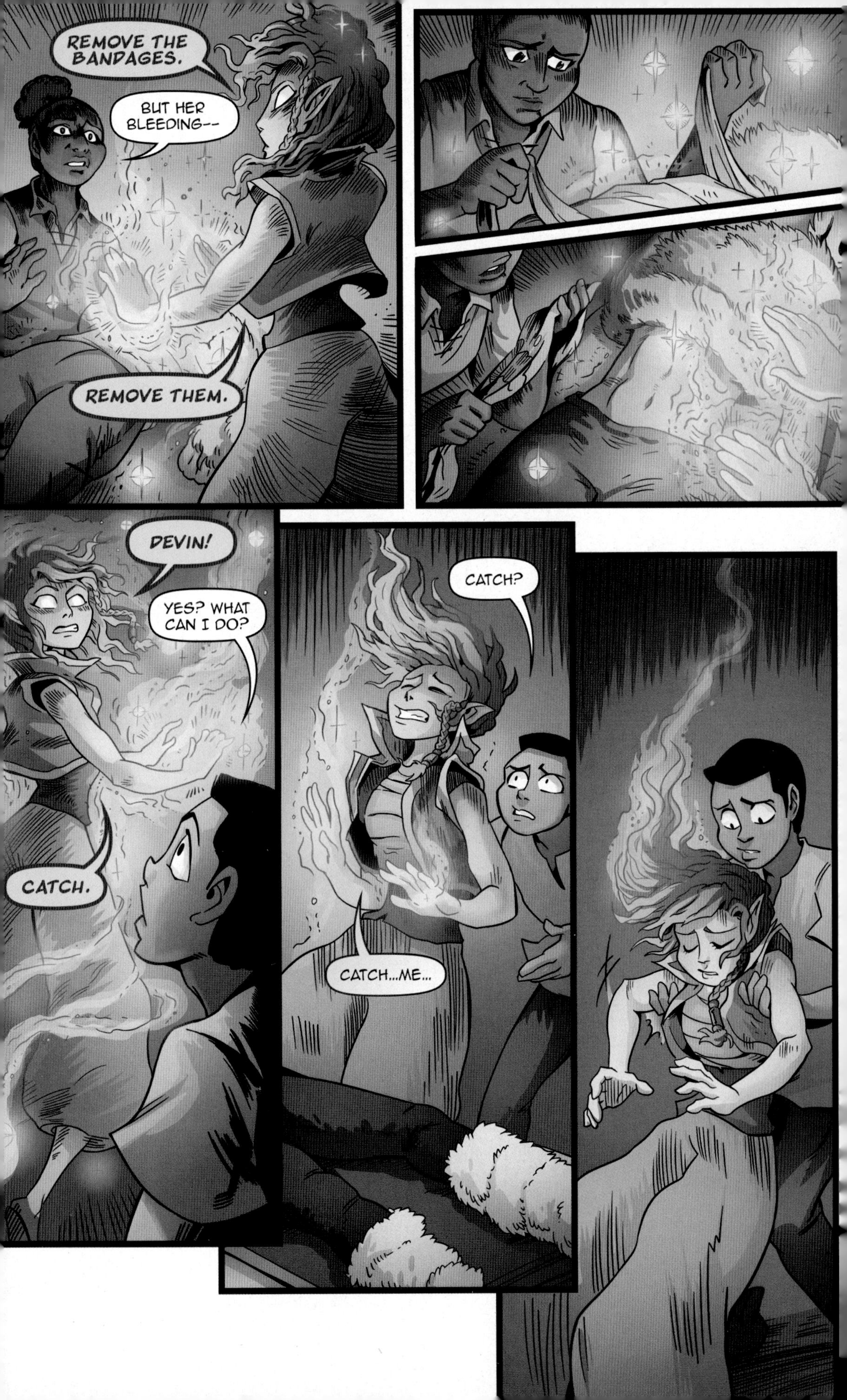
REMOVE THE BANDAGES.
BUT HER BLEEDING--
REMOVE THEM.
DEVIN!
YES? WHAT CAN I DO?
CATCH.
CATCH?
CATCH...ME...

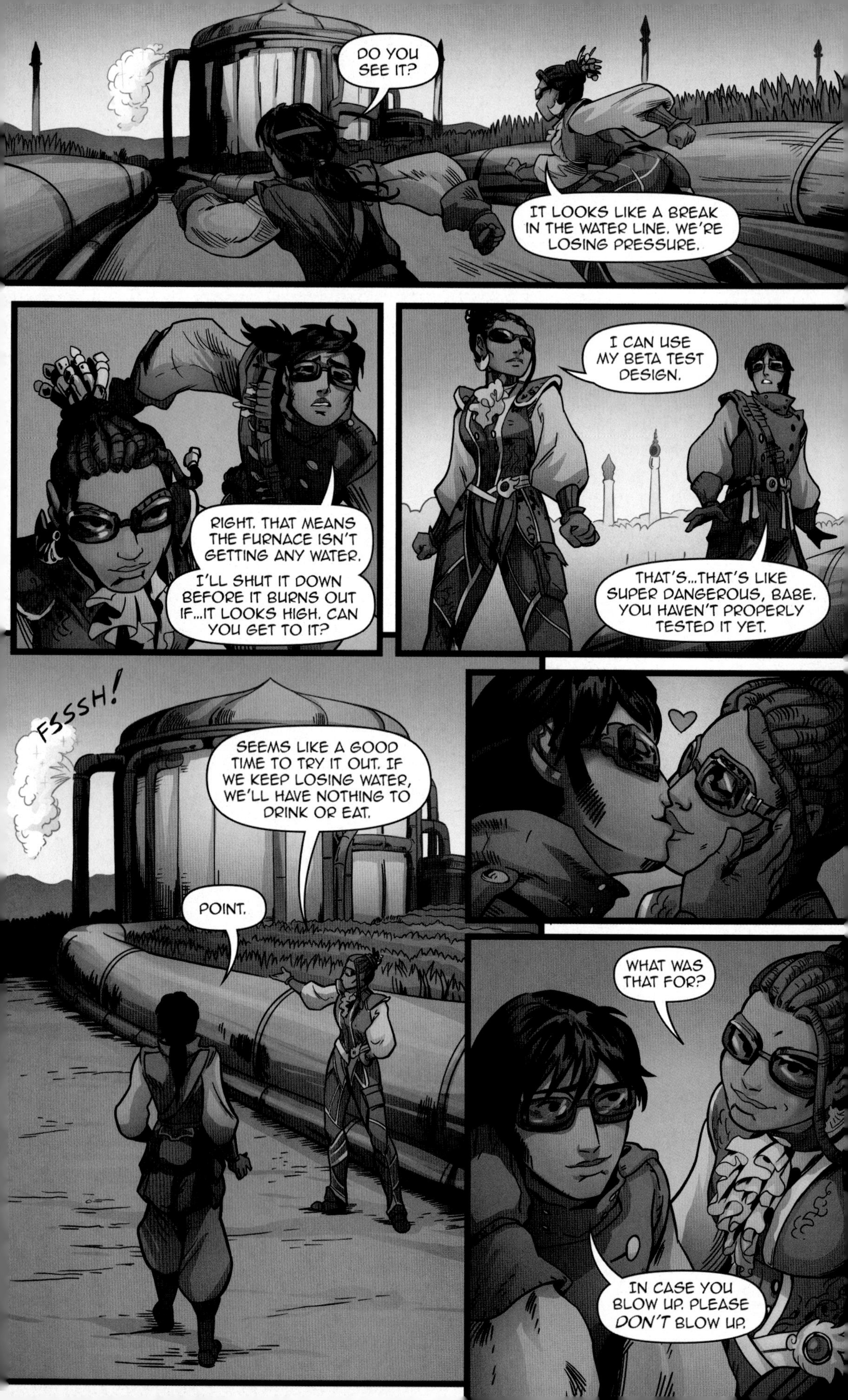
DO YOU SEE IT?
IT LOOKS LIKE A BREAK IN THE WATER LINE. WE'RE LOSING PRESSURE.
RIGHT. THAT MEANS THE FURNACE ISN'T GETTING ANY WATER.
I'LL SHUT IT DOWN BEFORE IT BURNS OUT IF...IT LOOKS HIGH. CAN YOU GET TO IT?
I CAN USE MY BETA TEST DESIGN.
THAT'S...THAT'S LIKE SUPER DANGEROUS, BABE. YOU HAVEN'T PROPERLY TESTED IT YET.
FSSSH!
SEEMS LIKE A GOOD TIME TO TRY IT OUT. IF WE KEEP LOSING WATER, WE'LL HAVE NOTHING TO DRINK OR EAT.
POINT.
WHAT WAS THAT FOR?
IN CASE YOU BLOW UP. PLEASE *DON'T* BLOW UP.

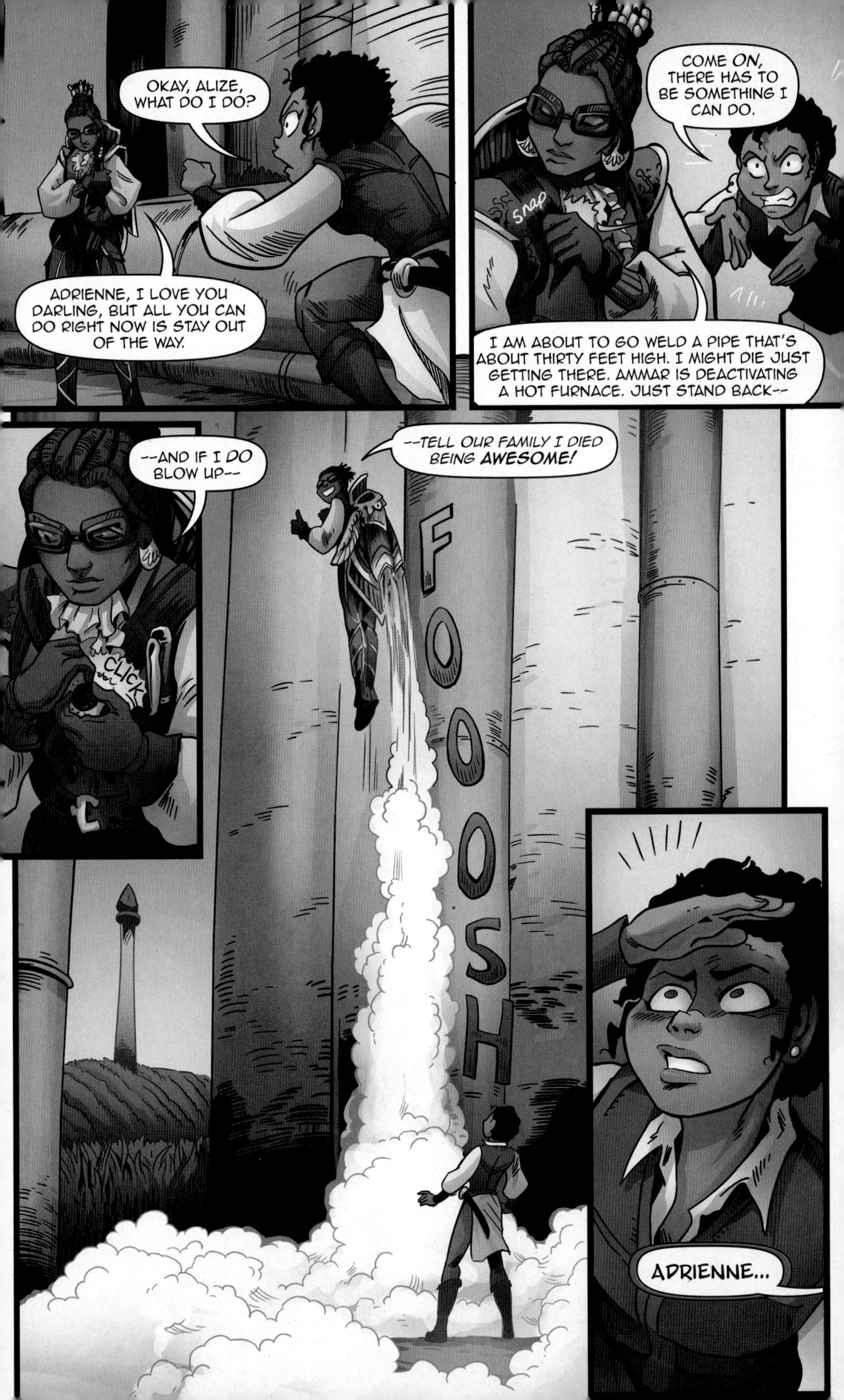
OKAY, ALIZE, WHAT DO I DO?
ADRIENNE, I LOVE YOU DARLING, BUT ALL YOU CAN DO RIGHT NOW IS STAY OUT OF THE WAY.
COME ON, THERE HAS TO BE SOMETHING I CAN DO.
SNAP
I AM ABOUT TO GO WELD A PIPE THAT'S ABOUT THIRTY FEET HIGH. I MIGHT DIE JUST GETTING THERE. AMMAR IS DEACTIVATING A HOT FURNACE. JUST STAND BACK--
--AND IF I DO BLOW UP--
CLICK
--TELL OUR FAMILY I DIED BEING AWESOME!
FOOOOSH
ADRIENNE...

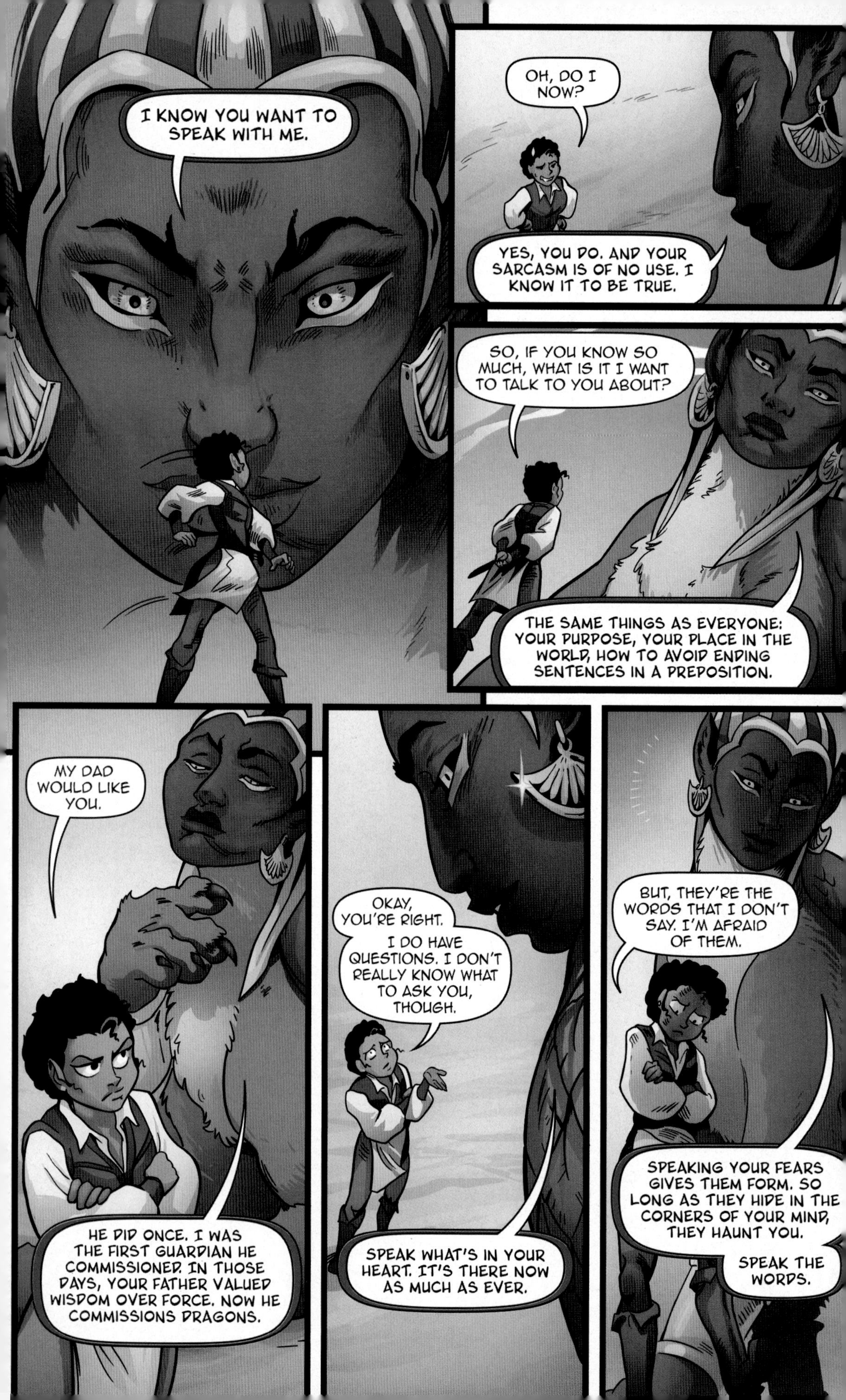
I KNOW YOU WANT TO SPEAK WITH ME.
OH, DO I NOW?
YES, YOU DO. AND YOUR SARCASM IS OF NO USE. I KNOW IT TO BE TRUE.
SO, IF YOU KNOW SO MUCH, WHAT IS IT I WANT TO TALK TO YOU ABOUT?
THE SAME THINGS AS EVERYONE: YOUR PURPOSE, YOUR PLACE IN THE WORLD, HOW TO AVOID ENDING SENTENCES IN A PREPOSITION.
MY DAD WOULD LIKE YOU.
HE DID ONCE. I WAS THE FIRST GUARDIAN HE COMMISSIONED. IN THOSE DAYS, YOUR FATHER VALUED WISDOM OVER FORCE. NOW HE COMMISSIONS DRAGONS.
OKAY, YOU'RE RIGHT.
I DO HAVE QUESTIONS. I DON'T REALLY KNOW WHAT TO ASK YOU, THOUGH.
SPEAK WHAT'S IN YOUR HEART. IT'S THERE NOW AS MUCH AS EVER.
BUT, THEY'RE THE WORDS THAT I DON'T SAY. I'M AFRAID OF THEM.
SPEAKING YOUR FEARS GIVES THEM FORM. SO LONG AS THEY HIDE IN THE CORNERS OF YOUR MIND, THEY HAUNT YOU.
SPEAK THE WORDS.

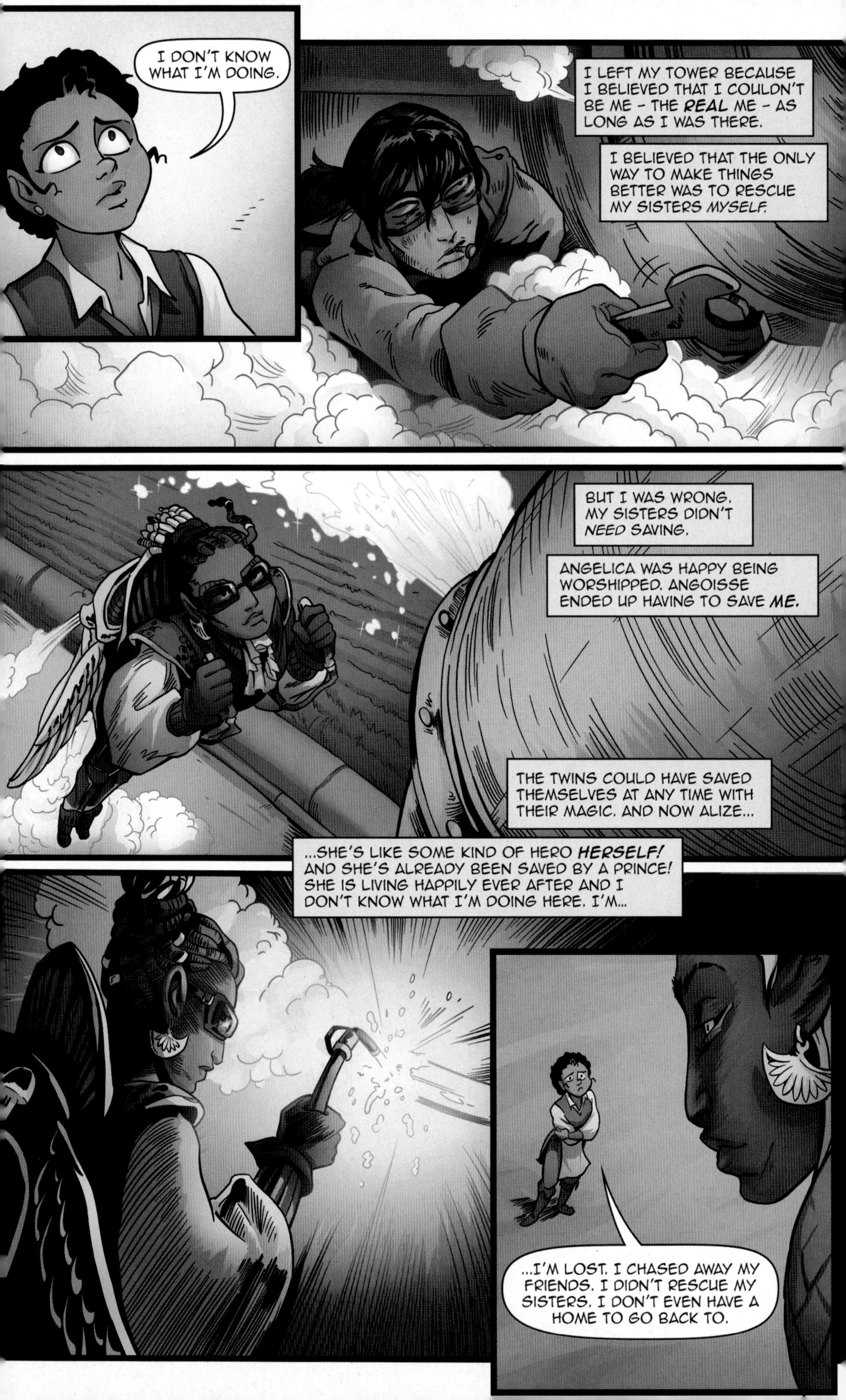
I DON'T KNOW WHAT I'M DOING.
I LEFT MY TOWER BECAUSE I BELIEVED THAT I COULDN'T BE ME - THE REAL ME - AS LONG AS I WAS THERE.
I BELIEVED THAT THE ONLY WAY TO MAKE THINGS BETTER WAS TO RESCUE MY SISTERS MYSELF.
BUT I WAS WRONG. MY SISTERS DIDN'T NEED SAVING.
ANGELICA WAS HAPPY BEING WORSHIPPED. ANGOISSE ENDED UP HAVING TO SAVE ME.
THE TWINS COULD HAVE SAVED THEMSELVES AT ANY TIME WITH THEIR MAGIC. AND NOW ALIZE...
...SHE'S LIKE SOME KIND OF HERO HERSELF! AND SHE'S ALREADY BEEN SAVED BY A PRINCE! SHE IS LIVING HAPPILY EVER AFTER AND I DON'T KNOW WHAT I'M DOING HERE. I'M...
...I'M LOST. I CHASED AWAY MY FRIENDS. I DIDN'T RESCUE MY SISTERS. I DON'T EVEN HAVE A HOME TO GO BACK TO.

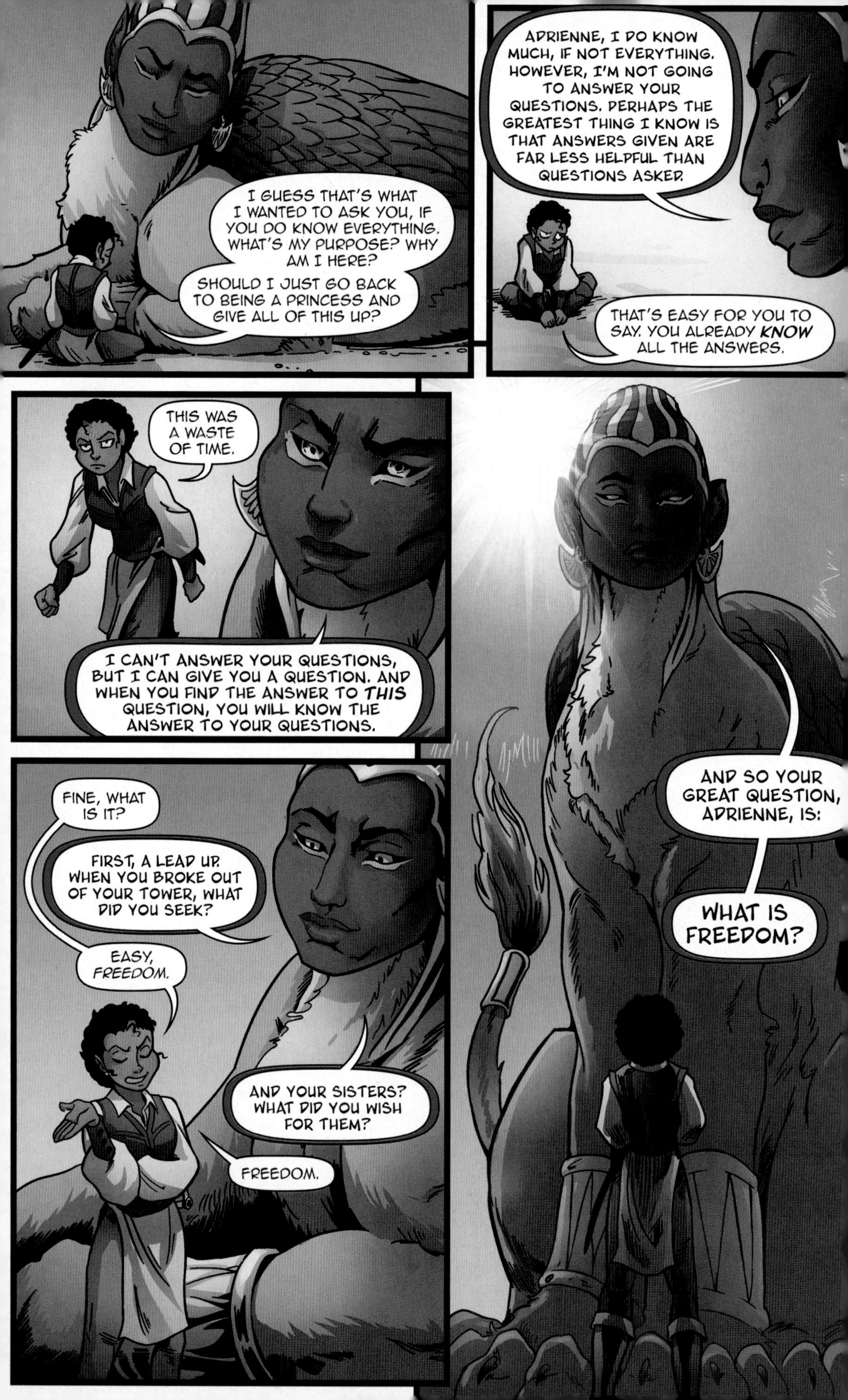
I GUESS THAT'S WHAT I WANTED TO ASK YOU, IF YOU DO KNOW EVERYTHING. WHAT'S MY PURPOSE? WHY AM I HERE?
SHOULD I JUST GO BACK TO BEING A PRINCESS AND GIVE ALL OF THIS UP?
ADRIENNE, I DO KNOW MUCH, IF NOT EVERYTHING. HOWEVER, I'M NOT GOING TO ANSWER YOUR QUESTIONS. PERHAPS THE GREATEST THING I KNOW IS THAT ANSWERS GIVEN ARE FAR LESS HELPFUL THAN QUESTIONS ASKED.
THAT'S EASY FOR YOU TO SAY. YOU ALREADY *KNOW* ALL THE ANSWERS.
THIS WAS A WASTE OF TIME.
I CAN'T ANSWER YOUR QUESTIONS, BUT I CAN GIVE YOU A QUESTION. AND WHEN YOU FIND THE ANSWER TO *THIS* QUESTION, YOU WILL KNOW THE ANSWER TO YOUR QUESTIONS.
FINE, WHAT IS IT?
FIRST, A LEAD UP. WHEN YOU BROKE OUT OF YOUR TOWER, WHAT DID YOU SEEK?
EASY, *FREEDOM.*
AND YOUR SISTERS? WHAT DID YOU WISH FOR THEM?
FREEDOM.
AND SO YOUR GREAT QUESTION, ADRIENNE, IS:
WHAT IS FREEDOM?

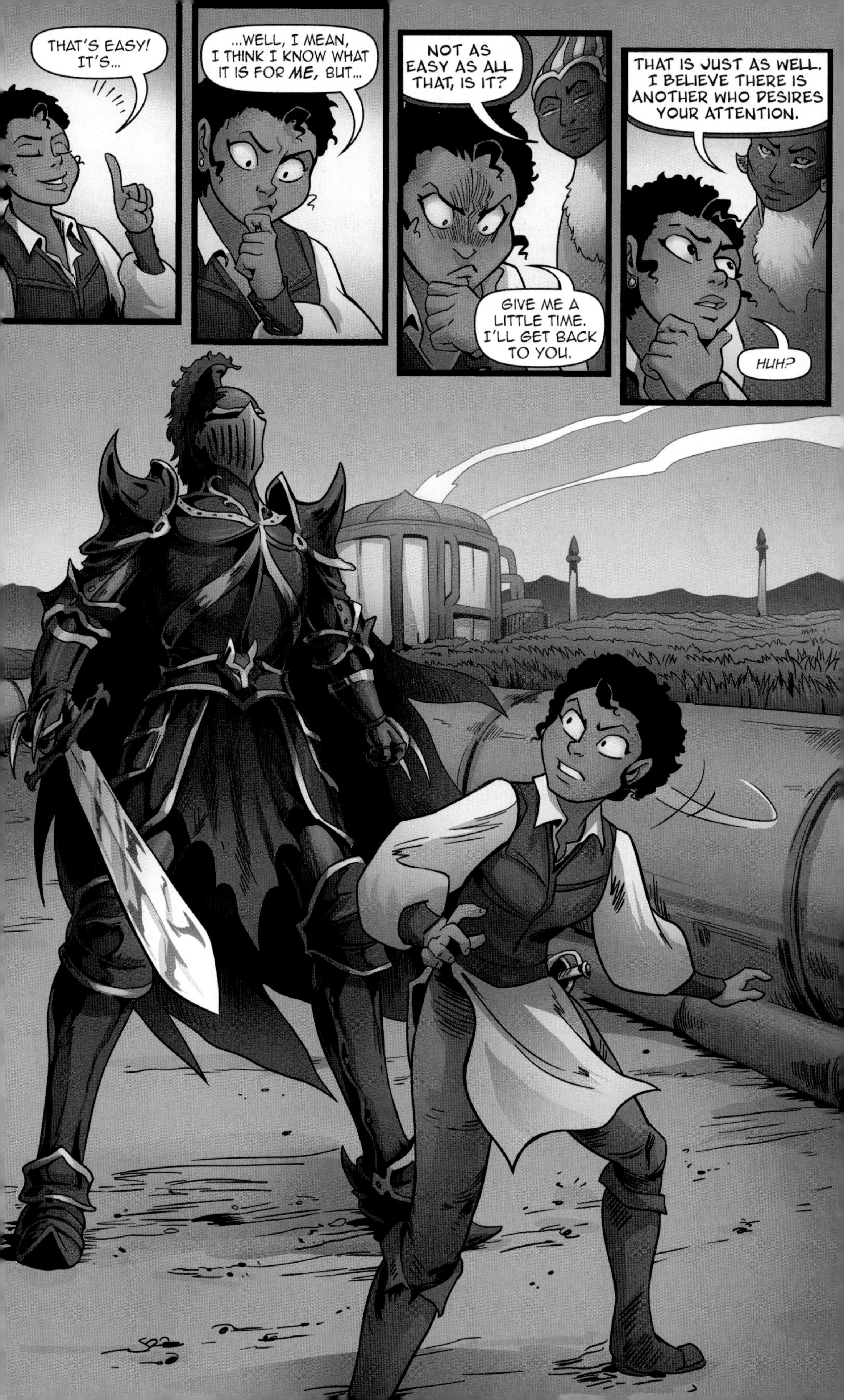
THAT'S EASY! IT'S...
...WELL, I MEAN, I THINK I KNOW WHAT IT IS FOR ME, BUT...
NOT AS EASY AS ALL THAT, IS IT?
GIVE ME A LITTLE TIME. I'LL GET BACK TO YOU.
THAT IS JUST AS WELL. I BELIEVE THERE IS ANOTHER WHO DESIRES YOUR ATTENTION.
HUH?

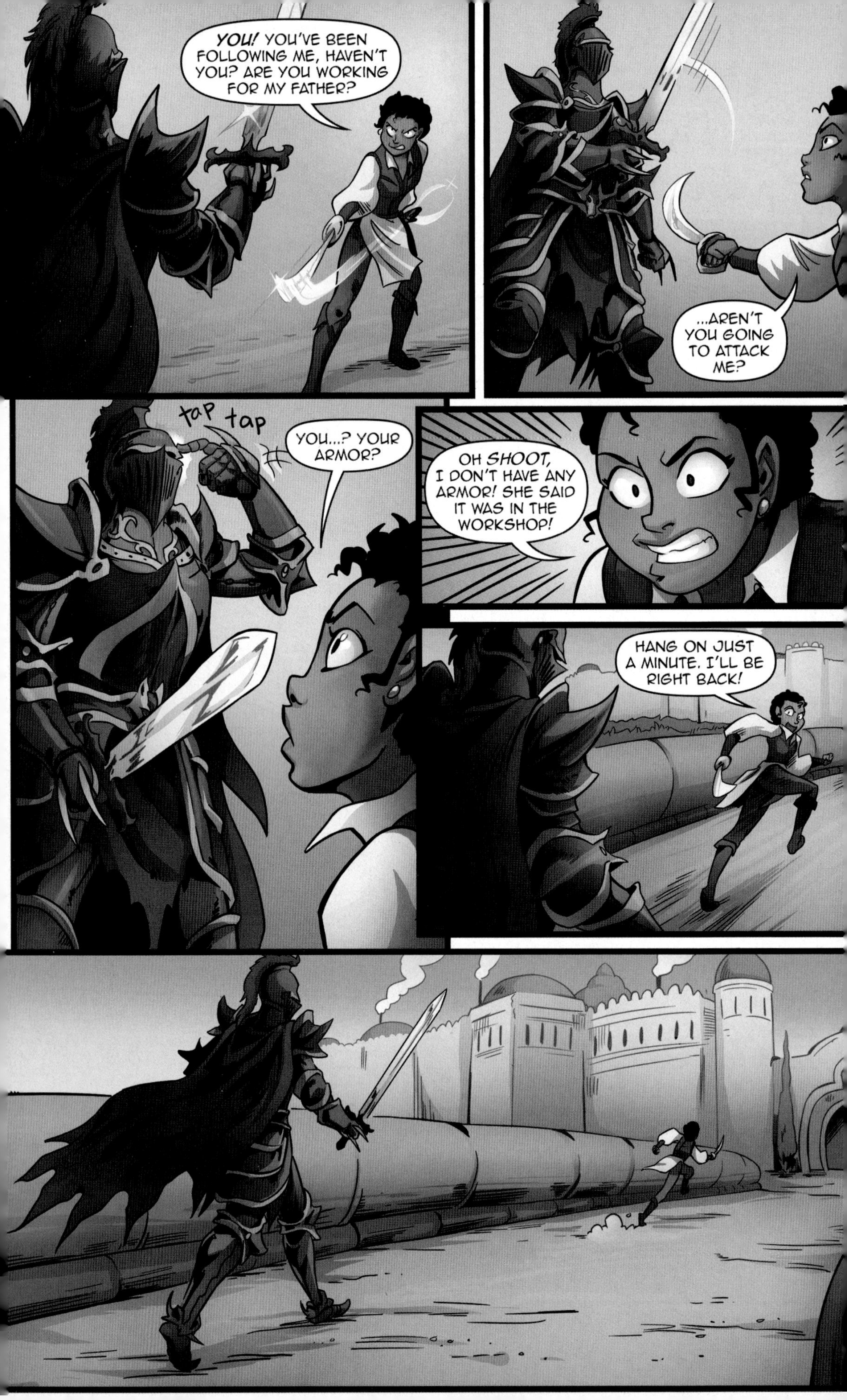
YOU! YOU'VE BEEN FOLLOWING ME, HAVEN'T YOU? ARE YOU WORKING FOR MY FATHER?
...AREN'T YOU GOING TO ATTACK ME?
tap tap
YOU...? YOUR ARMOR?
OH SHOOT, I DON'T HAVE ANY ARMOR! SHE SAID IT WAS IN THE WORKSHOP!
HANG ON JUST A MINUTE. I'LL BE RIGHT BACK!

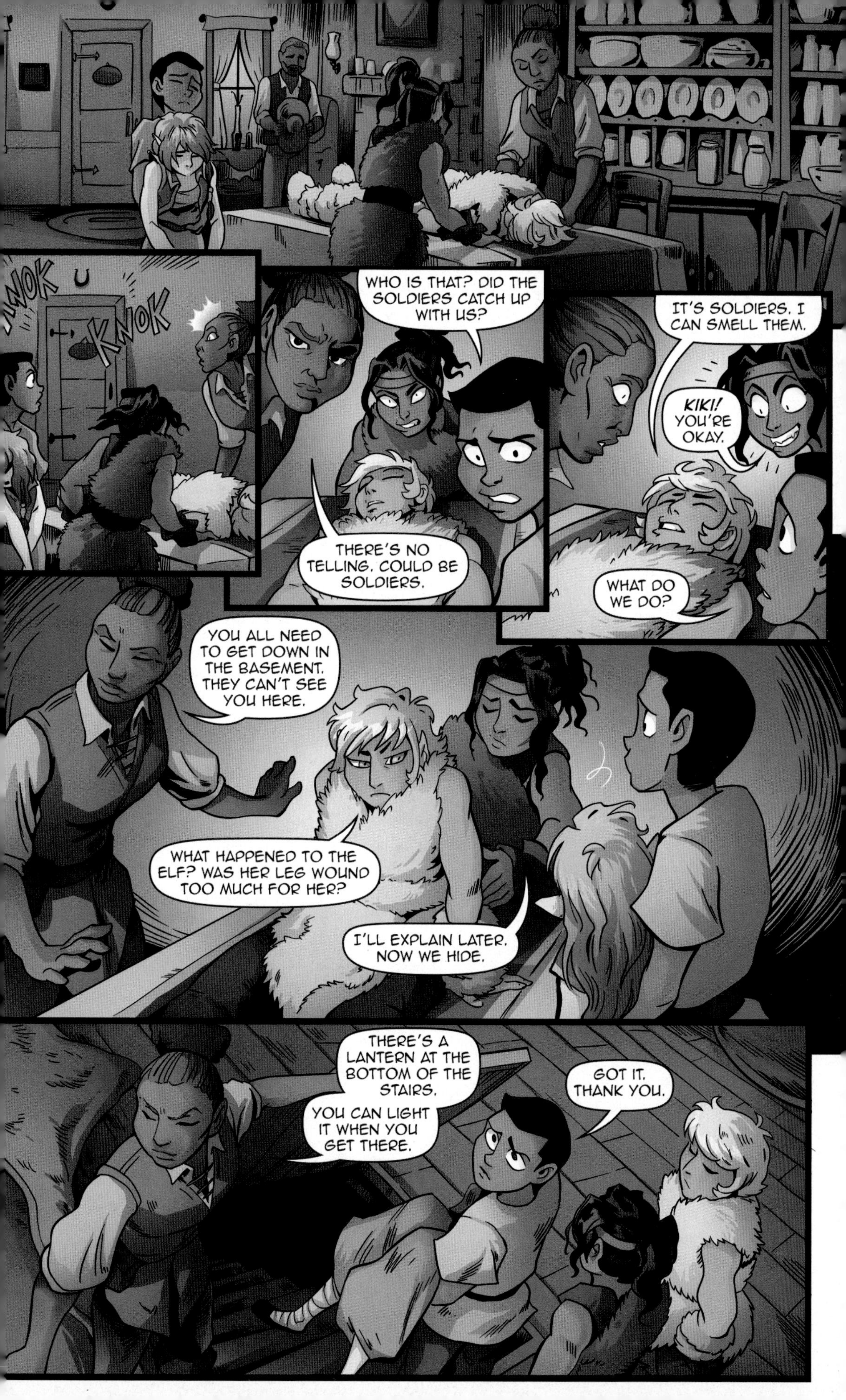
KNOK
KNOK
WHO IS THAT? DID THE SOLDIERS CATCH UP WITH US?
THERE'S NO TELLING. COULD BE SOLDIERS.
IT'S SOLDIERS. I CAN SMELL THEM.
KIKI! YOU'RE OKAY.
WHAT DO WE DO?
YOU ALL NEED TO GET DOWN IN THE BASEMENT. THEY CAN'T SEE YOU HERE.
WHAT HAPPENED TO THE ELF? WAS HER LEG WOUND TOO MUCH FOR HER?
I'LL EXPLAIN LATER. NOW WE HIDE.
THERE'S A LANTERN AT THE BOTTOM OF THE STAIRS.
YOU CAN LIGHT IT WHEN YOU GET THERE.
GOT IT. THANK YOU.

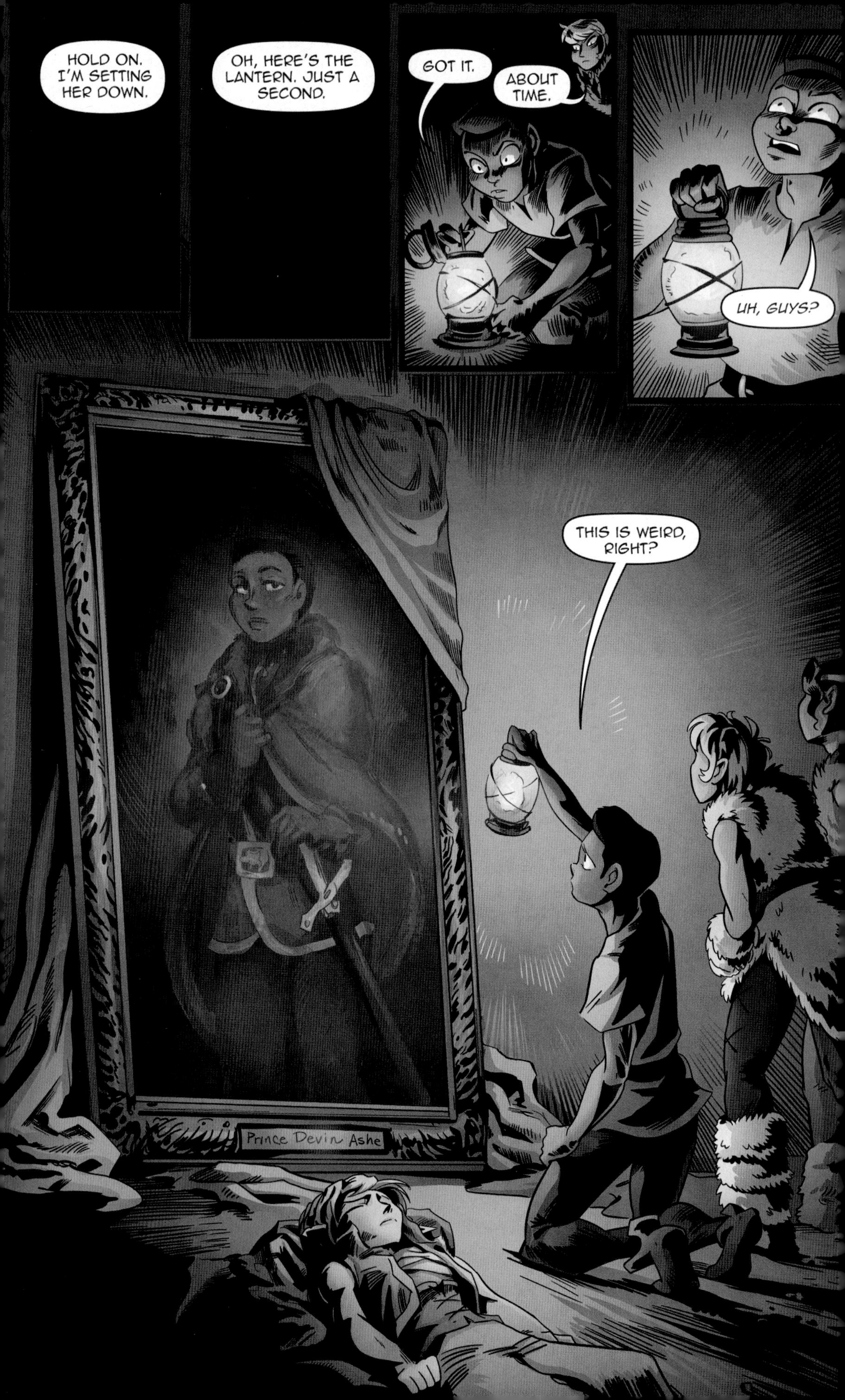
HOLD ON. I'M SETTING HER DOWN.
OH, HERE'S THE LANTERN. JUST A SECOND.
GOT IT.
ABOUT TIME.
UH, GUYS?
THIS IS WEIRD, RIGHT?
Prince Devin Ashe

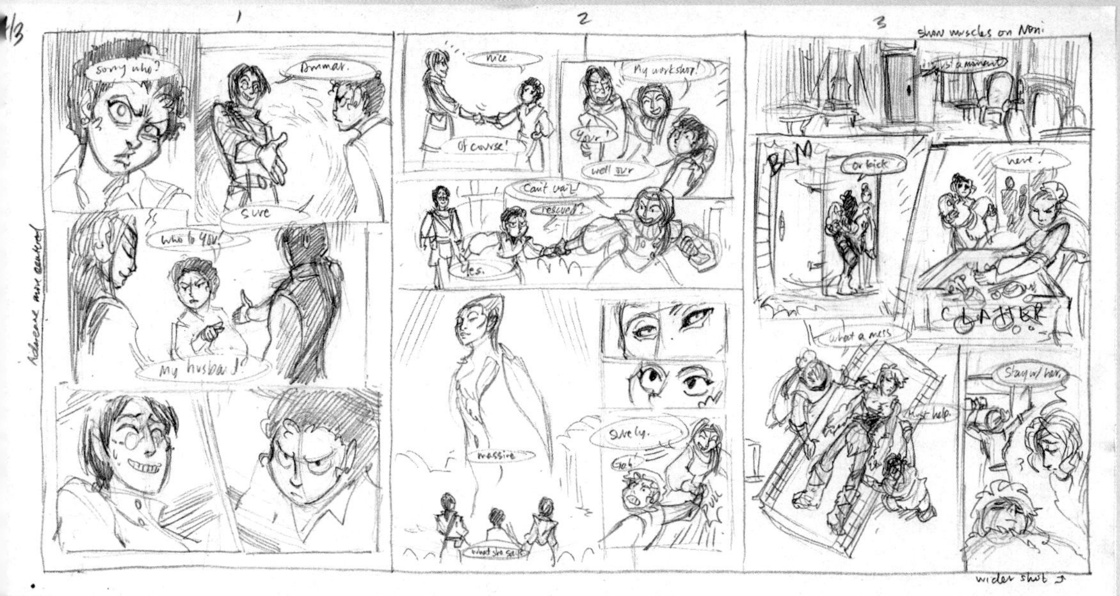
show muscles on Noni
sorry who?
Ammar.
sure
who to YOU
My husband!
nice
My workshop!
Of course!
well sir
Can't wait!
rescued?
Yes.
massive
surely.
BAM
CLATTER
what a mess
Stay w/ her.
wider shot

THUMBNAILS FOR PAGES 1 – 3

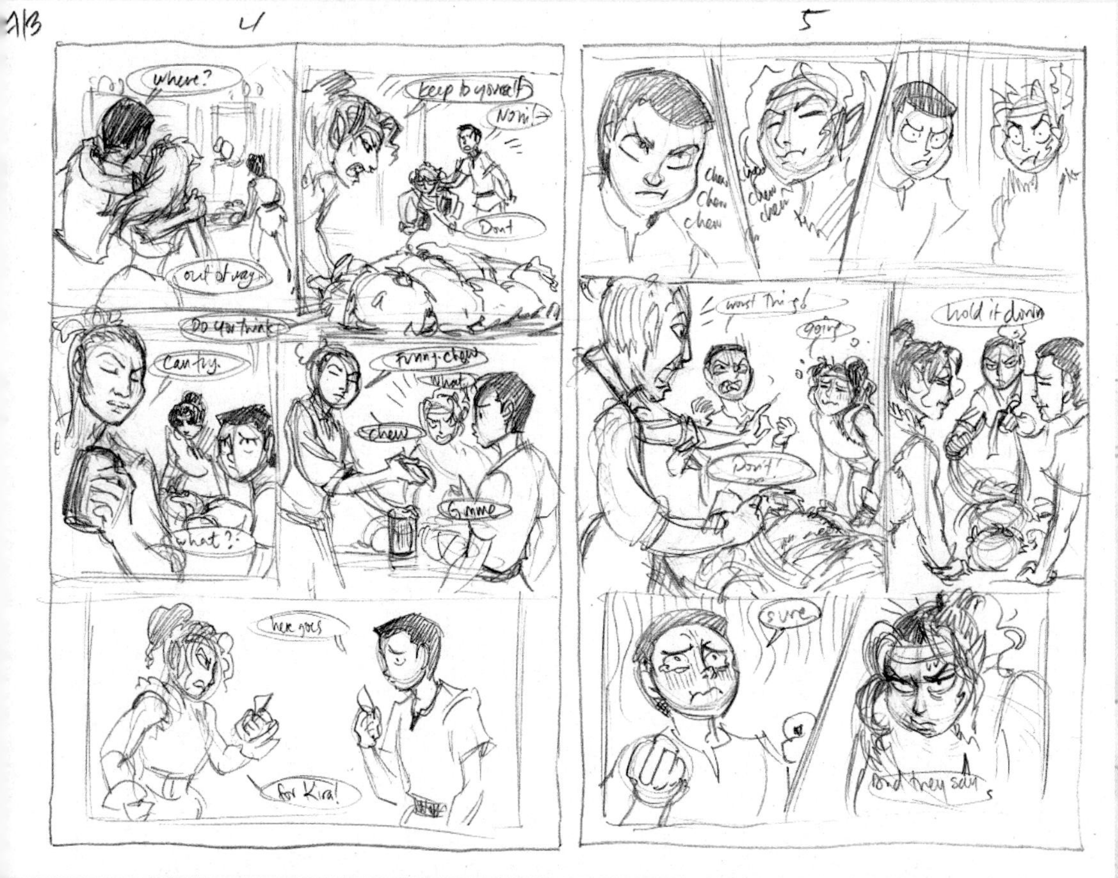
where?
out of way
keep to yourself
Noni!
Don't
Do you think
Can try.
what?
Funny-chew
What
chew
Gimme
here goes
for Kira!
chew
chew
chew
worst thing!
Don't!
hold it down
sure
and they say

THUMBNAILS FOR PAGES 4 – 5

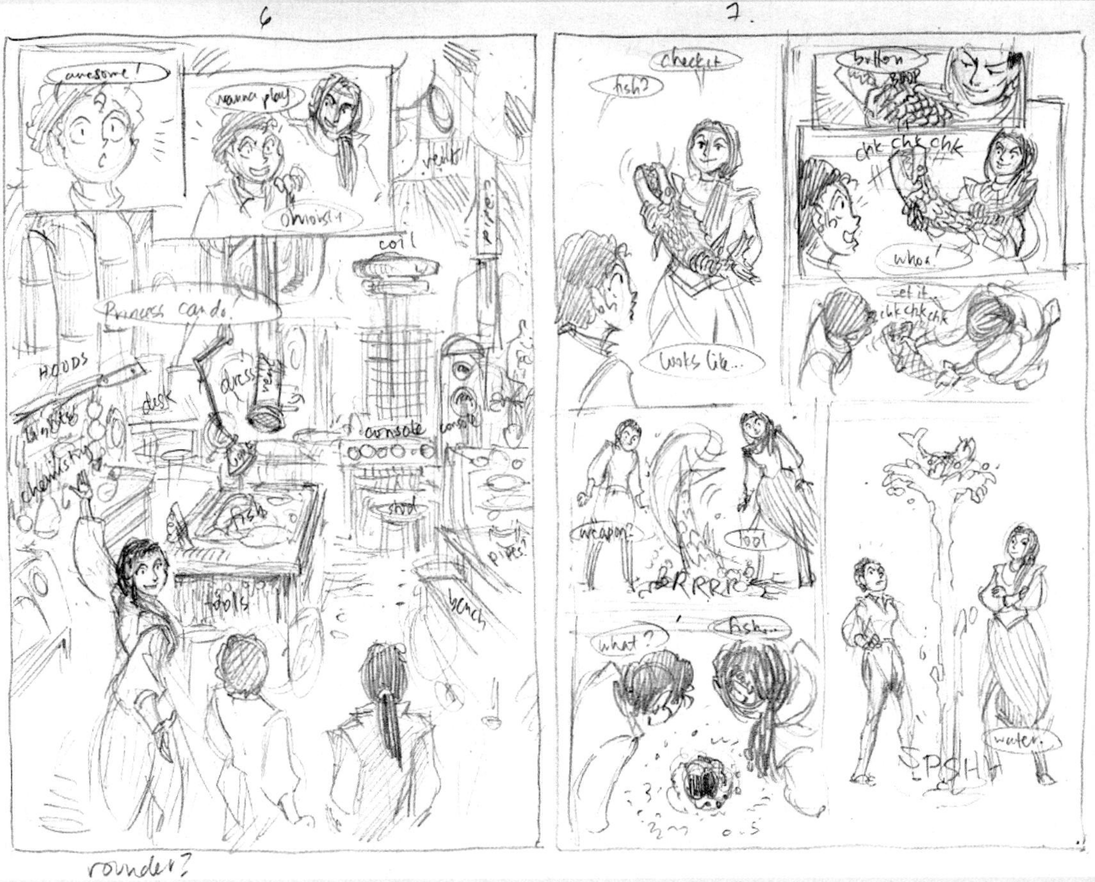
6
7.
awesome!
wanna play
coil
Princess can do.
HOODS
desk
dress
console
fish
tools
bench
check it
fish?
button
BOOP
chk chk chk
whoa!
looks like...
weapon?
tool
what?
fish...
water.
rounder?

THUMBNAILS FOR PAGES 6 – 7

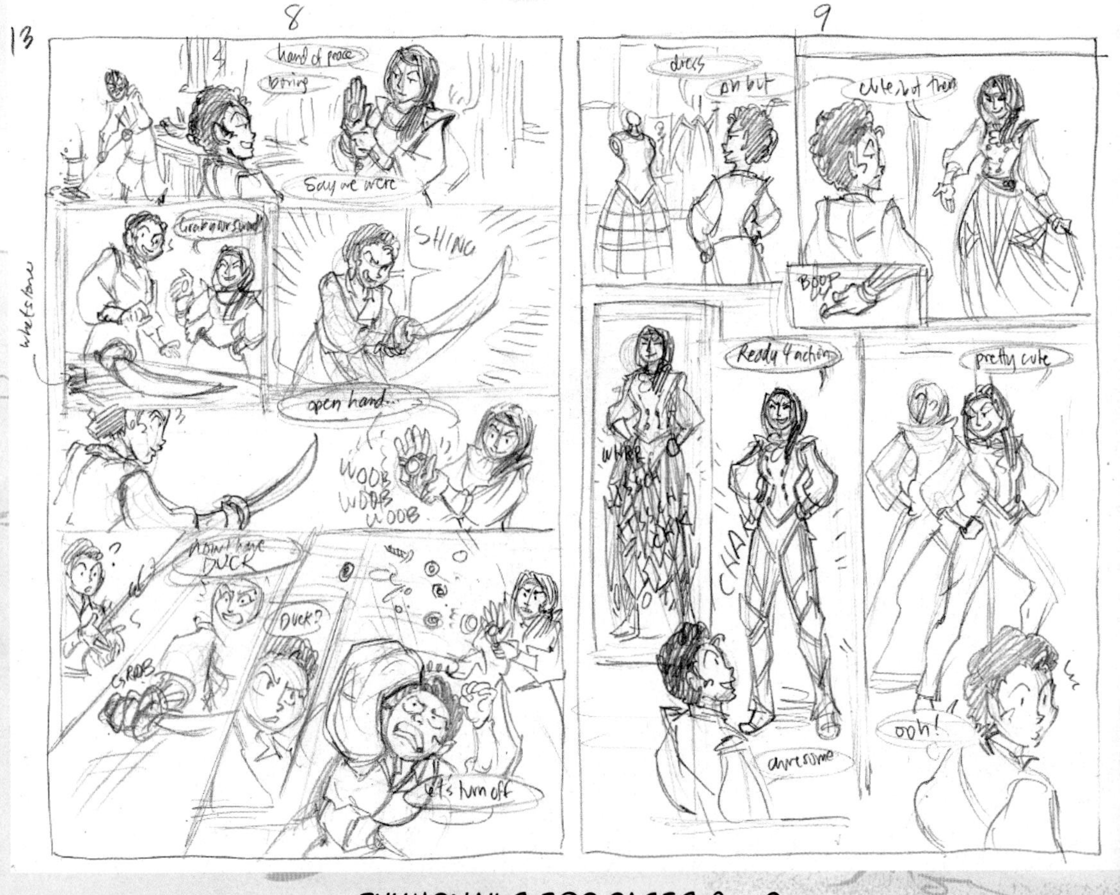
13
8
9
hand of peace
boring
say we were
SHING
open hand...
WOOB
WOOB
WOOB
DUCK
DUCK?
GRAB
let's turn off
dress
ah but
cute, but then
BOOP
Ready 4 action
pretty cute
ooh!
awesome

THUMBNAILS FOR PAGES 8 – 9

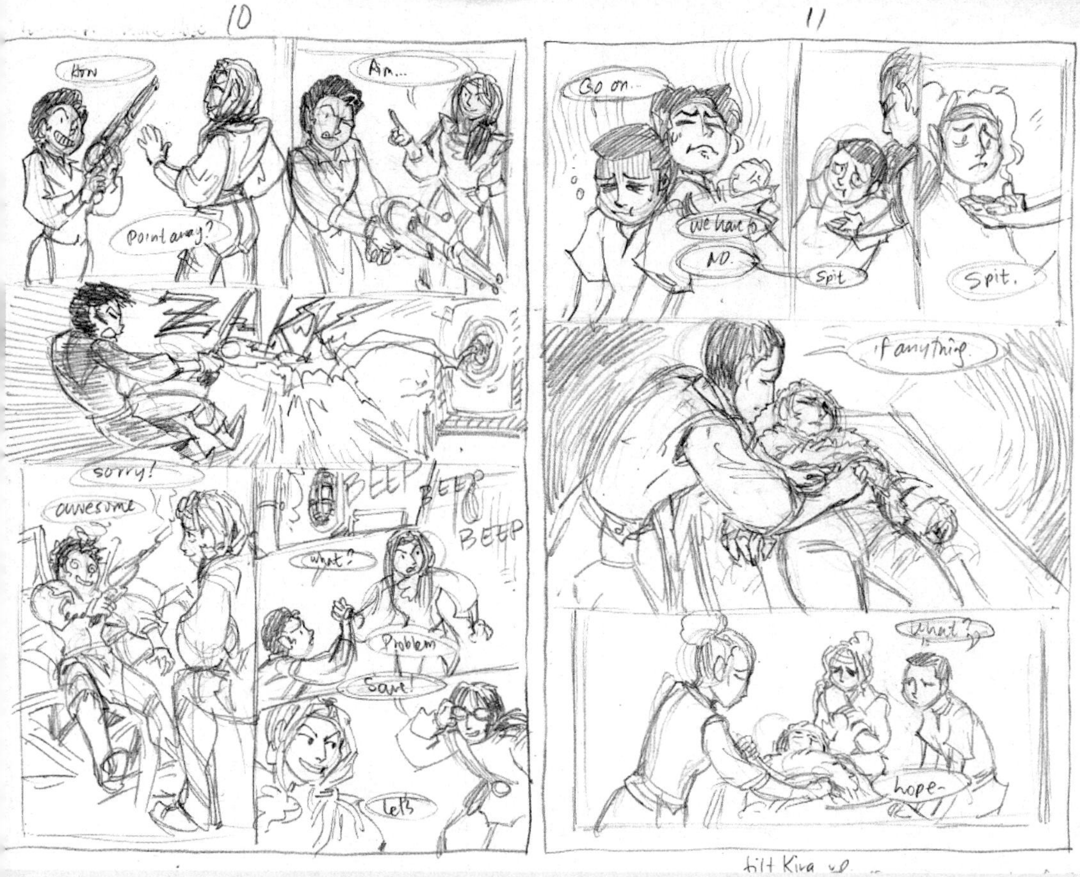
10
Hon
Am...
Point away?
sorry!
awesome
BEEP
BEEP
what?
Problem
Save!
lets
11
Go on...
We have to
NO.
Spit
Spit.
if anything.
What?
hope-

THUMBNAILS FOR PAGES 10 – 11

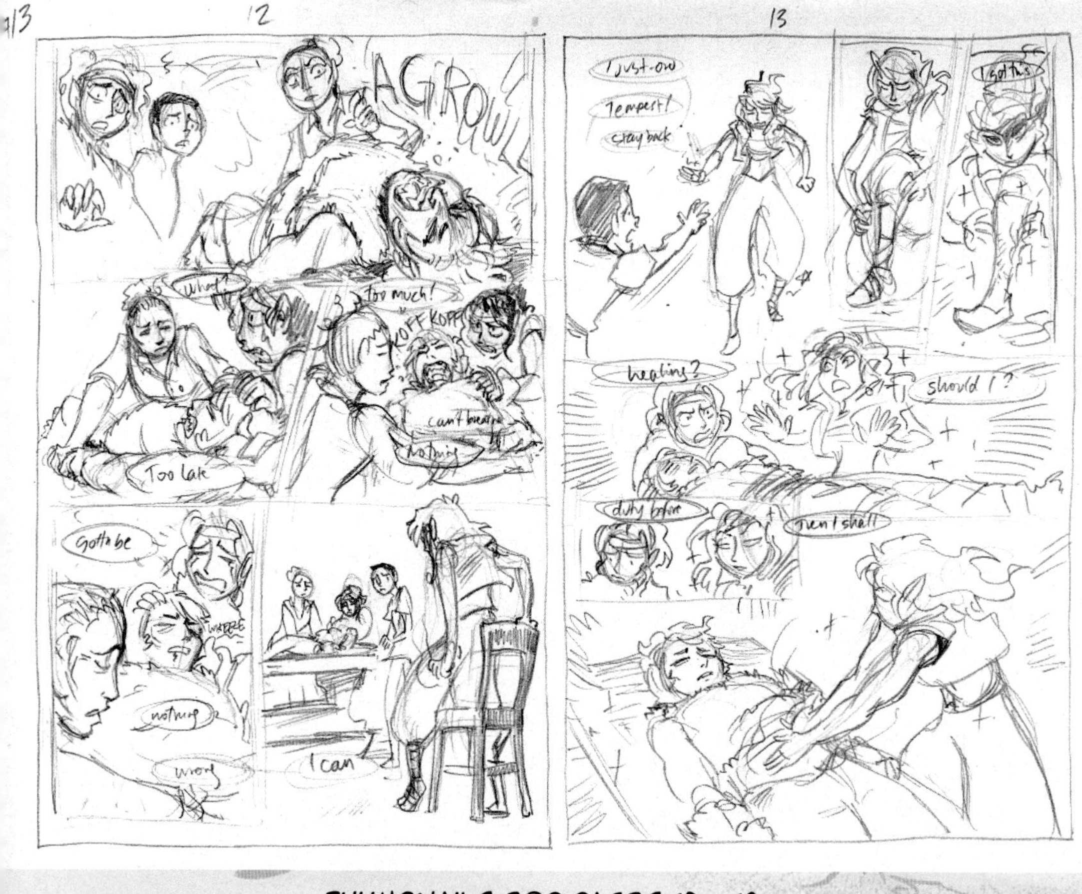
12
What?
too much!
can't breathe
nothing
Too late
Gotta be
nothing
wrong
I can
13
I just- ow
Tempest!
stay back
I got this
healing?
should I?
duty before
then I shall

THUMBNAILS FOR PAGES 12 – 13

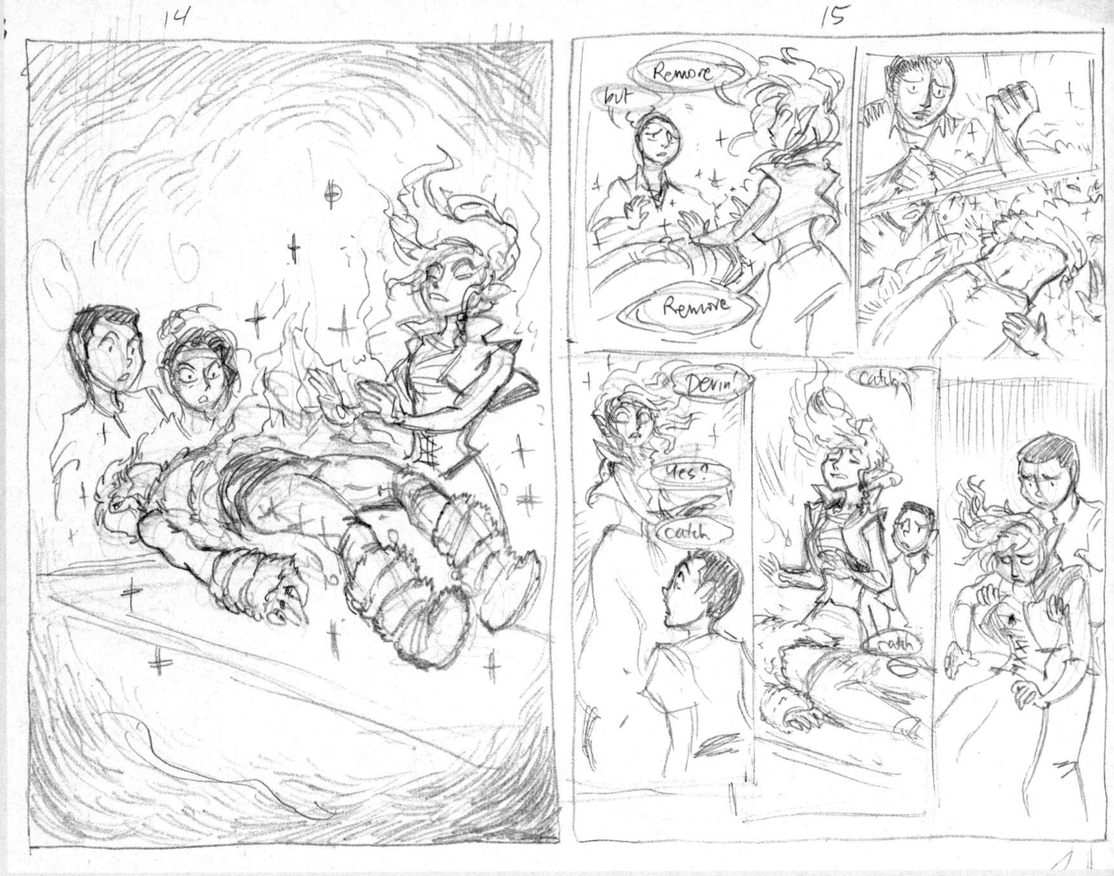
14
15
but
Remove
Remove
Devin!
Yes?
Catch
catch
catch

THUMBNAILS FOR PAGES 14 – 15

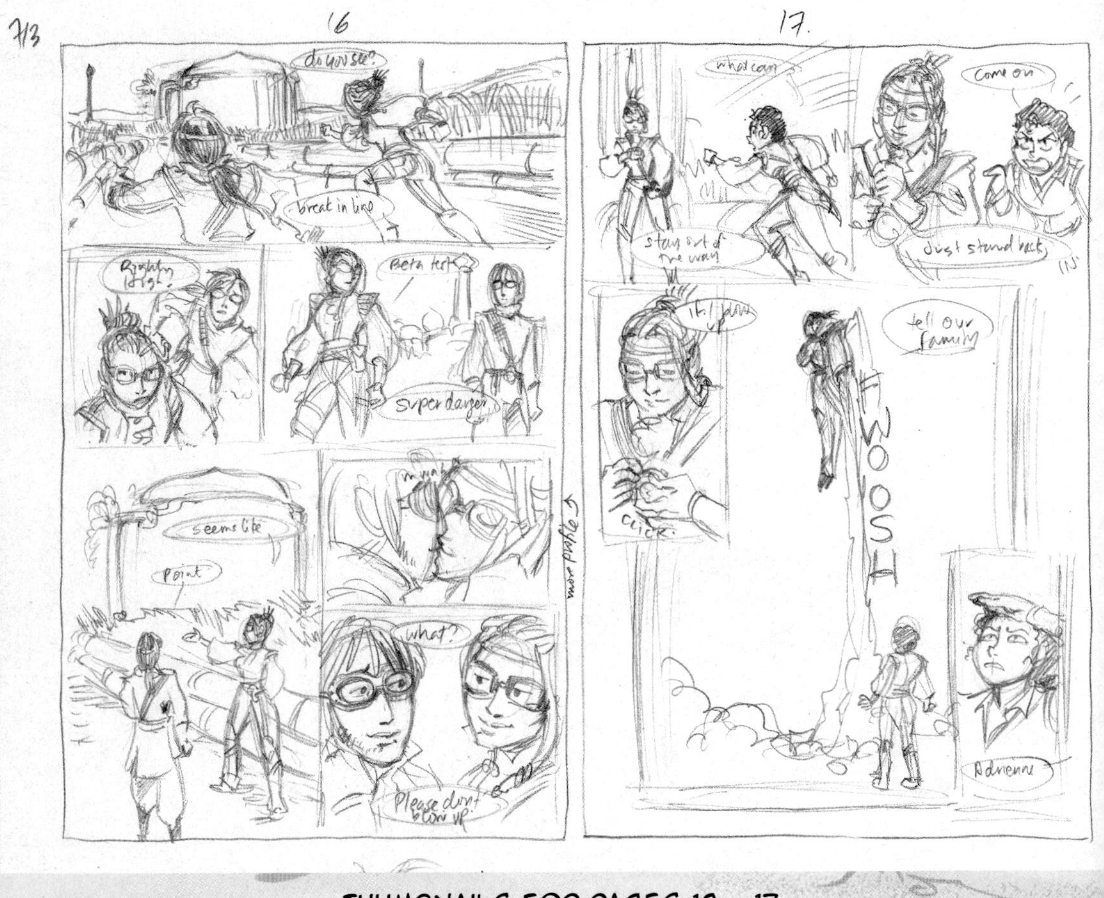
16
17.
do you see?
break in line
Beta test
super danger
seems like
point
what?
Please don't blow up
what can
stay out of the way
Come on
Just stand back
tell our family
click
WOOOSH
Adrienne

THUMBNAILS FOR PAGES 16 – 17

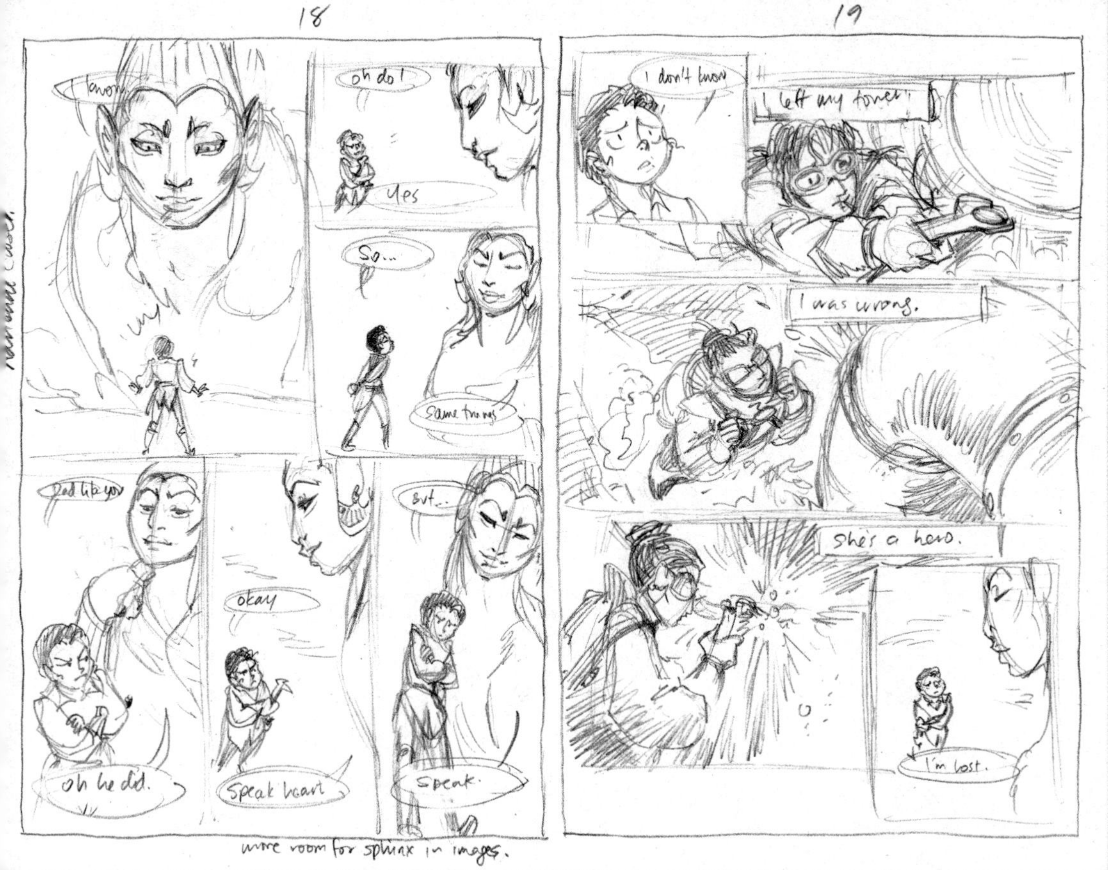
18
19
oh do!
Yes
So...
like you
okay
but...
oh he did.
Speak heart
Speak.
I don't know
I left my tower.
I was wrong.
She's a hero.
I'm lost.
more room for sphinx in images.

THUMBNAILS FOR PAGES 18 – 19

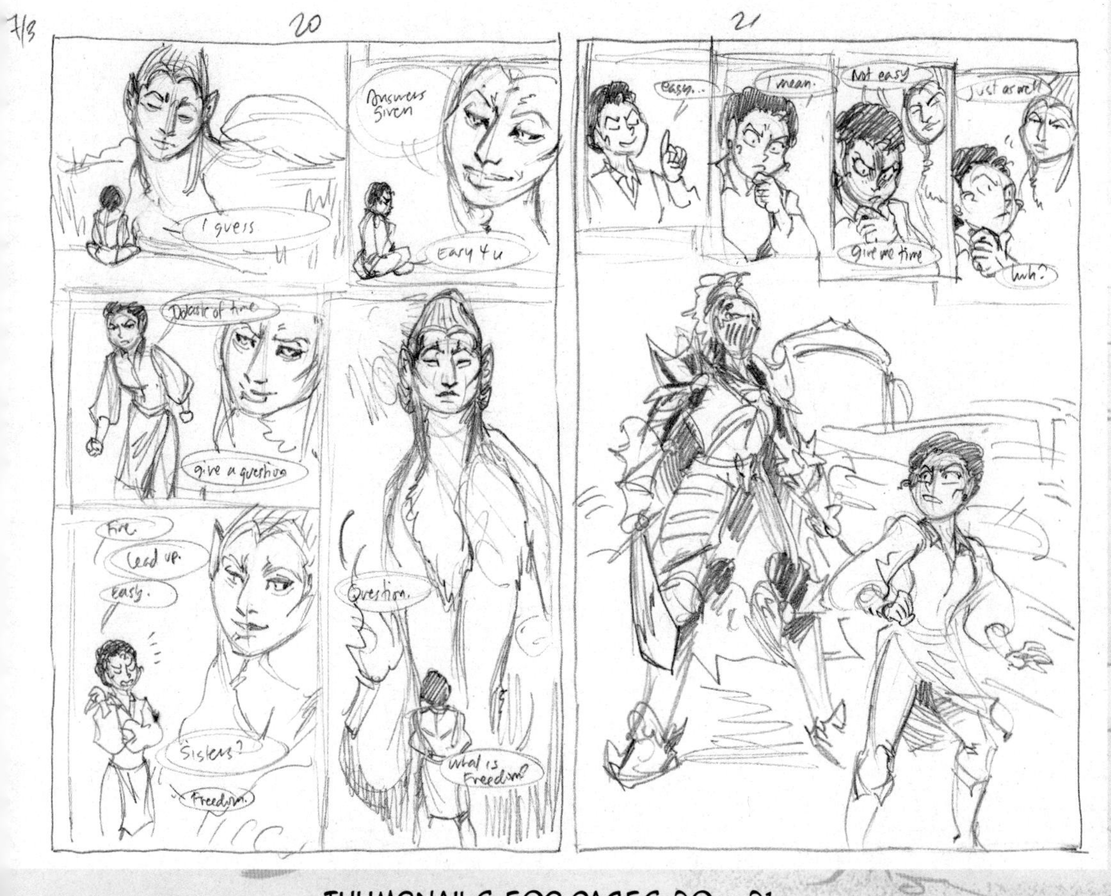
20
21
Answers Given
I guess
Easy 4 u
give a question
Fire.
Lead up.
Easy.
Question.
Sisters?
Freedom.
What is Freedom?
easy...
I mean.
Not easy
Just as well
Give me time
huh?

THUMBNAILS FOR PAGES 20 – 21

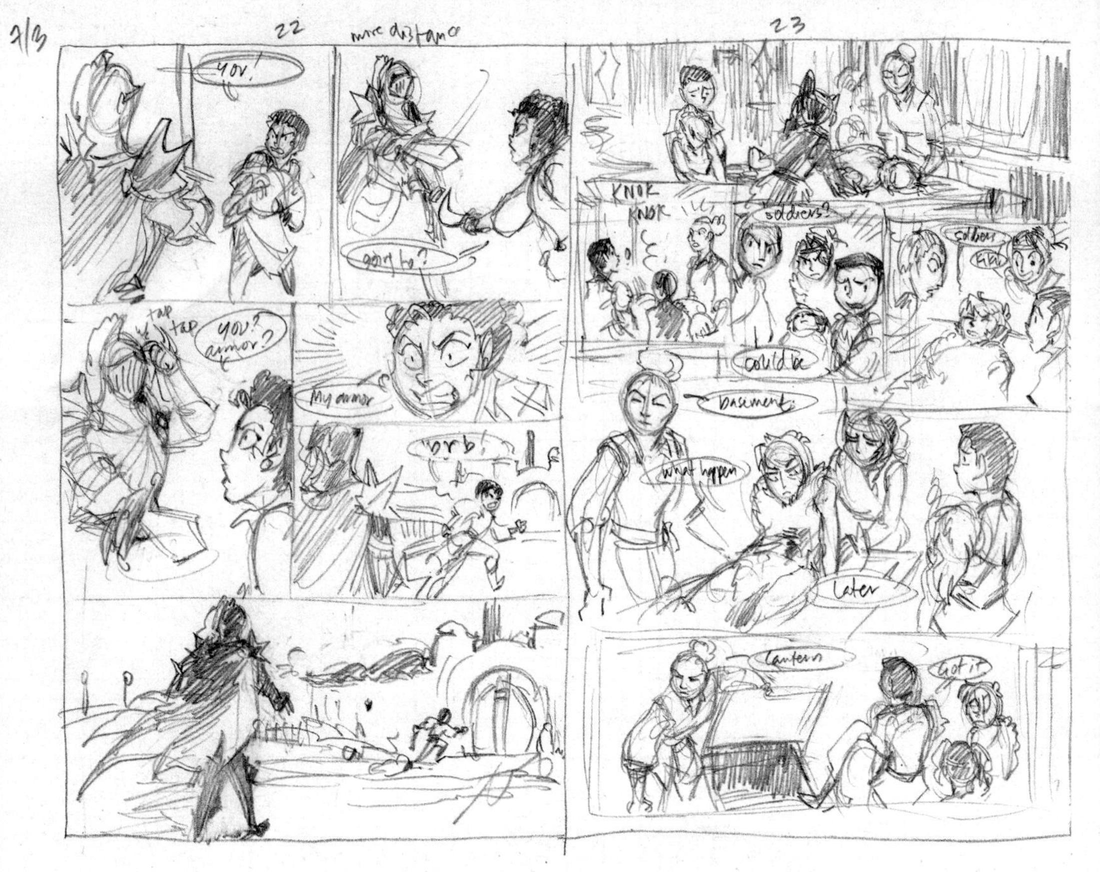
7/3
22
more distance
23
you!
tap tap
you? armor?
My armor
KNOK KNOK
soldiers?
could be
basement
what happen
Later
Lantern
Got it

THUMBNAILS FOR PAGES 22 – 23

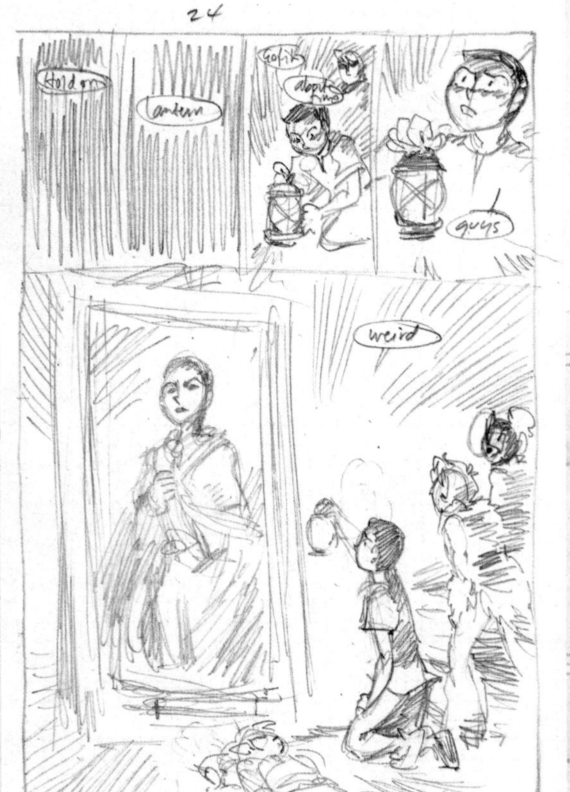
24
Hold on
Lantern
Got it
guys
weird

THUMBNAIL FOR PAGE 24

Chapter Four: The Legend of the Black Knight

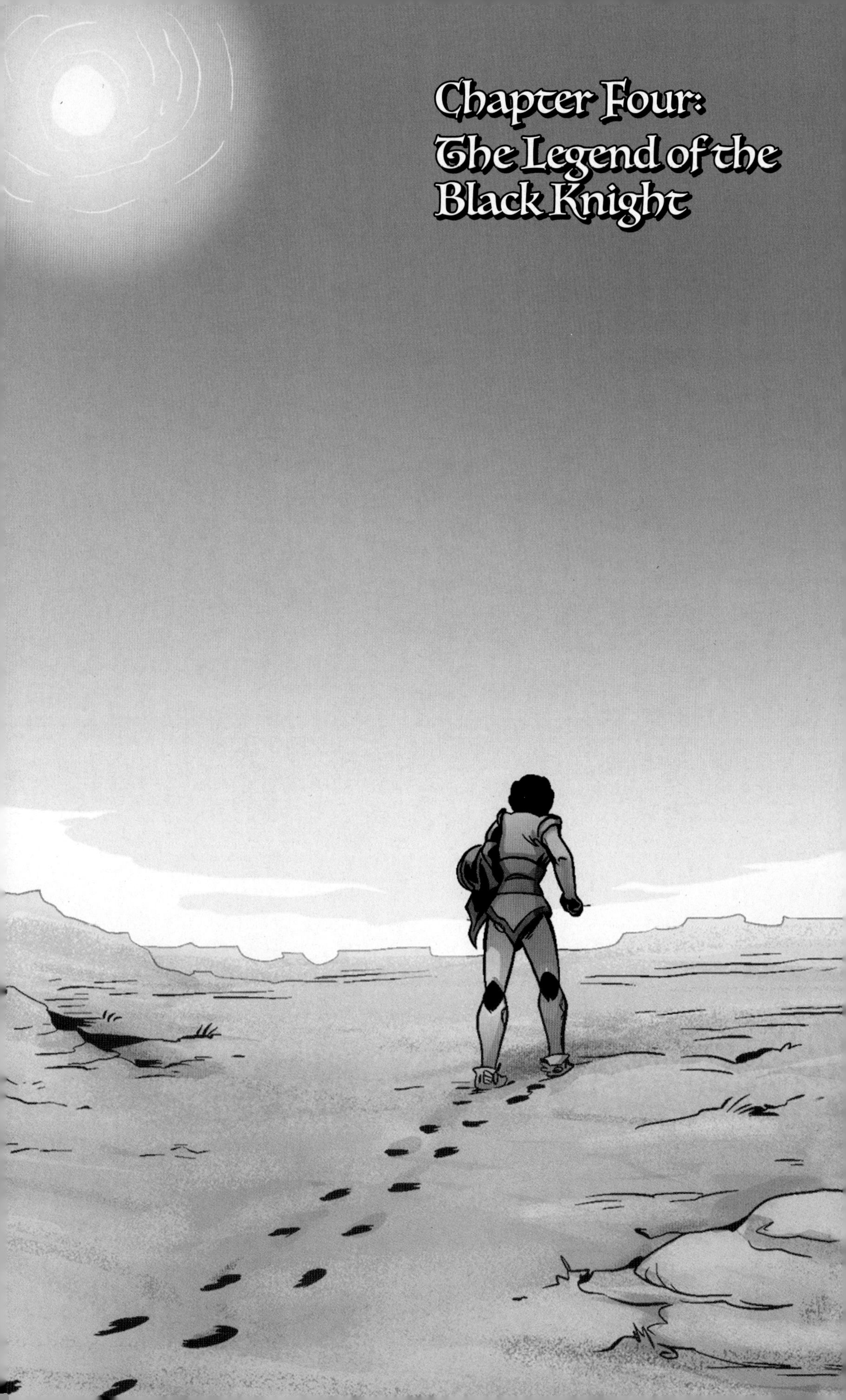

STORY:
Jeremy Whitley

PENCILS:
Emily Martin

INKS:
Christine Hipp

COLORS & LETTERS:
Brett Grunig

COVER A: Emily Martin   COVER B: Malia Knight

EDITORS:
Alicia Whitley (script)
Nicole D'Andria (comic)

Bryan Seaton: Publisher/ CEO • Shawn Gabborin: Editor In Chief
Jason Martin: Publisher-Danger Zone • Nicole D'Andria: Marketing Director/Editor
Danielle Davison: Executive Administrator • Chad Cicconi: Still Waiting For His Princess
Shawn Pryor: President of Creator Relations

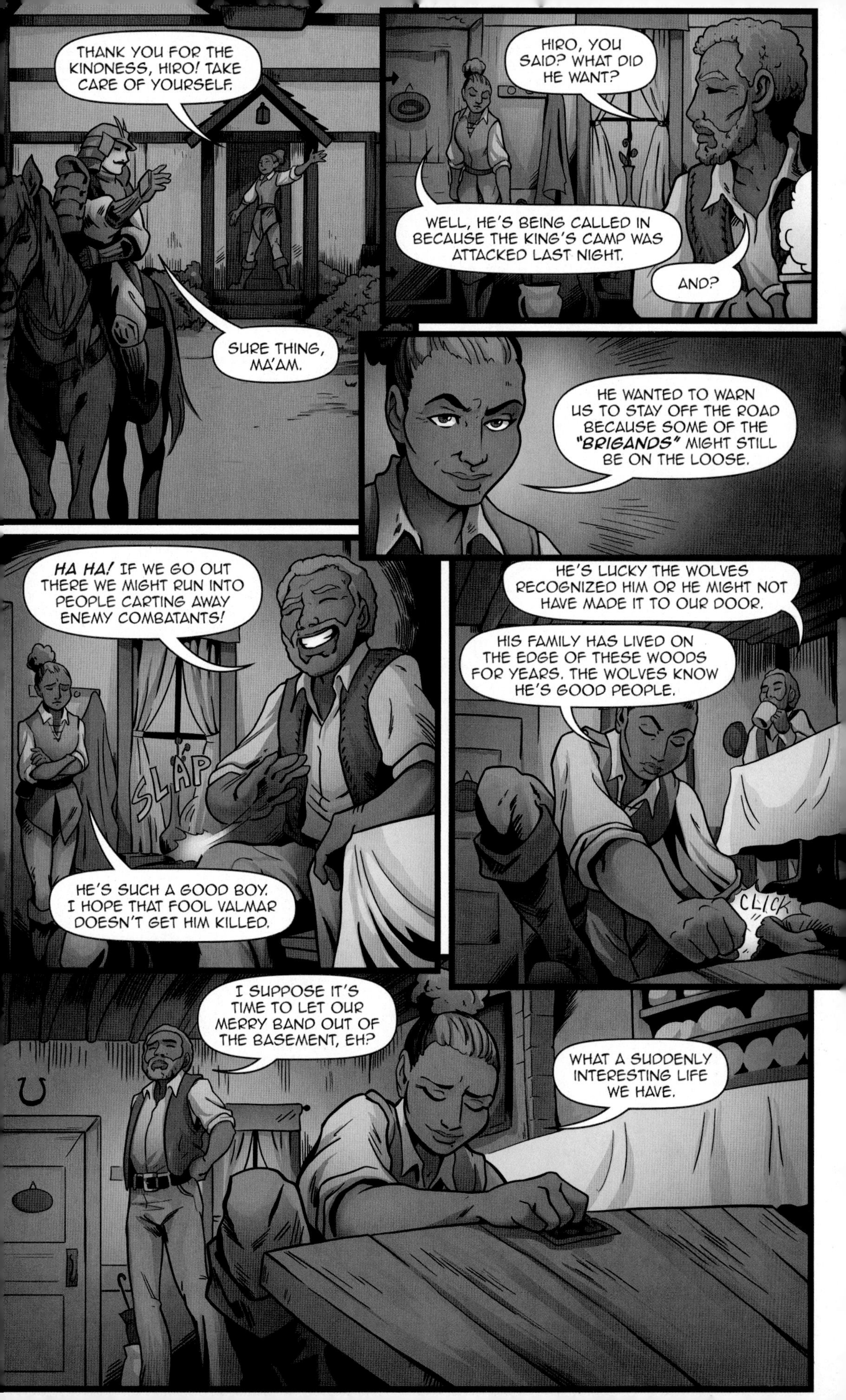

THANK YOU FOR THE KINDNESS, HIRO! TAKE CARE OF YOURSELF.
SURE THING, MA'AM.
HIRO, YOU SAID? WHAT DID HE WANT?
WELL, HE'S BEING CALLED IN BECAUSE THE KING'S CAMP WAS ATTACKED LAST NIGHT.
AND?
HE WANTED TO WARN US TO STAY OFF THE ROAD BECAUSE SOME OF THE "BRIGANDS" MIGHT STILL BE ON THE LOOSE.
HA HA! IF WE GO OUT THERE WE MIGHT RUN INTO PEOPLE CARTING AWAY ENEMY COMBATANTS!
SLAP
HE'S SUCH A GOOD BOY. I HOPE THAT FOOL VALMAR DOESN'T GET HIM KILLED.
HE'S LUCKY THE WOLVES RECOGNIZED HIM OR HE MIGHT NOT HAVE MADE IT TO OUR DOOR.
HIS FAMILY HAS LIVED ON THE EDGE OF THESE WOODS FOR YEARS. THE WOLVES KNOW HE'S GOOD PEOPLE.
CLICK
I SUPPOSE IT'S TIME TO LET OUR MERRY BAND OUT OF THE BASEMENT, EH?
WHAT A SUDDENLY INTERESTING LIFE WE HAVE.

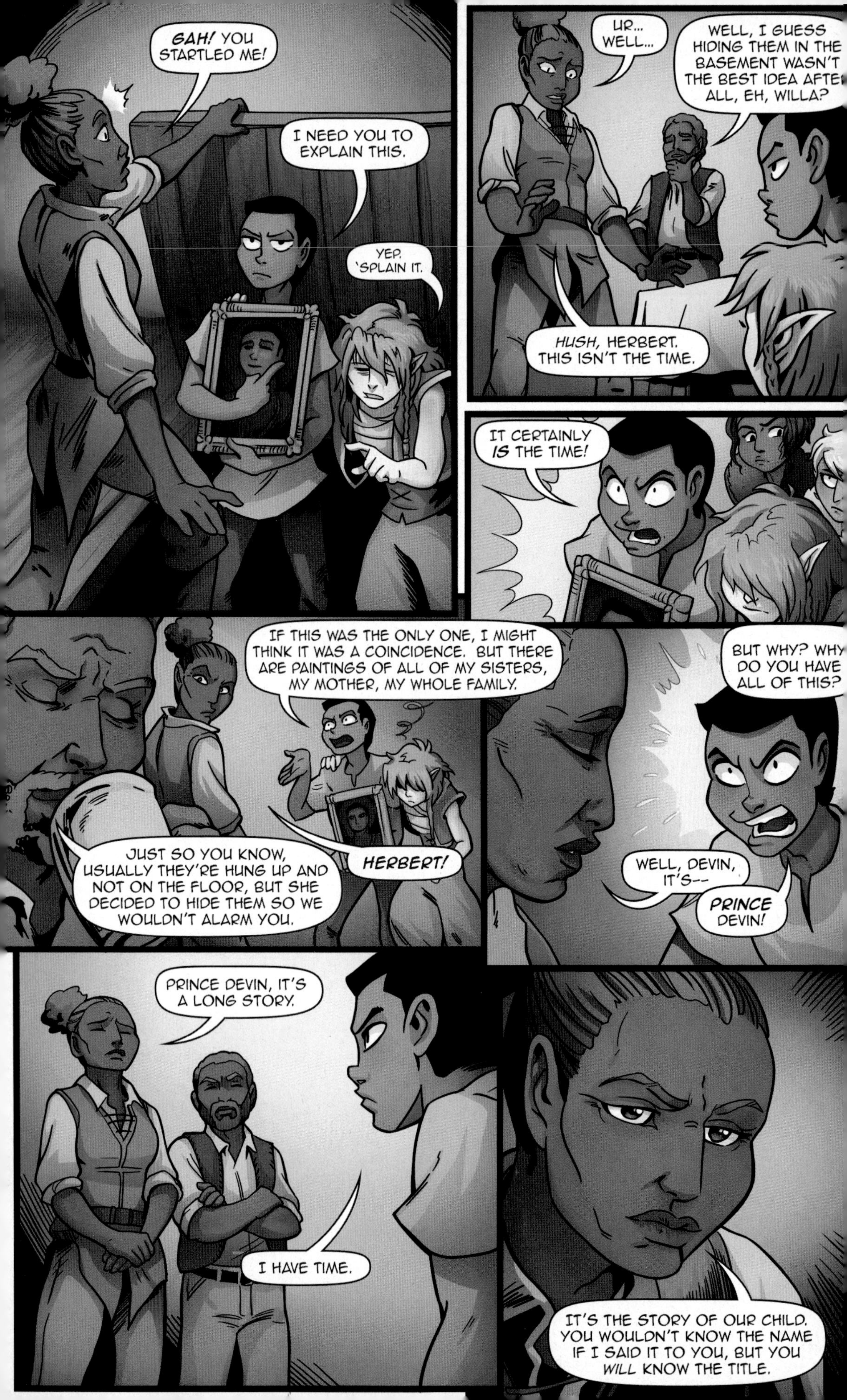
GAH! YOU STARTLED ME!
I NEED YOU TO EXPLAIN THIS.
YEP. 'SPLAIN IT.
UR... WELL...
WELL, I GUESS HIDING THEM IN THE BASEMENT WASN'T THE BEST IDEA AFTER ALL, EH, WILLA?
HUSH, HERBERT. THIS ISN'T THE TIME.
IT CERTAINLY IS THE TIME!
IF THIS WAS THE ONLY ONE, I MIGHT THINK IT WAS A COINCIDENCE. BUT THERE ARE PAINTINGS OF ALL OF MY SISTERS, MY MOTHER, MY WHOLE FAMILY.
JUST SO YOU KNOW, USUALLY THEY'RE HUNG UP AND NOT ON THE FLOOR, BUT SHE DECIDED TO HIDE THEM SO WE WOULDN'T ALARM YOU.
HERBERT!
BUT WHY? WHY DO YOU HAVE ALL OF THIS?
WELL, DEVIN, IT'S--
PRINCE DEVIN!
PRINCE DEVIN, IT'S A LONG STORY.
I HAVE TIME.
IT'S THE STORY OF OUR CHILD. YOU WOULDN'T KNOW THE NAME IF I SAID IT TO YOU, BUT YOU WILL KNOW THE TITLE.

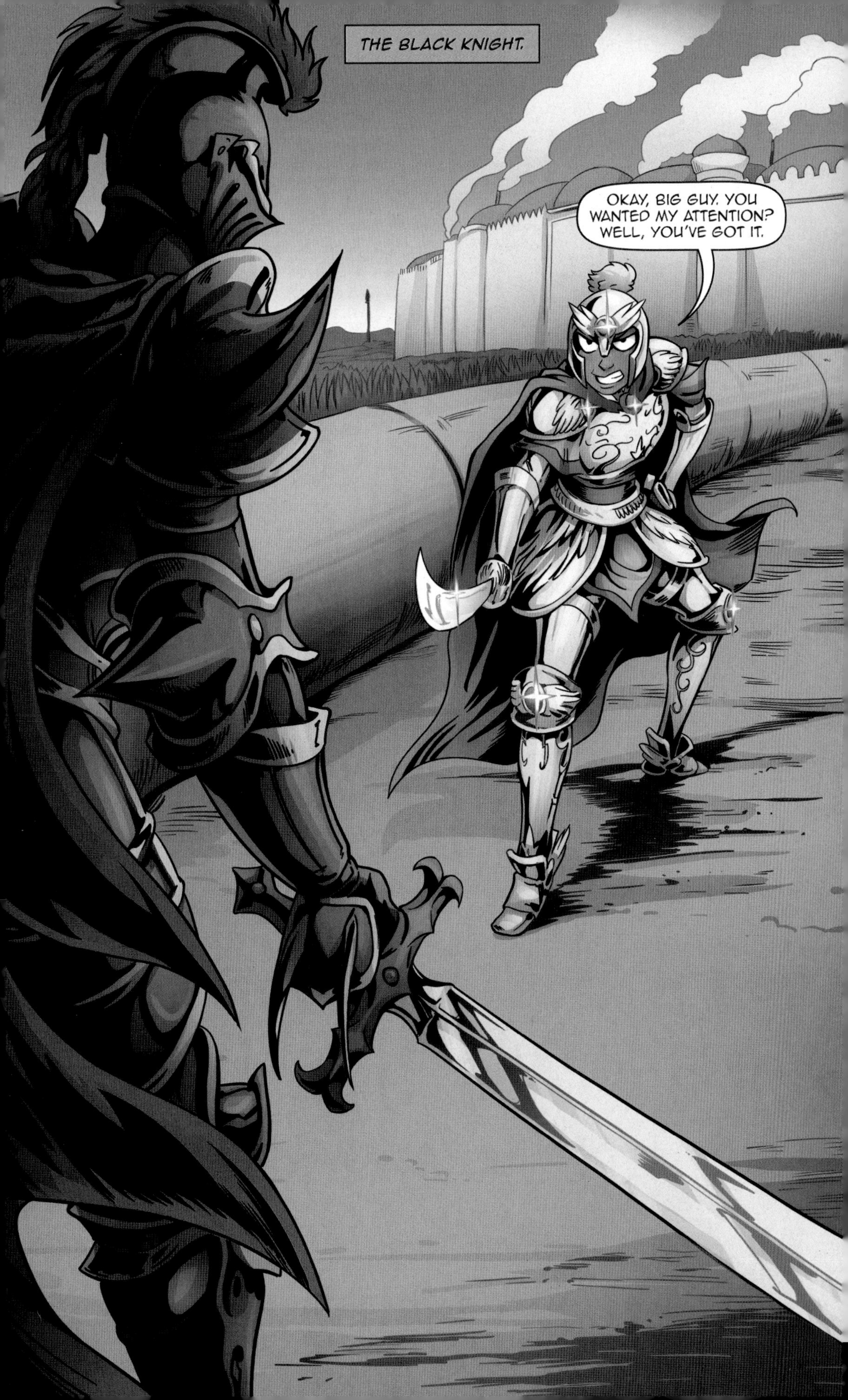
THE BLACK KNIGHT.
OKAY, BIG GUY. YOU WANTED MY ATTENTION? WELL, YOU'VE GOT IT.

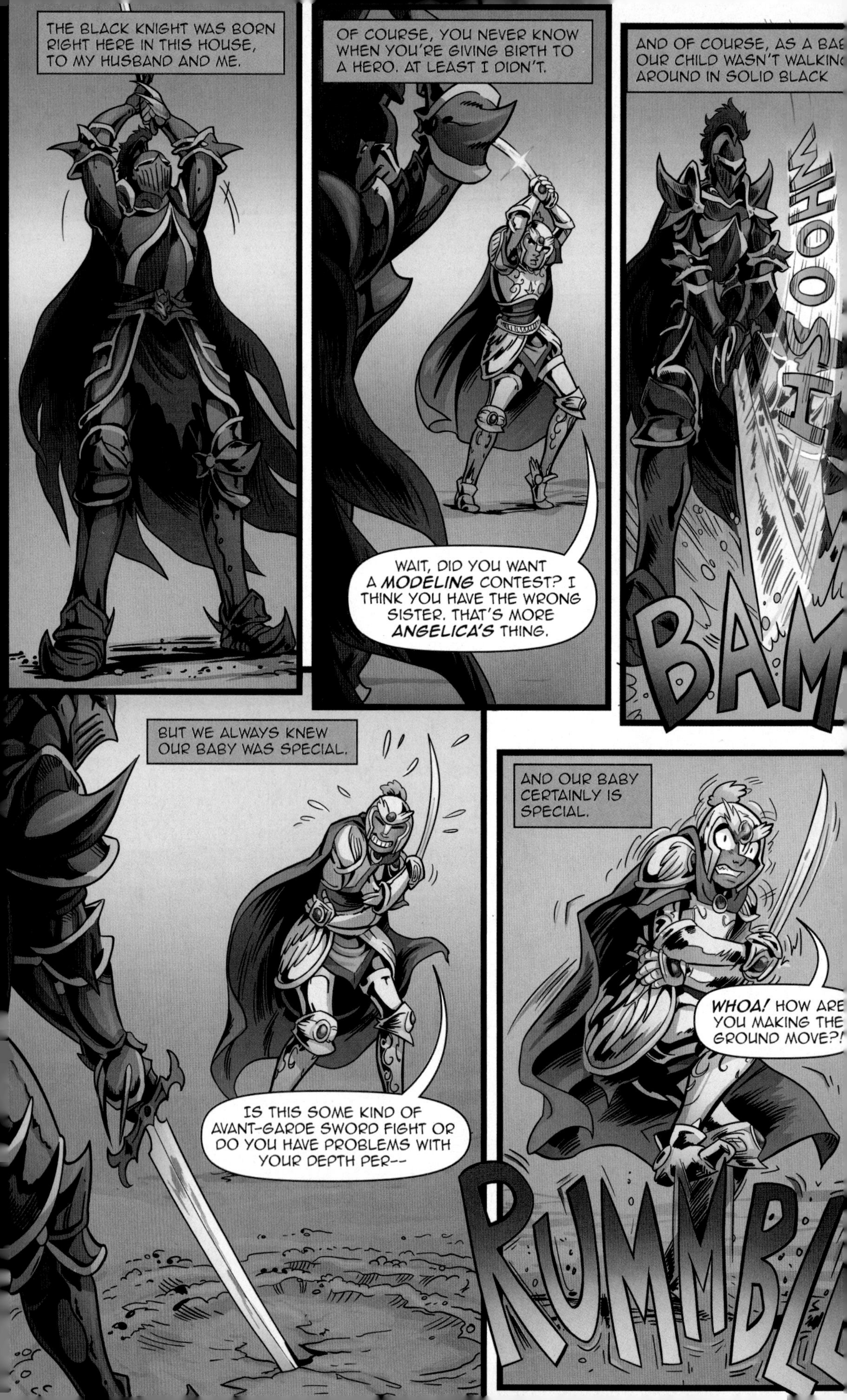
THE BLACK KNIGHT WAS BORN RIGHT HERE IN THIS HOUSE, TO MY HUSBAND AND ME.
OF COURSE, YOU NEVER KNOW WHEN YOU'RE GIVING BIRTH TO A HERO. AT LEAST I DIDN'T.
WAIT, DID YOU WANT A *MODELING* CONTEST? I THINK YOU HAVE THE WRONG SISTER. THAT'S MORE *ANGELICA'S* THING.
AND OF COURSE, AS A BAB OUR CHILD WASN'T WALKIN AROUND IN SOLID BLACK
WHOOSH
BAM
BUT WE ALWAYS KNEW OUR BABY WAS SPECIAL.
IS THIS SOME KIND OF AVANT-GARDE SWORD FIGHT OR DO YOU HAVE PROBLEMS WITH YOUR DEPTH PER--
AND OUR BABY CERTAINLY IS SPECIAL.
WHOA! HOW ARE YOU MAKING THE GROUND MOVE?!
RUMMBL

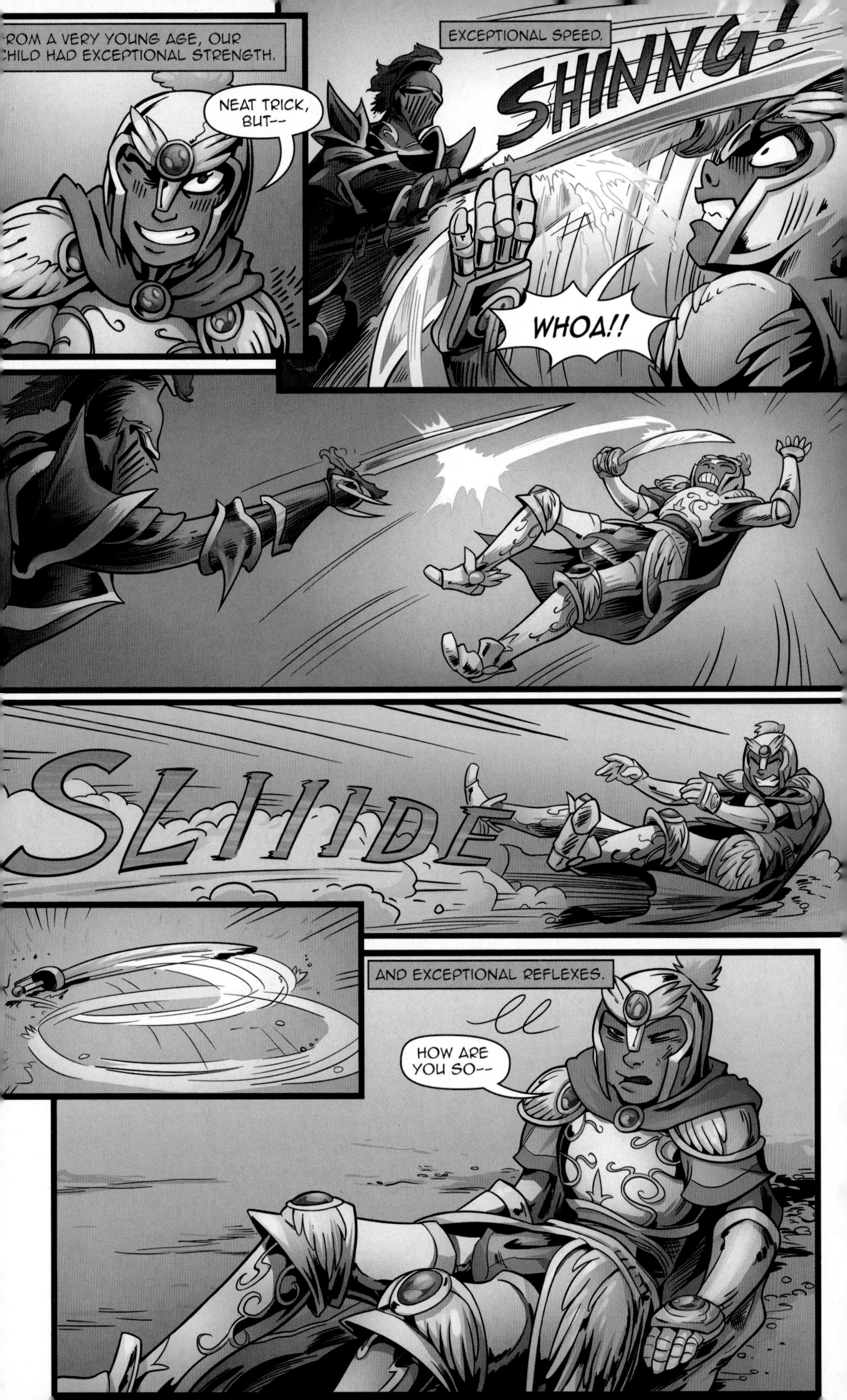
FROM A VERY YOUNG AGE, OUR CHILD HAD EXCEPTIONAL STRENGTH.
NEAT TRICK, BUT--
EXCEPTIONAL SPEED.
SHINNG!
WHOA!!
SLIIIDE
AND EXCEPTIONAL REFLEXES.
HOW ARE YOU SO--

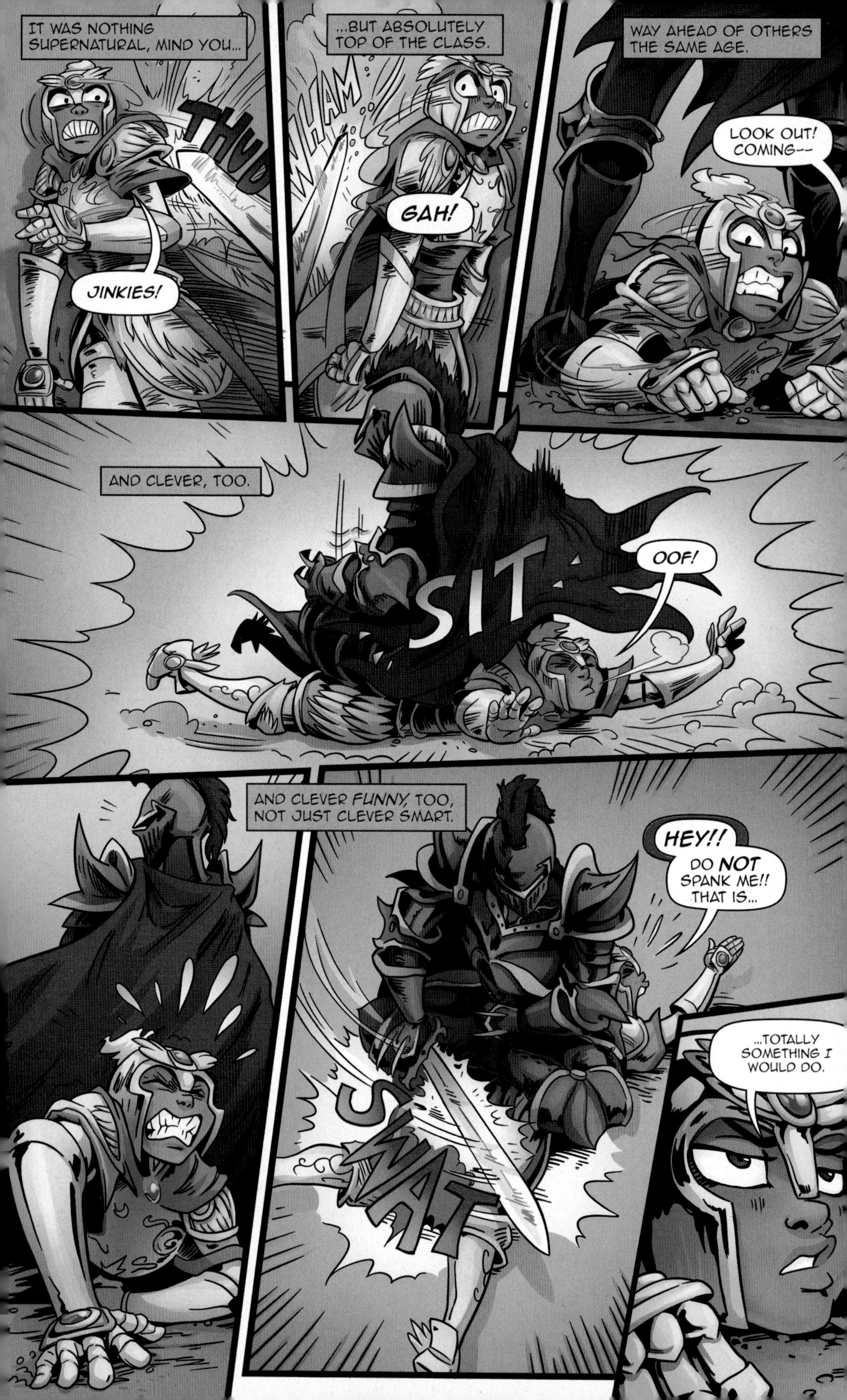

IT WAS NOTHING SUPERNATURAL, MIND YOU...
THUD
JINKIES!
...BUT ABSOLUTELY TOP OF THE CLASS.
THAM
GAH!
WAY AHEAD OF OTHERS THE SAME AGE.
LOOK OUT! COMING--
AND CLEVER, TOO.
SIT
OOF!
AND CLEVER *FUNNY*, TOO, NOT JUST CLEVER SMART.
HEY!!
DO **NOT** SPANK ME!! THAT IS...
SMAT
...TOTALLY SOMETHING I WOULD DO.

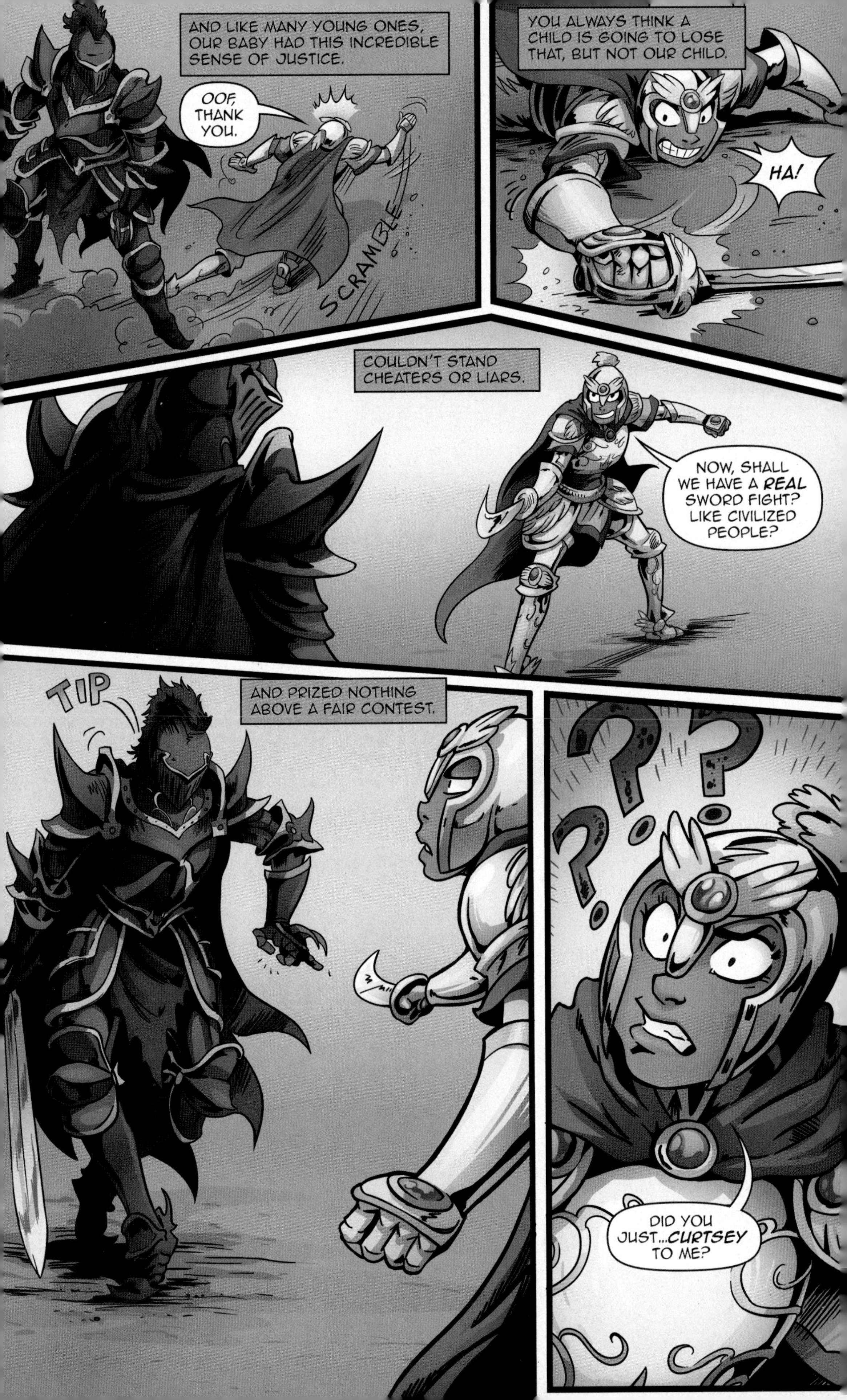
AND LIKE MANY YOUNG ONES, OUR BABY HAD THIS INCREDIBLE SENSE OF JUSTICE.
OOF, THANK YOU.
SCRAMBLE
YOU ALWAYS THINK A CHILD IS GOING TO LOSE THAT, BUT NOT OUR CHILD.
HA!
COULDN'T STAND CHEATERS OR LIARS.
NOW, SHALL WE HAVE A REAL SWORD FIGHT? LIKE CIVILIZED PEOPLE?
TIP
AND PRIZED NOTHING ABOVE A FAIR CONTEST.
DID YOU JUST...CURTSEY TO ME?

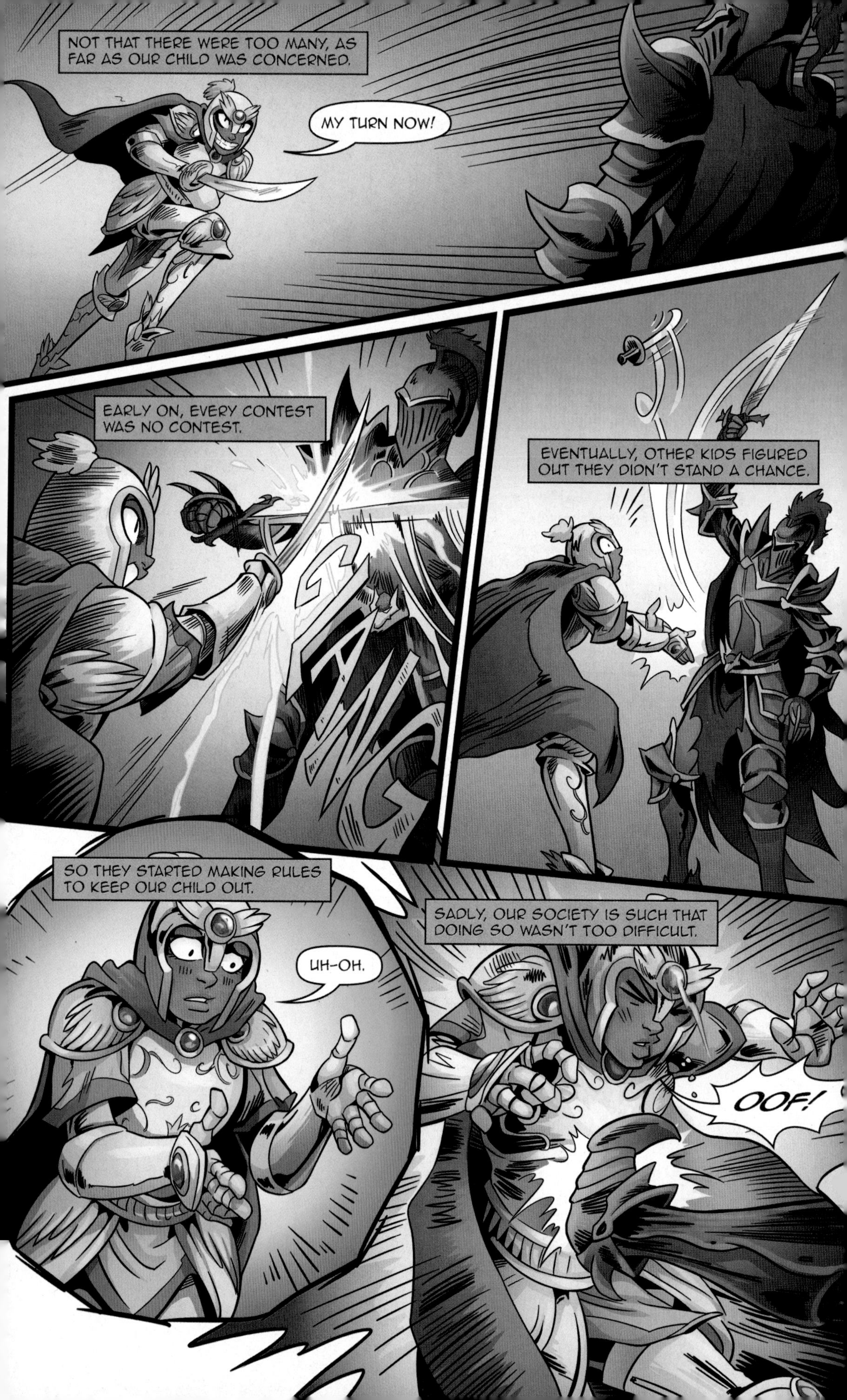
NOT THAT THERE WERE TOO MANY, AS FAR AS OUR CHILD WAS CONCERNED.
MY TURN NOW!
EARLY ON, EVERY CONTEST WAS NO CONTEST.
EVENTUALLY, OTHER KIDS FIGURED OUT THEY DIDN'T STAND A CHANCE.
SO THEY STARTED MAKING RULES TO KEEP OUR CHILD OUT.
UH-OH.
SADLY, OUR SOCIETY IS SUCH THAT DOING SO WASN'T TOO DIFFICULT.
OOF!

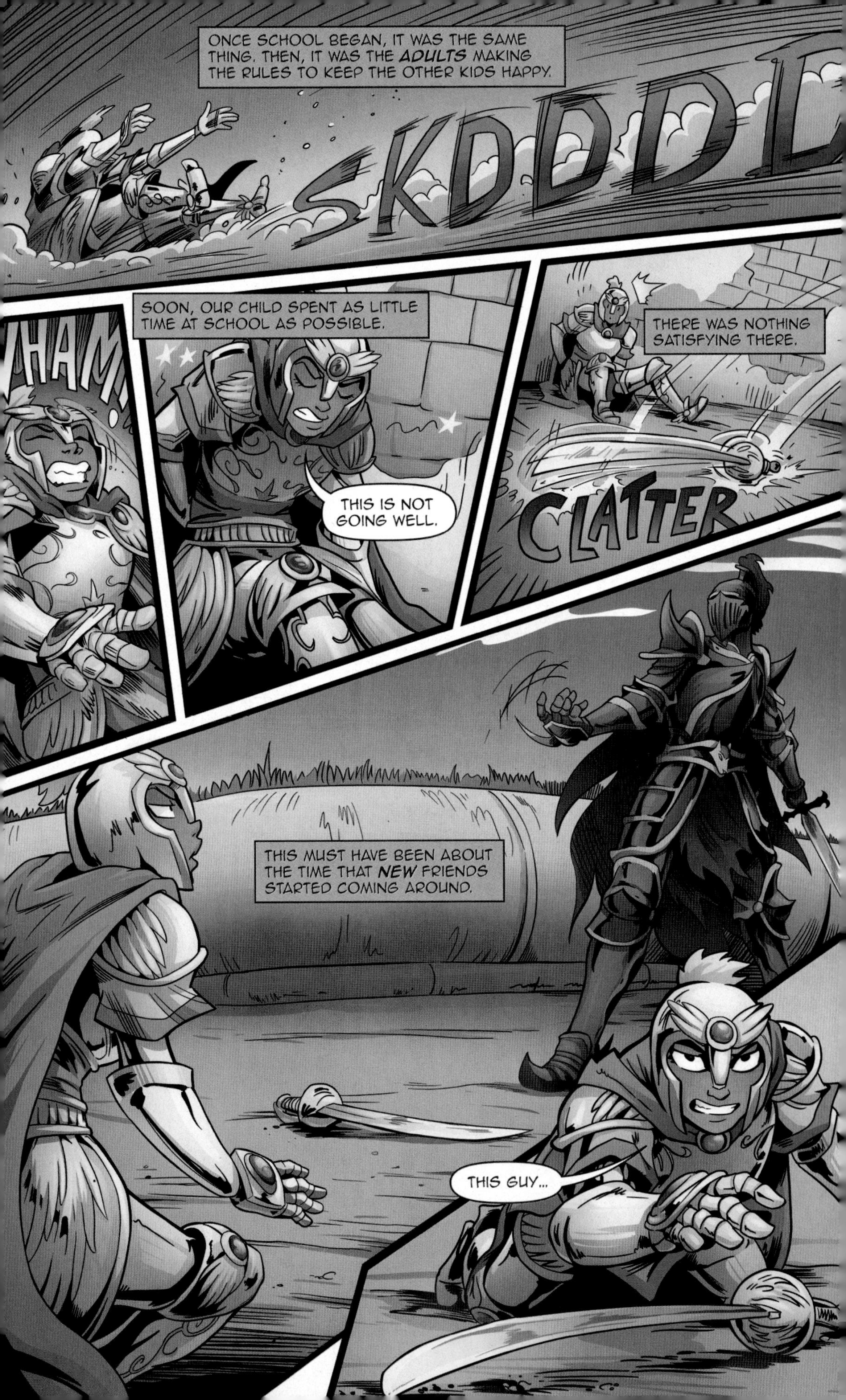
ONCE SCHOOL BEGAN, IT WAS THE SAME THING. THEN, IT WAS THE ADULTS MAKING THE RULES TO KEEP THE OTHER KIDS HAPPY.
SKDDDL
WHAM
SOON, OUR CHILD SPENT AS LITTLE TIME AT SCHOOL AS POSSIBLE.
THIS IS NOT GOING WELL.
THERE WAS NOTHING SATISFYING THERE.
CLATTER
THIS MUST HAVE BEEN ABOUT THE TIME THAT NEW FRIENDS STARTED COMING AROUND.
THIS GUY...

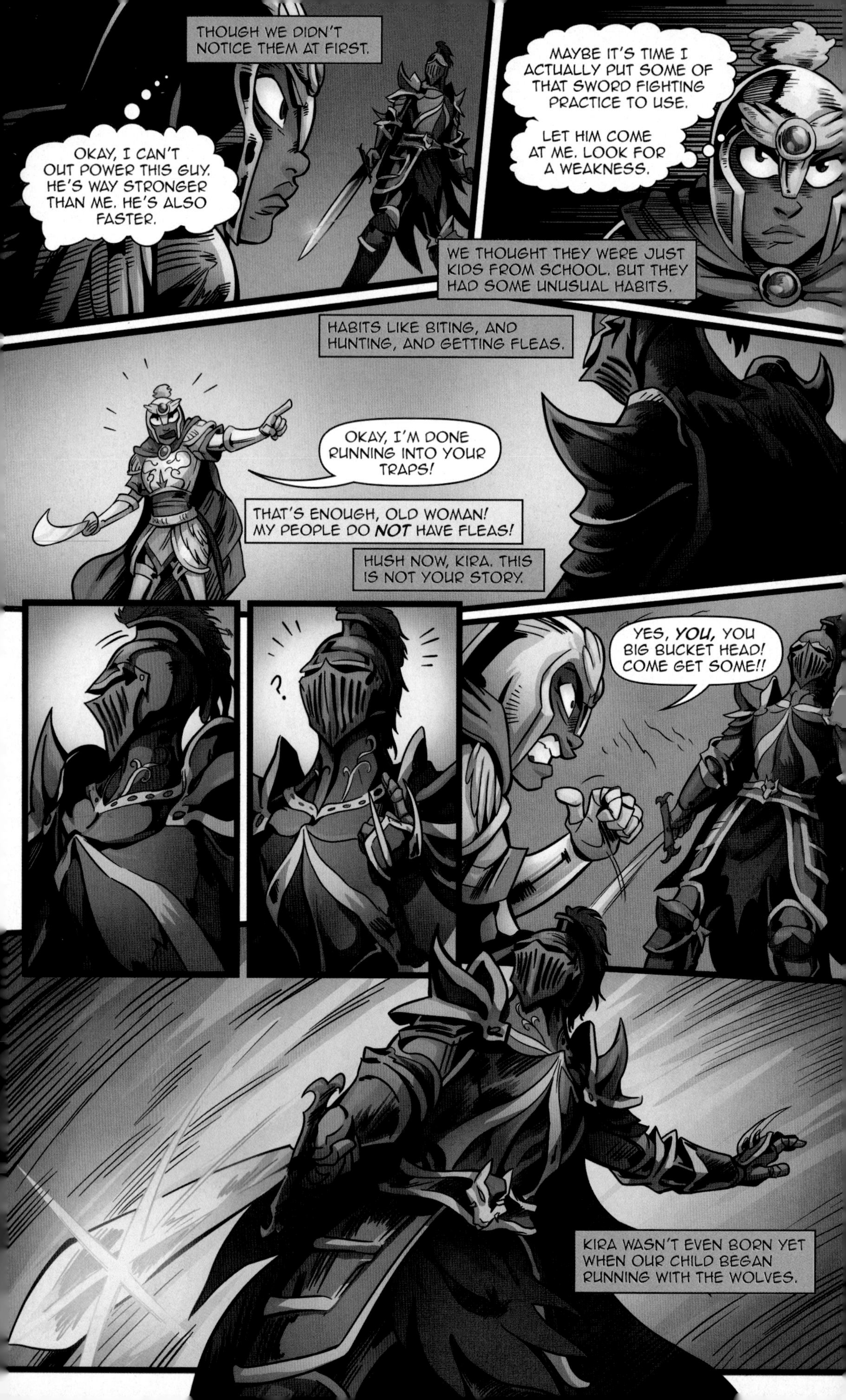
THOUGH WE DIDN'T NOTICE THEM AT FIRST.
OKAY, I CAN'T OUT POWER THIS GUY. HE'S WAY STRONGER THAN ME. HE'S ALSO FASTER.
MAYBE IT'S TIME I ACTUALLY PUT SOME OF THAT SWORD FIGHTING PRACTICE TO USE.
LET HIM COME AT ME. LOOK FOR A WEAKNESS.
WE THOUGHT THEY WERE JUST KIDS FROM SCHOOL. BUT THEY HAD SOME UNUSUAL HABITS.
HABITS LIKE BITING, AND HUNTING, AND GETTING FLEAS.
OKAY, I'M DONE RUNNING INTO YOUR TRAPS!
THAT'S ENOUGH, OLD WOMAN! MY PEOPLE DO **NOT** HAVE FLEAS!
HUSH NOW, KIRA. THIS IS NOT YOUR STORY.
?
YES, ***YOU,*** YOU BIG BUCKET HEAD! COME GET SOME!!
KIRA WASN'T EVEN BORN YET WHEN OUR CHILD BEGAN RUNNING WITH THE WOLVES.

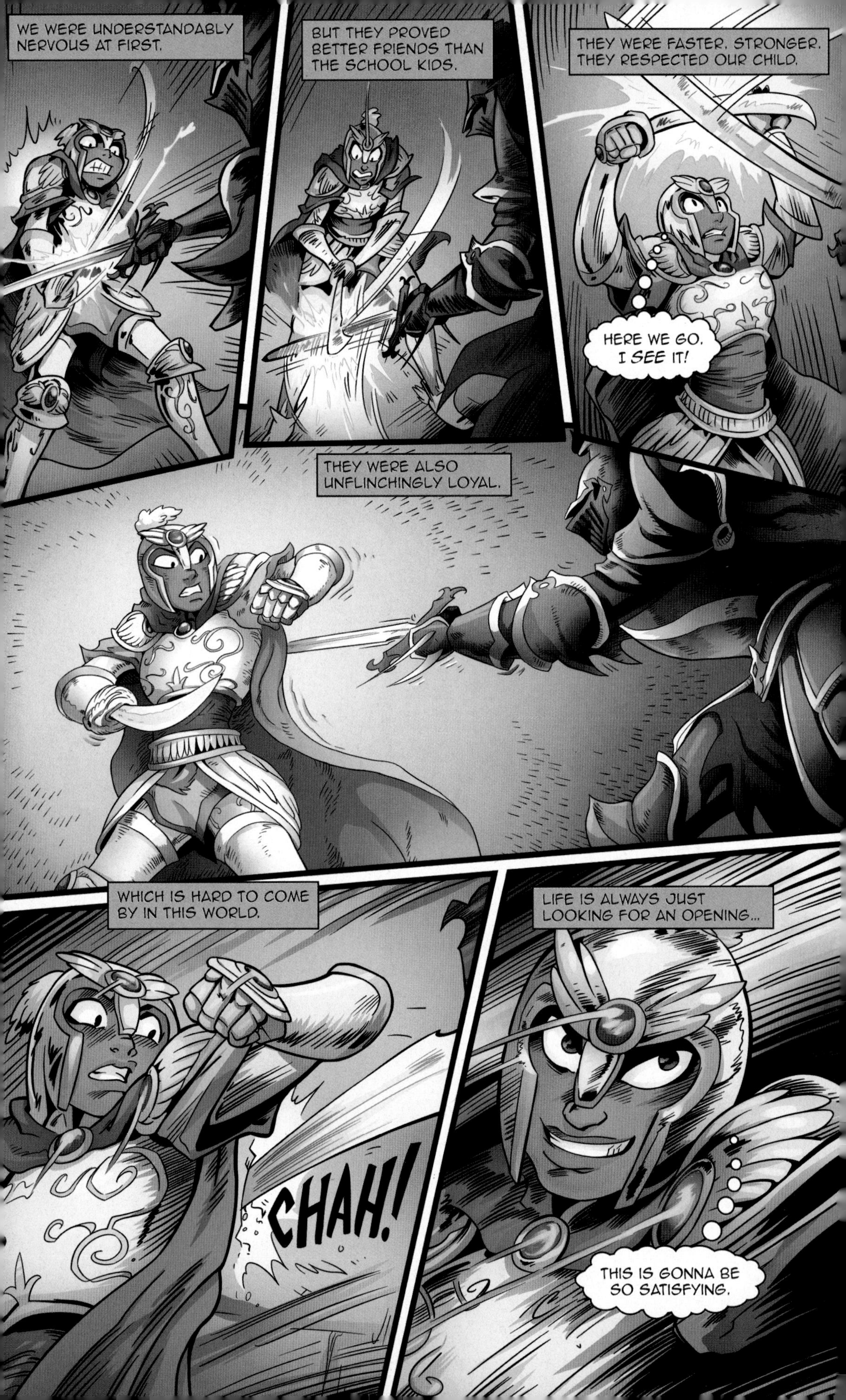
WE WERE UNDERSTANDABLY NERVOUS AT FIRST.
BUT THEY PROVED BETTER FRIENDS THAN THE SCHOOL KIDS.
THEY WERE FASTER. STRONGER. THEY RESPECTED OUR CHILD.
HERE WE GO. I SEE IT!
THEY WERE ALSO UNFLINCHINGLY LOYAL.
WHICH IS HARD TO COME BY IN THIS WORLD.
CHAH!
LIFE IS ALWAYS JUST LOOKING FOR AN OPENING...
THIS IS GONNA BE SO SATISFYING.

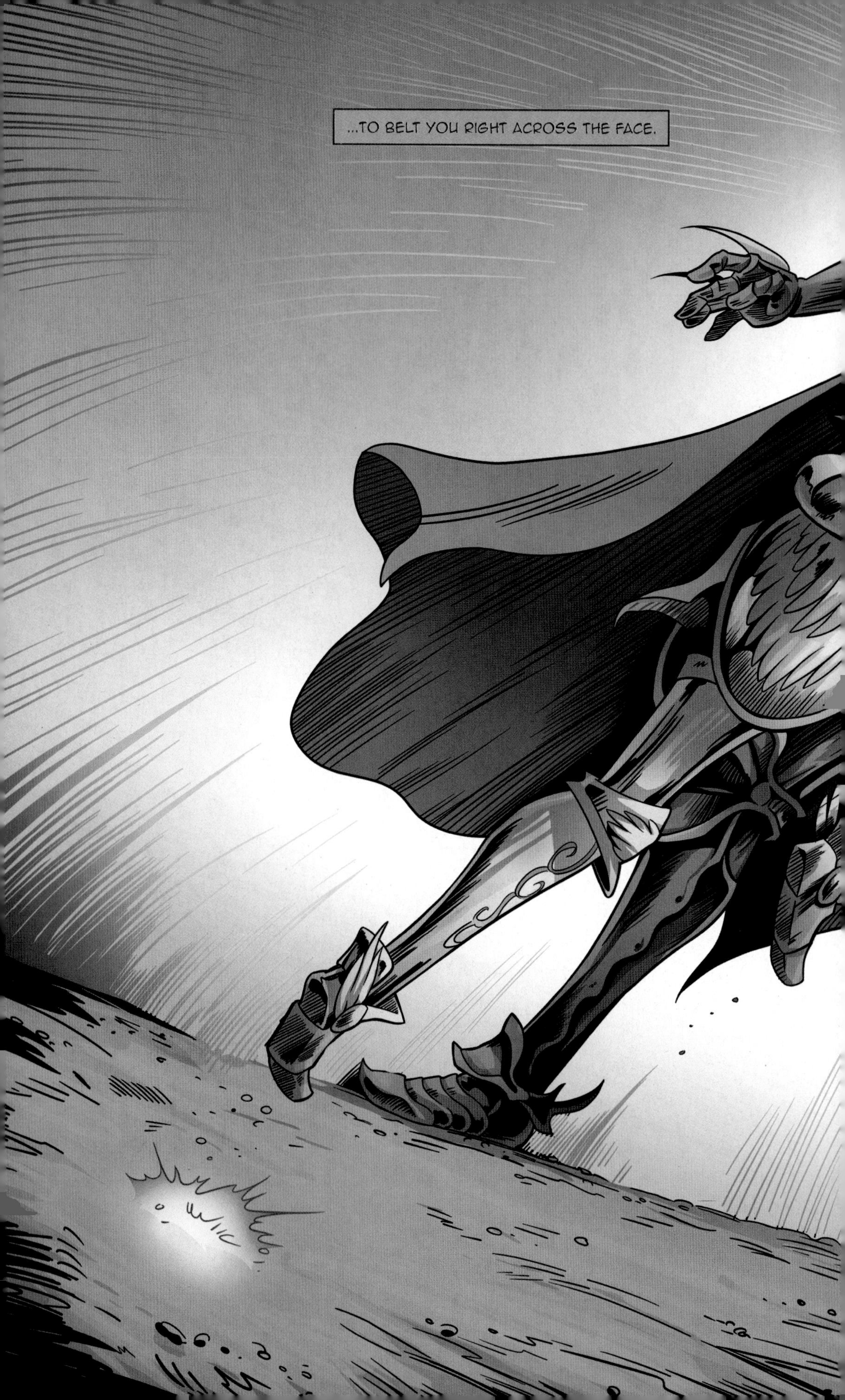
...TO BELT YOU RIGHT ACROSS THE FACE.

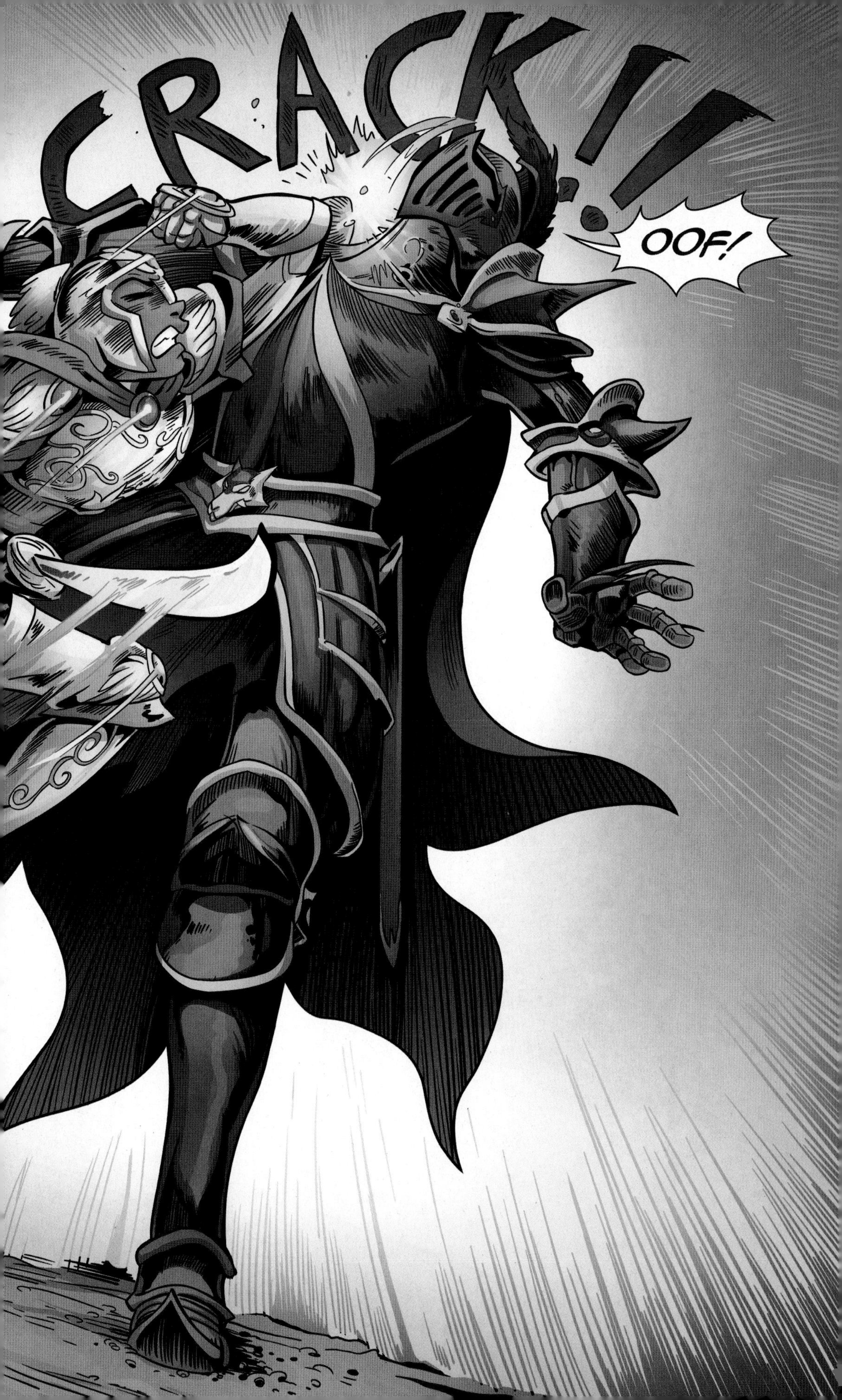
CRACK!!
OOF!

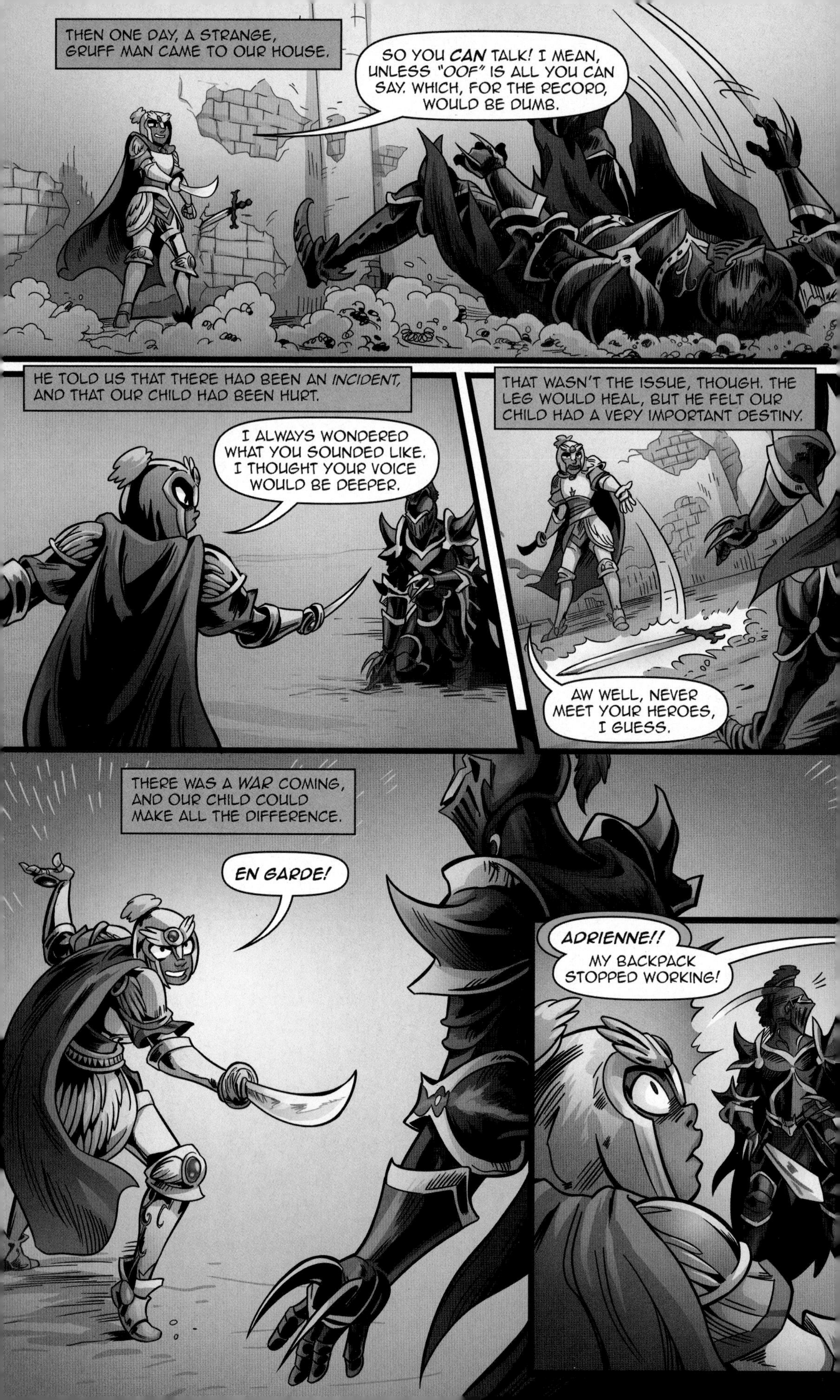
THEN ONE DAY, A STRANGE, GRUFF MAN CAME TO OUR HOUSE.
SO YOU *CAN* TALK! I MEAN, UNLESS *"OOF"* IS ALL YOU CAN SAY. WHICH, FOR THE RECORD, WOULD BE DUMB.
HE TOLD US THAT THERE HAD BEEN AN *INCIDENT,* AND THAT OUR CHILD HAD BEEN HURT.
I ALWAYS WONDERED WHAT YOU SOUNDED LIKE. I THOUGHT YOUR VOICE WOULD BE DEEPER.
THAT WASN'T THE ISSUE, THOUGH. THE LEG WOULD HEAL, BUT HE FELT OUR CHILD HAD A VERY IMPORTANT DESTINY.
AW WELL, NEVER MEET YOUR HEROES, I GUESS.
THERE WAS A *WAR* COMING, AND OUR CHILD COULD MAKE ALL THE DIFFERENCE.
EN GARDE!
ADRIENNE!! MY BACKPACK STOPPED WORKING!

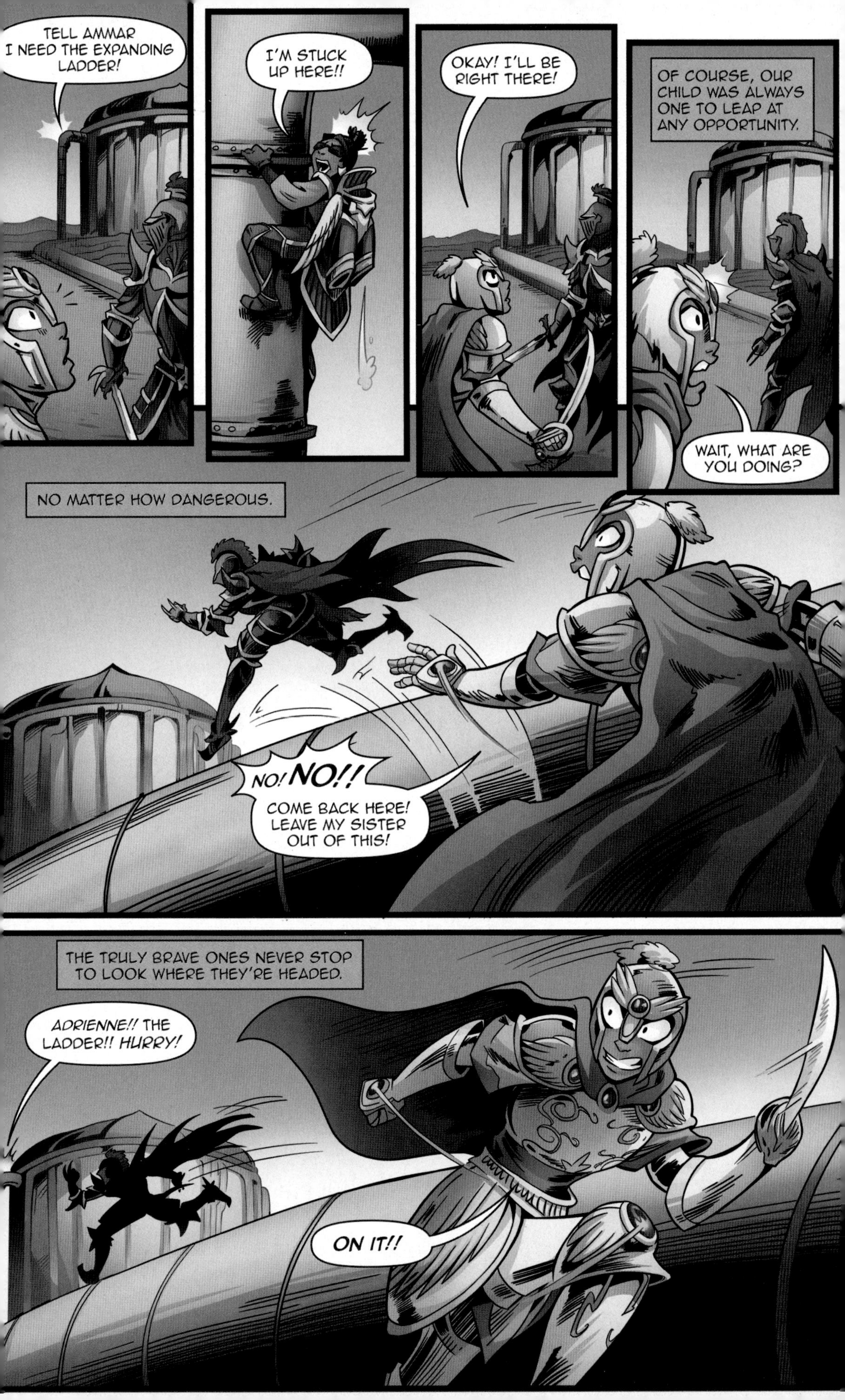
TELL AMMAR I NEED THE EXPANDING LADDER!
I'M STUCK UP HERE!!
OKAY! I'LL BE RIGHT THERE!
OF COURSE, OUR CHILD WAS ALWAYS ONE TO LEAP AT ANY OPPORTUNITY.
WAIT, WHAT ARE YOU DOING?
NO MATTER HOW DANGEROUS.
NO! NO!!
COME BACK HERE! LEAVE MY SISTER OUT OF THIS!
THE TRULY BRAVE ONES NEVER STOP TO LOOK WHERE THEY'RE HEADED.
ADRIENNE!! THE LADDER!! HURRY!
ON IT!!

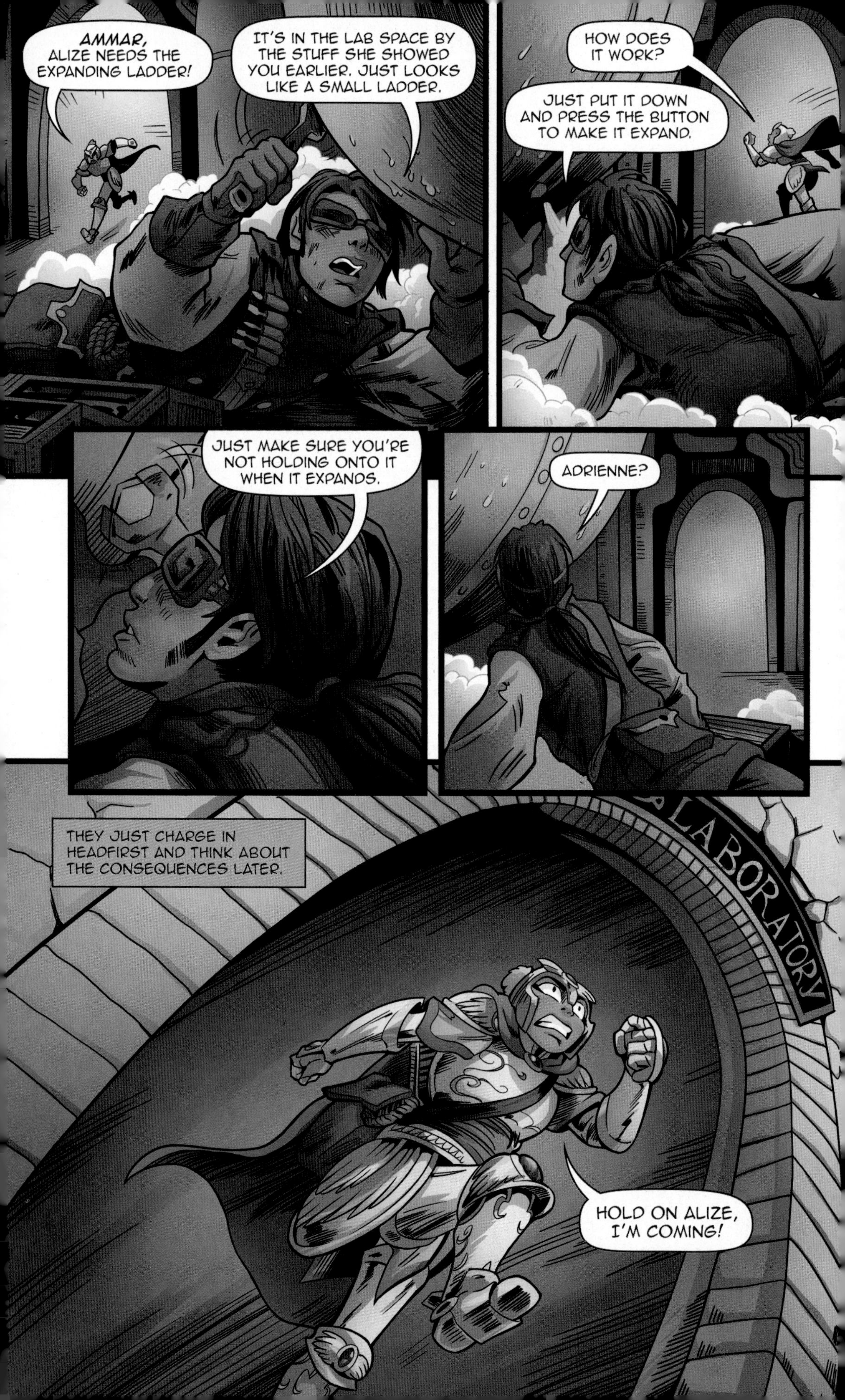
AMMAR, ALIZE NEEDS THE EXPANDING LADDER!
IT'S IN THE LAB SPACE BY THE STUFF SHE SHOWED YOU EARLIER. JUST LOOKS LIKE A SMALL LADDER.
HOW DOES IT WORK?
JUST PUT IT DOWN AND PRESS THE BUTTON TO MAKE IT EXPAND.
JUST MAKE SURE YOU'RE NOT HOLDING ONTO IT WHEN IT EXPANDS.
ADRIENNE?
THEY JUST CHARGE IN HEADFIRST AND THINK ABOUT THE CONSEQUENCES LATER.
LABORATORY
HOLD ON ALIZE, I'M COMING!

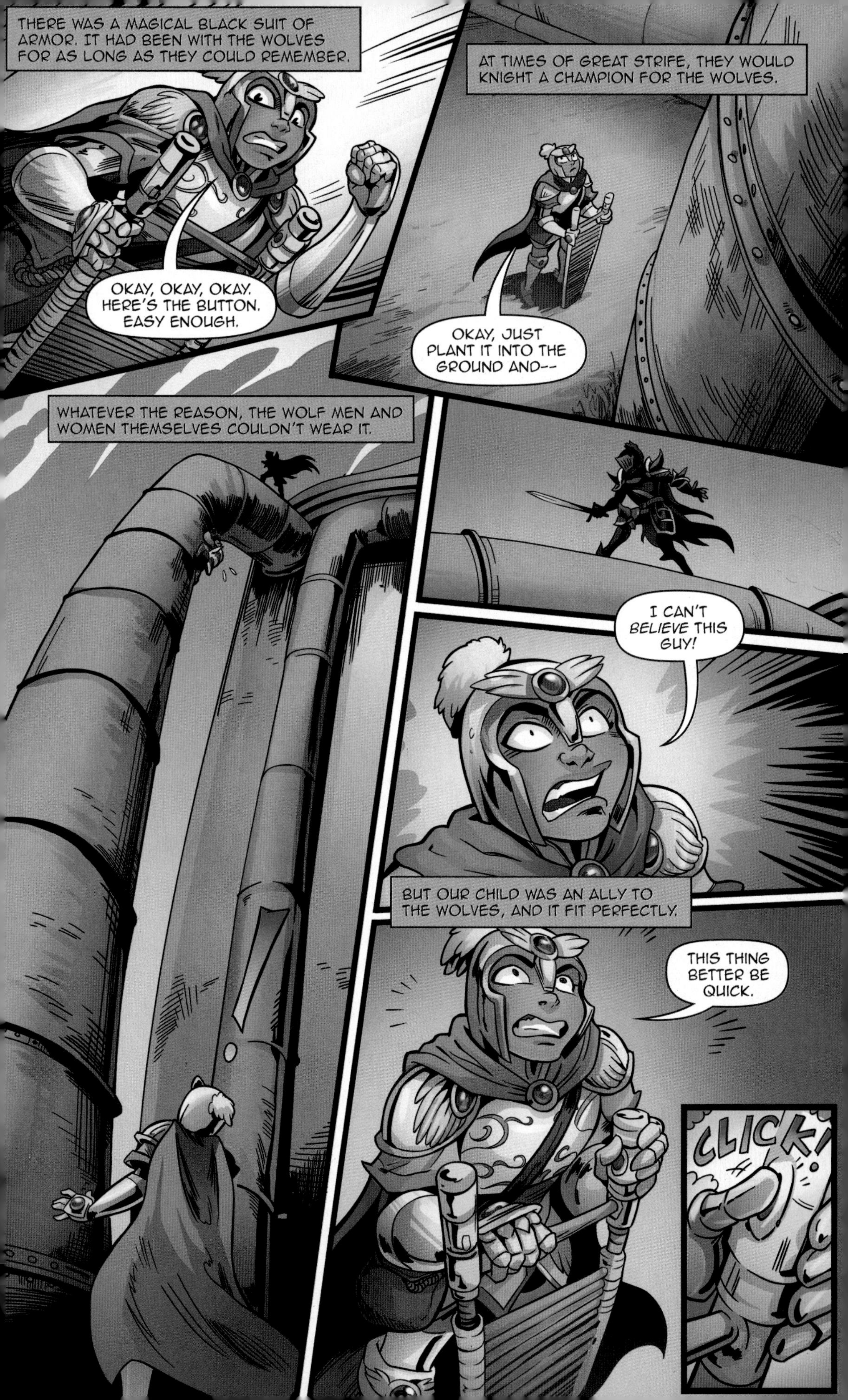
THERE WAS A MAGICAL BLACK SUIT OF ARMOR. IT HAD BEEN WITH THE WOLVES FOR AS LONG AS THEY COULD REMEMBER.
OKAY, OKAY, OKAY. HERE'S THE BUTTON. EASY ENOUGH.
AT TIMES OF GREAT STRIFE, THEY WOULD KNIGHT A CHAMPION FOR THE WOLVES.
OKAY, JUST PLANT IT INTO THE GROUND AND--
WHATEVER THE REASON, THE WOLF MEN AND WOMEN THEMSELVES COULDN'T WEAR IT.
I CAN'T BELIEVE THIS GUY!
BUT OUR CHILD WAS AN ALLY TO THE WOLVES, AND IT FIT PERFECTLY.
THIS THING BETTER BE QUICK.
CLICK!

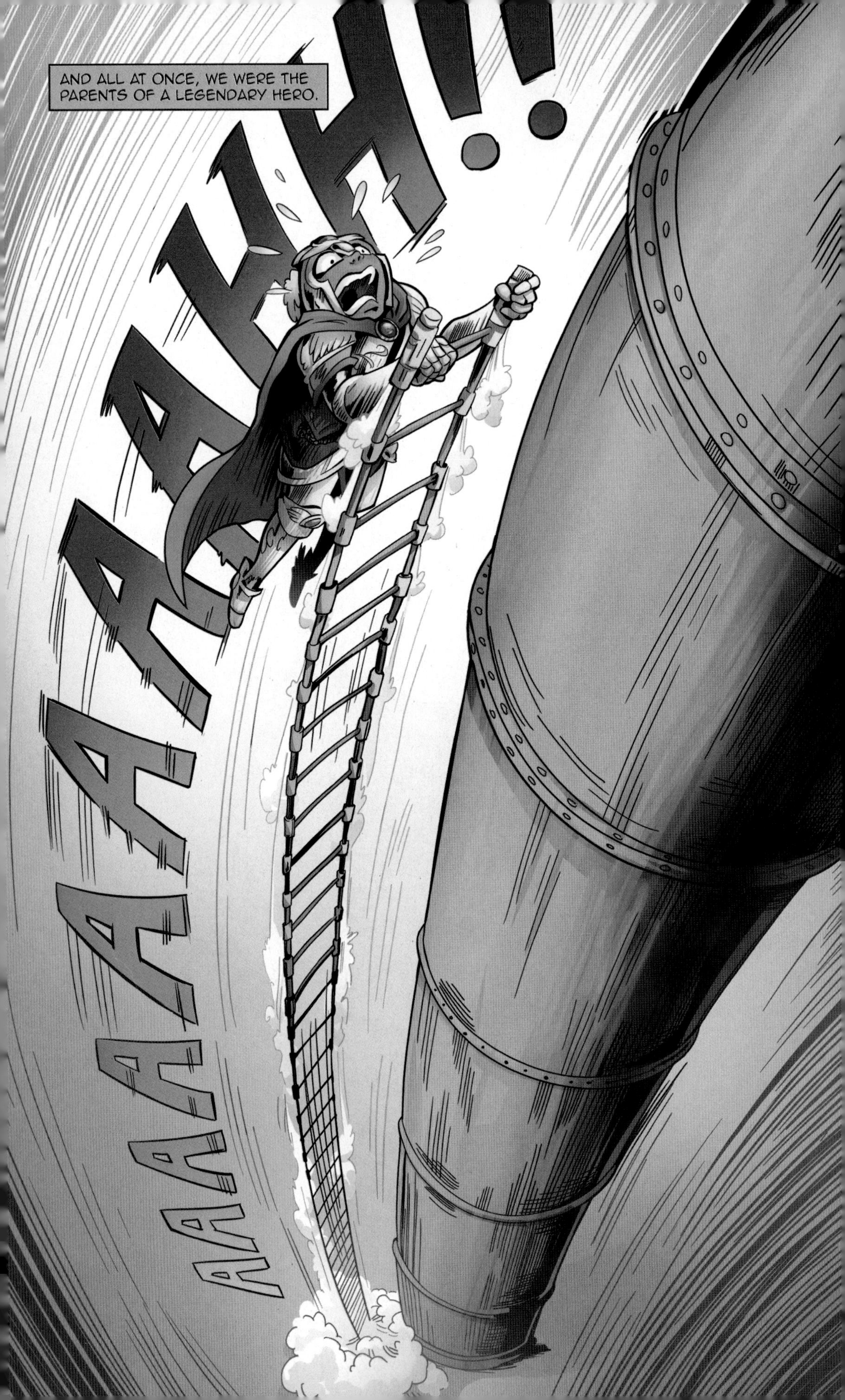
AND ALL AT ONCE, WE WERE THE PARENTS OF A LEGENDARY HERO.
AAAAAAAAAAHH!!!

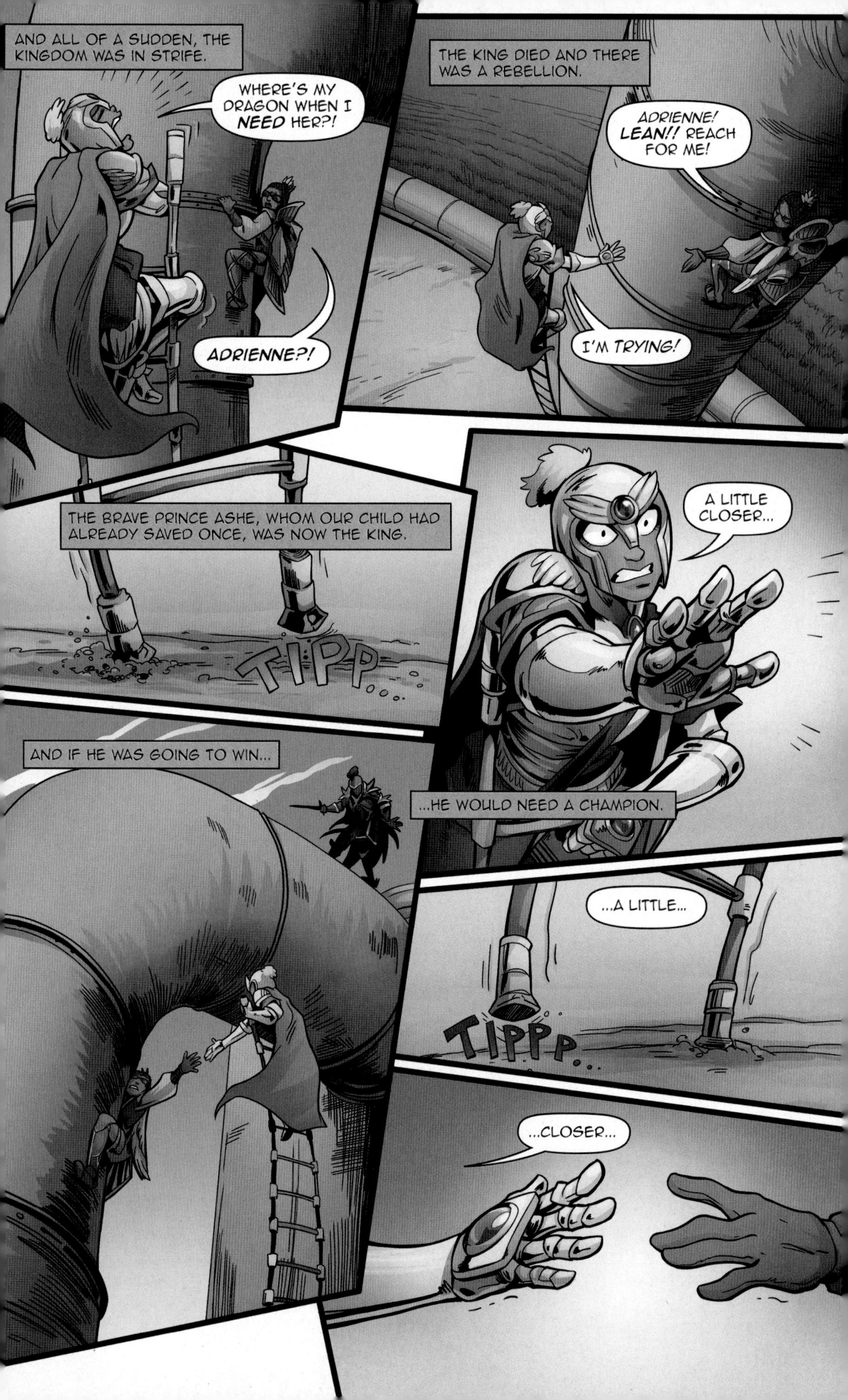
AND ALL OF A SUDDEN, THE KINGDOM WAS IN STRIFE.
WHERE'S MY DRAGON WHEN I NEED HER?!
ADRIENNE?!
THE KING DIED AND THERE WAS A REBELLION.
ADRIENNE! LEAN!! REACH FOR ME!
I'M TRYING!
THE BRAVE PRINCE ASHE, WHOM OUR CHILD HAD ALREADY SAVED ONCE, WAS NOW THE KING.
TIPP...
A LITTLE CLOSER...
AND IF HE WAS GOING TO WIN...
...HE WOULD NEED A CHAMPION.
...A LITTLE...
TIPPP...
...CLOSER...

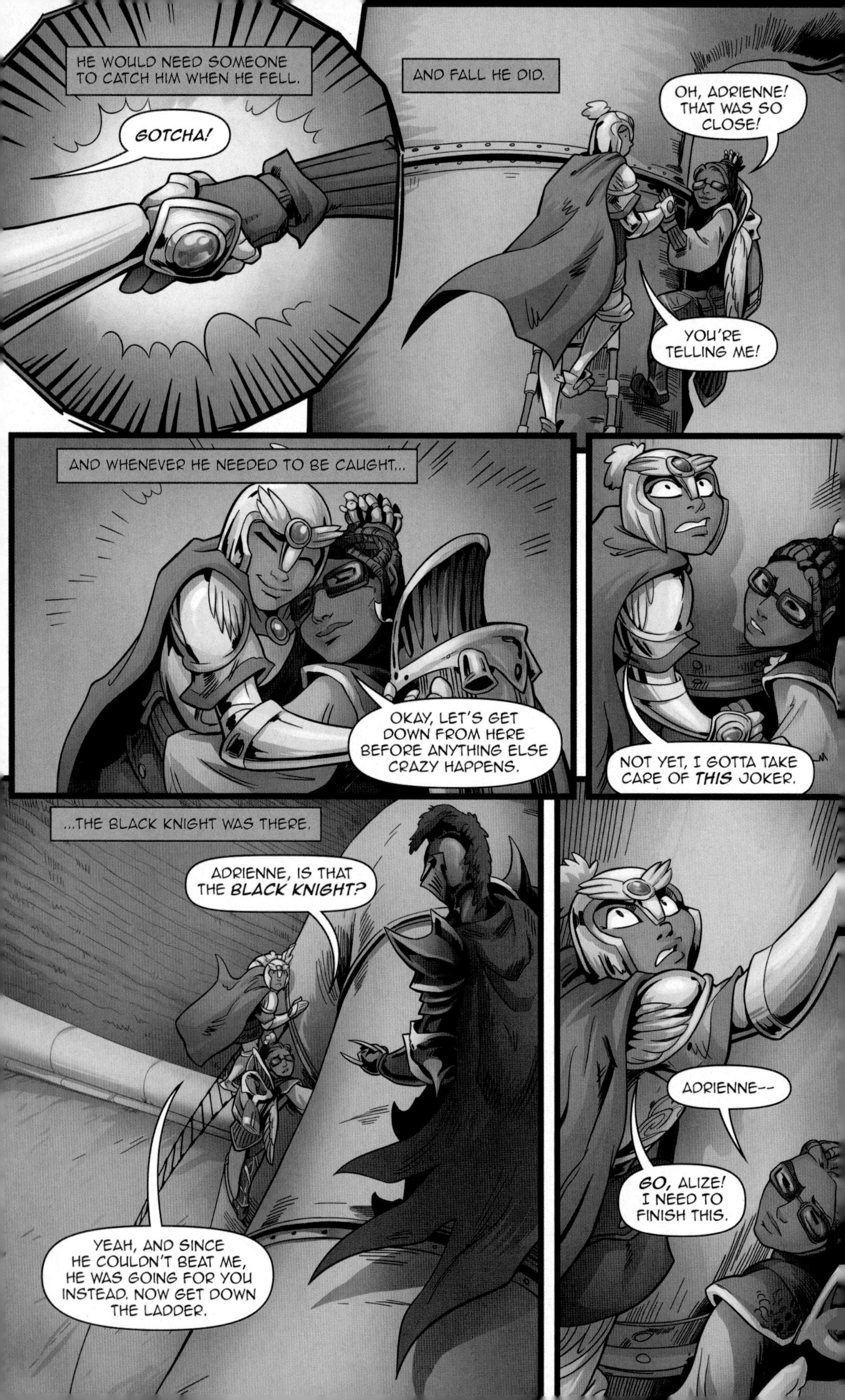
HE WOULD NEED SOMEONE TO CATCH HIM WHEN HE FELL.
GOTCHA!
AND FALL HE DID.
OH, ADRIENNE! THAT WAS SO CLOSE!
YOU'RE TELLING ME!
AND WHENEVER HE NEEDED TO BE CAUGHT...
OKAY, LET'S GET DOWN FROM HERE BEFORE ANYTHING ELSE CRAZY HAPPENS.
NOT YET, I GOTTA TAKE CARE OF THIS JOKER.
...THE BLACK KNIGHT WAS THERE.
ADRIENNE, IS THAT THE BLACK KNIGHT?
YEAH, AND SINCE HE COULDN'T BEAT ME, HE WAS GOING FOR YOU INSTEAD. NOW GET DOWN THE LADDER.
ADRIENNE--
GO, ALIZE! I NEED TO FINISH THIS.

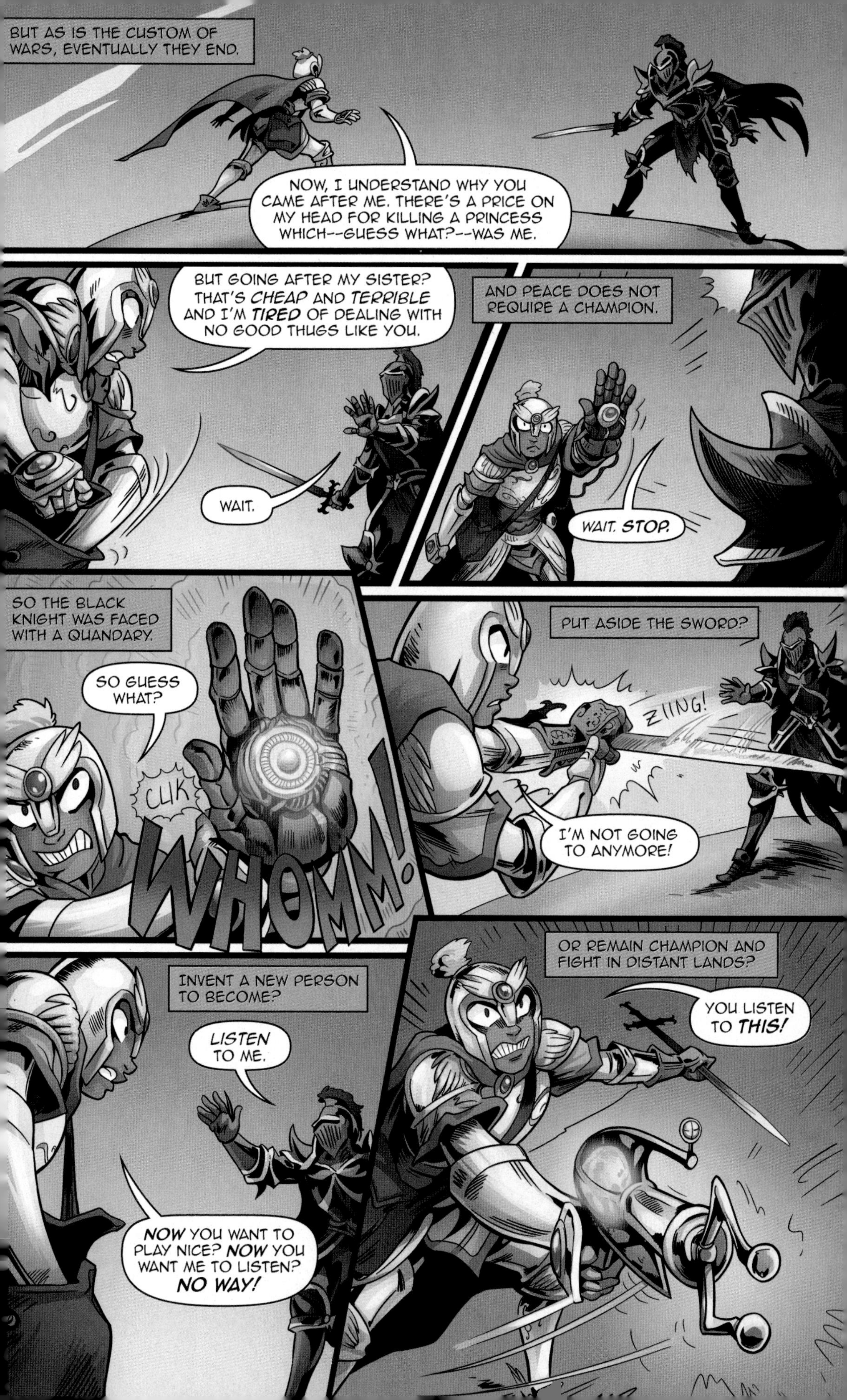
BUT AS IS THE CUSTOM OF WARS, EVENTUALLY THEY END.
NOW, I UNDERSTAND WHY YOU CAME AFTER ME. THERE'S A PRICE ON MY HEAD FOR KILLING A PRINCESS WHICH--GUESS WHAT?--WAS ME.
BUT GOING AFTER MY SISTER? THAT'S CHEAP AND TERRIBLE AND I'M TIRED OF DEALING WITH NO GOOD THUGS LIKE YOU.
WAIT.
AND PEACE DOES NOT REQUIRE A CHAMPION.
WAIT. STOP.
SO THE BLACK KNIGHT WAS FACED WITH A QUANDARY.
SO GUESS WHAT?
CLIK
WHOMM!
PUT ASIDE THE SWORD?
ZIING!
I'M NOT GOING TO ANYMORE!
INVENT A NEW PERSON TO BECOME?
LISTEN TO ME.
NOW YOU WANT TO PLAY NICE? NOW YOU WANT ME TO LISTEN? NO WAY!
OR REMAIN CHAMPION AND FIGHT IN DISTANT LANDS?
YOU LISTEN TO THIS!

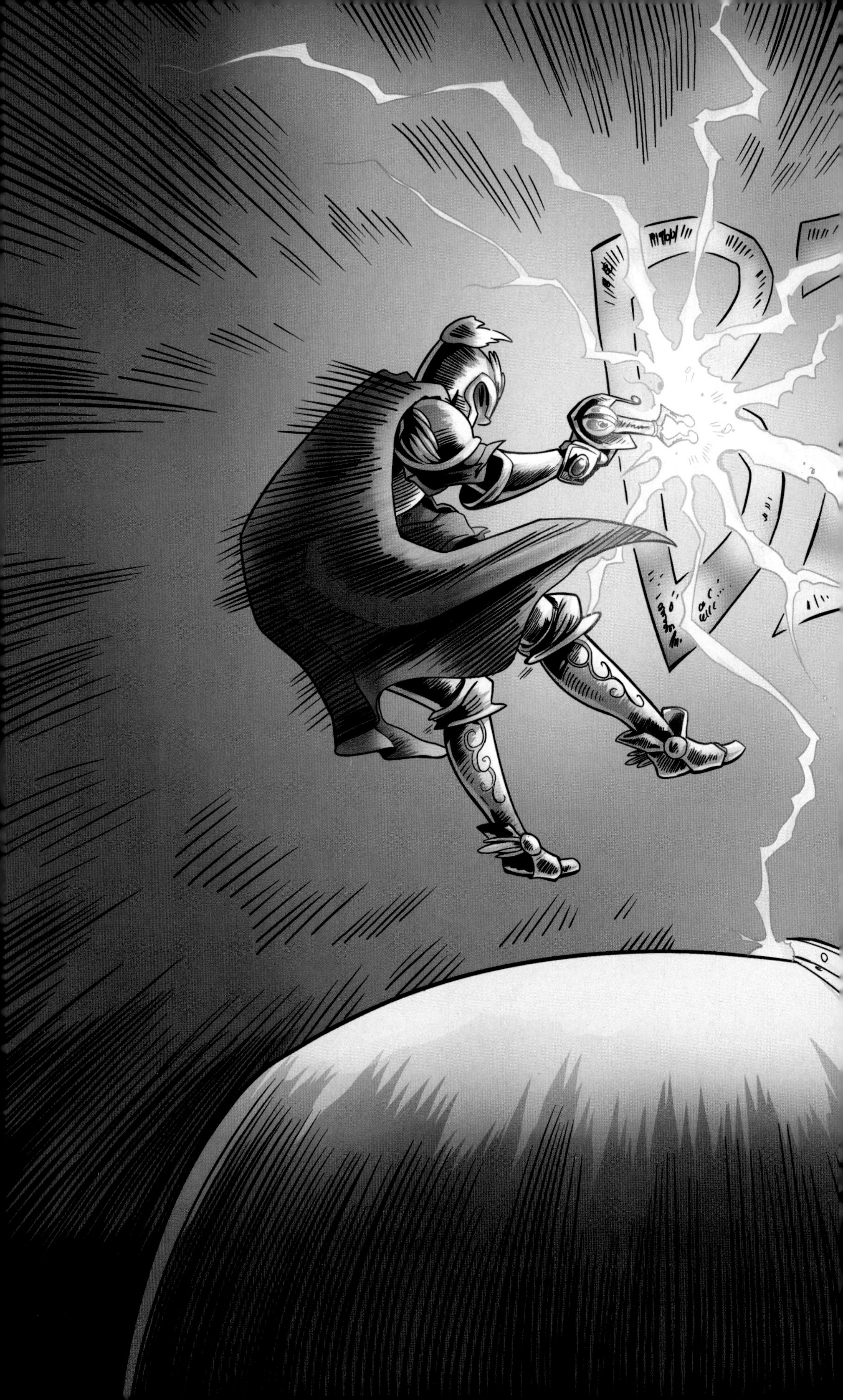

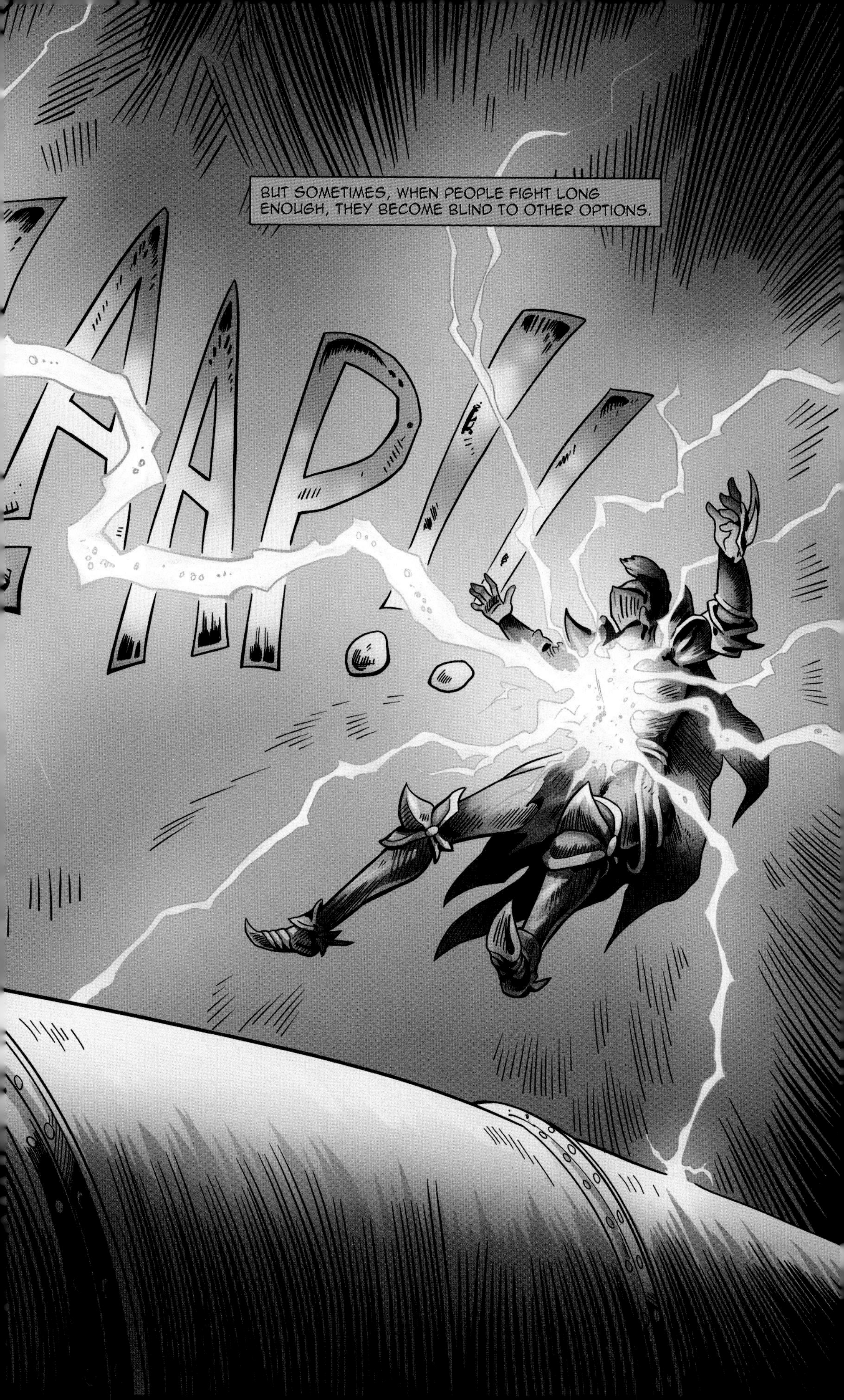
BUT SOMETIMES, WHEN PEOPLE FIGHT LONG ENOUGH, THEY BECOME BLIND TO OTHER OPTIONS.
AAP!!

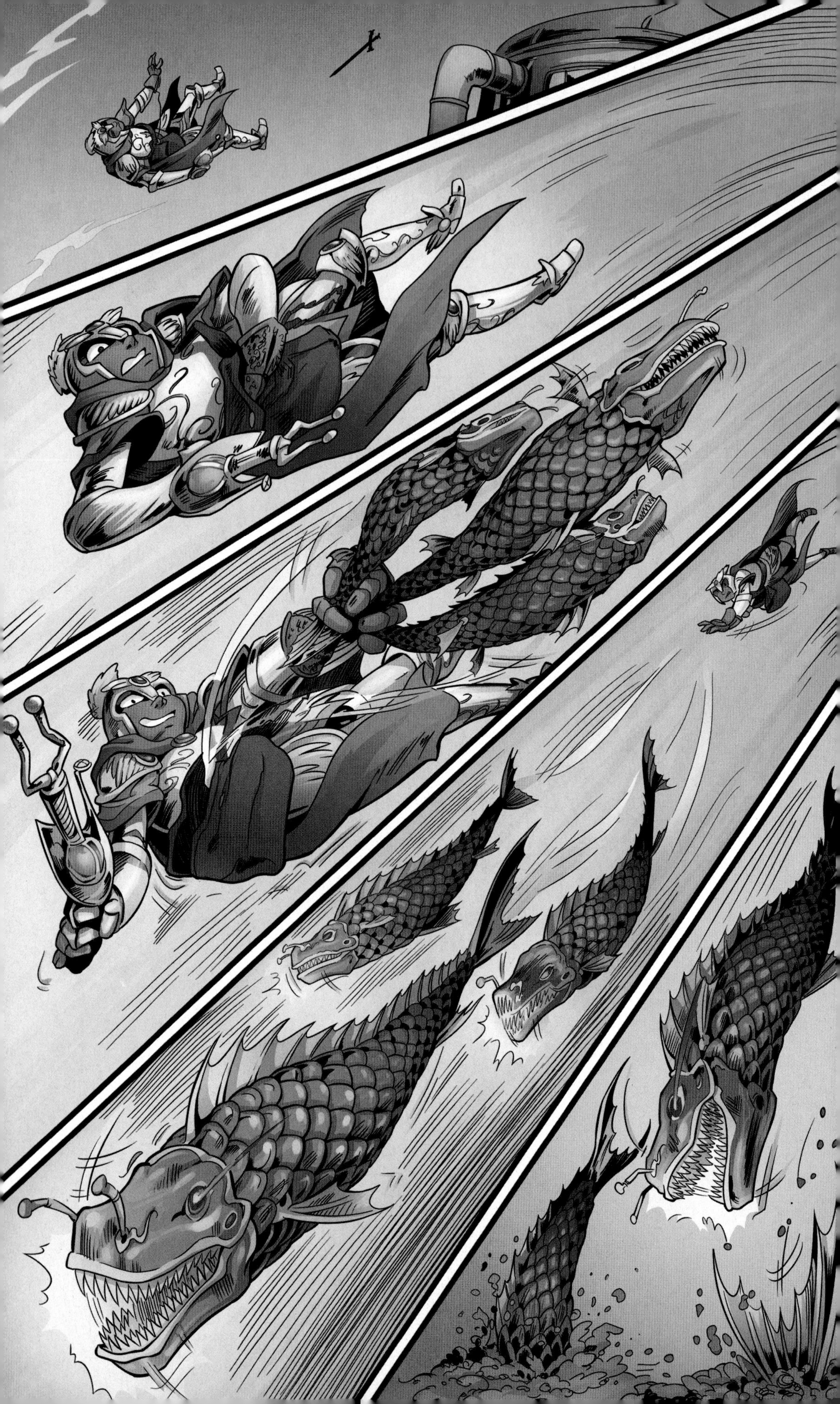

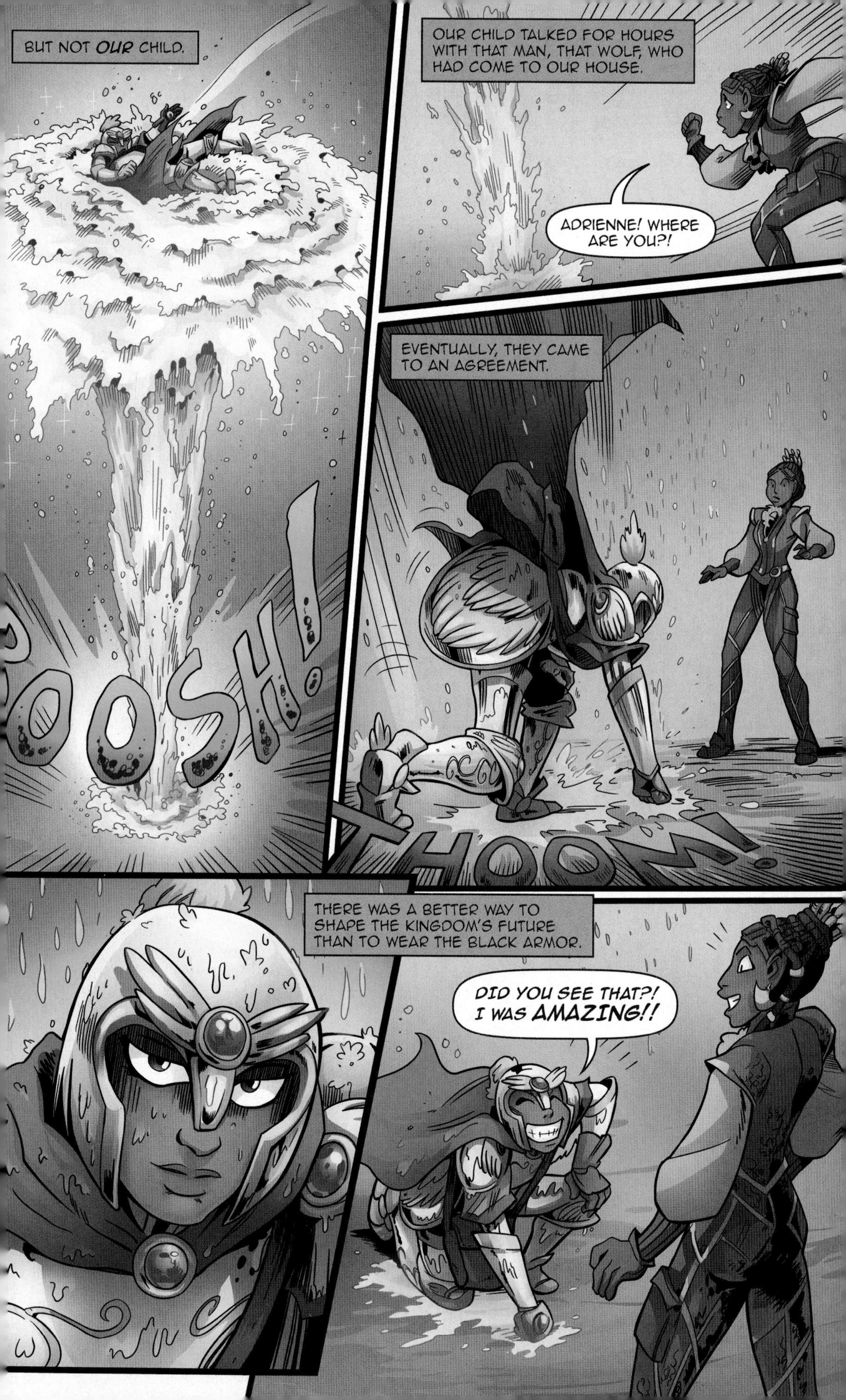
BUT NOT OUR CHILD.
FOOOSH!
OUR CHILD TALKED FOR HOURS WITH THAT MAN, THAT WOLF, WHO HAD COME TO OUR HOUSE.
ADRIENNE! WHERE ARE YOU?!
EVENTUALLY, THEY CAME TO AN AGREEMENT.
THOOM!
THERE WAS A BETTER WAY TO SHAPE THE KINGDOM'S FUTURE THAN TO WEAR THE BLACK ARMOR.
DID YOU SEE THAT?! I WAS AMAZING!!

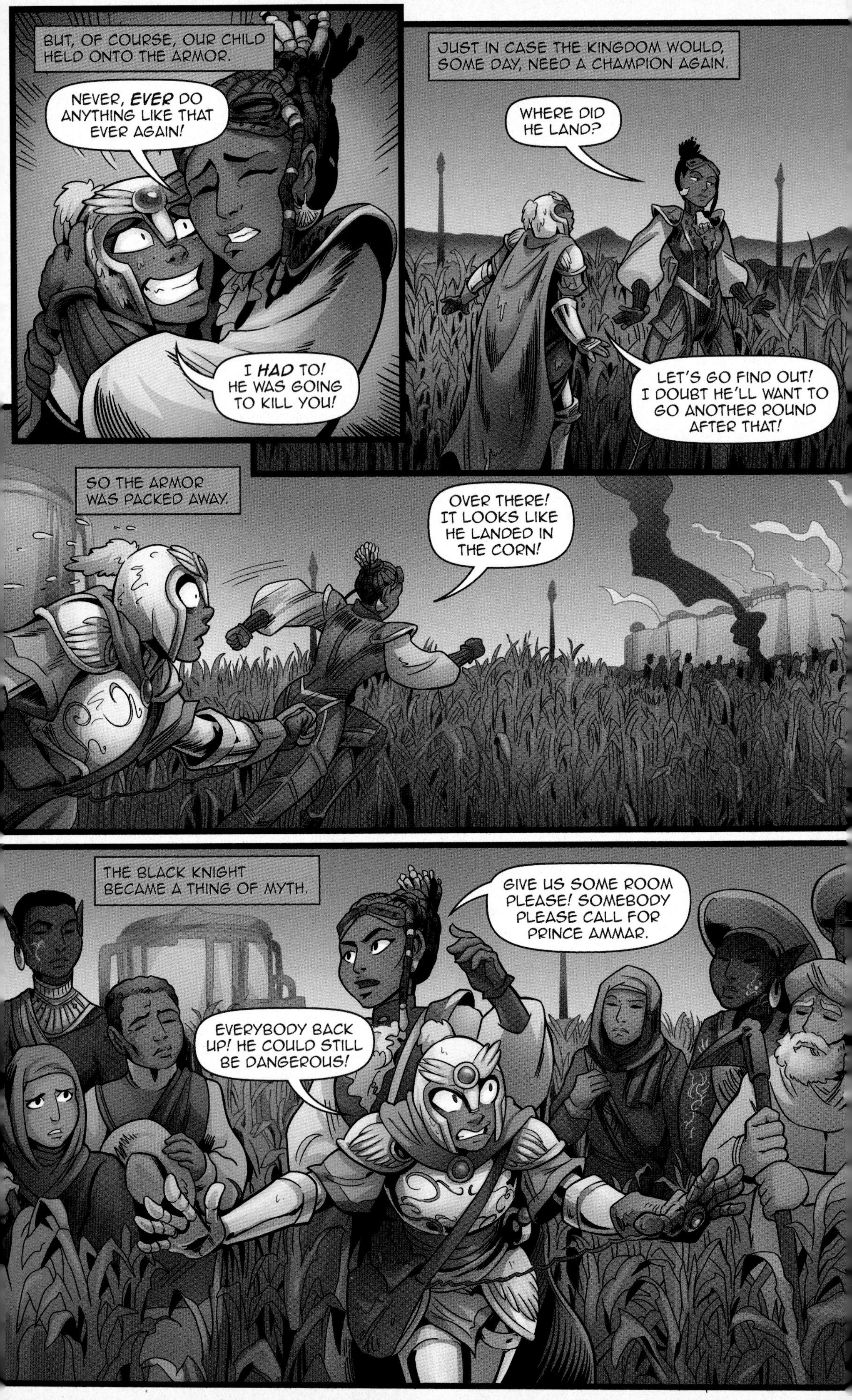
BUT, OF COURSE, OUR CHILD HELD ONTO THE ARMOR.
NEVER, **EVER** DO ANYTHING LIKE THAT EVER AGAIN!
I **HAD** TO! HE WAS GOING TO KILL YOU!
JUST IN CASE THE KINGDOM WOULD, SOME DAY, NEED A CHAMPION AGAIN.
WHERE DID HE LAND?
LET'S GO FIND OUT! I DOUBT HE'LL WANT TO GO ANOTHER ROUND AFTER THAT!
SO THE ARMOR WAS PACKED AWAY.
OVER THERE! IT LOOKS LIKE HE LANDED IN THE CORN!
THE BLACK KNIGHT BECAME A THING OF MYTH.
GIVE US SOME ROOM PLEASE! SOMEBODY PLEASE CALL FOR PRINCE AMMAR.
EVERYBODY BACK UP! HE COULD STILL BE DANGEROUS!

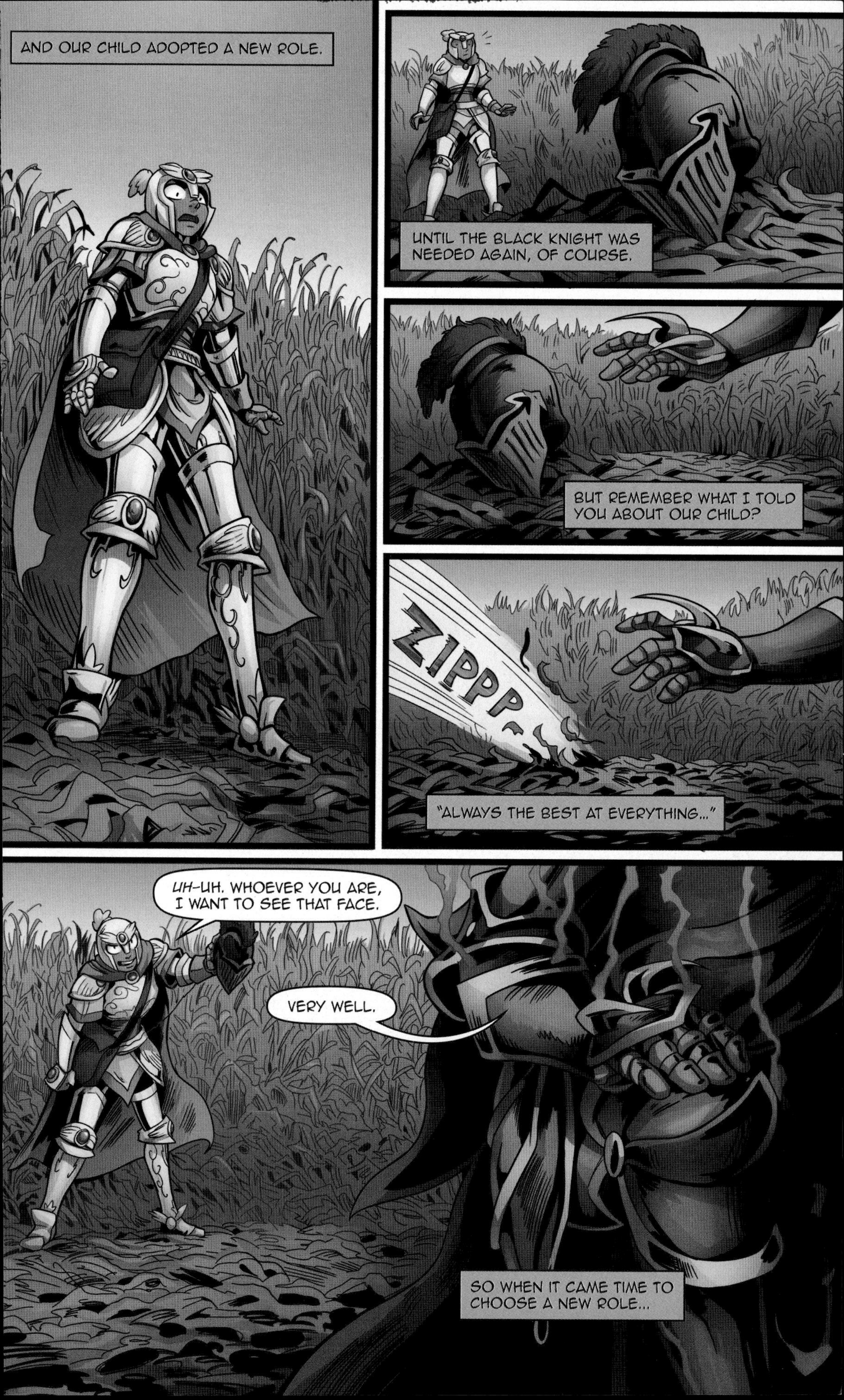
AND OUR CHILD ADOPTED A NEW ROLE.
UNTIL THE BLACK KNIGHT WAS NEEDED AGAIN, OF COURSE.
BUT REMEMBER WHAT I TOLD YOU ABOUT OUR CHILD?
ZIPPP
"ALWAYS THE BEST AT EVERYTHING..."
UH-UH. WHOEVER YOU ARE, I WANT TO SEE THAT FACE.
VERY WELL.
SO WHEN IT CAME TIME TO CHOOSE A NEW ROLE...

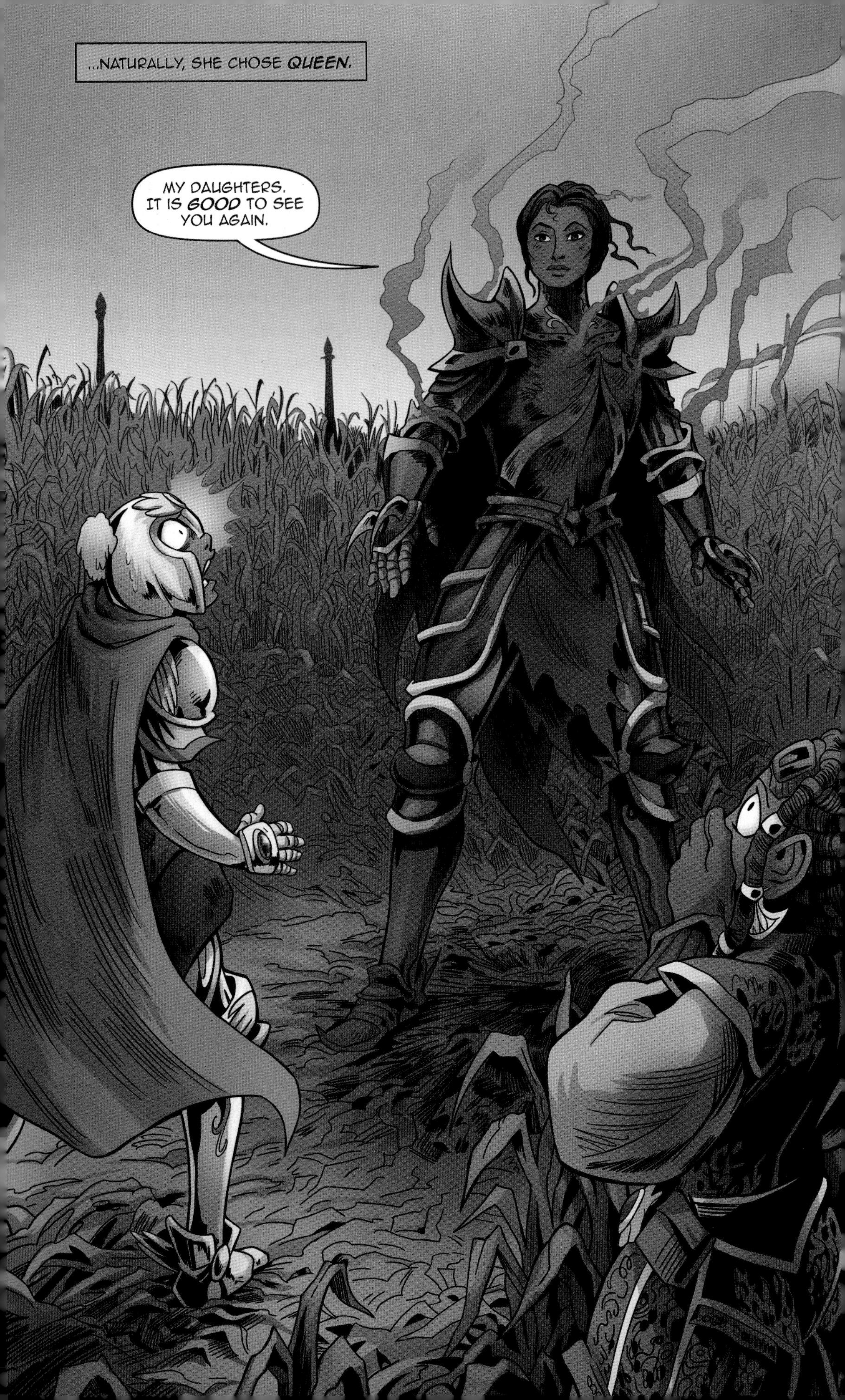
...NATURALLY, SHE CHOSE QUEEN.
MY DAUGHTERS. IT IS GOOD TO SEE YOU AGAIN.

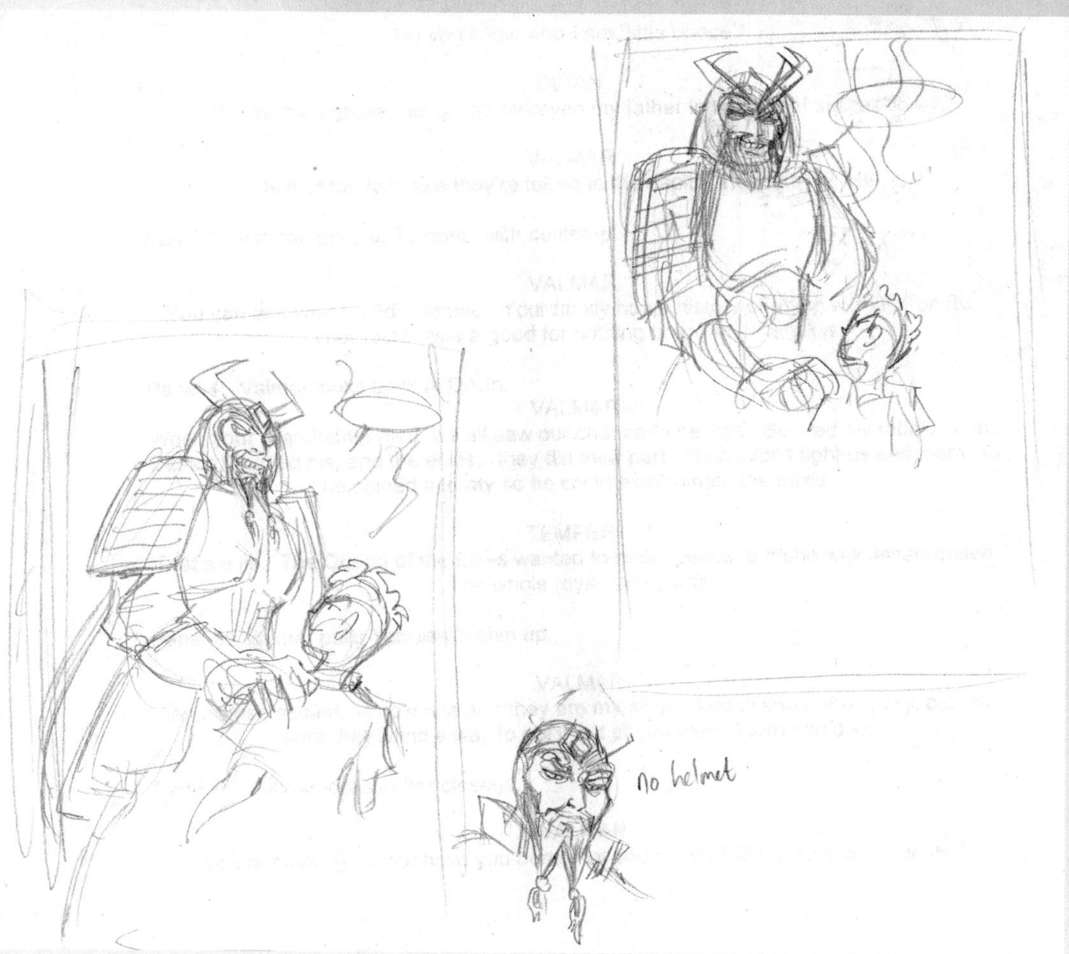
No helmet

VALMAR SKETCHES

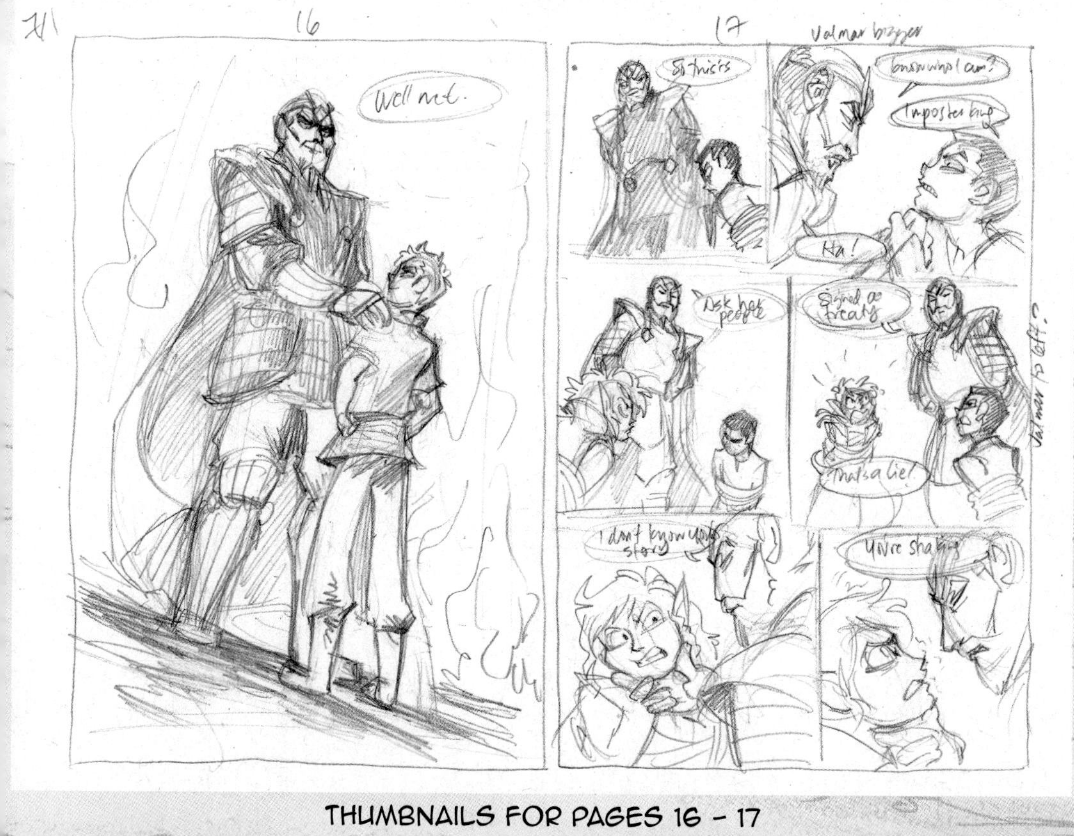
16
Well met.
17
Valmar bigger
So this is
Know who I am?
Imposter boy
Ha!
Ask her people
Signed a treaty
That's a lie!
Valmar to left?
I don't know your story
You're shaking

THUMBNAILS FOR PAGES 16 - 17

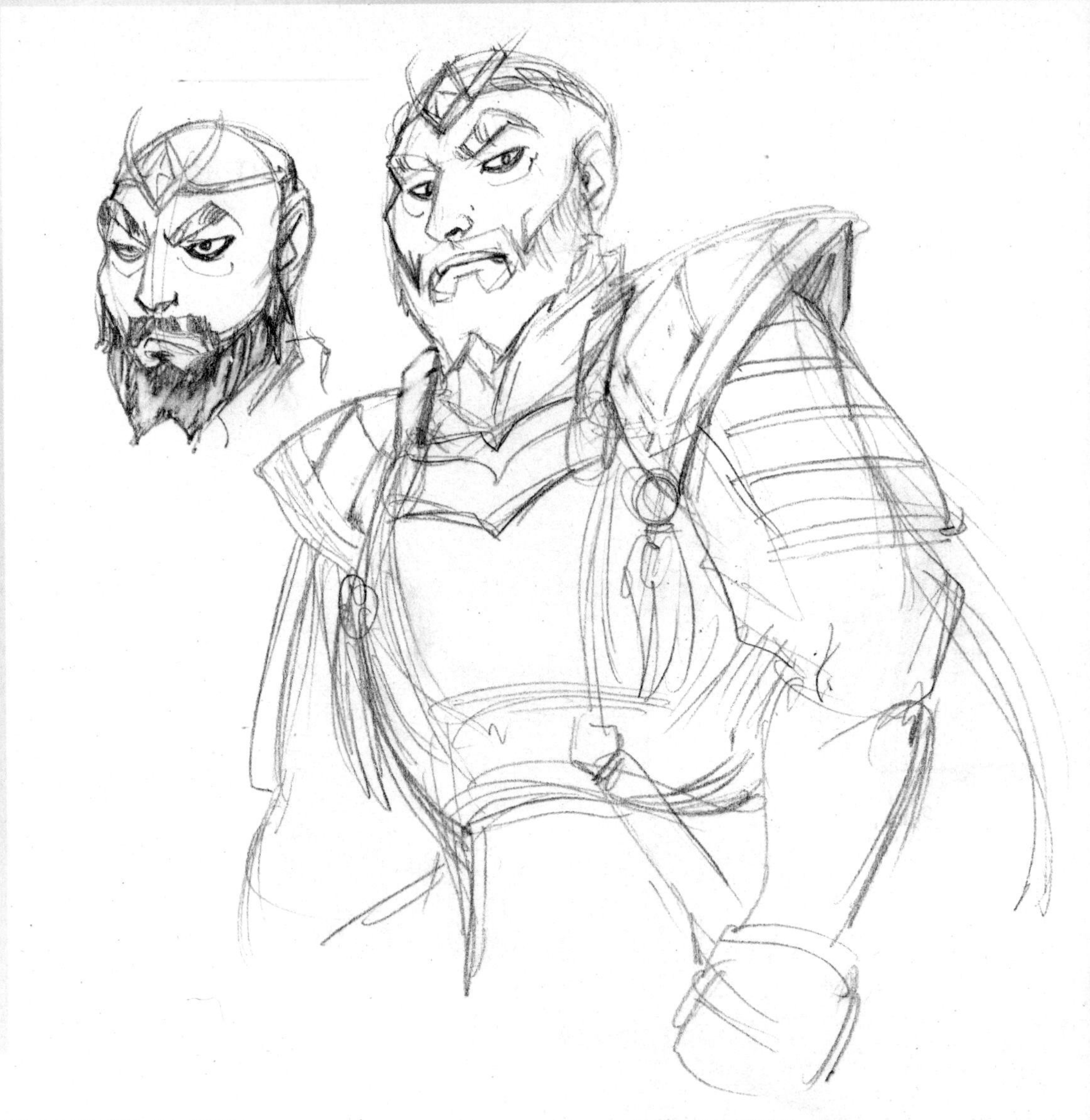

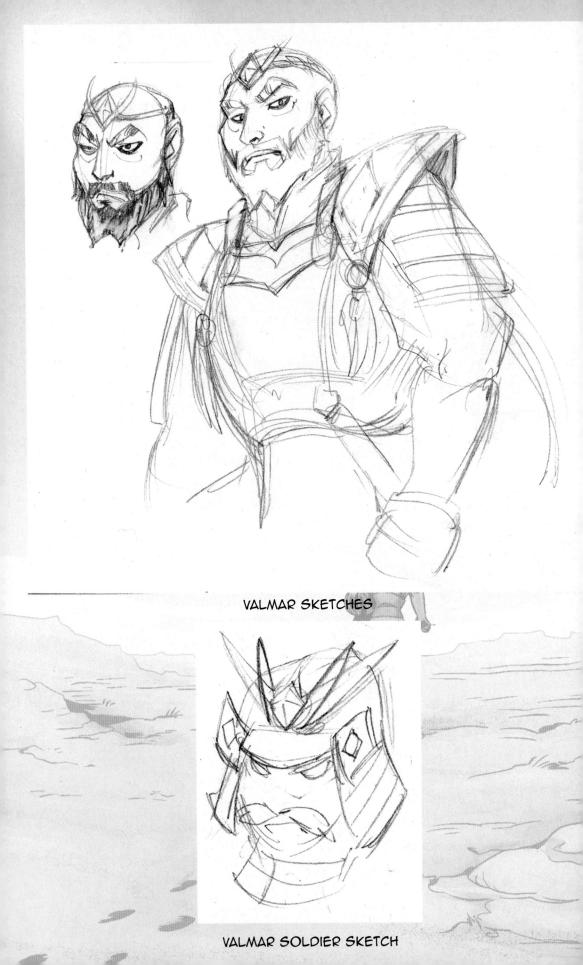

VALMAR SKETCHES

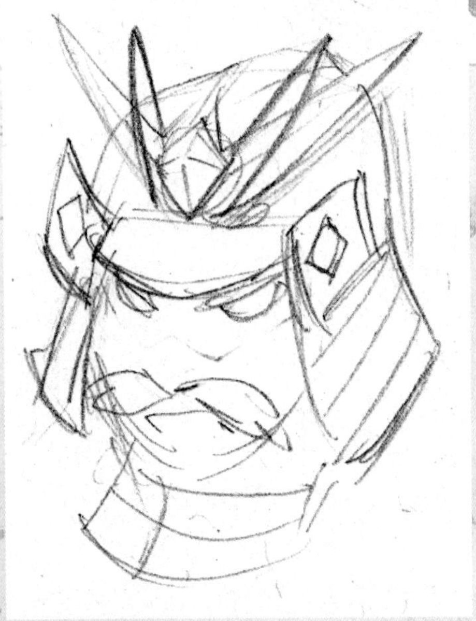

VALMAR SOLDIER SKETCH

Chapter Five: Into the Woods of the Wolves

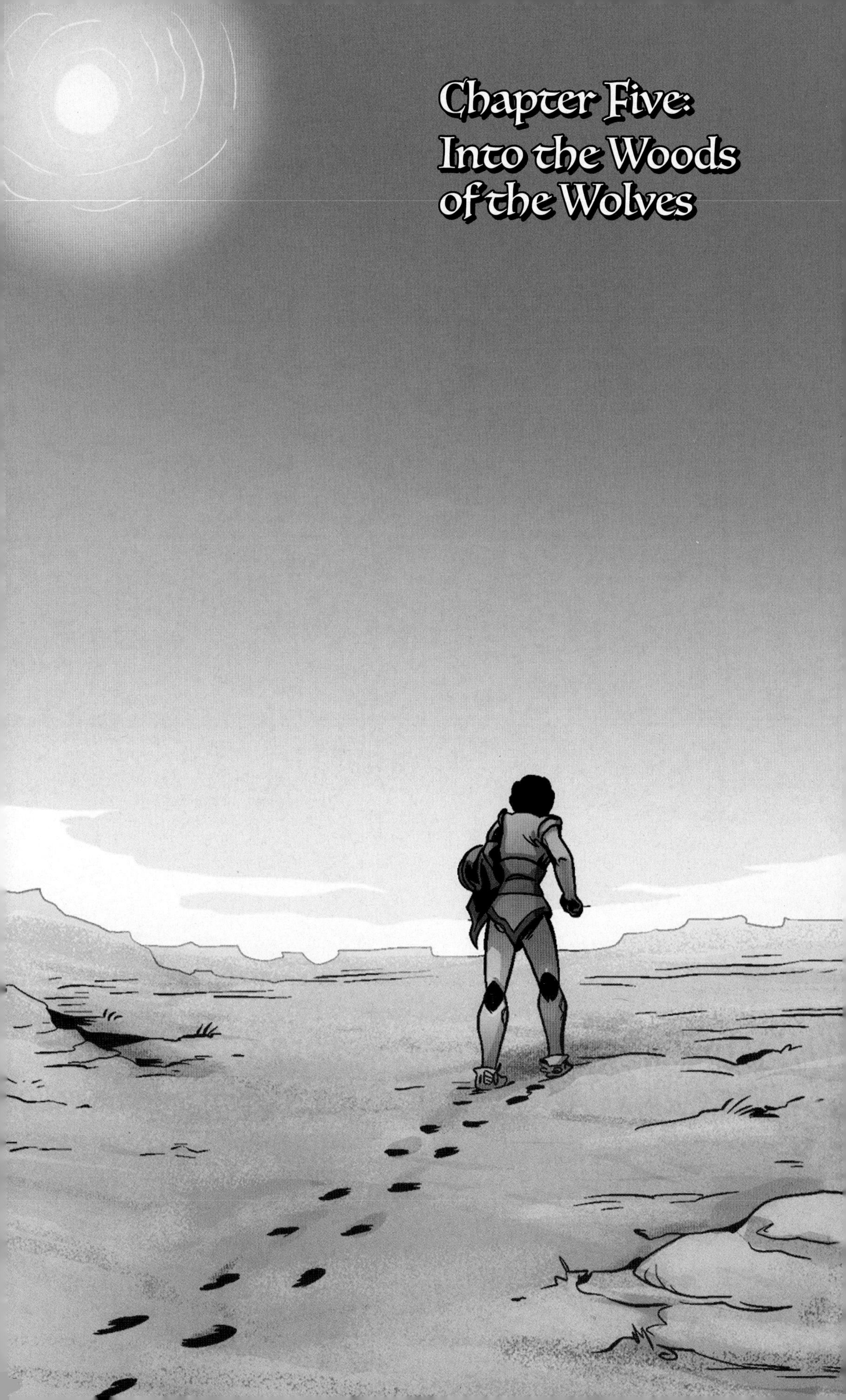

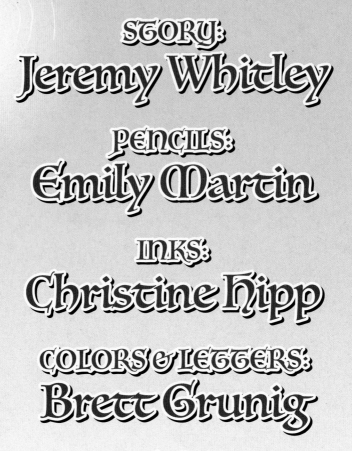

STORY:
Jeremy Whitley

PENCILS:
Emily Martin

INKS:
Christine Hipp

COLORS & LETTERS:
Brett Grunig

COVERA: Emily Martin

EDITORS:
Alicia Whitley (script)
Nicole D'Andria (comic)

Bryan Seaton: Publisher/ CEO • **Shawn Gabborin:** Editor In Chief
Jason Martin: Publisher-Danger Zone • **Nicole D'Andria:** Marketing Director/Editor
Jessica Lowrie: Social Media Czar • **Danielle Davison:** Executive Administrator
Chad Cicconi: Still Waiting For His Princess • **Shawn Pryor:** President of Creator Relations

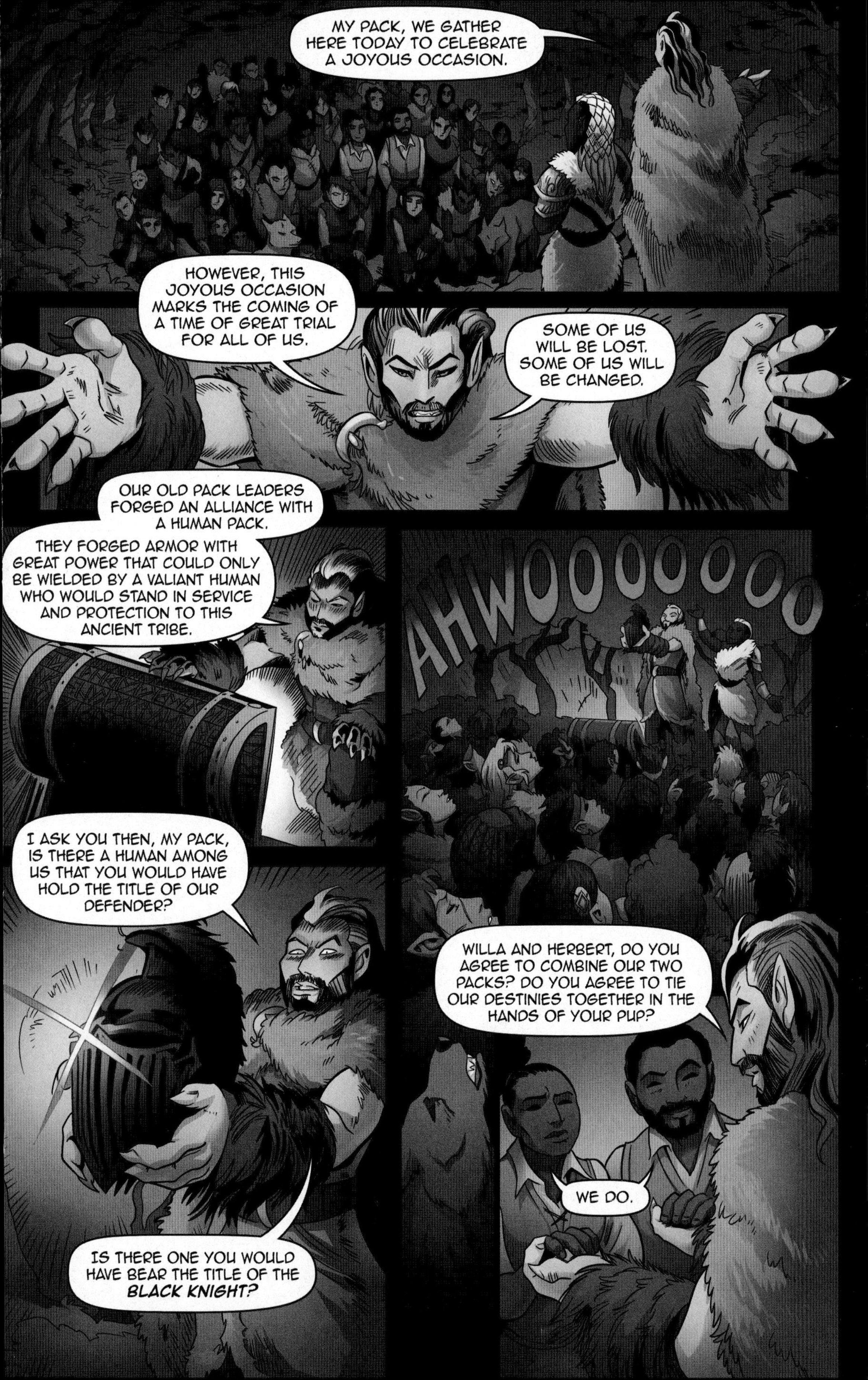
MY PACK, WE GATHER HERE TODAY TO CELEBRATE A JOYOUS OCCASION.
HOWEVER, THIS JOYOUS OCCASION MARKS THE COMING OF A TIME OF GREAT TRIAL FOR ALL OF US.
SOME OF US WILL BE LOST. SOME OF US WILL BE CHANGED.
OUR OLD PACK LEADERS FORGED AN ALLIANCE WITH A HUMAN PACK.
THEY FORGED ARMOR WITH GREAT POWER THAT COULD ONLY BE WIELDED BY A VALIANT HUMAN WHO WOULD STAND IN SERVICE AND PROTECTION TO THIS ANCIENT TRIBE.
I ASK YOU THEN, MY PACK, IS THERE A HUMAN AMONG US THAT YOU WOULD HAVE HOLD THE TITLE OF OUR DEFENDER?
IS THERE ONE YOU WOULD HAVE BEAR THE TITLE OF THE *BLACK KNIGHT?*
AHWOOOOOOO
WILLA AND HERBERT, DO YOU AGREE TO COMBINE OUR TWO PACKS? DO YOU AGREE TO TIE OUR DESTINIES TOGETHER IN THE HANDS OF YOUR PUP?
WE DO.

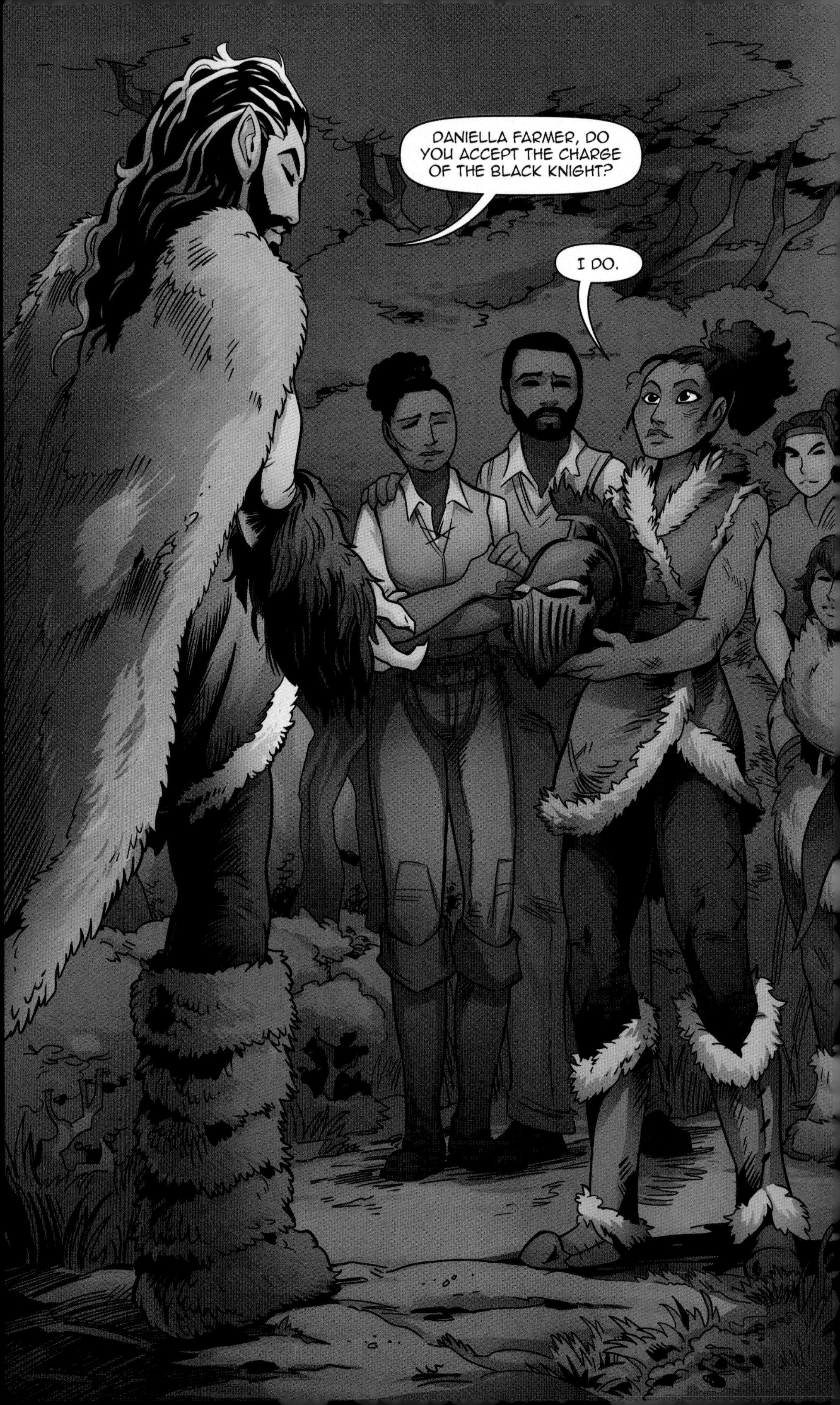
DANIELLA FARMER, DO YOU ACCEPT THE CHARGE OF THE BLACK KNIGHT?
I DO.

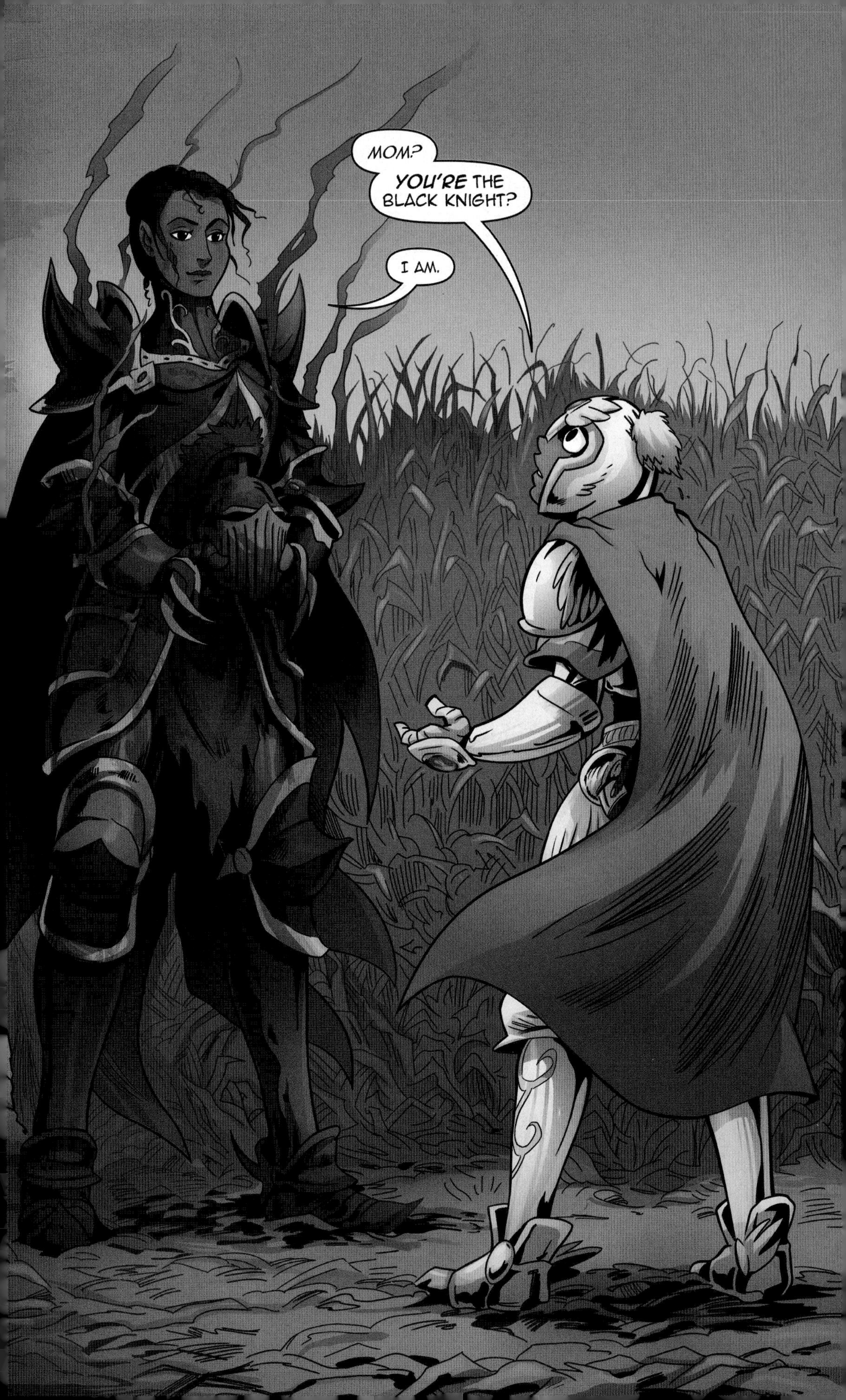
MOM?
YOU'RE THE BLACK KNIGHT?
I AM.

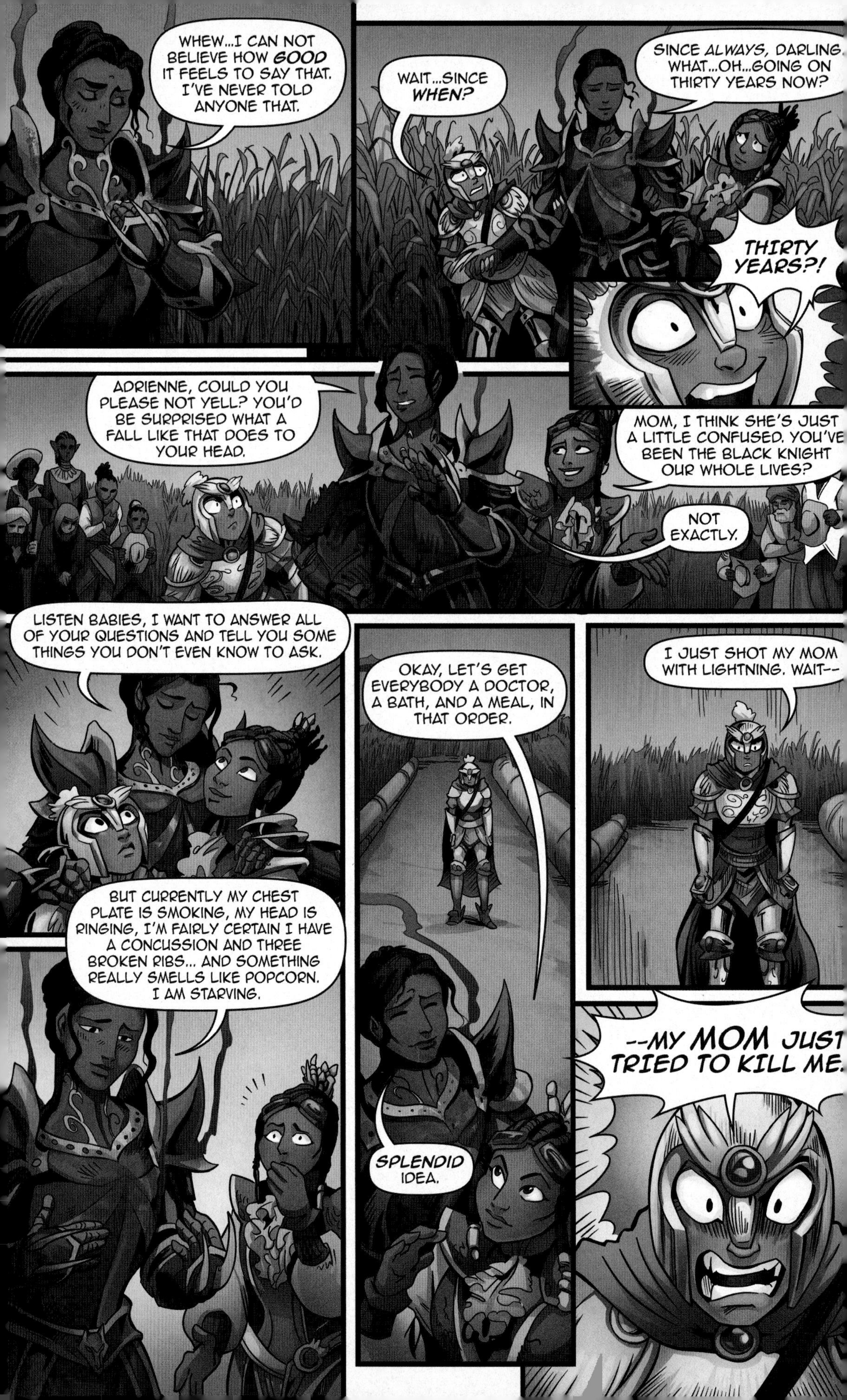
WHEW...I CAN NOT BELIEVE HOW GOOD IT FEELS TO SAY THAT. I'VE NEVER TOLD ANYONE THAT.
WAIT...SINCE WHEN?
SINCE ALWAYS, DARLING. WHAT...OH...GOING ON THIRTY YEARS NOW?
THIRTY YEARS?!
ADRIENNE, COULD YOU PLEASE NOT YELL? YOU'D BE SURPRISED WHAT A FALL LIKE THAT DOES TO YOUR HEAD.
MOM, I THINK SHE'S JUST A LITTLE CONFUSED. YOU'VE BEEN THE BLACK KNIGHT OUR WHOLE LIVES?
NOT EXACTLY.
LISTEN BABIES, I WANT TO ANSWER ALL OF YOUR QUESTIONS AND TELL YOU SOME THINGS YOU DON'T EVEN KNOW TO ASK.
BUT CURRENTLY MY CHEST PLATE IS SMOKING, MY HEAD IS RINGING, I'M FAIRLY CERTAIN I HAVE A CONCUSSION AND THREE BROKEN RIBS... AND SOMETHING REALLY SMELLS LIKE POPCORN. I AM STARVING.
OKAY, LET'S GET EVERYBODY A DOCTOR, A BATH, AND A MEAL, IN THAT ORDER.
SPLENDID IDEA.
I JUST SHOT MY MOM WITH LIGHTNING. WAIT--
--MY MOM JUST TRIED TO KILL ME.

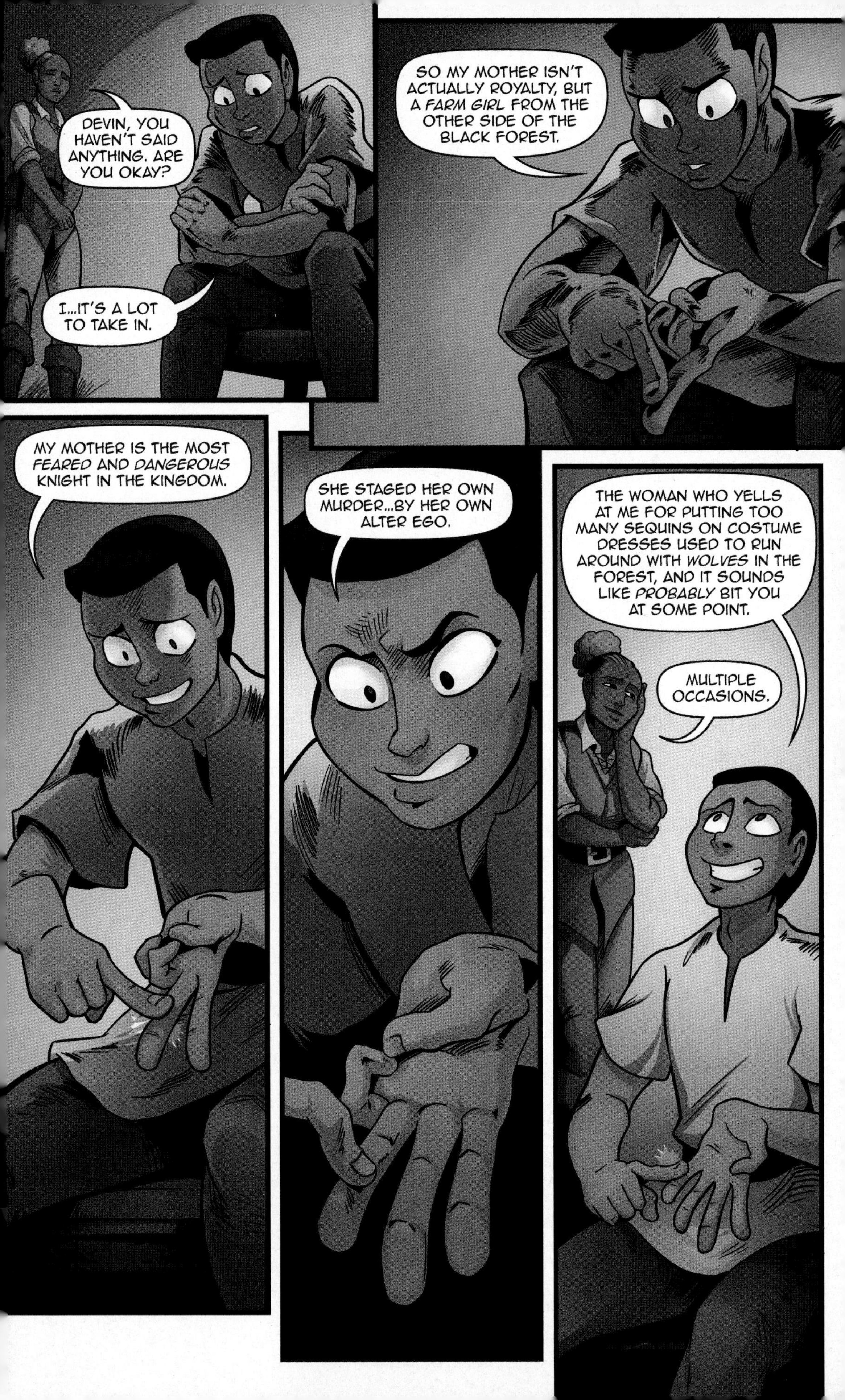
DEVIN, YOU HAVEN'T SAID ANYTHING. ARE YOU OKAY?
I...IT'S A LOT TO TAKE IN.
SO MY MOTHER ISN'T ACTUALLY ROYALTY, BUT A *FARM GIRL* FROM THE OTHER SIDE OF THE BLACK FOREST.
MY MOTHER IS THE MOST *FEARED* AND *DANGEROUS* KNIGHT IN THE KINGDOM.
SHE STAGED HER OWN MURDER...BY HER OWN ALTER EGO.
THE WOMAN WHO YELLS AT ME FOR PUTTING TOO MANY SEQUINS ON COSTUME DRESSES USED TO RUN AROUND WITH *WOLVES* IN THE FOREST, AND IT SOUNDS LIKE *PROBABLY* BIT YOU AT SOME POINT.
MULTIPLE OCCASIONS.

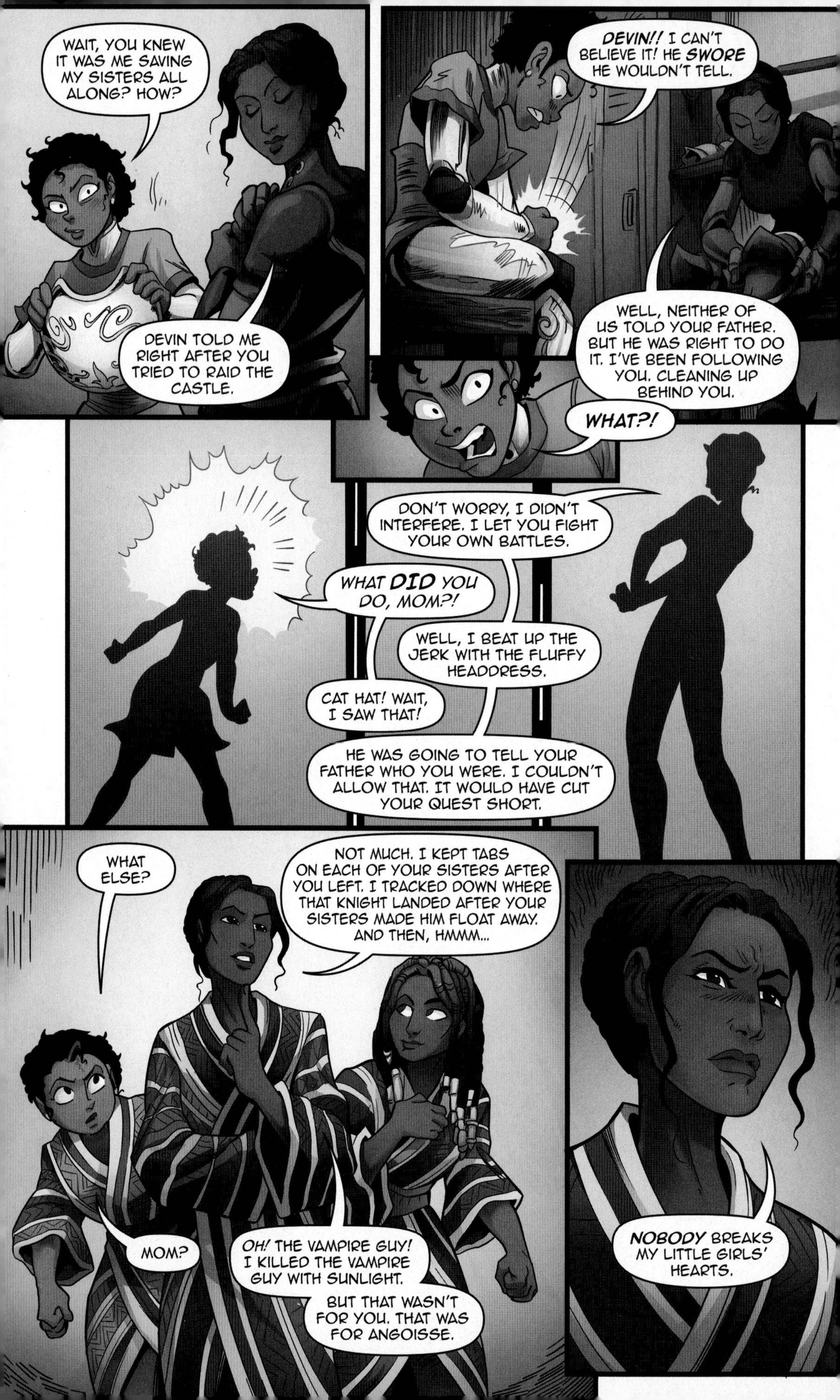

WAIT, YOU KNEW IT WAS ME SAVING MY SISTERS ALL ALONG? HOW?
DEVIN TOLD ME RIGHT AFTER YOU TRIED TO RAID THE CASTLE.
DEVIN!! I CAN'T BELIEVE IT! HE SWORE HE WOULDN'T TELL.
WELL, NEITHER OF US TOLD YOUR FATHER. BUT HE WAS RIGHT TO DO IT. I'VE BEEN FOLLOWING YOU. CLEANING UP BEHIND YOU.
WHAT?!
DON'T WORRY, I DIDN'T INTERFERE. I LET YOU FIGHT YOUR OWN BATTLES.
WHAT DID YOU DO, MOM?!
WELL, I BEAT UP THE JERK WITH THE FLUFFY HEADDRESS.
CAT HAT! WAIT, I SAW THAT!
HE WAS GOING TO TELL YOUR FATHER WHO YOU WERE. I COULDN'T ALLOW THAT. IT WOULD HAVE CUT YOUR QUEST SHORT.
WHAT ELSE?
NOT MUCH. I KEPT TABS ON EACH OF YOUR SISTERS AFTER YOU LEFT. I TRACKED DOWN WHERE THAT KNIGHT LANDED AFTER YOUR SISTERS MADE HIM FLOAT AWAY. AND THEN, HMMM...
MOM?
OH! THE VAMPIRE GUY! I KILLED THE VAMPIRE GUY WITH SUNLIGHT.
BUT THAT WASN'T FOR YOU. THAT WAS FOR ANGOISSE.
NOBODY BREAKS MY LITTLE GIRLS' HEARTS.

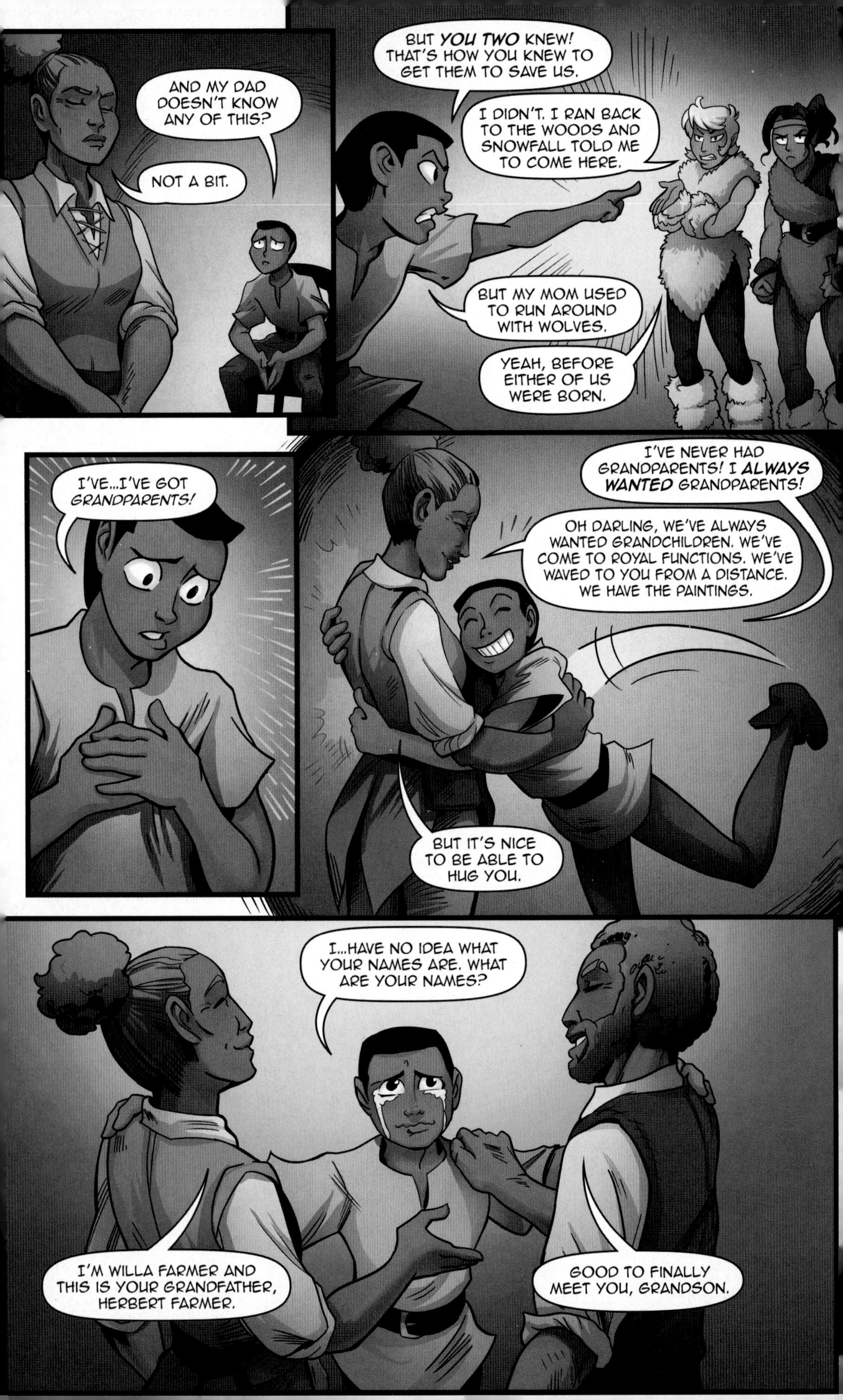
AND MY DAD DOESN'T KNOW ANY OF THIS?
NOT A BIT.
BUT ***YOU TWO*** KNEW! THAT'S HOW YOU KNEW TO GET THEM TO SAVE US.
I DIDN'T. I RAN BACK TO THE WOODS AND SNOWFALL TOLD ME TO COME HERE.
BUT MY MOM USED TO RUN AROUND WITH WOLVES.
YEAH, BEFORE EITHER OF US WERE BORN.
I'VE...I'VE GOT GRANDPARENTS!
I'VE NEVER HAD GRANDPARENTS! I ***ALWAYS WANTED*** GRANDPARENTS!
OH DARLING, WE'VE ALWAYS WANTED GRANDCHILDREN. WE'VE COME TO ROYAL FUNCTIONS. WE'VE WAVED TO YOU FROM A DISTANCE. WE HAVE THE PAINTINGS.
BUT IT'S NICE TO BE ABLE TO HUG YOU.
I...HAVE NO IDEA WHAT YOUR NAMES ARE. WHAT ARE YOUR NAMES?
I'M WILLA FARMER AND THIS IS YOUR GRANDFATHER, HERBERT FARMER.
GOOD TO FINALLY MEET YOU, GRANDSON.

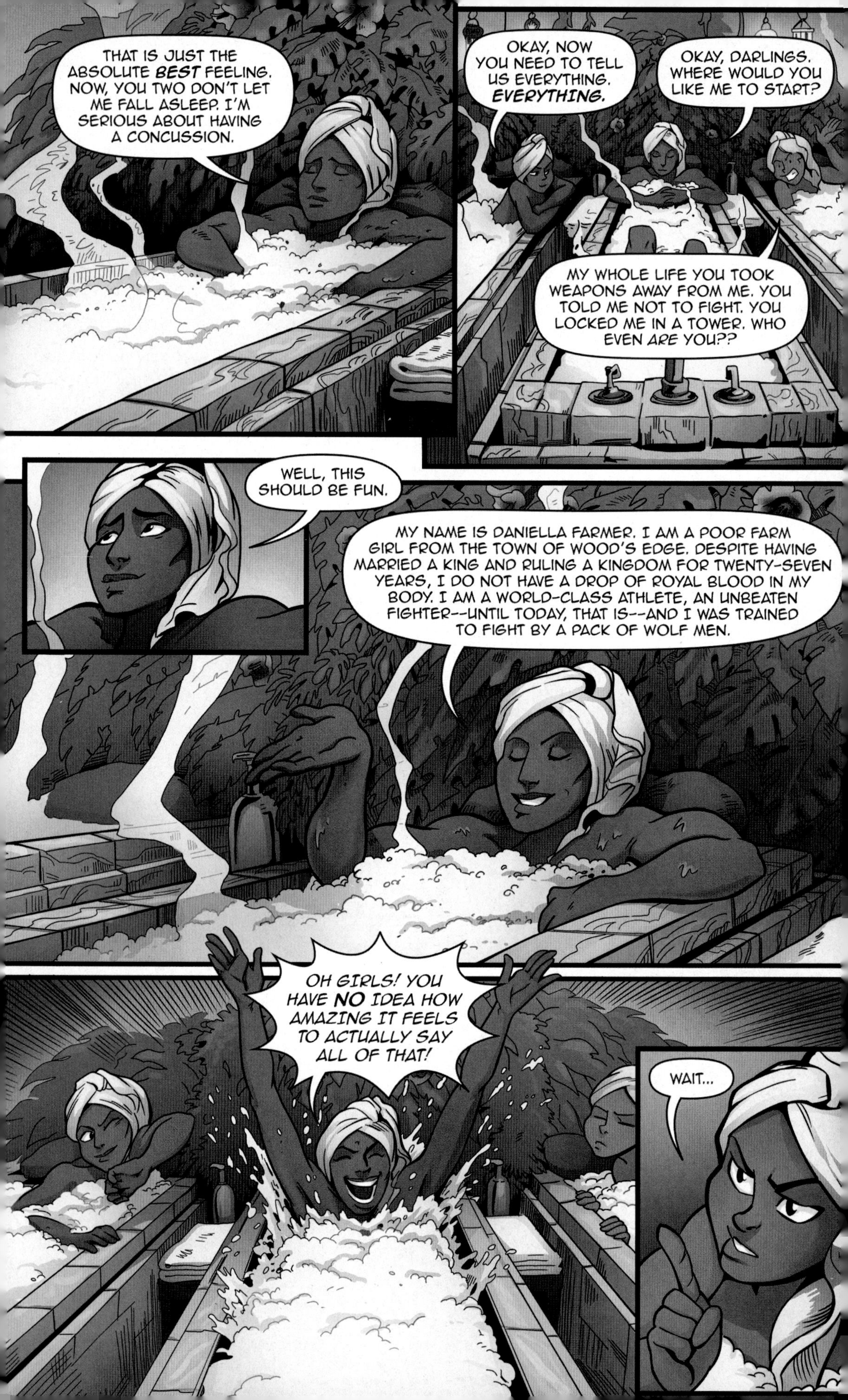
THAT IS JUST THE ABSOLUTE **BEST** FEELING. NOW, YOU TWO DON'T LET ME FALL ASLEEP. I'M SERIOUS ABOUT HAVING A CONCUSSION.
OKAY, NOW YOU NEED TO TELL US EVERYTHING. ***EVERYTHING.***
OKAY, DARLINGS. WHERE WOULD YOU LIKE ME TO START?
MY WHOLE LIFE YOU TOOK WEAPONS AWAY FROM ME. YOU TOLD ME NOT TO FIGHT. YOU LOCKED ME IN A TOWER. WHO EVEN *ARE* YOU??
WELL, THIS SHOULD BE FUN.
MY NAME IS DANIELLA FARMER. I AM A POOR FARM GIRL FROM THE TOWN OF WOOD'S EDGE. DESPITE HAVING MARRIED A KING AND RULING A KINGDOM FOR TWENTY-SEVEN YEARS, I DO NOT HAVE A DROP OF ROYAL BLOOD IN MY BODY. I AM A WORLD-CLASS ATHLETE, AN UNBEATEN FIGHTER--UNTIL TODAY, THAT IS--AND I WAS TRAINED TO FIGHT BY A PACK OF WOLF MEN.
OH GIRLS! YOU HAVE **NO** IDEA HOW AMAZING IT FEELS TO ACTUALLY SAY ALL OF THAT!
WAIT...

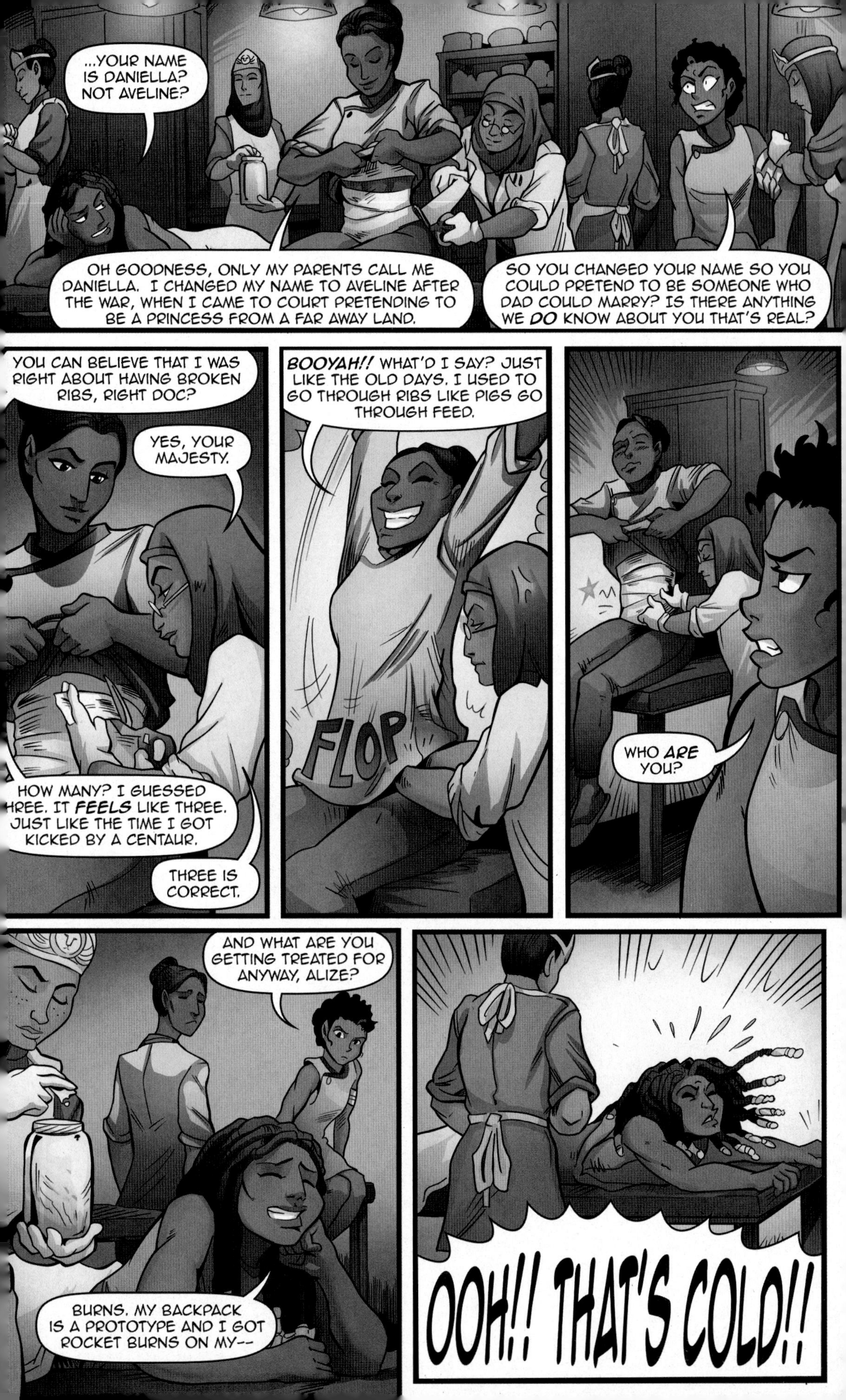
...YOUR NAME IS DANIELLA? NOT AVELINE?
OH GOODNESS, ONLY MY PARENTS CALL ME DANIELLA. I CHANGED MY NAME TO AVELINE AFTER THE WAR, WHEN I CAME TO COURT PRETENDING TO BE A PRINCESS FROM A FAR AWAY LAND.
SO YOU CHANGED YOUR NAME SO YOU COULD PRETEND TO BE SOMEONE WHO DAD COULD MARRY? IS THERE ANYTHING WE *DO* KNOW ABOUT YOU THAT'S REAL?
YOU CAN BELIEVE THAT I WAS RIGHT ABOUT HAVING BROKEN RIBS, RIGHT DOC?
YES, YOUR MAJESTY.
HOW MANY? I GUESSED THREE. IT *FEELS* LIKE THREE. JUST LIKE THE TIME I GOT KICKED BY A CENTAUR.
THREE IS CORRECT.
BOOYAH!! WHAT'D I SAY? JUST LIKE THE OLD DAYS. I USED TO GO THROUGH RIBS LIKE PIGS GO THROUGH FEED.
FLOP
WHO *ARE* YOU?
AND WHAT ARE YOU GETTING TREATED FOR ANYWAY, ALIZE?
BURNS. MY BACKPACK IS A PROTOTYPE AND I GOT ROCKET BURNS ON MY--
OOH!! THAT'S COLD!!

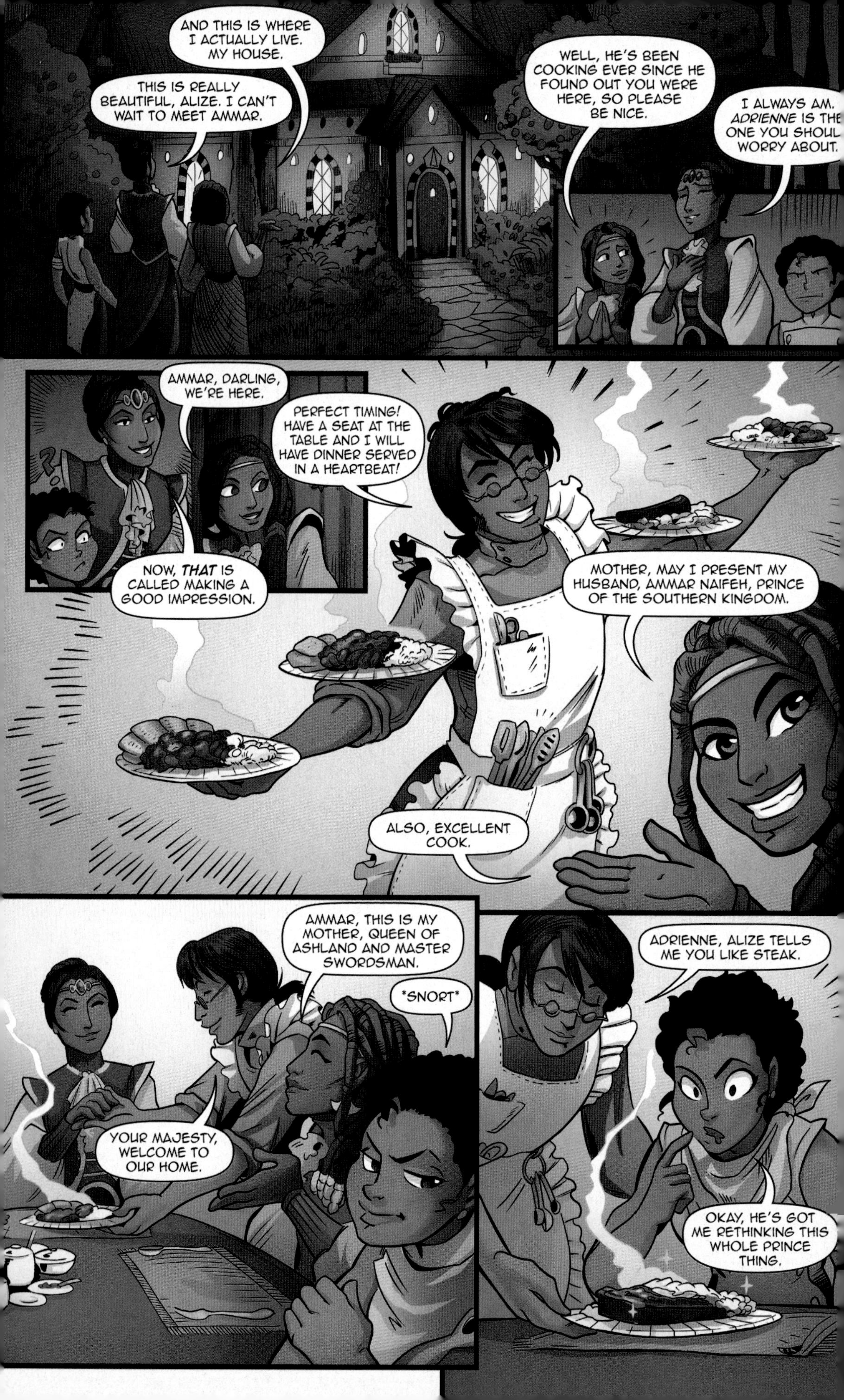
AND THIS IS WHERE I ACTUALLY LIVE. MY HOUSE.
THIS IS REALLY BEAUTIFUL, ALIZE. I CAN'T WAIT TO MEET AMMAR.
WELL, HE'S BEEN COOKING EVER SINCE HE FOUND OUT YOU WERE HERE, SO PLEASE BE NICE.
I ALWAYS AM. ADRIENNE IS THE ONE YOU SHOUL WORRY ABOUT.
AMMAR, DARLING, WE'RE HERE.
PERFECT TIMING! HAVE A SEAT AT THE TABLE AND I WILL HAVE DINNER SERVED IN A HEARTBEAT!
NOW, THAT IS CALLED MAKING A GOOD IMPRESSION.
MOTHER, MAY I PRESENT MY HUSBAND, AMMAR NAIFEH, PRINCE OF THE SOUTHERN KINGDOM.
ALSO, EXCELLENT COOK.
AMMAR, THIS IS MY MOTHER, QUEEN OF ASHLAND AND MASTER SWORDSMAN.
SNORT
YOUR MAJESTY, WELCOME TO OUR HOME.
ADRIENNE, ALIZE TELLS ME YOU LIKE STEAK.
OKAY, HE'S GOT ME RETHINKING THIS WHOLE PRINCE THING.

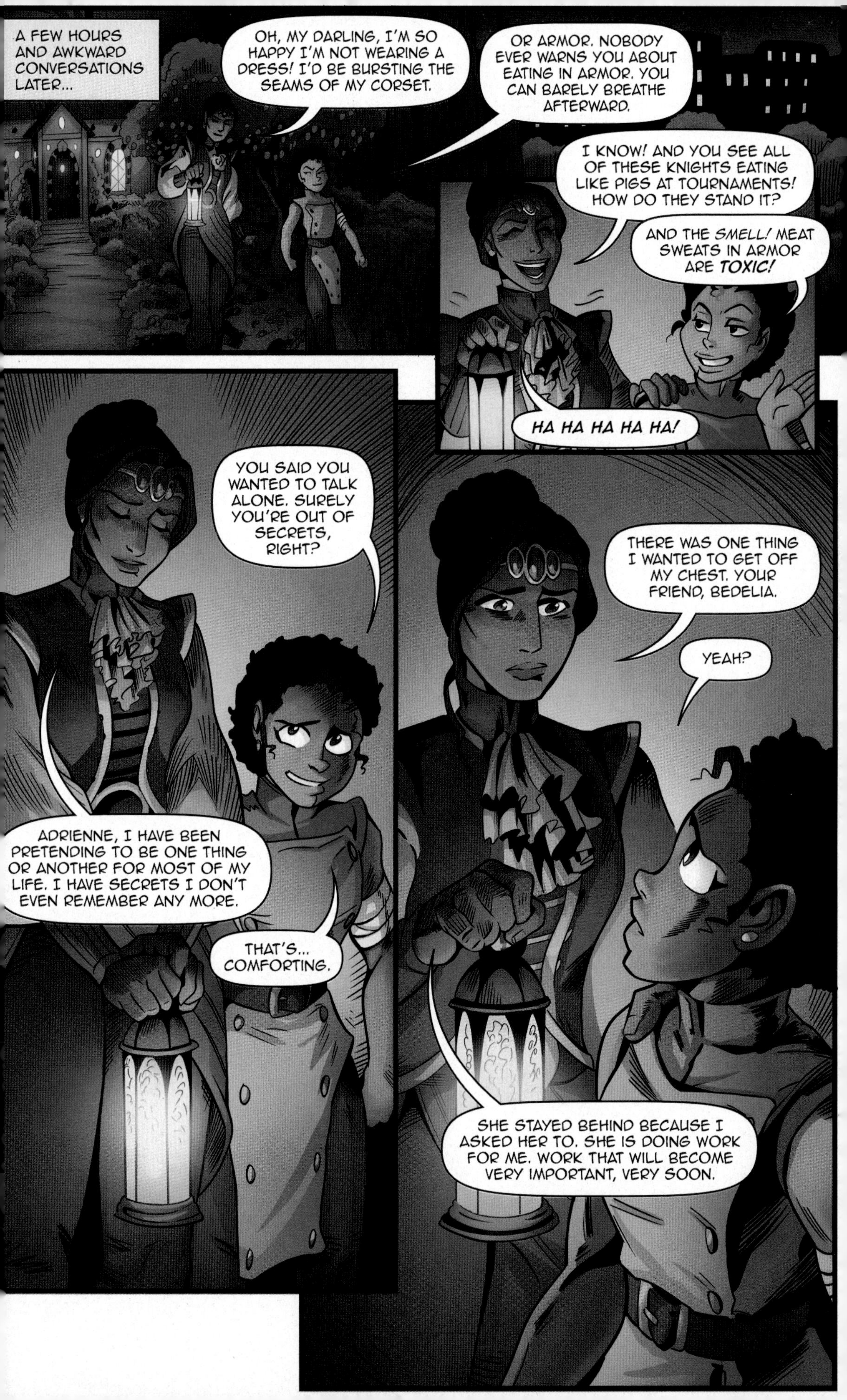
A FEW HOURS AND AWKWARD CONVERSATIONS LATER...
OH, MY DARLING, I'M SO HAPPY I'M NOT WEARING A DRESS! I'D BE BURSTING THE SEAMS OF MY CORSET.
OR ARMOR. NOBODY EVER WARNS YOU ABOUT EATING IN ARMOR. YOU CAN BARELY BREATHE AFTERWARD.
I KNOW! AND YOU SEE ALL OF THESE KNIGHTS EATING LIKE PIGS AT TOURNAMENTS! HOW DO THEY STAND IT?
AND THE *SMELL!* MEAT SWEATS IN ARMOR ARE ***TOXIC!***
HA HA HA HA HA!
YOU SAID YOU WANTED TO TALK ALONE. SURELY YOU'RE OUT OF SECRETS, RIGHT?
ADRIENNE, I HAVE BEEN PRETENDING TO BE ONE THING OR ANOTHER FOR MOST OF MY LIFE. I HAVE SECRETS I DON'T EVEN REMEMBER ANY MORE.
THAT'S... COMFORTING.
THERE WAS ONE THING I WANTED TO GET OFF MY CHEST. YOUR FRIEND, BEDELIA.
YEAH?
SHE STAYED BEHIND BECAUSE I ASKED HER TO. SHE IS DOING WORK FOR ME. WORK THAT WILL BECOME VERY IMPORTANT, VERY SOON.

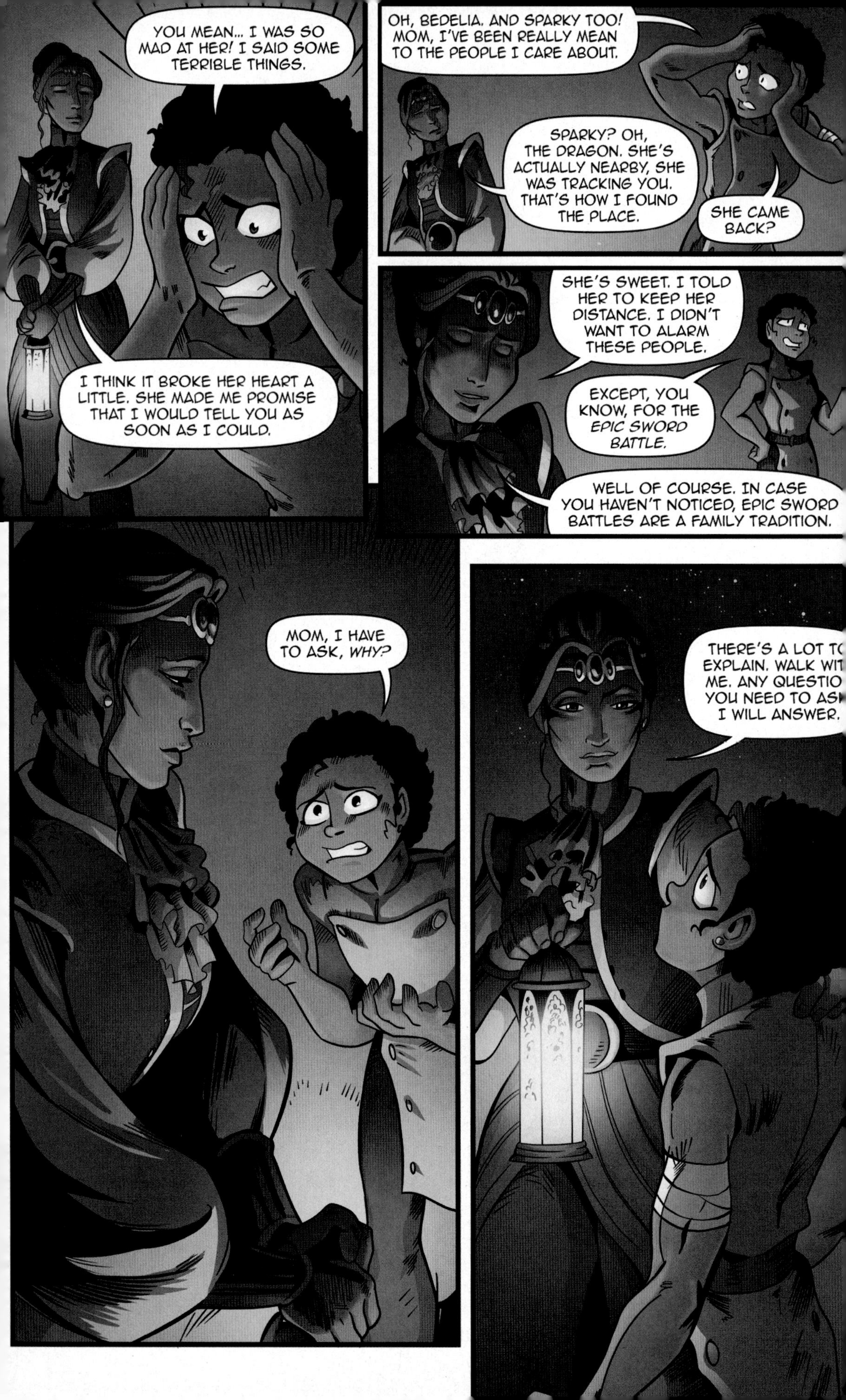

YOU MEAN... I WAS SO MAD AT HER! I SAID SOME TERRIBLE THINGS.
I THINK IT BROKE HER HEART A LITTLE. SHE MADE ME PROMISE THAT I WOULD TELL YOU AS SOON AS I COULD.
OH, BEDELIA. AND SPARKY TOO! MOM, I'VE BEEN REALLY MEAN TO THE PEOPLE I CARE ABOUT.
SPARKY? OH, THE DRAGON. SHE'S ACTUALLY NEARBY, SHE WAS TRACKING YOU. THAT'S HOW I FOUND THE PLACE.
SHE CAME BACK?
SHE'S SWEET. I TOLD HER TO KEEP HER DISTANCE. I DIDN'T WANT TO ALARM THESE PEOPLE.
EXCEPT, YOU KNOW, FOR THE *EPIC SWORD BATTLE.*
WELL OF COURSE. IN CASE YOU HAVEN'T NOTICED, EPIC SWORD BATTLES ARE A FAMILY TRADITION.
MOM, I HAVE TO ASK, *WHY?*
THERE'S A LOT T EXPLAIN. WALK WIT ME. ANY QUESTIO YOU NEED TO AS I WILL ANSWER.

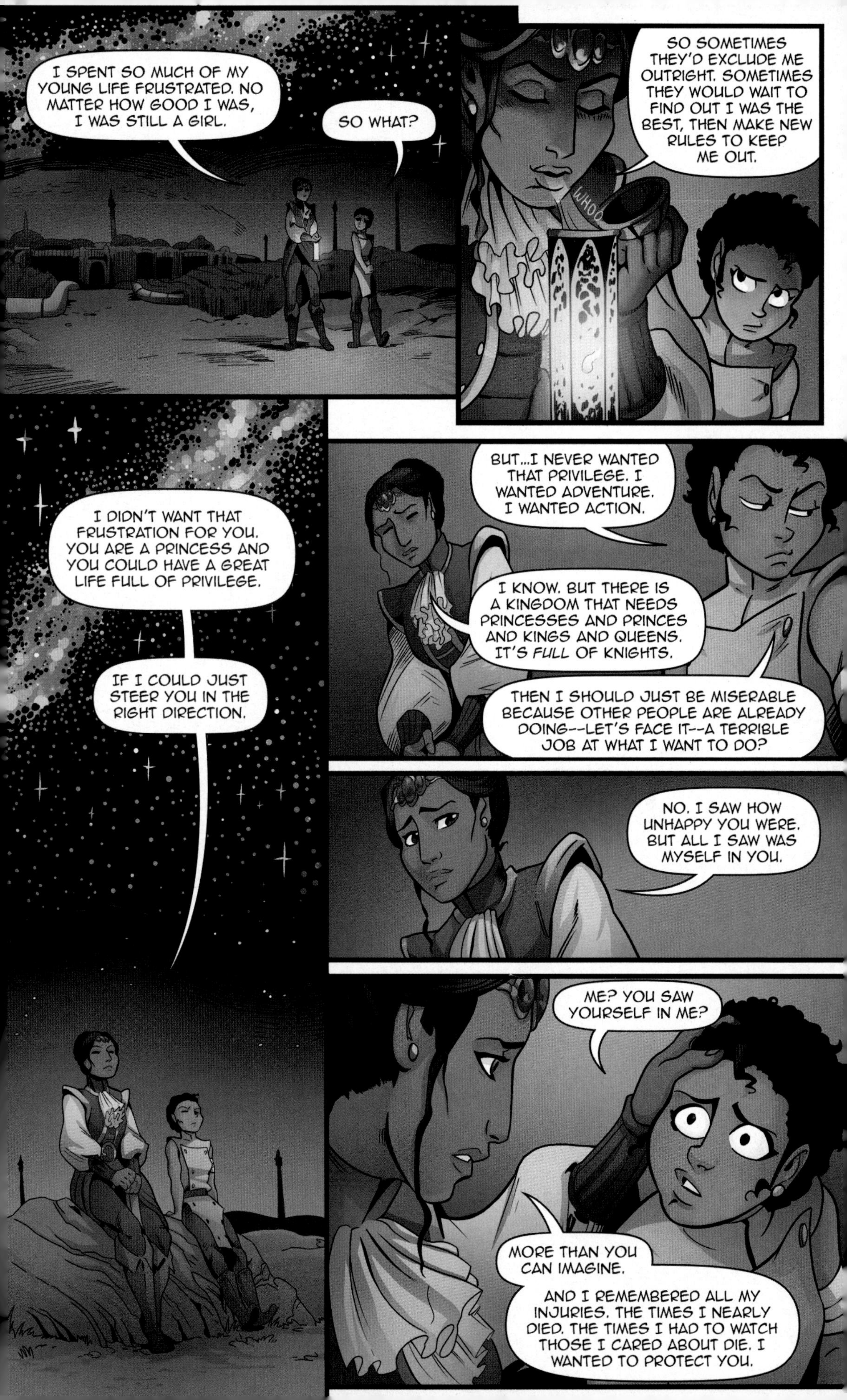

I SPENT SO MUCH OF MY YOUNG LIFE FRUSTRATED. NO MATTER HOW GOOD I WAS, I WAS STILL A GIRL.
SO WHAT?
SO SOMETIMES THEY'D EXCLUDE ME OUTRIGHT. SOMETIMES THEY WOULD WAIT TO FIND OUT I WAS THE BEST, THEN MAKE NEW RULES TO KEEP ME OUT.
WHOO
I DIDN'T WANT THAT FRUSTRATION FOR YOU. YOU ARE A PRINCESS AND YOU COULD HAVE A GREAT LIFE FULL OF PRIVILEGE.
IF I COULD JUST STEER YOU IN THE RIGHT DIRECTION.
BUT...I NEVER WANTED THAT PRIVILEGE. I WANTED ADVENTURE. I WANTED ACTION.
I KNOW. BUT THERE IS A KINGDOM THAT NEEDS PRINCESSES AND PRINCES AND KINGS AND QUEENS. IT'S *FULL* OF KNIGHTS.
THEN I SHOULD JUST BE MISERABLE BECAUSE OTHER PEOPLE ARE ALREADY DOING--LET'S FACE IT--A TERRIBLE JOB AT WHAT I WANT TO DO?
NO. I SAW HOW UNHAPPY YOU WERE. BUT ALL I SAW WAS MYSELF IN YOU.
ME? YOU SAW YOURSELF IN ME?
MORE THAN YOU CAN IMAGINE.
AND I REMEMBERED ALL MY INJURIES. THE TIMES I NEARLY DIED. THE TIMES I HAD TO WATCH THOSE I CARED ABOUT DIE. I WANTED TO PROTECT YOU.

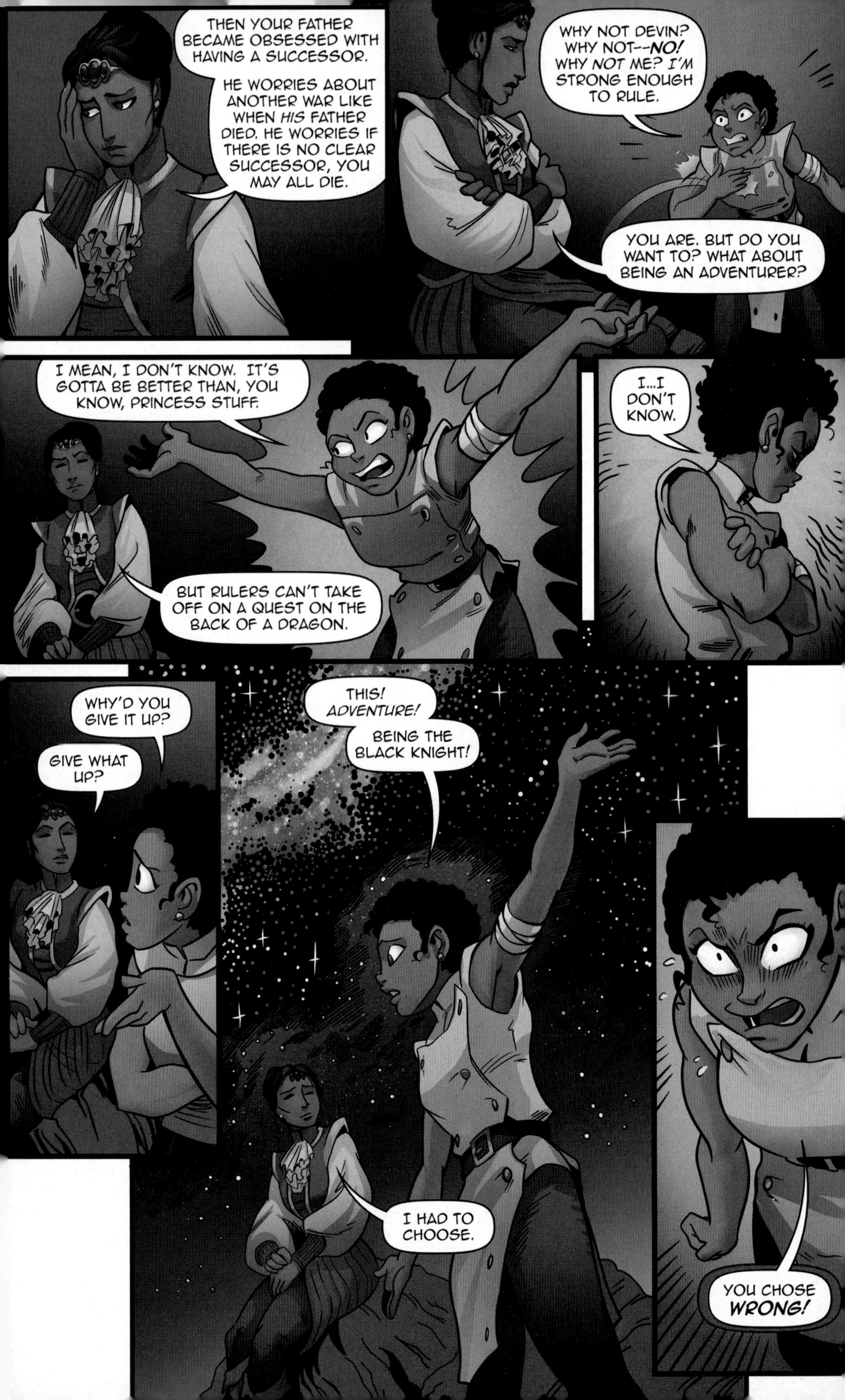
THEN YOUR FATHER BECAME OBSESSED WITH HAVING A SUCCESSOR.
HE WORRIES ABOUT ANOTHER WAR LIKE WHEN *HIS* FATHER DIED. HE WORRIES IF THERE IS NO CLEAR SUCCESSOR, YOU MAY ALL DIE.
WHY NOT DEVIN? WHY NOT--**NO!** WHY *NOT* ME? *I'M* STRONG ENOUGH TO RULE.
YOU ARE. BUT DO YOU WANT TO? WHAT ABOUT BEING AN ADVENTURER?
I MEAN, I DON'T KNOW. IT'S GOTTA BE BETTER THAN, YOU KNOW, PRINCESS STUFF.
BUT RULERS CAN'T TAKE OFF ON A QUEST ON THE BACK OF A DRAGON.
I...I DON'T KNOW.
WHY'D YOU GIVE IT UP?
GIVE WHAT UP?
THIS! *ADVENTURE!*
BEING THE BLACK KNIGHT!
I HAD TO CHOOSE.
YOU CHOSE ***WRONG!***

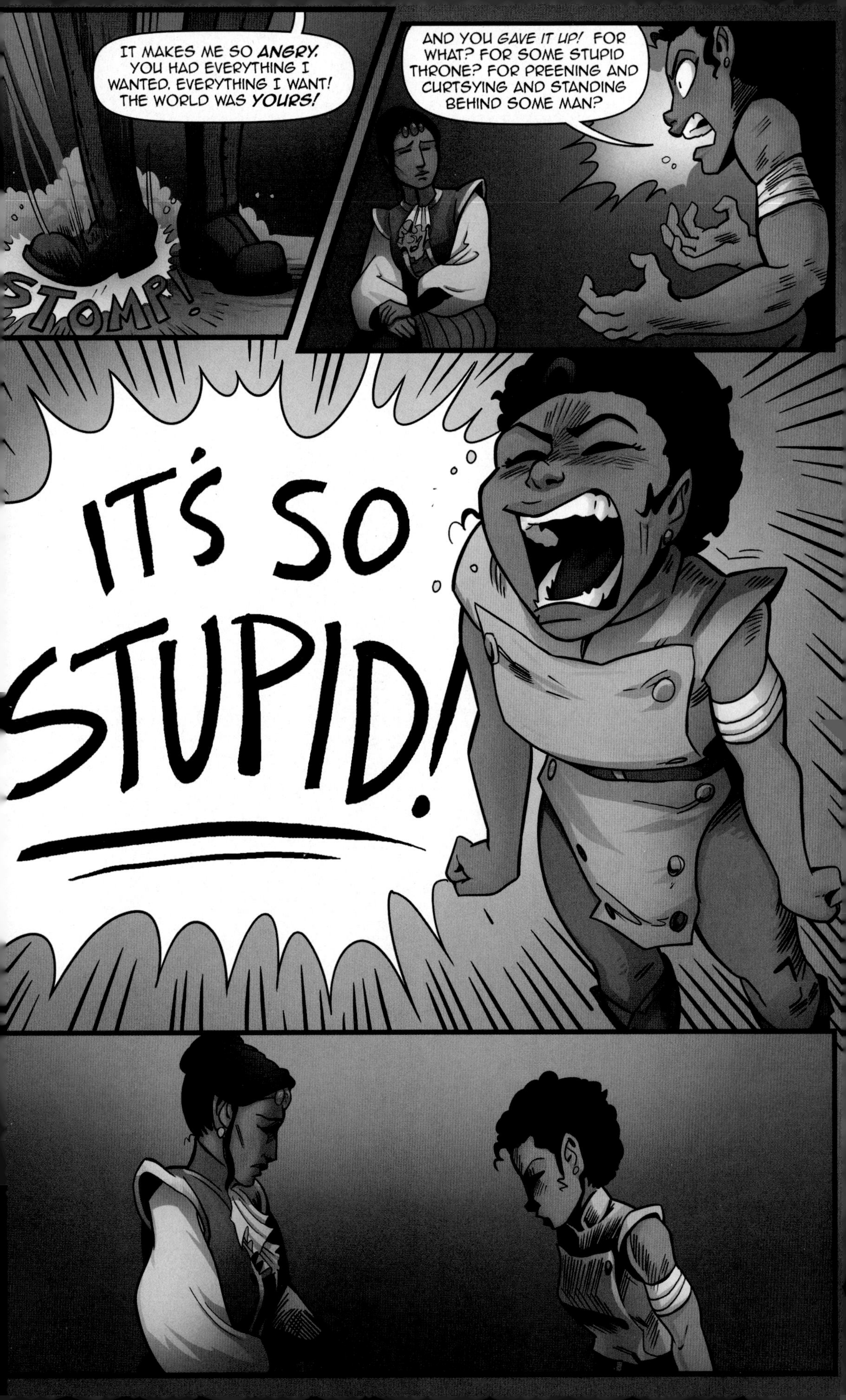
IT MAKES ME SO ANGRY. YOU HAD EVERYTHING I WANTED. EVERYTHING I WANT! THE WORLD WAS YOURS!
STOMP!
AND YOU GAVE IT UP! FOR WHAT? FOR SOME STUPID THRONE? FOR PREENING AND CURTSYING AND STANDING BEHIND SOME MAN?
IT'S SO STUPID!

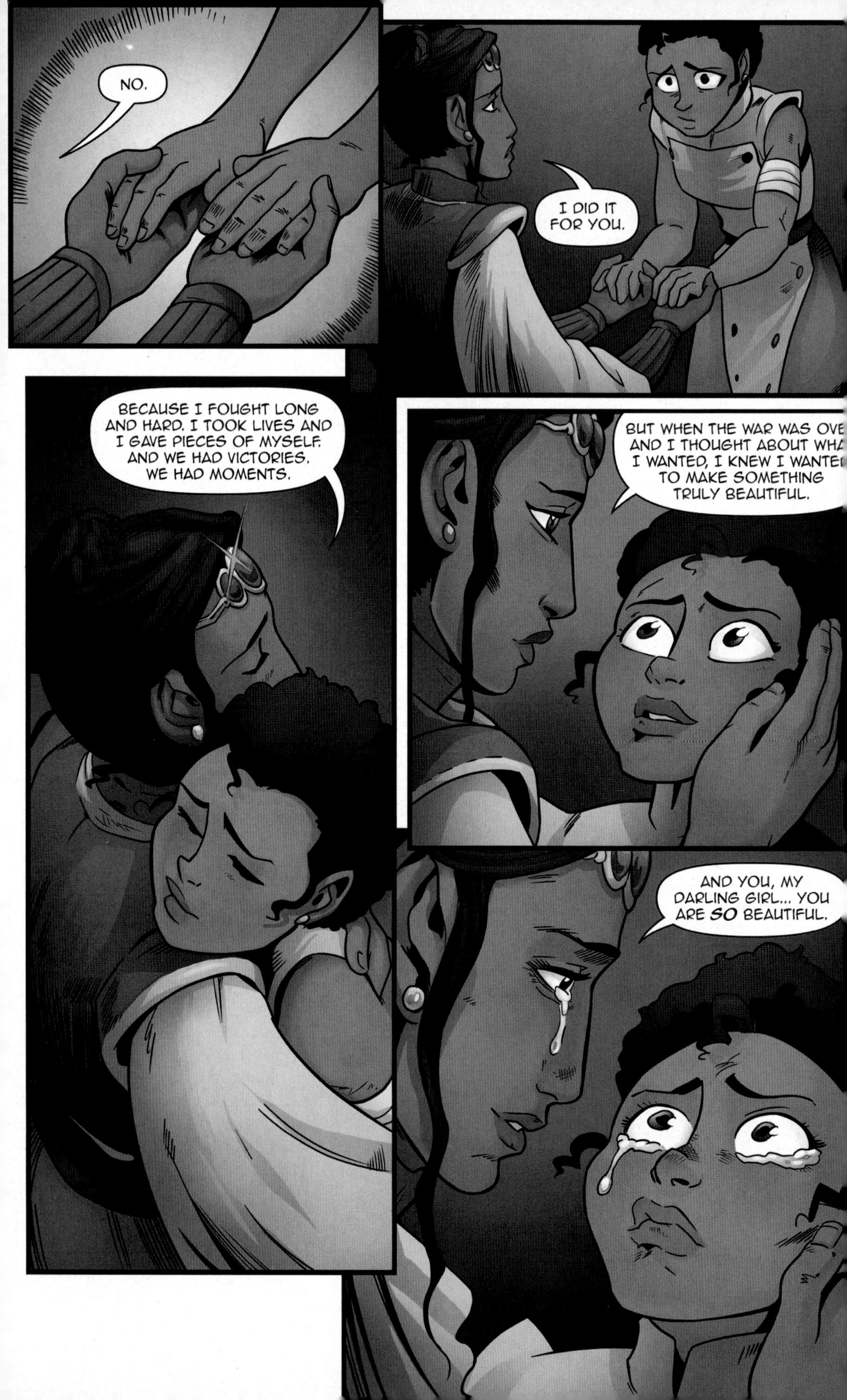
NO.
I DID IT FOR YOU.
BECAUSE I FOUGHT LONG AND HARD. I TOOK LIVES AND I GAVE PIECES OF MYSELF. AND WE HAD VICTORIES. WE HAD MOMENTS.
BUT WHEN THE WAR WAS OVE AND I THOUGHT ABOUT WHA I WANTED, I KNEW I WANTE TO MAKE SOMETHING TRULY BEAUTIFUL.
AND YOU, MY DARLING GIRL... YOU ARE SO BEAUTIFUL.

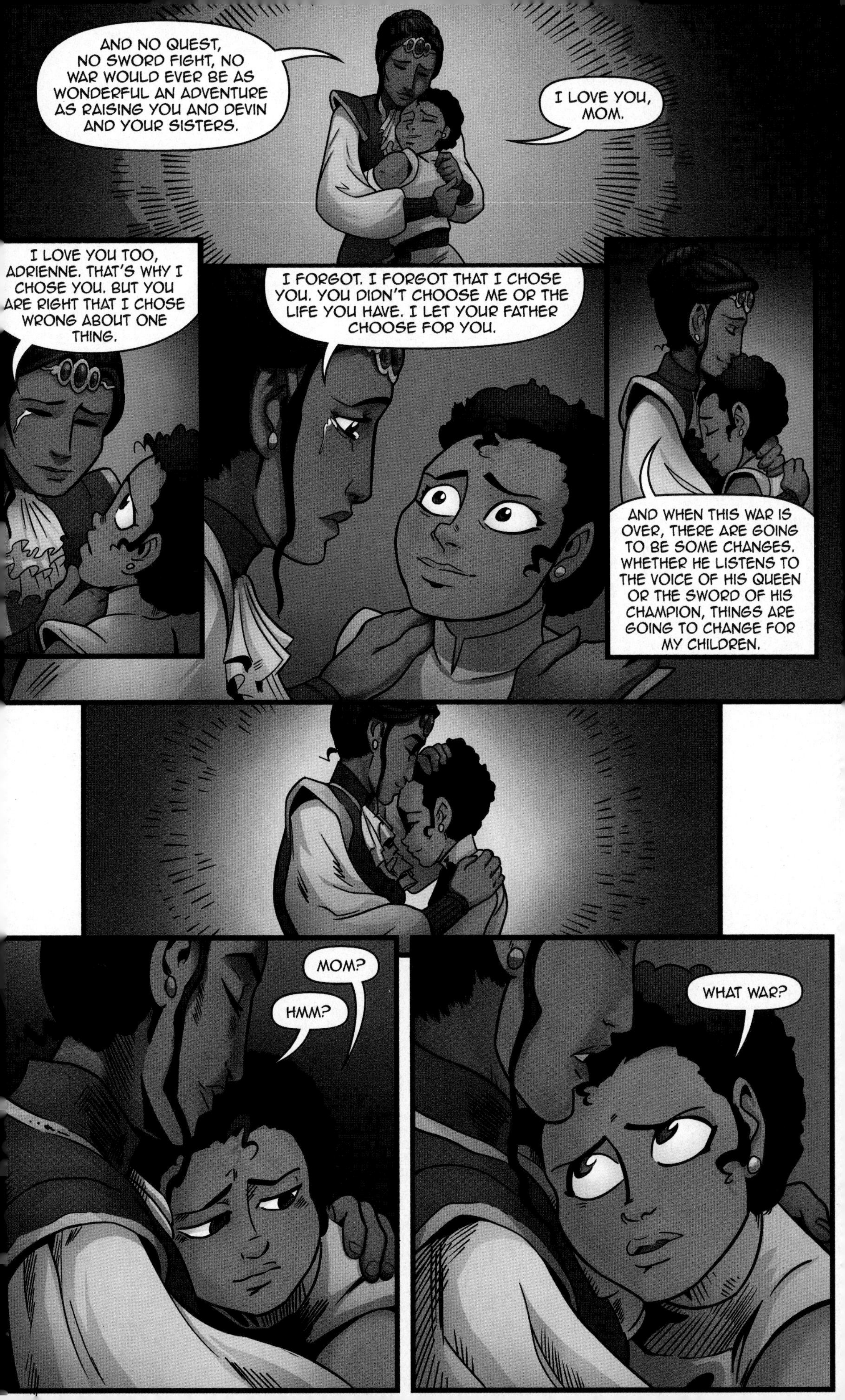
AND NO QUEST, NO SWORD FIGHT, NO WAR WOULD EVER BE AS WONDERFUL AN ADVENTURE AS RAISING YOU AND DEVIN AND YOUR SISTERS.
I LOVE YOU, MOM.
I LOVE YOU TOO, ADRIENNE. THAT'S WHY I CHOSE YOU. BUT YOU ARE RIGHT THAT I CHOSE WRONG ABOUT ONE THING.
I FORGOT. I FORGOT THAT I CHOSE YOU. YOU DIDN'T CHOOSE ME OR THE LIFE YOU HAVE. I LET YOUR FATHER CHOOSE FOR YOU.
AND WHEN THIS WAR IS OVER, THERE ARE GOING TO BE SOME CHANGES. WHETHER HE LISTENS TO THE VOICE OF HIS QUEEN OR THE SWORD OF HIS CHAMPION, THINGS ARE GOING TO CHANGE FOR MY CHILDREN.
MOM?
HMM?
WHAT WAR?

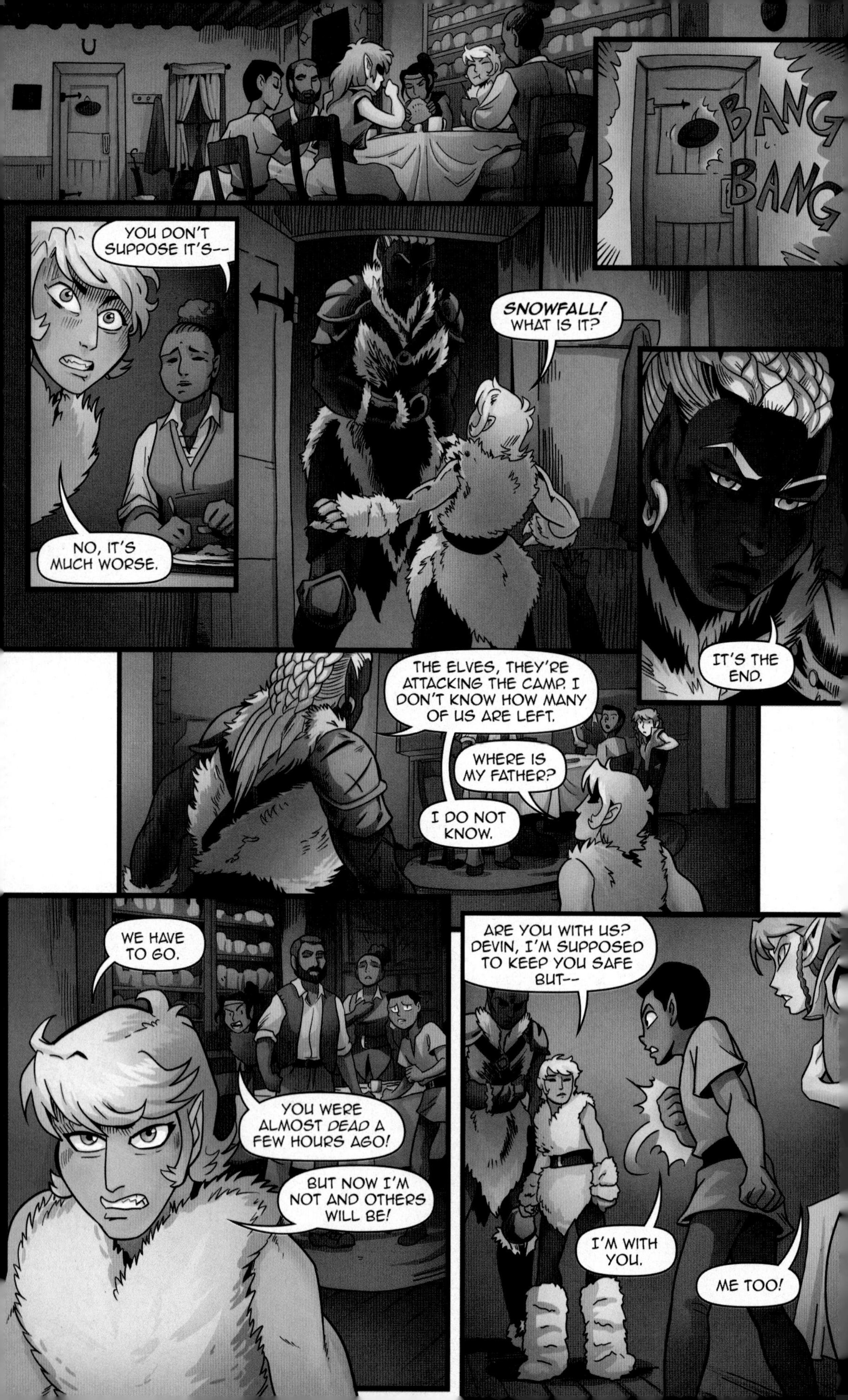
BANG
BANG
YOU DON'T SUPPOSE IT'S--
NO, IT'S MUCH WORSE.
SNOWFALL! WHAT IS IT?
IT'S THE END.
THE ELVES, THEY'RE ATTACKING THE CAMP. I DON'T KNOW HOW MANY OF US ARE LEFT.
WHERE IS MY FATHER?
I DO NOT KNOW.
WE HAVE TO GO.
YOU WERE ALMOST DEAD A FEW HOURS AGO!
BUT NOW I'M NOT AND OTHERS WILL BE!
ARE YOU WITH US? DEVIN, I'M SUPPOSED TO KEEP YOU SAFE BUT--
I'M WITH YOU.
ME TOO!

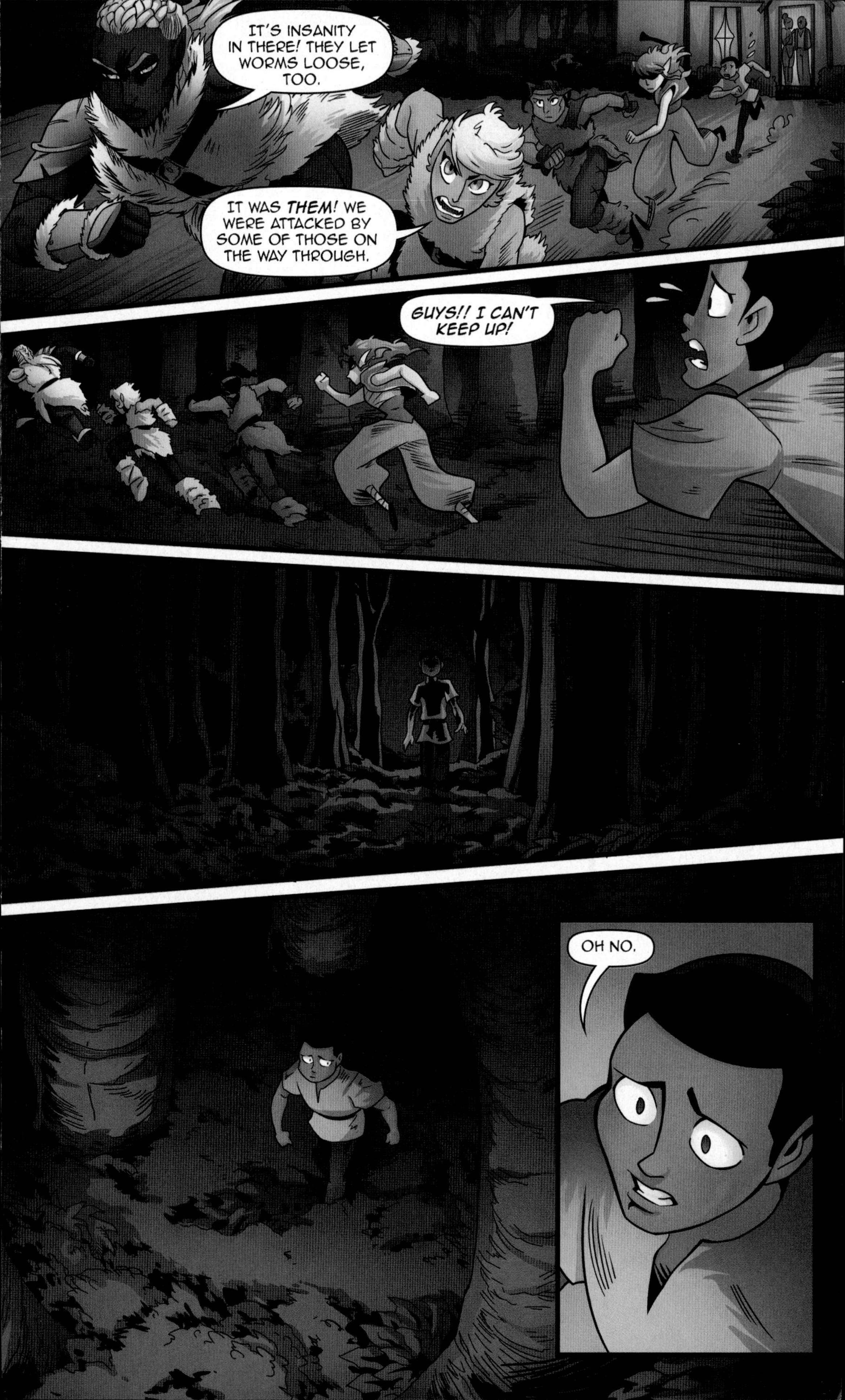
IT'S INSANITY IN THERE! THEY LET WORMS LOOSE, TOO.
IT WAS *THEM*! WE WERE ATTACKED BY SOME OF THOSE ON THE WAY THROUGH.
GUYS!! I CAN'T KEEP UP!
OH NO.

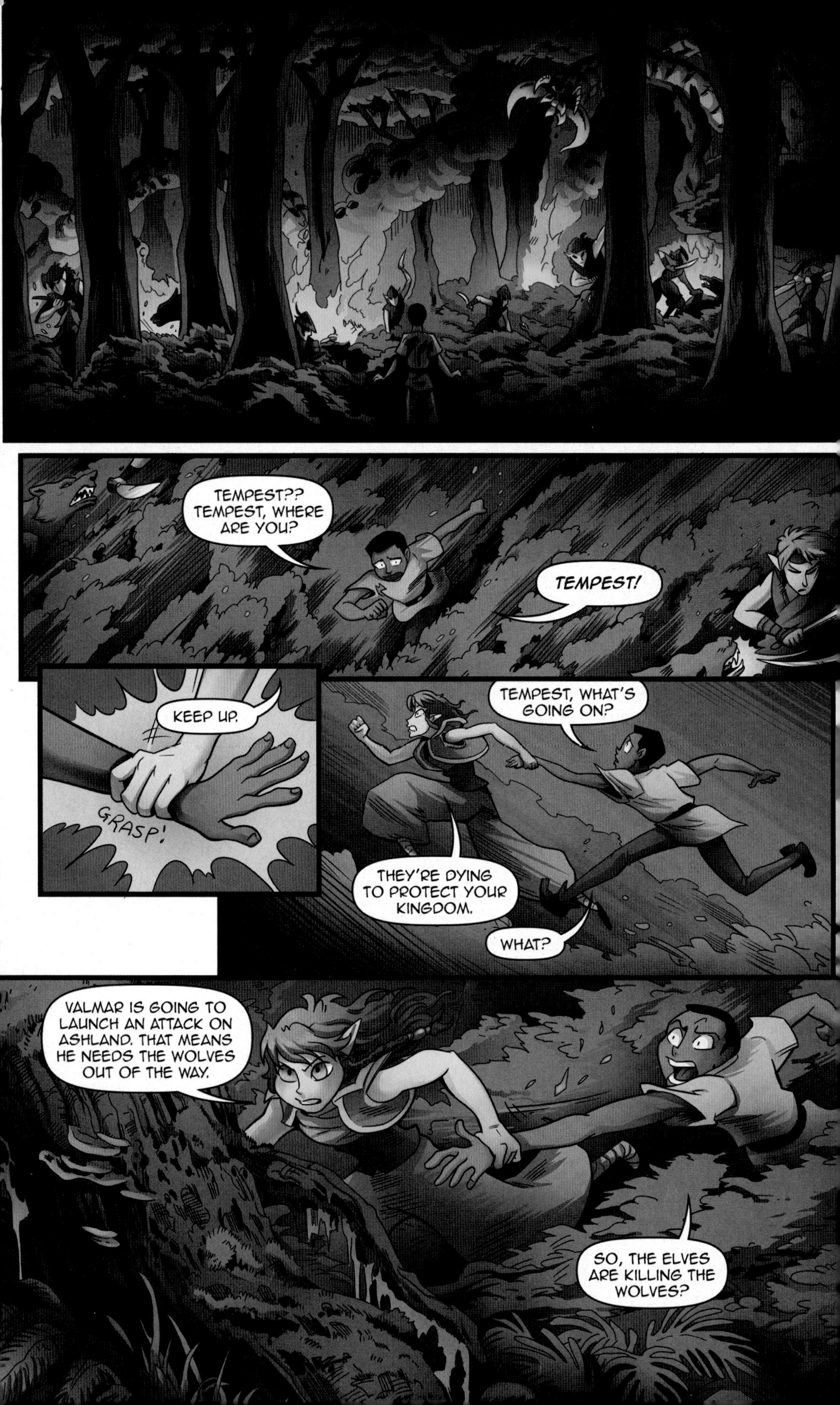
TEMPEST?? TEMPEST, WHERE ARE YOU?
TEMPEST!
KEEP UP.
GRASP!
TEMPEST, WHAT'S GOING ON?
THEY'RE DYING TO PROTECT YOUR KINGDOM.
WHAT?
VALMAR IS GOING TO LAUNCH AN ATTACK ON ASHLAND. THAT MEANS HE NEEDS THE WOLVES OUT OF THE WAY.
SO, THE ELVES ARE KILLING THE WOLVES?

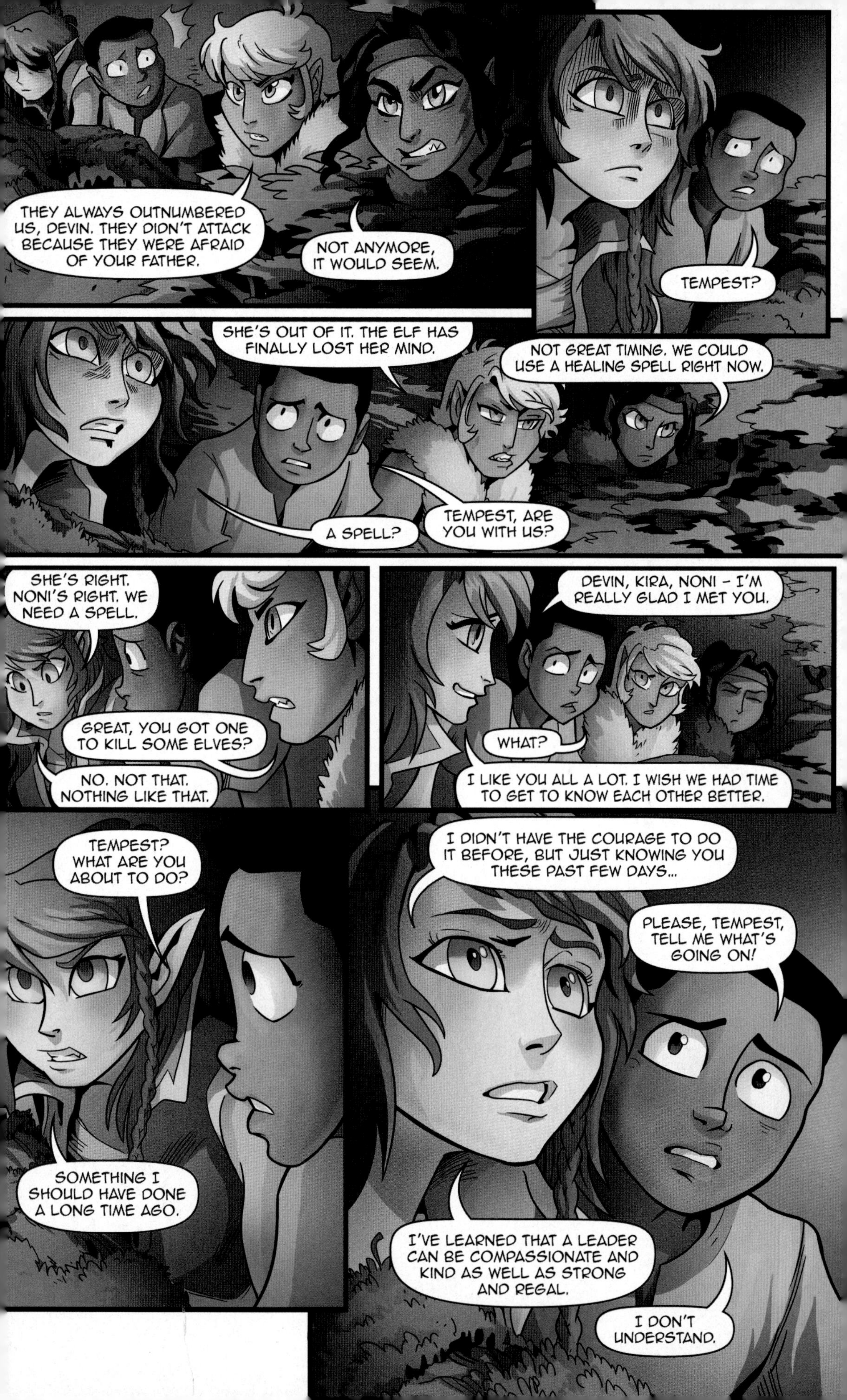

THEY ALWAYS OUTNUMBERED US, DEVIN. THEY DIDN'T ATTACK BECAUSE THEY WERE AFRAID OF YOUR FATHER.
NOT ANYMORE, IT WOULD SEEM.
TEMPEST?
SHE'S OUT OF IT. THE ELF HAS FINALLY LOST HER MIND.
NOT GREAT TIMING. WE COULD USE A HEALING SPELL RIGHT NOW.
TEMPEST, ARE YOU WITH US?
A SPELL?
SHE'S RIGHT. NONI'S RIGHT. WE NEED A SPELL.
GREAT, YOU GOT ONE TO KILL SOME ELVES?
NO. NOT THAT. NOTHING LIKE THAT.
DEVIN, KIRA, NONI – I'M REALLY GLAD I MET YOU.
WHAT?
I LIKE YOU ALL A LOT. I WISH WE HAD TIME TO GET TO KNOW EACH OTHER BETTER.
TEMPEST? WHAT ARE YOU ABOUT TO DO?
SOMETHING I SHOULD HAVE DONE A LONG TIME AGO.
I DIDN'T HAVE THE COURAGE TO DO IT BEFORE, BUT JUST KNOWING YOU THESE PAST FEW DAYS...
PLEASE, TEMPEST, TELL ME WHAT'S GOING ON!
I'VE LEARNED THAT A LEADER CAN BE COMPASSIONATE AND KIND AS WELL AS STRONG AND REGAL.
I DON'T UNDERSTAND.

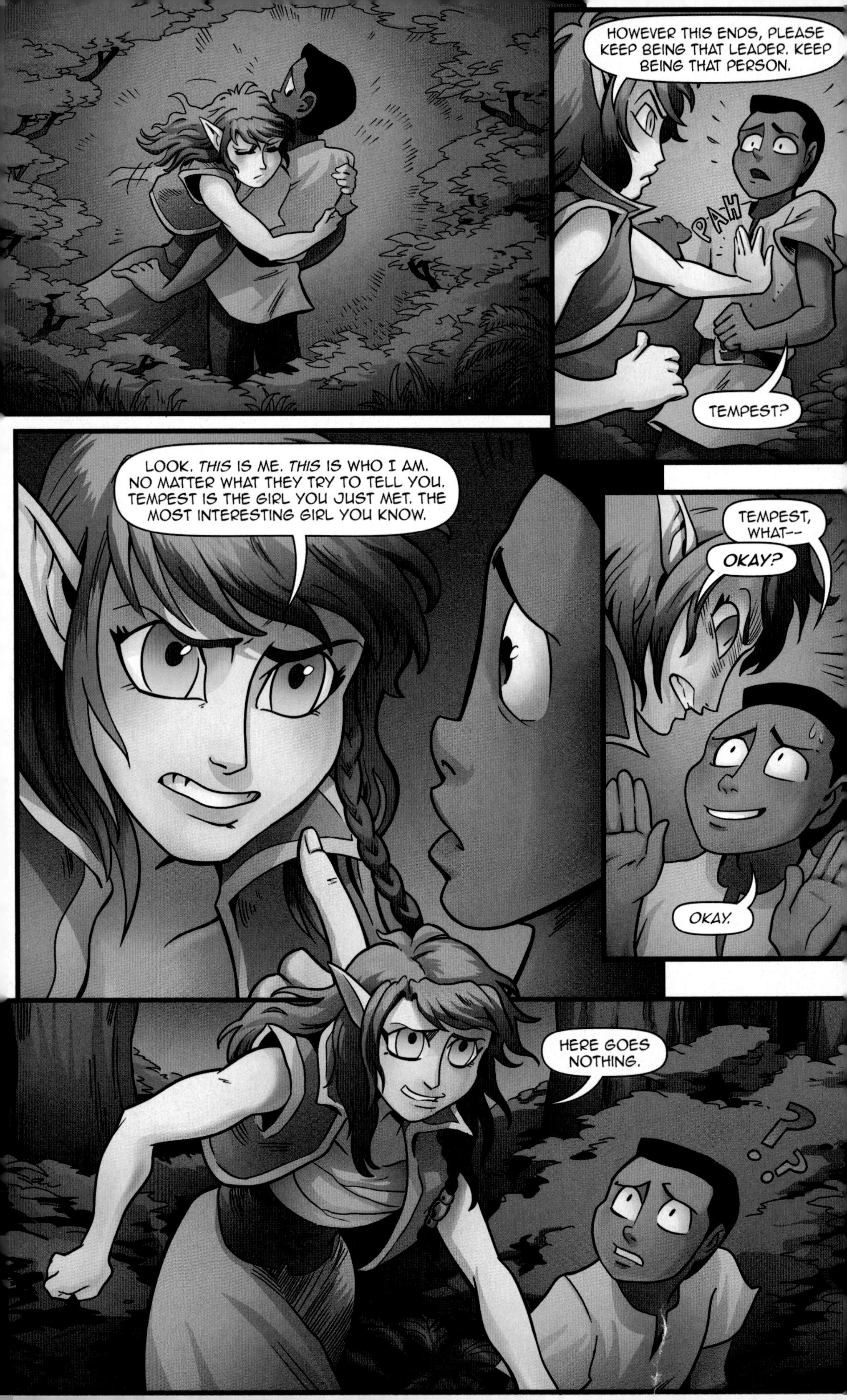
HOWEVER THIS ENDS, PLEASE KEEP BEING THAT LEADER. KEEP BEING THAT PERSON.
PAH
TEMPEST?
LOOK. *THIS* IS ME. *THIS* IS WHO I AM. NO MATTER WHAT THEY TRY TO TELL YOU. TEMPEST IS THE GIRL YOU JUST MET. THE MOST INTERESTING GIRL YOU KNOW.
TEMPEST, WHAT--
OKAY?
OKAY.
HERE GOES NOTHING.
?
?

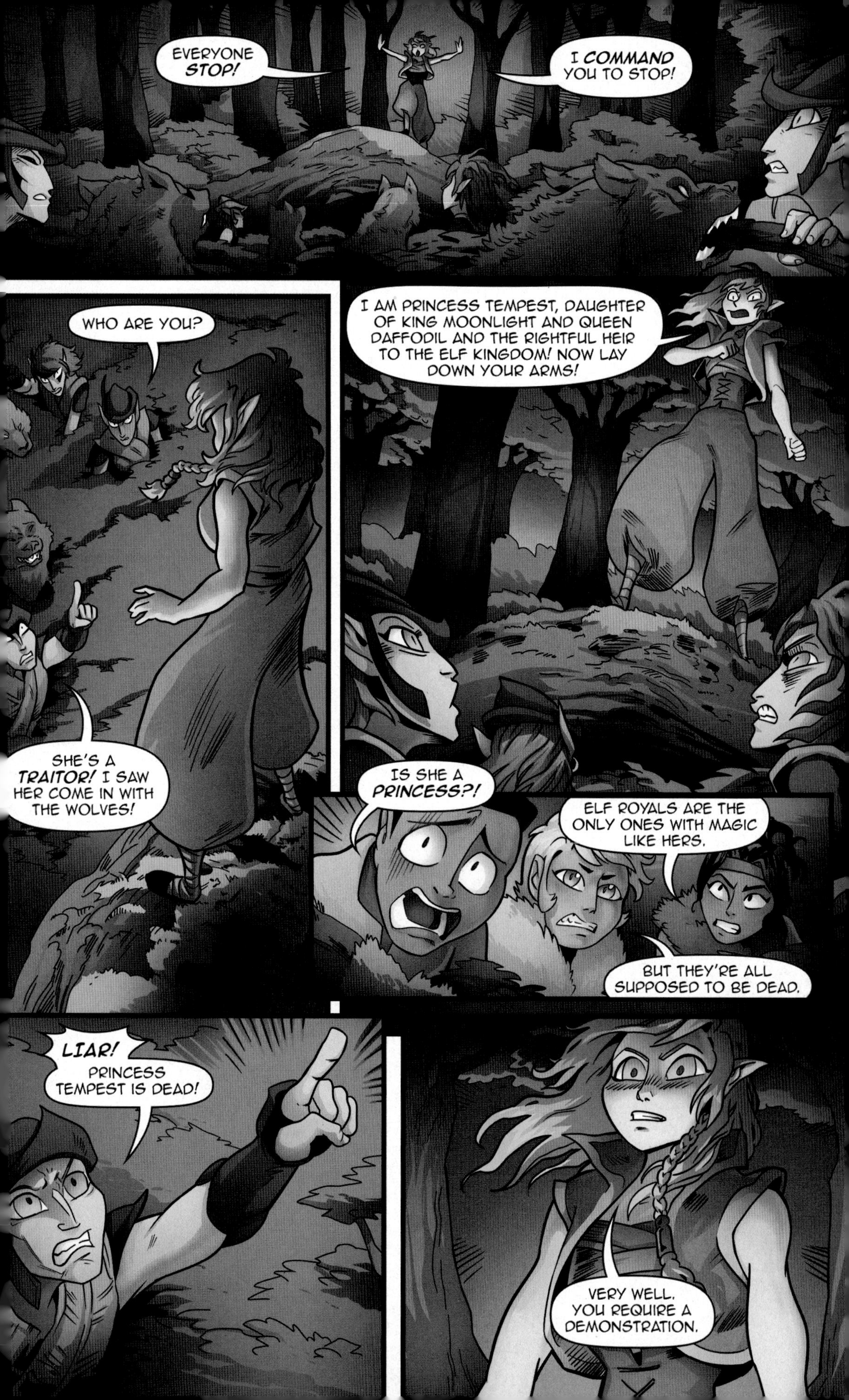
EVERYONE STOP!
I COMMAND YOU TO STOP!
WHO ARE YOU?
I AM PRINCESS TEMPEST, DAUGHTER OF KING MOONLIGHT AND QUEEN DAFFODIL AND THE RIGHTFUL HEIR TO THE ELF KINGDOM! NOW LAY DOWN YOUR ARMS!
SHE'S A TRAITOR! I SAW HER COME IN WITH THE WOLVES!
IS SHE A PRINCESS?!
ELF ROYALS ARE THE ONLY ONES WITH MAGIC LIKE HERS.
BUT THEY'RE ALL SUPPOSED TO BE DEAD.
LIAR! PRINCESS TEMPEST IS DEAD!
VERY WELL. YOU REQUIRE A DEMONSTRATION.

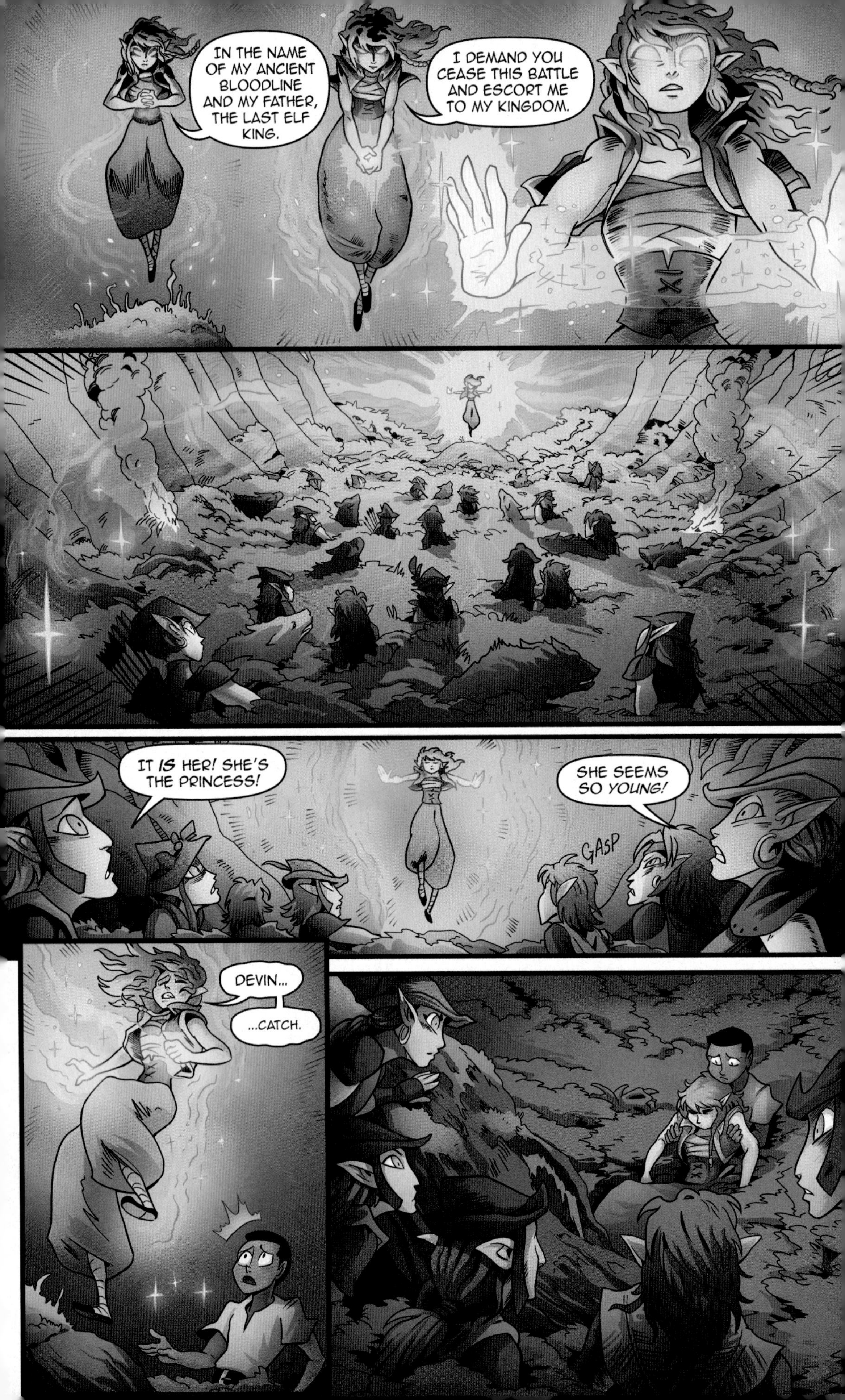
IN THE NAME OF MY ANCIENT BLOODLINE AND MY FATHER, THE LAST ELF KING.
I DEMAND YOU CEASE THIS BATTLE AND ESCORT ME TO MY KINGDOM.
IT *IS* HER! SHE'S THE PRINCESS!
SHE SEEMS SO *YOUNG!*
GASP
DEVIN...
...CATCH.

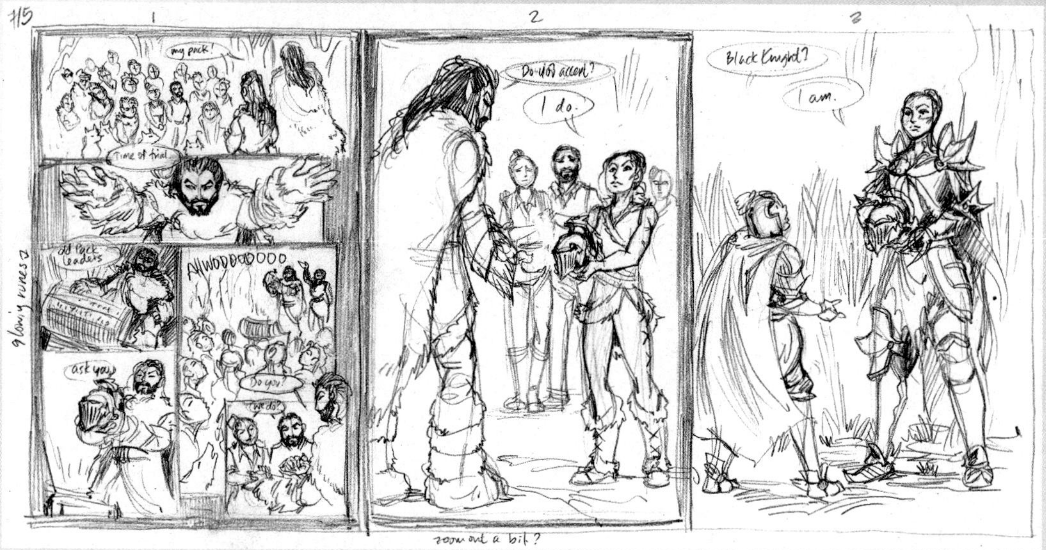
7/5
1
my pack!
Time of trial
old pack leaders
AHWOOOOOOOO
ask you
Do you?
glowing runes
2
Do you accept?
I do.
zoom out a bit?
3
Black Knight?
I am.

THUMBNAILS FOR PAGES 1 – 3

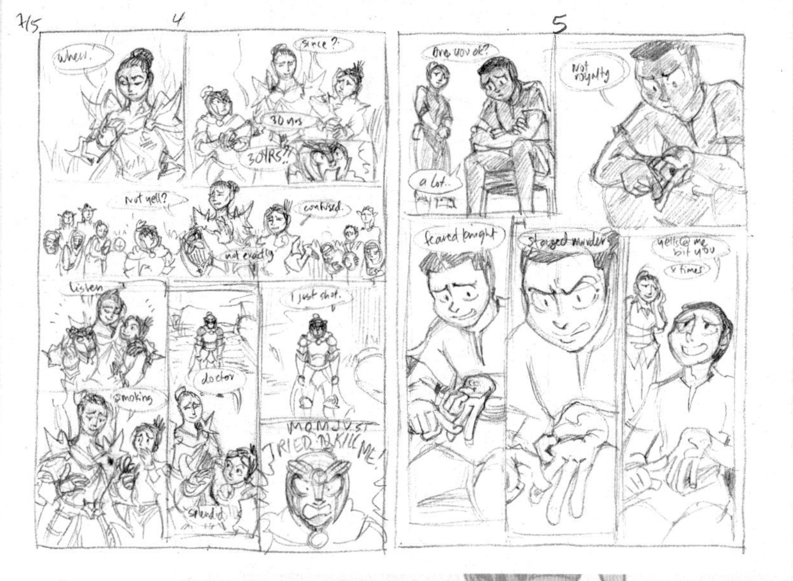
7/5
4
When!
Since?
30 yrs
30 YRS!!
not yell?
confused
not exactly
listen
I just shot
doctor
smoking
splendid
MOM JUST TRIED TO KILL ME!
5
Are you ok?
not royalty
a lot
feared knight
staged murder
x times

THUMBNAILS FOR PAGES 4 – 5

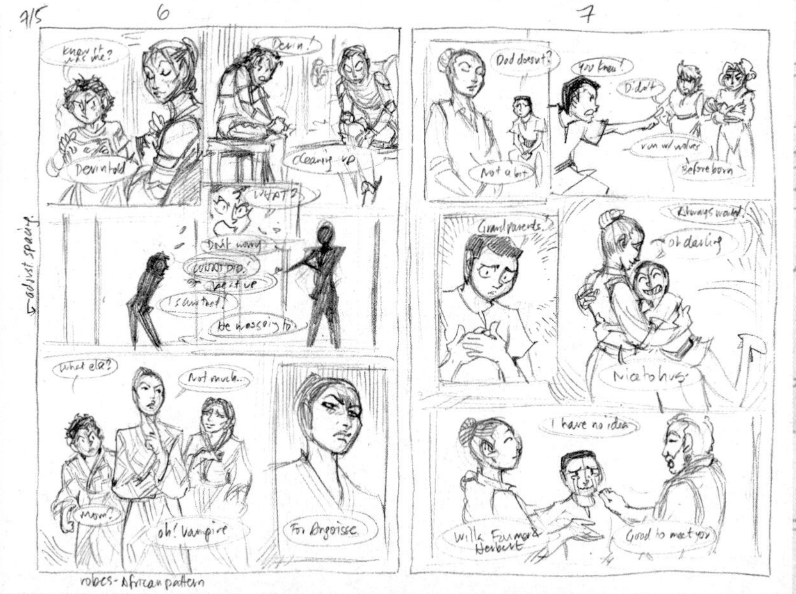
7/5
6
Devin!
Devin told
cleaning up
WHAT?
Don't worry
adjust spacing
What else?
Not much...
Mom?
oh! vampire
robes- African pattern
7
Dad doesn't?
You knew!
Not a bit
before born
Grandparents?
oh darling
I have no idea
Good to meet you

THUMBNAILS FOR PAGES 6 – 7

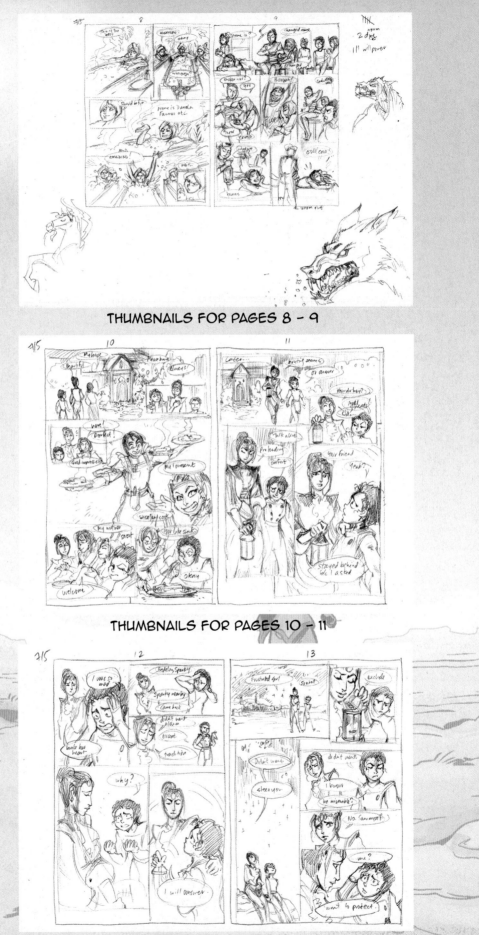

THUMBNAILS FOR PAGES 8 - 9

THUMBNAILS FOR PAGES 10 - 11

THUMBNAILS FOR PAGES 12 - 13

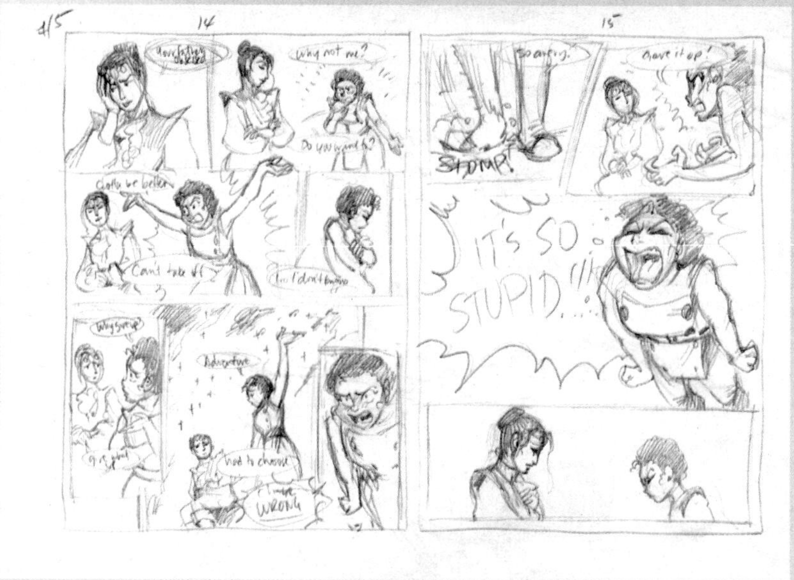
14
15
Why not me?
Do you want to?
Gotta be better
Can't take it!
Adventure
had to choose
WRONG
Give it up!
STOMP!
IT'S SO STUPID!!!

THUMBNAILS FOR PAGES 14 – 15

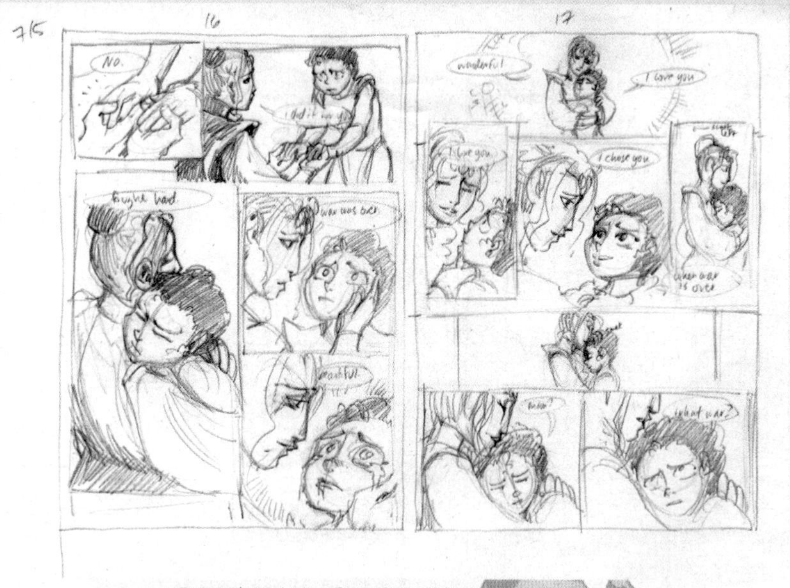
16
17
No.
war was over
I love you
I chose you
When war is over
what war?

THUMBNAILS FOR PAGES 16 – 17

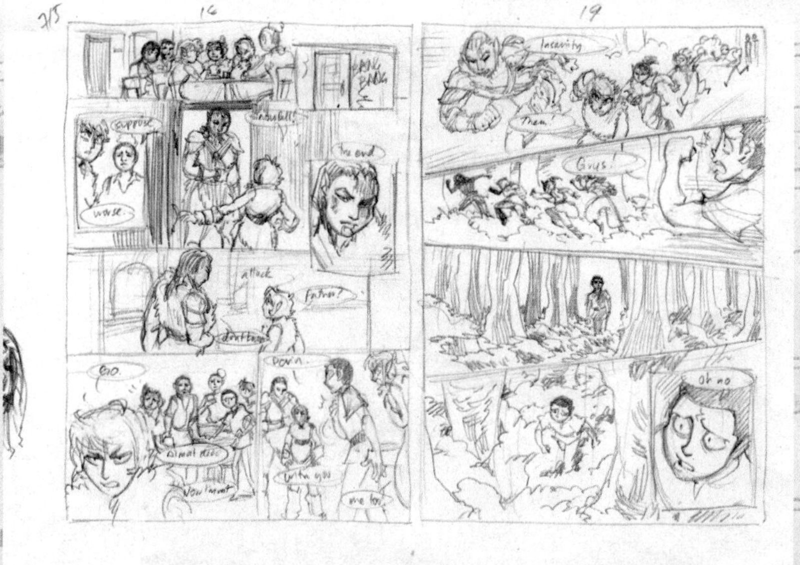
19
Surprise
worse.
The end
attack
Father?
Go.
Down.
With you
Me too
Them!
Guys!
Oh no

THUMBNAILS FOR PAGES 18 – 19

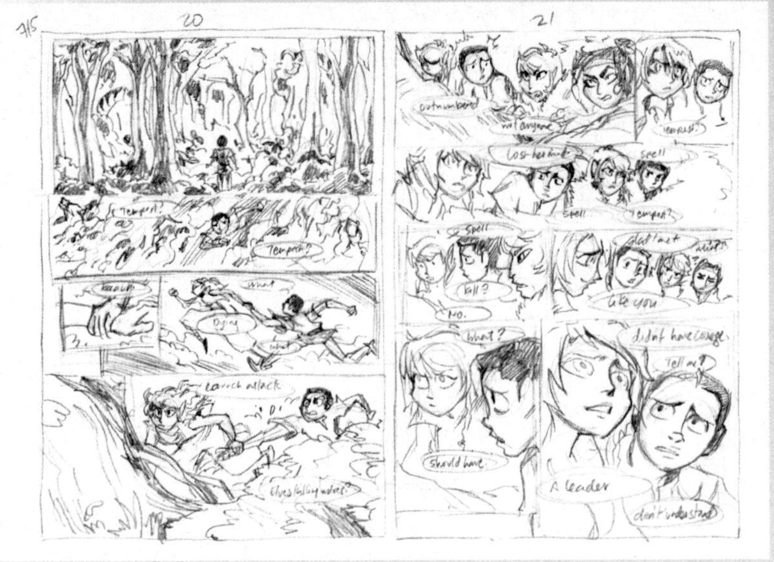
20
21
Tempest?
Spell
Like you
Should have
A leader
don't understand

THUMBNAILS FOR PAGES 20 - 21

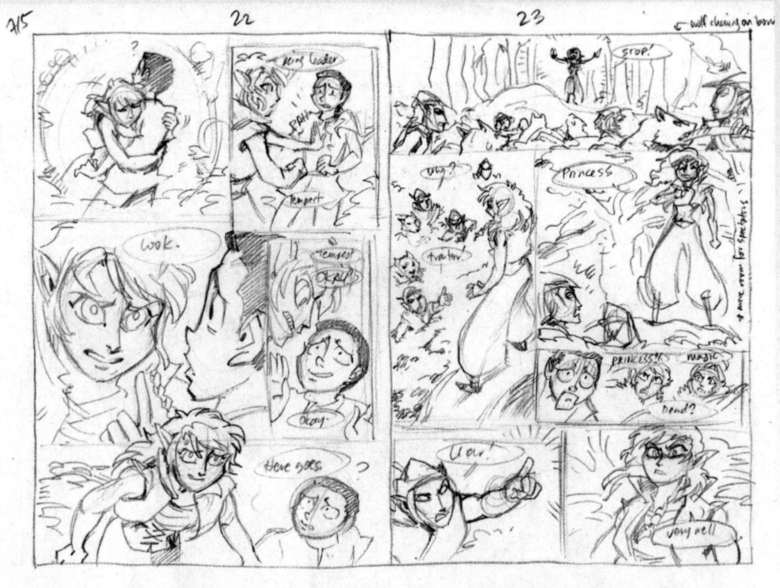
22
23
STOP!
Princess
Look.
Tempest
Okay
Here goes
PRINCESS?!
MAGIC
Dead?
very well

THUMBNAILS FOR PAGES 22 - 23

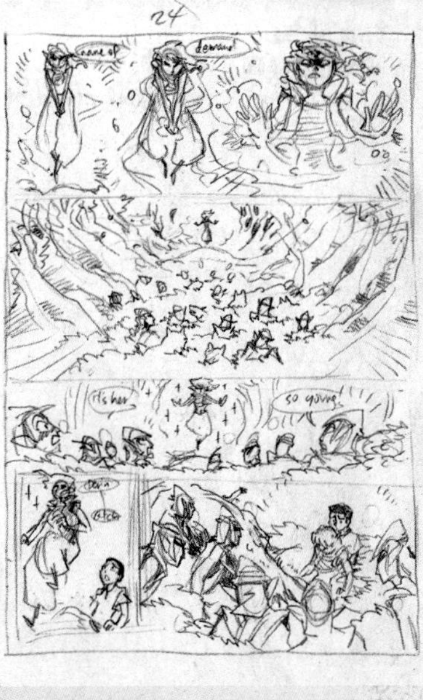
24

THUMBNAIL FOR PAGE 24

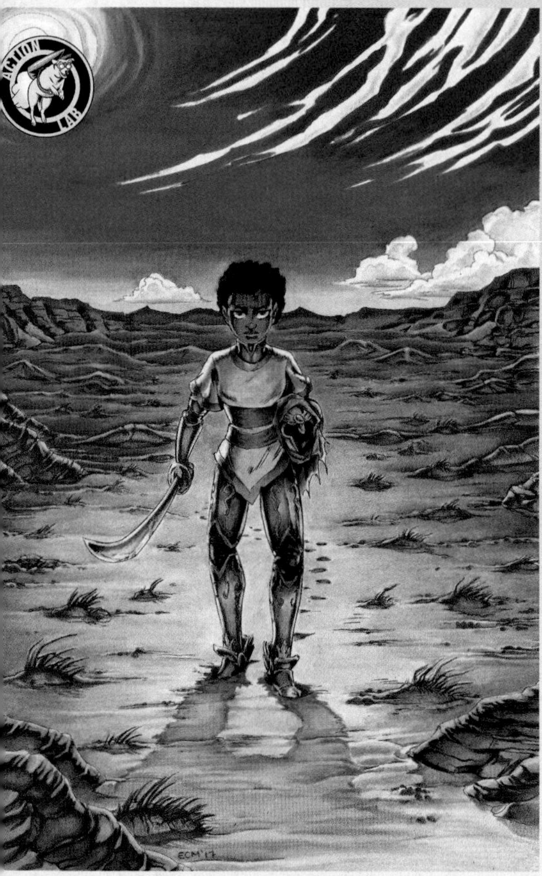

ISSUE #1 (COVER A)
EMILY MARTIN

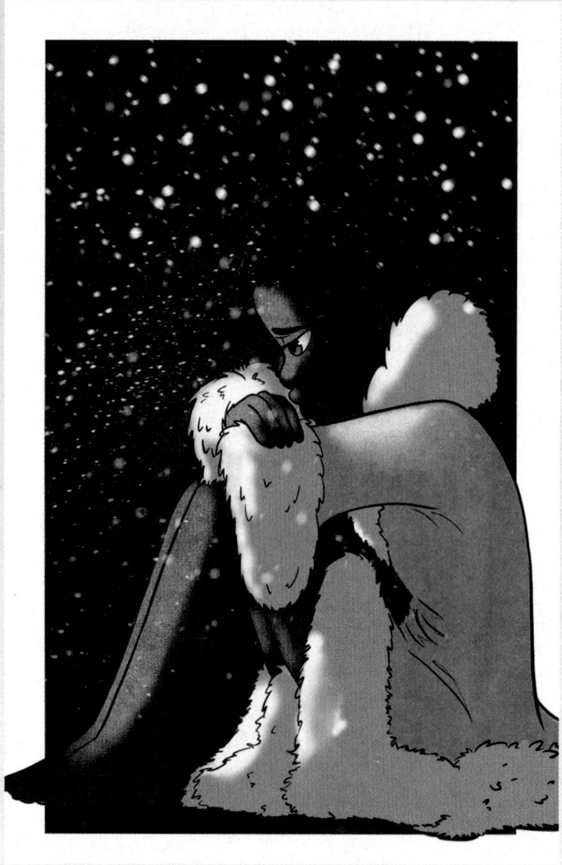

ISSUE #1 (COVER B)
ONYINYE ANAKOR

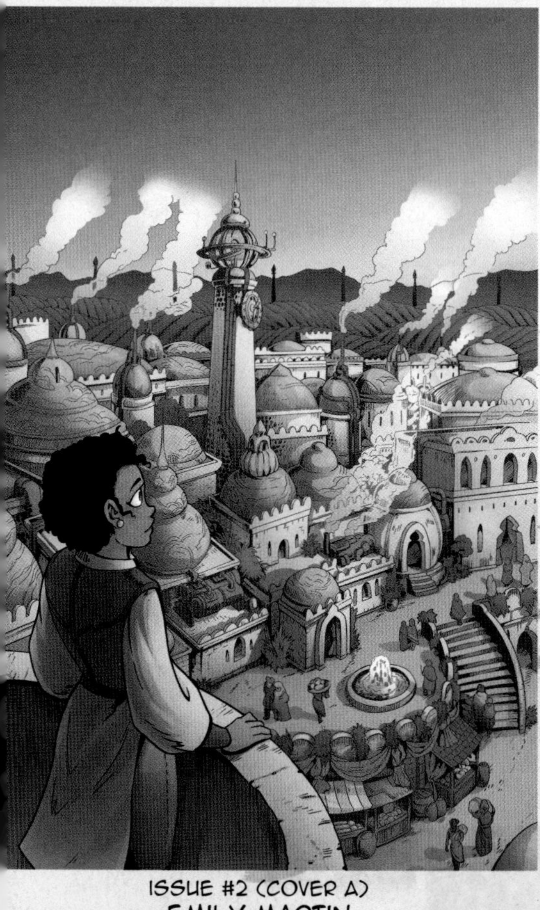

ISSUE #2 (COVER A)
EMILY MARTIN

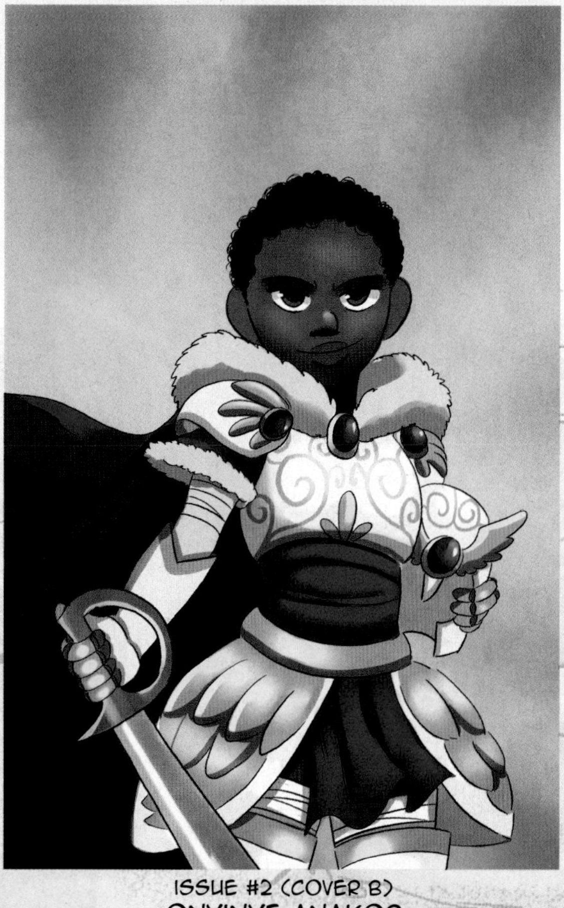

ISSUE #2 (COVER B)
ONYINYE ANAKOR

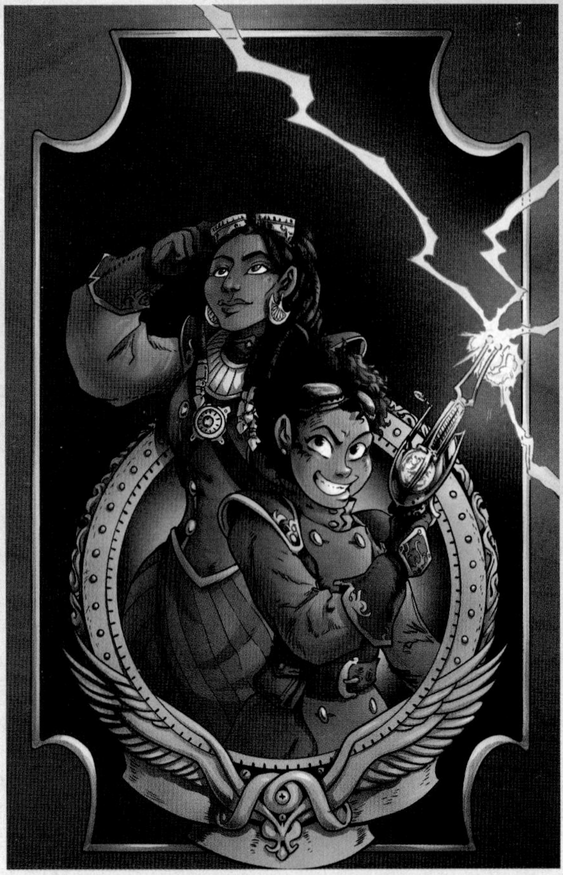

ISSUE #3 (COVER A)
EMILY MARTIN

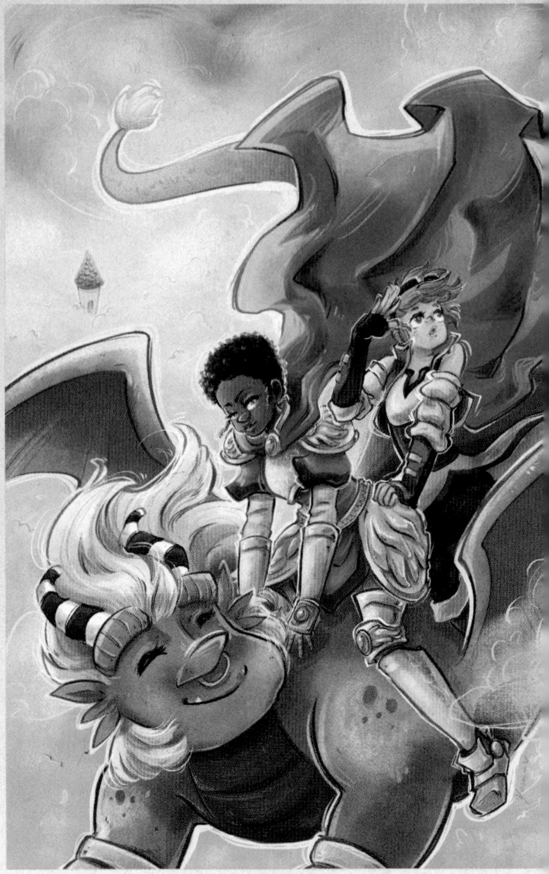

ISSUE #3 (COVER B)
YESENIA MOISES

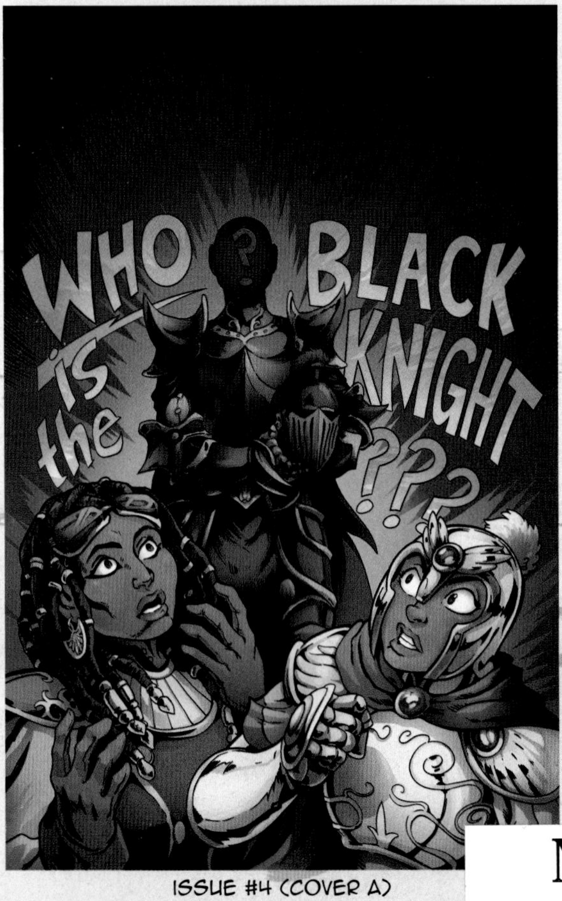
WHO is the BLACK KNIGHT???

ISSUE #4 (COVER A)
EMILY MARTIN

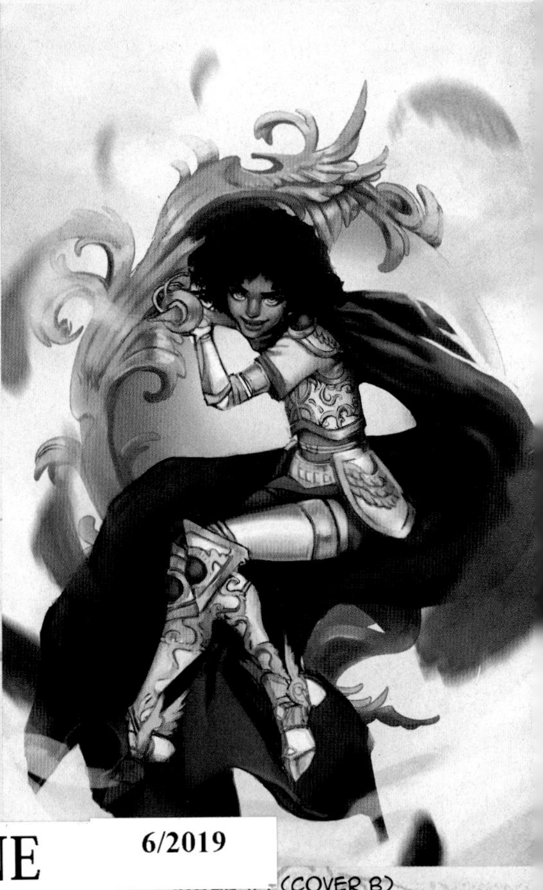

(COVER B)
MALIA KNIGHT